DARK HARBOUR

DAVID HOSP

PAN BOOKS

First published in the US 2005 by Grand Central Publishing, New York

First published in the UK 2010 by Pan Books
an imprint of Pan Macmillan, a division of Macmillan Publishers Limited
Pan Macmillan, 20 New Wharf Road, London N1 9RR
Basingstoke and Oxford
Associated companies throughout the world
www.panmacmillan.com

ISBN 978-1-4472-2831-8

1 3 5 7 9 8 6 4 2

A CIP catalogue record for this book is available from
the British Library.

Printed in the UK by CPI Group (UK) Ltd, Croydon, CR0 4YY

DARK HARBOUR

David Hosp is a trial lawyer who finds time to write his novels on his daily commute by boat across Boston Harbour. He lives with his wife and family in the city.

Acclaim for David Hosp

'This is a knock out; Grisham with passion, even a touch of the great Michael Connelly thrown in . . . It crackles from the first page to the last and never lets up for a second'

Daily Mail

'Hosp is a born storyteller, a master of quirky character and detail who enthrals through the simple, but elusive, expedient of never seeming to write a dull sentence'

Daily Telegraph [Review]

'With a clever, believable plot, *Among Thieves* is one of those thrillers that propels the reader through to the last page, leaving them thoroughly exhilarated' *Waterstone's Books Quarterly*

'Accomplished legal thriller writer' *Bookseller*

'This novel by a Boston attorney is not only brilliant . . . but handled with page-igniting panache'

Daily Telegraph Top 50 Summer Reads 2009

'Explodes in the first chapter and catapults the reader through forty-four more. Hosp hits the trifecta – brilliant, brawny, and totally believable'

David Baldacci

Also by David Hosp

Among Thieves
The Betrayed
Innocence

PROLOGUE

Monday, September 12, 2005

Ed Tannery leaned back into the vinyl seat as the commuter train pulled out of the station. He couldn't remember ever having been so tired.

"How's the baby?" Harry Makin asked. The two of them had been riding the train together for three years. They were similar cogs in the great economic engine of corporate America: white, male, early thirties, married, blue suit, white shirt, red tie—just two among more than a thousand hardworking souls on the 7:34 a.m. train winding its way through the suburban sprawl west of Boston.

"She's great," Tannery replied. "I just wish she was sleeping better."

"Yeah, well, get used to it, buddy. If you had any illusions about getting a good night's sleep anytime in the next three months, you may as well abandon them."

Tannery smiled. "It's worth it, though."

Harry laughed. "Tell me that when she's sixteen and she's not coming home at night anymore because she's dating someone like you."

"No problem. I've already applied for a gun license."

Harry laughed again and closed his eyes, turning his head toward the window, away from Tannery. Tannery enjoyed riding to work with Harry. He understood that silence could be a commuter's best friend, and recognized the difference between light banter and incessant chatter.

The two men sat quietly next to each other as the train gathered speed. That particular day, a respectful silence seemed appropriate. It had been exactly four years and a day since the world had changed so drastically.

They'd both known several people who perished in the attack on the World Trade Center. The financial community was small and inbred, and the ripples that spread across their industry in the wake of the loss were still deeply felt.

"I thought you were going to take the day off," Harry commented after a while, his eyes still closed. Tannery's company allowed its employees to take September 11 as a floating holiday in memory of the great tragedy. Because the eleventh fell on Sunday, they had been given the option of taking the Monday off in remembrance of the dark anniversary.

"Nah, I've got too much going on. I couldn't." That wasn't exactly true. The baby was only two weeks old, and Tannery hadn't logged any vacation time yet. He could have skipped work that day. But the markets were down, and he was young and ambitious; he was unwilling to give ground to his competitors. Besides, Amy seemed to be doing great with the baby, and he was planning on taking a week off in the beginning of October—the most beautiful time of year in New England. *Go*, Amy had told him, *and then you can really relax when we're on vacation*. So he'd gone.

Harry grunted his understanding and sank deeper into his seat, desperate to augment what little sleep he got at home contending with two children of his own. There just never seemed to be enough time in the day.

Sitting on the train, a part of Ed Tannery knew he'd made a

mistake. The baby would never be this young again, and he would never get this time back. At the same time, he had responsibilities now. He had to make sure he provided for his young family.

He took a photograph out of his jacket pocket and held it up. Amy stared out at him from the delivery room, sweaty and tired, but radiant. In her arms lay their newborn baby, only minutes old, still sticky and red and grumpy. Tannery put the picture back into his breast pocket and patted his chest. He closed his eyes as a tired smile spread across his face. He'd have a lifetime with them, he thought.

Three rows ahead of Ed Tannery, Alhari Al Sadria sat with his eyes glued to the window, following the train's path parallel to the highway.

He had short, neatly trimmed black hair, a thin mustache, and an olive complexion. Most people assumed he was Spanish, or perhaps Greek. In fact, Sadria had been born and raised in Tunisia on the shores near the ancient city of Carthage. As a boy, he'd played in the turquoise waters of the Mediterranean and watched the barbarians from Italy, France, and America claim the small African nation street by street, building by building, and family by family. It was there that he came under the influence of Nisar Ben Mohammad Namur, an outspoken mullah who shared Sadria's contempt for Westerners. The great teacher had taken Sadria's adolescent disenchantment and molded it with care into a hatred that burned with blind passion.

In 1996, Sadria had arrived in the United States as a twenty-year-old college student, ready to study computer science at Boston University. He graduated near the top of his class and earned a spot in a master's program at MIT. Upon receiving his degree, he turned down doctoral program offers from several top universities, choosing instead to enter the private sector. A large consulting company hired him and expedited the visa paperwork so he could stay in the country. In the two years since, he'd ridden this same train every morning. Never again, he knew.

The call had come two weeks before. To anyone eavesdropping, the conversation with his old friend in Tunisia would have sounded innocent enough. They spoke of Sadria's family and the goings-on in his old seaside town on the Mediterranean. They talked about the top African and European football stars and the latest matches. They laughed about the times they'd enjoyed when they were boys, and about the future. The conversation was so relaxed and natural that Sadria almost missed the signal.

"We're having an anniversary party," his friend said.

"Really?" Sadria's breath caught in his chest.

"Yes, and we'd like you to join us."

Sadria couldn't believe it. He'd waited so long to hear such instructions that he'd ceased to believe they'd ever come. His manufactured life in the United States had become his reality. He found himself unable to talk, and the pause on the phone was noticeable.

"Do you think you'll be able to make it?" His friend's voice was still nonchalant, but Sadria could feel the urgency from half a world away. Buoyed by the importance of his task, Sadria found his voice.

"Of course, my brother. I'm already counting the moments until we can embrace each other again around the warmth of the desert fire. I know it will be soon." With that, Sadria's course was set.

Now the culmination of nine years of waiting and planning and thinking was at hand. Sadria looked up toward the front of the car at the young man in the bright blue uniform. He couldn't be more than twenty years old, and was of no concern. He was a member of the newly formed Massachusetts Transportation Safety Commission Guard Unit, which had been thrown together in haste when the American federal government blindly put up billions of dollars for states to use in developing homeland defense strategies. Fearful of losing out on the funding, politicians had fallen over one another to come up with pork-barrel schemes for "improved security." The Guard Unit officers assigned to the transit rails were, Sadria knew, nothing more than window dressing.

At the same time, the security wizards and political hacks had failed to recognize the real weaknesses in transport security. As a result, it had been child's play for Sadria to sneak into the rail yard at night and attach bundles of explosives to the bottom of each of the train's twelve cars. The hole he'd cut in the simple chain-link fence would be discovered later in the day, and the shouting and finger-pointing would begin. But by then it would be too late.

The explosives were set on a two-second delayed detonation sequence, running from the back car to the front, where he was. In his pocket he held the detonator that would start the chain reaction. He was amazed that his palm wasn't sweaty, and he took that as a sign from Allah that his cause was just and he would be rewarded. He found peace in his belief that he would indeed be reunited with his old friend soon.

Sadria looked out the window again. The train had reached its top speed and was headed toward a sharp turn near Newton Corner. If his calculations were correct, each car would explode and separate in sequence, slipping the rails in a fury. Death would not be confined to the train itself. It would be carried off the tracks by each railcar, enveloping pedestrians, passing cars, and nearby buildings. It would be glorious.

As the train entered the curve, Sadria took a deep breath and said a silent prayer. Then he flipped the switch.

At first he thought there'd been a malfunction, and he feared he had failed his brothers at his most important moment. He lamented that he wouldn't be able to regain the respect of the movement, and that his place in heaven was no longer certain. He was deep in despair when he heard the first explosion. It was distant, coming from the rear of the train. Two seconds later there was another, closer this time. Then another, and another. His heart was filled with joy as the explosions became deafening. The eleventh explosion rocked the car just behind his, and he was no longer able to contain his excitement.

"Allahu Akhbar!" he shouted at the top of his lungs. He was barely able to get the words out before the final explosion ripped through the train's front car, the fireball burning straight through his clothes and melting the flesh from his face, reducing it to an eternal grimace.

Three rows behind, Ed Tannery had only a moment to grasp one final time at his jacket pocket to feel the outlines of the photograph that held the image of his wife and their infant daughter.

CHAPTER ONE

August 2006

Her body was found on a Sunday evening. It might have been discovered earlier, but floating in Boston Harbor it blended in with the logs and tires and trash that spilled over from the city.

She was the seventh, or so they thought at the time. Two weeks had passed since the sixth, and people were holding their breath, greedy in their anticipation. Not since the days when the Boston Strangler prowled his way across Beacon Hill had a singular fear so titillated New Englanders.

She was found by a police officer—Officer Paul Stone—who stumbled on her, almost literally. Twenty-two years old and fresh from the police academy, he spent his afternoons on foot patrol along the piers at the edge of South Boston—"Southie," as it was known to the locals. It was a lousy assignment. Directly across Fort Point Channel from downtown Boston, the edge of Southie was lifeless on the weekends, particularly in the heat of late August. The Boston World Trade Center was deserted, as were the new Convention Center and the Federal Courthouse. Other than those outcast buildings, the area was dominated by warehouses, parking lots, and storage facilities, the majority of which were shut down on Sundays. Stone felt as if he were in some postapocalyptic version of his hometown as he patrolled up and down the center of empty streets.

He walked halfway across the abandoned Northern Avenue Bridge at around seven o'clock. It was nearing dusk and most of the lights were on in the skyscrapers in front of him. Many were of the fluorescent variety, beaming out unfriendly from office towers where the lights seemed to burn around the clock, but others glowed from apartment buildings, shimmering along the city's edge and easing the evening's transition. At the bridge's center, he took one last look at the financial district, then turned and followed his patrol route back toward Southie.

The top of his shirt was open to the summer heat as he walked back along the bridge, but there was very little wind. A nice sea breeze might have made the beat more bearable, but the water was still and silent, and he cursed the heat as his collar rode up on his neck, soaked through with sweat.

It was high tide, and the piers seemed peaceful. The sunset over his shoulder cast a flat, pre-dusk light on the shoreline, highlighting the pockets of garbage floating by the shore along the harbor's embankments.

One particular clump caught Stone's eye; a dark mass stuck on a piling twenty yards or so east of the bridge. A metal object in the center of the lump was clinging unnaturally high on the piling. It had found the last rays of sunlight and was reflecting them right into Stone's eyes. He followed the glimmer out of boredom and curiosity, leaving the bridge, turning left, and walking along the shoreline.

When he came to the piling, he leaned over the embankment to take a look.

He could see the object now. It was a watch—a nice one, too. A Movado. The crisp silver casing that formed the simple, understated watch face still held the sunlight from the west. Stone was no longer focused on the watch itself, though; his attention was riveted on the wrist to which it was attached. It was delicate yet firm, and extended up from the water, supporting a slim hand that seemed to be reaching for help. It was so desperate in its pose that Stone's heart skipped a beat, and he reached over the harbor wall to grab hold. It was foolish, he realized, but he did it out of reflex and instinct. The cold, dead feel of the skin returned him to reality and he jerked himself back.

As he let go of the hand, the wrist slipped off its catch on the piling and the entire dark mass rolled over in the water. Stone found himself staring straight down into the face of a woman submerged just inches below the water's surface. Her eyes were open, as if to take one final look at the late summer sky. She was dressed in what looked like a tight-fitting black outfit, and around her neck was a bright red ribbon holding a gold crucifix in place at the top of her chest. Stone had the feeling that she was staring at him, and his heart skipped again when he looked into her eyes. They were clear blue, and they were mesmerizing. Later that night, in trying to recall the entirety of the incident, his only specific recollection would be of those eyes.

He stumbled back from the edge of the embankment and reached for his radio. He was about to call the precinct when a wave of nausea overtook him and he lunged toward the nearest bushes.

After he'd taken a moment to compose himself, he picked up his radio again. "Dispatch, this is Patrol Twelve. I've got a DB Code Thirty in the harbor. Right by the Northern Avenue Bridge, south side. Over."

It seemed like hours before the call was answered. "Patrol Twelve, this is dispatch, could you repeat that?"

"Yeah, I've got a body floating in the goddamned harbor! Caucasian female. Looks like she's in her twenties or thirties. Is that you, Kate?" Stone was friendly with the dispatcher. They'd both grown up in Southie, as had many of the cops in the precinct, and she'd gone to school with his older brother.

"Yeah, it's me, Paul. Don't touch anything. I'm gonna get a team down there to take over on crime scene. Just make damn sure no one goes near the area."

"That shouldn't be too much of a problem. It's just me and the seagulls down here, and I'm sure as hell not going swimming with a stiff."

There was silence on the other end of the radio for a few moments, and after a while Stone started to get nervous. The humidity was oppressive, and he could feel his uniform sticking to his body, bunching uncomfortably in the crevices where his limbs met his torso. It was as if the air was pushing in on him; a stress test draining his arms and legs of their strength as the sweat ran in streams down his back and chest. He began to have the feeling that someone was watching him from a distance, but there was no movement along the waterfront, and he assumed it was just his imagination.

"Kate?" he said into his handset. There was no answer. He walked to the edge of the harbor and looked over the embankment again. The harbor-lady was still there, looking up at him in apparent indifference.

"Kate, you there?" he repeated. He could hear the edge in his voice and he hoped that it wouldn't be obvious back at the station house. He didn't really care, though. He was feeling spooked.

"Yeah, Paul, hold on a minute." Kate's voice calmed him down a little. "Okay," she said after a brief pause. "We've got the task force from Area A-1 on the way down. They should be there in a couple of minutes."

"Okay, I'll be here."

There was another pause. Then, unable to contain her curiosity, Kate asked the question. "Is it him?"

"I don't know, Kate. Red choker. Gold cross. Yeah, I'd say it's probably him. It's just a guess, though."

Kate didn't respond. Stone stood for a moment, looking down at the lifeless figure in the water. Then he sat down on the embankment to wait in silence.

CHAPTER TWO

Police detective lieutenant Linda Flaherty looked at her watch. She hated Mondays. Always had. It sometimes struck her as odd that the hatred remained despite the fact that, in her line of work, Mondays held no particular significance. Weekends offered no break in the investigative cycle. On "the job," Fridays blended into Saturdays and Sundays into Mondays without any distinction. Nevertheless, she hated Mondays, and, standing in the medical examiner's cutting room at eight forty-five in the morning, she knew that this particular Monday was going to be a bad one.

She'd gotten the call at seven-thirty on Sunday evening: *Number Seven has been found.* She'd been at her desk, poring over the case files on the first six victims, looking for anything to grab on to that might bring her some redemption. That was what you did when you were the lead investigator on a case involving a serial killer—you searched for redemption. Until the case was solved and the bastard was rotting in jail, you were a failure, and every new victim was hung around your neck with a weight few could comprehend. So you searched through everything you had for that one clue that might break the case and keep the weight from dragging you down forever.

She wasn't finding anything when the call came in.

Flaherty was the first on the task force to arrive on the scene. A young officer she didn't know was sitting at the edge of the harbor when she pulled up. He stood as soon as he saw her car pulling into the vacant lot near the water. Two police vans from the crime scene unit pulled in behind her.

"What d'ya got?" she shouted to the officer as she got out of her car.

"Dead woman," the officer replied. He sounded nervous. "She's right over here at the edge of the water."

Flaherty walked to the embankment and looked over the edge. This type of grim scene no longer had the power to shock her, but she felt her chest hitch involuntarily as she looked down at the corpse floating by the piling. The tide was still high, and she hadn't expected the woman's body to be as close as it was. When she peered over the embankment, she was looking straight into the most penetrating eyes she'd ever seen. They were pale blue, and they stared up at her with such vibrancy that she almost thought the woman was alive. She must have been beautiful, Flaherty thought. Any amount of time in the water violates a corpse's integrity, and Flaherty could already see the blue swelling around the eyes and lips where the body had begun to decompose and bloat. But even in this deteriorated condition, she could tell that the woman had once been stunning.

"Is this how you found her?" Flaherty's voice was rough, concealing her shock.

Stone hesitated.

"What's your name?" Flaherty's voice betrayed an anger she couldn't explain. Not waiting for an answer, she read the name off the tag on his shirt, just below the badge that was still so new it shined even in the waning light. "*Stone*? Is that how you found her?" This time she got right up to his face and raised her voice to a bark. In her years on the force, she'd learned that, as an attractive woman, this was the best way to gain an advantage over the testosterone factories that populated the ranks. They had no idea how to respond short of physical violence, and the professional inappropriateness of violence against women had been so drilled into them that they were most often left without any defense. She also knew that if she gave a rookie any time to think, he'd tell her what he thought she wanted to hear rather than the truth. Better to frighten him out of using what few brain cells he probably had.

"I'm going to ask you one more time"—she was loud enough now that some of the crime scene team could hear her, and they were looking over nervously—"is that how you found her?"

"Not exactly," Stone finally admitted.

"What do you mean, 'not exactly'?" Her voice was not as loud, but the edge was still there, sharp enough to cut through any rookie's bravado.

"She was more on her side, facedown in the water. Her arm was sticking straight up, so I grabbed her hand and she rolled over."

"Why the hell did you grab her hand?"

"I don't know, I thought I could help her. I thought she needed help."

"Well, you were right, she did need help . . . about a goddamned day and a half ago from the look of her."

Stone was silent but continued to look Flaherty straight in the eyes. He knew he probably should have left the body alone, but he'd grabbed the hand out of reflex, to try and save the woman. As illogical as it seemed now, it wasn't something he was ashamed of.

Flaherty continued to stare back at him, too. She was pissed off, but not at Stone. She was just taking her anger out on him because he happened to be there. She was pissed off at *him*—the one the media had taken to calling "Little Jack." Some snot-nosed beat reporter at the *Herald* had started using the moniker because all of the victims had been prostitutes and the killer had eviscerated each of them, much like Jack the Ripper. Other reporters, lacking originality, had adopted the title, and it had stuck.

Flaherty suddenly wondered how long it had been since she'd had a decent night's sleep. Not since she'd taken over the task force. There was a lot of political pressure that came with the job. Boston was held in the grip of a serial killer, and every politician with legs was running for cover, looking for someone to take the fall as the bodies piled up.

She sighed. "Don't worry about it too much, Stone. We're probably not going to get much from this crime scene anyway. He kills them someplace else before he dumps the bodies." She shrugged. "And you can't dust the harbor for fingerprints."

"No ma'am." Stone didn't smile or show relief. His face was impassive, but he continued to hold Flaherty's look straight in the eye. His self-assurance was unsettling.

"All right," Flaherty said. "Clear out of here and let the lab boys do their work. Just make sure you have a written report on my desk by six a.m."

"Yes ma'am." Stone nodded and gave a stiff salute before he finally broke eye contact and walked away slowly. Flaherty watched him go, then leaned over the embankment again to look at the woman in the harbor.

She stayed at the crime scene for a while, watching the technicians photograph and record every detail. As she suspected, it was a useless exercise, but then, you never knew what was going to break open a case. When it was clear there'd be no immediate revelations at the crime scene, she left.

It was past midnight when she returned to her tiny apartment fifteen blocks from the downtown Boston police station where she spent almost all of her time. She caught a couple of hours of sleep, then rose early to be at the ME's office to see the entire autopsy. She looked at her watch again, noting it was after the scheduled nine o'clock start for the procedure.

Dr. Tim Farmalant, the chief coroner, finally entered the cutting room. He'd kept her waiting on purpose. It wasn't personal; he did it to everyone. It was his way of making sure everyone knew he ran the show in the Medical Examiner's office, and if you wanted anything done, you were at his mercy.

Other than his obsession with administrative power, Farmalant was the antithesis of the stereotypical coroner. He was tall and handsome, with blond hair whipped back in a styled coif and bright blue eyes. Even under the blue-green of the fluorescent lights in the ancient government building, the depth of his tan was evident.

He smiled at Flaherty as he walked in. It was the type of smile she was used to seeing from men—warm and friendly, but with a hint of lechery lurking underneath. At first his passes had angered her, but Farmalant was so deliberately transparent that she decided to humor him, and even to play along when it gained her an advantage. It was harmless, she told herself, by way of an excuse to assuage the guilt that bit at the feminism she'd been forced to conceal throughout her career. The truth was, she also found it flattering.

"Linda," he said in his most charming voice. "It's good to see you again, even under these circumstances." He reached toward her and took her hand, bringing it up to his lips and kissing it lightly.

Flaherty shook her head in mock disgust. "Doctor, you have the most romantic sense of timing."

"My timing might be better if you would have dinner with me sometime."

Flaherty pointed to the body on the steel table, still covered with a sheet. "I'll tell you what, Doc. You get me something I can use to catch the asshole who did this, and I'll not only go to dinner with you, I'll buy."

Farmalant raised his eyebrows. "You know how I love a challenge."

He walked over to the steel table, letting his critical eye drift over the body even as it was still covered with a white antiseptic sheet. The whole scene made Flaherty shiver in spite of herself. Necessary though it was, an autopsy always struck her as the final insult to a murder victim. Stripped of her life, the woman on the table no longer qualified for the most basic protections against intrusion. What the police would learn might lead to her killer. Then again, it might not. One thing was certain, though: the autopsy would pull back the curtain on her final secrets. The most personal and carefully guarded pieces of herself would become fodder for review and speculation—and often ridicule—around watercoolers and bars once the rank and file learned about them. Necessary, yes. Kind, no. This was the part of her job she hated most.

With one fluid motion, Tim Farmalant's gloved hand tore the sheet off the body and let it float gently to the floor. "Let's begin, shall we?" He winked at Flaherty as he picked up a surgical saw and leaned over the dead woman's body.

CHAPTER THREE

Scott T. Finn, Esq., stood at the window of his downtown office. It was small, little more than a cubicle with four walls, as were all of the associates' offices at the venerable law firm of Howery, Black & Longbothum, PC, but the large window behind the desk offered a beautiful view of the harbor and South Boston. Once he made partner, he'd get a much bigger office, he knew.

He rubbed his hand over the stubble that covered his chin. He'd have to take care of that before any of the partners came in. That was fine. He kept a razor and shaving cream in his desk drawer, along with Advil and Alka-Seltzer.

It had been a long weekend. It was amazing to him that two days could feel so long. He'd crammed too much drinking into too little time, and he was paying for it now. He needed to stop drinking so much, he knew. He needed to start acting like the seventh-year associate at Howery, Black he was. Finn thought back to the madness of his youth on the streets of Charlestown and marveled at how far he'd come. It seemed like a short time ago that he and his crew were running errands for the local crime bosses. It had been a matter of survival, but he had always felt that it wasn't a part of who he was meant to be. After that fateful night, he knew he had to get out, and that was just what he'd done.

He'd fought the odds to get to college, and finished in four years, despite working two jobs at the same time. That was followed by law school in Suffolk University's night program, and then a twenty-thousand-dollar-a-year job as a public defender. He'd probably be there still if he hadn't been noticed by a well-connected prosecutor who told his friend Preston Holland, the managing partner at Howery, Black, that he'd recently come up against one of the finest young courtroom lawyers he'd seen in years. With that recommendation, Finn was able to get a job at the white-shoe law firm, where his salary had immediately increased to one hundred and thirty thousand dollars a year.

Now, six years later, he was only one year away from making partner if everything went according to plan. And while there were certainly no guarantees, he knew he was catching the attention of some of the more influential senior partners, and had even become a protégé of Preston Holland himself, which gave him an advantage over most of the other associates. In a law firm where roughly one out of thirty starting associates managed to make partner, he felt like his chances were better than fifty-fifty, and he was going to do everything he could to increase those odds. He could already taste victory.

Maybe then he could relax a little. Maybe then the hole he'd felt throughout his life would fill in, and he could put his past behind him.

But first he had to shave.

He also had to apologize to Natalie. He'd acted like a jackass toward her on Friday night, and he needed to make sure he hadn't caused any permanent damage to their friendship. Natalie Caldwell was his closest ally at the firm, and he relied on her to get through the hard times. She was a couple of years behind him, but she had been at the Justice Department for two years before coming to Howery, and she was regarded as a star in her own right. He'd been drawn to her from the moment she joined the firm, and she to him, though less compulsively. For a brief period, just after she joined the firm, they'd been more than friends. It had hurt when she ended it, and they hadn't been as close since, but she was still a better friend to him than anyone else.

Their drinks date on Friday had been a disaster. They'd started out well enough; they got a table at the International and ordered margaritas. They hadn't spent much time alone together since she'd ended their tryst, and he quickly realized how much he'd missed her company. She was funny and open, playfully licking salt from the rim of her glass and laughing seductively. "I've missed this," she said, echoing Finn's thoughts.

"Missed what?" Finn asked, hesitant.

"This," Natalie said. "You and me alone, talking to each other. When was the last time you and I really let our hair down together?"

"I don't know," Finn answered, but it was a lie. He remembered exactly, and it had been a very long time.

"Well, I'm glad we're doing it again." Natalie raised her glass in a toast, and Finn could feel the eyes of every man in the bar following her every move, wondering who she was, and how they might be lucky enough to be with someone like her.

By the third drink, Finn was feeling a little light-headed, and it seemed as if he'd been transported back in time to when he and Natalie had been intimate. He felt sure she was feeling the same way. She seemed comfortable, and yet she kept casting sideways glances at him, her smile suggesting a hidden agenda. In his state, Finn easily convinced himself that her agenda was reconciliation.

By the time he started on his fourth margarita, he'd decided to take a chance. As she was laughing her way through their conversation, closing her eyes and doubling over toward him, he leaned in and kissed her cheek, gently, but with determination. It clearly startled her, and she stiffened, pulling away.

"What's wrong?" he asked.

She looked almost scared, and a little bit angry, as though Finn had broken her trust, and he realized instantly he'd misread her. "I told you a long time ago, we're just friends," she said. Finn felt his face redden, and then, worse, he recognized her look of pity. She softened her tone somewhat. "Look, you're a great guy, Finn, but I've moved on."

"Hey, I know that, Nat. I was just kidding around."

She hesitated. "I'm seeing someone else now."

He looked away from her, knowing he wouldn't react well to the news. "That's great," he said, realizing how forced the words seemed. "Really, I'm happy for you. Who's the lucky guy?" As soon as the question left his lips he regretted asking. It was bad enough she was seeing someone else; he realized he didn't really want to know the details.

She shook her head. "I couldn't tell you if I wanted to. He's older," she said, "and there are complications. But he's been really good for me, teaching me a lot." She continued talking, but Finn was no longer listening. The drinks and his mortification caught up with him quickly, and his light-headedness quickly turned to nausea. He tried to focus on the television above the bar, just to get his bearings, but it was no use, he had to get out of there. As she continued talking, he pulled out two twenty-dollar bills and laid them on the table.

"What are you doing?" she asked, interrupting her monologue.

"Listen, Nat, I'm sorry, but I'm feeling a little under the weather. The tequila's hitting me a little harder than I thought it would," Finn responded. "This should cover our drinks, and then some."

"You can't be serious."

"I know, I feel bad about it, but I've really got to head out. I guess I just can't drink the way I used to when we . . . when I was younger."

"But I have something I need to talk to you about," Natalie protested. "I really need your help. That was the reason I asked you to meet me tonight."

Finn forced a laugh. "You mean it wasn't just for the pleasure of my company?" He heard his voice, and it sounded petty and weak. He had to get out of there before she lost all respect for him. He pasted a smile on his face and patted her on the shoulder clumsily. "I really am sorry, but I feel like shit. Let's do this another time—maybe we can get together for lunch early next week, okay?" She didn't respond, but just looked up at him with an expression of hurt that made him want to take her in his arms. He had to leave. "Okay then, I'll see you Monday."

As he walked out the front door, he turned to look at her, and she flashed him a look of anger that settled in his memory even through the alcohol. He knew he'd have trouble sleeping well again until he made things right between them. After all, in spite of their problems, they were still good friends.

That she would in fact forgive him was not a question in his mind. She'd understand, he knew. That was the thing about their relationship; strained though it was at times, they understood each other. Finn knew he'd never have made it this far in the rarefied environs of Howery, Black if he hadn't had Natalie Caldwell to turn to. She'd *have* to forgive him.

Shaking himself free from the memories of Friday night, Finn picked up the phone and dialed her extension. The phone rang four times before the automated voice-mail system picked up. He put the phone back down. *No point leaving her a message.* He'd catch her when she got in. An apology might go over better in person anyway.

He turned back toward the window and looked out over the

harbor again. From his vantage he could see police lines set up near the edge of the rusted Northern Avenue Bridge, close to the Federal Courthouse, where he spent much of his time. *That must be where they found Little Jack's latest victim.* Like everyone else in Boston, he'd followed the investigation for the past few months. With the infamous Red Sox curse no longer holding his attention, the saga of murder was one of the few entertainments left in the newspapers. He looked down on the few police officers that were still at the scene, covering every inch of the lot as though they might actually find something useful. *Poor bastards.*

He took a deep breath as he surveyed the rest of the harbor and the islands that lay to the south, running their way down toward the tony shoreline suburbs and beyond to Cape Cod. Yeah, things were about as good as they could get from up here on the forty-fourth floor. He just had to make it through the next year or so, then he could relax a little. He raised his arms in a stretch, smiling as he did.

Then he pulled out the razor and shaving cream from his top desk drawer and padded down to the men's room.

CHAPTER FOUR

"His taste has gotten better," said Farmalant.

Flaherty was examining the pile of clothes and personal effects on the table in the corner of the room and wasn't listening. "What?" she asked.

"Little Jack," he said. "His taste in prostitutes has gotten better. The first six we had in here were in pretty ragged shape—even before he got to them. Malnourished, needle tracks up the arms, scars, the works. But this one's a real beauty. Clean, pretty, nice musculature. Maybe he figures that, with his new fame, he can afford call girls instead of streetwalkers?"

Flaherty couldn't tell whether Farmalant was kidding, but she made a mental note to have someone do a quick check of the different escort services around the city.

"She's even got expensive clothes," Farmalant pointed out, nodding at the table in front of Flaherty.

It was true; Flaherty had already noticed it. The leather skirt she'd been wearing was from Giordano's, a chic fashion boutique on Newbury Street. The matching leather jacket didn't have a store label, but it was a Ferragamo design. Even the lingerie, which made up the rest of the outfit, was high-quality: stockings and a garter belt from Victoria's Secret, and a satin bustier from Saks. There were no panties, Flaherty noticed without surprise.

"Anything come in with her besides the clothes?" she asked.

"That's pretty much it," Farmalant replied. "No wallet, no credit cards, no purse. Just the pack of matches we found in her jacket pocket over there."

Flaherty picked up the matches lying on the corner of the table. The cover was entirely black except for a bright red imprint of a lipstick kiss emblazoned in the middle.

"The Kiss Club," Flaherty said.

"What?"

"The matches. They're from the Kiss Club in the leather district. It's a pickup joint owned by one of Whitey Bulger's old crew. Sleazy, but in an upscale sort of way. It's very popular with high-end hookers looking for out-of-towners with some money to spend. It draws in the local scumbags, but it also gets some of the yuppies looking for a night out on the wild side."

"Sounds pretty sketchy. I'm surprised you'd turn a blind eye to someplace like that, Detective. That doesn't seem like your style."

Flaherty shrugged. "Not my call. I work homicide, not vice. Besides, I think people are afraid of who we might find in there if we ever raided the place."

Farmalant nodded and turned back toward the autopsy table. He flipped the switch on the microphone that hung around his neck to record his observations.

"The deceased is a female, Caucasian, approximately twenty-eight to thirty-five years old. Body length has been recorded at sixty-eight and a quarter inches; weight before incision is one hundred and twenty-two pounds, seven ounces. Fingerprints have been taken, as have external prelims. Judging from the state of rigor and the level of decomposition at the time the body was found, the time of death has been estimated between one and four a.m. on Saturday morning.

"The deceased has a large incision in her chest and abdomen, running from the top of her sternum to approximately two inches above her navel. There's significant lividity at the edges of the wound at the bottom, much less at the top. It's apparent that the sternum has been cleaved and the rib cage opened. The wound has been partially sewn together with what appears to be either a light fishing line or a heavy surgical suture. I'm proceeding to open the stitches, and I'm spreading the rib cage to examine the chest cavity.

"There's significant surface damage to both lungs, as well as to the trachea. The damage appears to have been caused by a straight blade with a fine edge, possibly a surgical scalpel."

Farmalant switched off his microphone. "He's losing his patience," he said to Flaherty.

"What do you mean?"

"Well, he's never been what I would consider a skilled surgeon. I mean, I wouldn't want him operating on me. But he's always shown a reasonable amount of proficiency. He's known what he's after, and where to get it. In the past there's been relatively little damage to the other organs. This is a hatchet job by comparison."

"You think he may have rushed this one?"

"It's possible. But we still haven't established that this woman's killer is in fact Little Jack." He turned the microphone back on. "I'm now separating the lungs to reveal the thoracic cavity." He paused as he ran his hands around the insides of the body. "There's a defined severance of the aorta at approximately one-quarter inch. There's a similar severance of the pulmonary artery. There's significant arterial and tissue damage to the surrounding area." He paused again and looked at Flaherty. "The deceased's heart has been completely removed."

"Little Jack," Flaherty said under her breath.

"Little Jack," Farmalant repeated. He didn't realize his microphone was still on.

Back in Farmalant's office, Flaherty sat in one of the doctor's matching leather chairs. He'd clearly bought these himself, she thought. The city didn't spring for such luxuries.

"I thought we might be dealing with a copycat when I saw the damage to the lungs," Farmalant was saying. "It just didn't seem like Little Jack's work." He said it casually enough, but to Flaherty it still felt like a sharp jab.

"We haven't told the press about the missing hearts, though. So how could a copycat have known what to mimic?"

"Yeah, it doesn't make sense. Still . . ."

"If somebody *had* leaked something like that, it would have been in every newspaper in Boston. We haven't even told everyone on the task force. That's on a need-to-know basis. It's hard to see how the information about the hearts could have gotten out when we're even keeping it from our own guys." Flaherty leaned back and looked at the ceiling. The truth was, she didn't want to consider the possibility that they had a copycat on the loose. That would mean they had two serial killers to catch. The thought was more than she could bear.

"You're probably right," the coroner admitted. He said it without conviction, though.

"I've gotta get this guy. Did you see anything in there that might give us some direction?"

"Not really. Just what we already know. We're almost certainly dealing with a white male in his twenties or thirties. All of the victims have been prostitutes, so there may be some sort of moral or retributive motive. And the skillful cutting of the previous six victims suggests it's someone with at least some medical training. Finally, given the location where the bodies have been found, it's likely our boy lives or works either in downtown Boston or in Southie."

"Thanks," Flaherty said. "You just summarized my last memo."

"Like I said, I don't have anything you don't already know."

Just then the door to Farmalant's office banged open. Detective Tom Kozlowski stood at the threshold. He was short and squat, but powerfully built. It looked for a moment like he wasn't going to get his shoulders through. As usual, his graying hair was mussed and his collar was crooked. A thick, ugly scar ran from the corner of his left eye halfway down his cheek. He was an old-school cop in every way, and he and Flaherty had been partners for three years. His skill at the job kept him on the force, but his temperament kept him from advancing. Since they'd been partnered together, Flaherty had been promoted twice, while Kozlowski had remained a detective sergeant.

"I've got something for you," he said. His voice was low and gravelly from four decades of cigarettes. He seemed tired in that immovable sort of way that comes only after cops reach twenty years on the force and have locked in their pensions. It gives them a certain resistance to the pressures that bear down on them on a daily basis. Kozlowski had passed his twenty years more than half a decade ago. "I had the tech guys put a rush on Jane Doe's fingerprints."

"Did we get lucky?" Flaherty was leaning forward in the plush leather chair now.

"Sort of. I guess it depends on your point of view."

"Let me guess," the medical examiner interrupted. "Numerous arrests for solicitation? Maybe one or two for indecent exposure or disturbing the peace, right?"

"Close, but not quite, Doc." Kozlowski looked at Flaherty, hesitant to reveal his information in front of Farmalant, who wasn't technically on the task force.

"Well?" Flaherty prodded.

"Actually, she was in the FBI database."

"FBI?" Farmalant raised an eyebrow.

"Yeah." Kozlowski nodded grimly. "Turns out she was once a federal prosecutor."

"She was *what*?" Flaherty almost fell out of the comfortable leather chair.

Kozlowski nodded. "Unless the system is completely screwed up, the lady lying on that table is former assistant United States attorney Natalie J. Caldwell."

Flaherty took a deep breath, blowing it out through puffed cheeks in a massive sigh. "Aw shit," she said finally.

"Yeah," Kozlowski agreed. "Shit."

CHAPTER FIVE

Finn had no idea where the day had gone. He'd started reading deposition transcripts in one of his cases, and by the time he looked up it was after three. *I guess time really does fly when you're having fun*, he thought with a note of sarcasm. Sadly, there was nothing fun about what he was reading. There, in front of his eyes, was the testimony that would likely send one of the firm's clients to jail. It was a securities fraud case, and the firm was representing one of the principals at a Fortune 500 company, the stock value of which had fallen eighty-five percent in five months. The particular executive they were representing, Paul Miller, had gotten his hand caught in the cookie jar—up to his elbow, actually—trading on insider information as his company crashed around his feet.

Rich people baffled Finn. Miller had stashed away tens of millions of dollars already, and management had created enough golden parachutes for everyone in the upper echelons. Even if the company flew straight into the ground, Miller was sure to land gently in the middle of his ten-acre estate on Martha's Vineyard, where he could spend the rest of his days living in luxury off the interest in his holdings. Apparently, that hadn't been enough. When Miller saw the writing on the wall, he began dumping his company holdings. And as if that wasn't bad enough, he was also shorting the stock, making millions by betting that the company's stock would go down. It wasn't just criminal; it was criminally stupid. Finn shook his head. *How could he have possibly thought he wouldn't get caught?* Even the street thugs Finn once represented as a public defender would have laughed at the man's idiocy.

Ah well, Finn sighed. This was what he'd signed up for when he came to play in the big leagues. Regular folks couldn't afford the fees that generated his salary. Not even the innocent ones—particularly not the innocent ones. Only the fabulously wealthy could afford to break the law, secure in the knowledge that the brilliant legal minds at Howery, Black & Longbothum, PC, would work tirelessly to protect them from any hint of justice.

And Finn and his colleagues would probably get Miller off in the end. They'd cut a deal with the Securities and Exchange Commission and the feds, and their guy would walk with a fine and a slap on the wrist. Afterward, the partners would marvel at Finn's brilliance as they lunched at Hamersley's or Locke-Ober, and Finn's salary would continue to grow. As hard as it was to stomach, he knew there were worse ways to make a living.

The buzzer on his phone brought him out of his trance. He hit the intercom button. "What is it, Nancy?"

"There are two people out here who want to talk to you." His secretary lowered her voice to a whisper. "They have badges," she said quietly.

"Badges?"

"Yes."

"What do they want?"

"All they'll tell me is that they want to speak with you."

"All right, you can bring them in, but buzz me in five minutes and pretend you're reminding me about a meeting."

Badges. For a moment, Finn considered the possibility that

the folks from the SEC were ready to pitch a settlement in the Miller case, but he was on good terms with Sarah Golden, the lead prosecutor, and she would have called to set up a meeting.

As a lawyer, he shouldn't have been bothered by badges. He certainly had dealt with the police all the time when he was in the Public Defender's office, and he should have gotten over his fear of the law. But badges still reminded him of some of the darker moments of his youth, before he gained control of his life. He took a deep breath and straightened his tie as Nancy brought the two badges in.

Finn's first reaction was one of shock. The woman who followed Nancy through the door was stunning. She had shoulder-length dark hair, brushed back neatly in a simple but stylish manner, and the face and figure of a model. It made him reevaluate his notion of what it meant to be one of Boston's Finest. For just a moment he let himself believe this might be a pleasant experience.

Then he noticed the Neanderthal behind her. He was much more typical, Finn thought grimly. He was shorter than Finn, but much thicker—particularly through the shoulders and chest. Finn estimated him to be at least ten years older, but suspected that it had been a hard decade—the kind that produces a particularly hard man. The man gave the impression of being someone you wouldn't want to mess with.

"Mr. Finn?" Detective Flaherty said. She was smiling, but her voice contained a strange lilt that sounded almost like sympathy. It unnerved Finn. "My name is Lieutenant Linda Flaherty with the Boston Police Department. This is my partner, Detective Tom Kozlowski. We'd like to take a moment of your time, if that's all right?"

"Yes. Please, sit down." Finn gestured toward the two small wooden armchairs that were crammed together in the tiny space opposite his desk. They were nondescript, functional units mass-produced for hundreds of thousands of similar small offices around the country. Still an associate, Finn was rarely called on to host clients in his office, so only the bare necessities were provided. Flaherty took the chair closest to the wall. The hulk she was with squeezed himself into the chair next to the door. He looked almost comical, and the absurdity made Finn feel more at ease.

"What can I do for you?" he asked, smiling at the brunette.

"We'd like to ask you a few questions," she said, somewhat gently.

"Yes, my secretary told me. I can assure you that, whatever it is, I didn't do it. I've got witnesses." Finn hoped his joke would help lighten the mood. It didn't. Flaherty's smile was indulgent at best, and Kozlowski just kept staring straight through the back of Finn's head.

"Mr. Finn," she began again.

"Please, it's just Finn. Nobody ever calls me 'Mister.'"

"Mr. Finn, we need to ask you some questions about Natalie Caldwell."

That got Finn's attention. He'd been craned forward over his desk, trying to draw the officers in and establish some rapport. He immediately leaned back in his chair when he heard Natalie's name. He was protective by nature, and he didn't like the idea of the police asking him questions about a friend.

His change in attitude must have been apparent, because he noticed his visitors exchange a look. The chess game had begun. He smiled again, forcing himself this time.

"What do you want to know about Nat?" He'd learned long ago that it was always better to be the one asking questions, and he'd developed a reflex of going on the offensive when confronted with an interrogation. He wondered what Natalie had done wrong. Most likely, she'd pissed off somebody down at City Hall, he thought. She had an aggressive personality, and most men hated dealing with assertive women. As a consequence, she often made enemies. She must have really stepped on somebody's toes this time for them to send two cops out asking questions. The thought amused him, and he suddenly felt better-equipped to deal with the meeting.

"Well, let's start with when you last saw her?"

Finn regarded the attractive brunette and silently counted to five. It was another technique he'd learned over the years; always control the pace of the questioning—it throws people off. He didn't change his expression or look away. He simply looked straight at her until he reached five.

"Why would you want to know when I last saw her?"

"We're conducting an investigation that involves her. Mr. Holland, the head of your firm, indicated you've been her closest colleague, so we thought we should start with you."

"Really? An investigation involving her? Could you be a little more specific? Maybe that would help." He was toying with her now, and enjoying it. God, she was pretty.

"Well, we'd really like to start out by determining when it was you saw her last."

Just then the buzzer sounded. *Right on time.* "Yes, Nancy?" he said into the receiver. He paused as though getting some important news. "Oh, that's right, thank you for reminding me." He hung up the phone and looked at the officers. "I'm going to have to run to a meeting in a moment. Look, if it's an investigation involving Natalie, maybe you should start by talking to her. Her office is right around the corner. Have you stopped by to see if she's in there?" It was time to get rid of these two. As much as he was enjoying the joust with this good-looking cop, he had work to do and didn't want to say anything that might put Natalie in a jam.

"No, we haven't. We're pretty sure she's not in there."

"How would you know if you haven't looked?" Finn flashed them his most condescending smartass lawyer smile. *This ought to get rid of them.*

It was Kozlowski who finally answered. It was the first time he'd spoken. "Because we found her body floating in Boston Harbor last night."

He said it so simply, so utterly without passion or feeling or sympathy, that Finn convinced himself that he must have misheard. He *must* have. That was the only logical explanation. Even if Finn was being a prick, which he was, the police wouldn't joke about something like that, particularly not to a lawyer. It would invite a lawsuit. No, it couldn't have been a joke, and that meant Finn must have misheard the giant squeezed into the chair in front of him, because the only other explanation was that Nat was actually . . .

He looked at Flaherty again, and she had the same sympathetic look on her face that she wore when she walked into the office. All at once, Finn knew it wasn't a joke, and that he hadn't misheard Kozlowski.

"What the hell are you talking about?" he demanded. He meant for it to come out forcefully, as though if he were belligerent enough, he could prevent what Kozlowski said from being true. He heard his own voice as a whisper, though.

"I'm very sorry, Mr. Finn," Flaherty said. "We believe we found Ms. Caldwell's body in the harbor yesterday evening. We're investigating the circumstances of her death."

"You 'believe'? You mean you're not sure?" Finn felt his heart flicker, only to have Kozlowski stomp on it again.

"The body's fingerprints match those on record for Ms. Caldwell with the FBI. As you probably know, she had no parents or immediate family, so we haven't found anyone to make a positive ID yet, but we're ninety-nine percent sure."

Flaherty cut off Kozlowski's cruelty. "Again, we're very sorry, Mr. Finn, but we do need to ask you some questions."

Finn could hear the blood rushing through his ears. The pretty lieutenant was still talking, but he couldn't make out her words. His world had narrowed and his brain was blocking out everything; everything except that one sentence that kept repeating over and over: *We're investigating the circumstances of her death*. The rhythm of the words tortured him and kept him from focusing on anything else.

"Wait," Finn interrupted Flaherty in midsentence. "You found her in the harbor?"

"Yes, she was . . ." But Finn had tuned her out again. He got up and took two steps over to the floor-to-ceiling window in his office. He looked across the channel and saw the yellow police tape still walling off an area near the bridge, but there was only one officer still there. For the most part the activity from the morning had ceased.

"It was Natalie, wasn't it?" Finn asked without turning around.

"I'm sorry?" Flaherty asked, not comprehending.

"It was Natalie they were talking about in the papers, wasn't it? Number Seven. It was her. Little Jack did this, didn't he?"

"We're not sure at this point."

"The papers seemed sure this morning."

Flaherty sighed. "Yeah, well, this kind of thing makes better copy if it's a serial killer, doesn't it? And it's possible it *is* the same guy; that's certainly something we're looking at. At this point, though, we're just trying to conduct the most complete investigation we can."

Finn was still staring out the window at the crime scene across the channel. All at once it hit him. He wouldn't have the chance to apologize for his behavior at the bar on Friday. She couldn't forgive him. It wouldn't be all right.

"That's why we need your help," Flaherty said, trying to penetrate his grief.

He took a deep breath and put on his game face before turning around.

"What can I do?" he asked.

CHAPTER SIX

"Last Friday night," he said. "Evening, actually. We went out for a couple of drinks." The detectives were still in his office. Finn was sitting at his desk again, having composed himself.

"This was with people from the office?" Flaherty asked. Both she and Kozlowski had taken out notebooks and were scribbling away.

"Not really people, just Nat and me."

"Was that normal? The two of you going out to drink alone after work?" This time it was Kozlowski, and there seemed to be some insinuation in the question.

"We're lawyers," Finn said simply. "We *all* drink."

"How long were you out for?" Flaherty asked.

"Several hours, but I was only with Natalie for an hour or so. We had separate social lives, so we were just having a couple of drinks after work. To unwind, you know?"

Kozlowski gave a grunt. Finn couldn't tell whether it was a grunt of understanding or of judgment, but he was beyond caring what the Neanderthal thought.

"What time did you see her last?" At least Flaherty seemed to have some sensitivity.

"I left the bar at around seven or so. We were out at the International, right across the street."

"Did she tell you what her plans were for the rest of the weekend?"

Finn thought for a moment. "I'm pretty sure she had a date, but she didn't give me an itinerary or anything like that."

"Did she tell you who the date was with?"

"She didn't. She had a new boyfriend, I think, but he was older, and I guess I didn't really approve, so she didn't go into it."

Flaherty and Kozlowski shared another look. Kozlowski asked the next question. "You don't know anything about this guy?"

Finn thought back to his conversation with Natalie. She'd been talking about her new man in veiled terms, but he'd tuned her out. He'd been too busy dealing with his own emotions. In his memory, he could hear her voice in the background of his own thoughts, but he couldn't make out what she had said. "Like I said, I got the impression he was older, but that's about it," he said at last.

"What was your relationship with Ms. Caldwell?" Again, it was Kozlowski, and his voice had a bite to it that annoyed Finn.

"We were colleagues," he said flatly.

"That it?" Kozlowski pressed.

Finn breathed in slowly as he considered the question. "No, that's not it," he said after a pause. "We were friends." He turned back to Flaherty. "Are we done here? It's turned into a pretty crappy day."

Flaherty nodded. "I think that's all we need at the moment, but I do have a favor to ask."

"I can't wait."

"As I said before, we haven't been able to get a positive identification—yet." She paused, as though unsure whether to follow through with her request. Finn could read the question on her face, though.

"You've got to be kidding. You want me to ID her body?"

"I know it's not pleasant, but we need to do this if we're going to progress with the investigation. I would think you would want to do that for your friend."

Finn rolled his eyes. He couldn't bear the thought of having to look at Natalie's dead body. He would have much preferred to remember her the way she was when she was alive: vibrant, vital, and beautiful. But something about what Flaherty said struck a chord. It wasn't so much the investigation he was worried about; it was that she didn't have any family. Natalie was an only child and she'd lost her parents when she was young. Finn was an orphan, and had never known his parents. The absence of family was one of the things they shared; a bond that others probably wouldn't understand, but that kept them together even when there was tension between them. He couldn't let her death go unacknowledged by the one person who really cared about her. That would be too much of a betrayal.

He also still harbored the desperate hope, in the back of his mind, that they'd made a mistake. Maybe she wasn't really dead. He knew he'd never really accept her death unless he saw her with his own eyes.

"All right, let's go," he said, standing up and grabbing his suit jacket. When he got to the door a thought struck him. He turned around and looked at Flaherty. She was less than an arm's length away from him in the small office and he could smell her perfume.

"I thought Little Jack only killed prostitutes. Why would he have killed Natalie?"

Flaherty hesitated, trying to phrase her answer delicately. "She was dressed provocatively. He might have mistaken her for something she wasn't."

Finn closed his eyes again and dropped his chin into his chest. He was silent for a moment as he fought off a wave of memories. He knew he had to put them aside if he was going to get through this. He could do it; he'd done it before. It was a part of the survival skills he'd learned at a young age. Psychiatrists called it "compartmentalization": the ability to separate feelings, memories, and tasks. It was a useful skill in dealing with difficult issues while still leading a useful, productive, even successful life. Finn was an expert at it.

He took two more deep breaths, then lifted his head.

"Okay, I'm ready."

The three arrived at the ME's office twenty minutes later. As they walked down the corridor to where the junior coroner had laid out Natalie's body, Flaherty realized that she felt sorry for Finn—and that was rare for her. When you spend your time wading hip deep in human tragedy, you become numb to the pain of those around you. You have to in order to survive. You say the right things to the grieving widows, and you wear the proper facial expressions to convince the victims' families of your sincere and heartfelt condolences, but you never really let it in.

For some reason, this was different. Maybe it was because she'd seen something in the dead woman's eyes the first time she looked over the embankment wall at the body floating in the water. Flaherty felt like she'd glimpsed the woman Natalie Caldwell had been: strong, confident, unapologetic. It was an image Flaherty identified with as a woman in a brutally unforgiving, predominantly male profession. And now, watching Scott Finn's face, she saw her intuition confirmed. In seeming homage to Caldwell's strength, he didn't wail or cry the way so many others did when confronted by death. Nor did he look away when the sheet was pulled back. His expression was stoic and reserved, with just a slight twitch at the corner of his eye, and a drawing together of his lips.

"That's her," he said. He reached out his hand and stroked her hair. It was matted and stiff, as though to provide further evidence of her death. His eyes watered, but he kept the tears from falling. "I'm sorry, Nat," he said. Then he pulled his hand away.

Flaherty nodded at the junior coroner, who pulled up the sheet over Natalie Caldwell's face and carefully slid her body back into the refrigerated drawer that had become her home. When the drawer closed, a latch caught with a loud crack that signaled finality. Flaherty watched Finn as he continued to stare at the drawer's door, lost in thought. Once again, she felt sorry for him.

"Thank you for doing this," she said, putting her hand on his shoulder. "I know it wasn't easy."

"Is that all you need?" Finn asked, still staring with empty eyes at the door that had swallowed his friend.

"Yeah, that should do it for now."

"You'll be around if we need to ask you any questions, right?" Kozlowski asked. Flaherty cringed. Her partner had the sensitivity of a pit bull.

Finn's gaze moved from the drawer to Kozlowski, narrowing as it bore straight through his forehead. Flaherty saw the change instantly. The grief that had been there only a moment before had been replaced by something else. Rage. Finn's face reflected an anger so intense that Flaherty thought for a moment he might actually attack Kozlowski. It was a determined rage, and Flaherty didn't like it. She stepped in between the two men.

"We'll contact you if we need anything else," she said to Finn.

He turned and looked at her. His eyes softened a bit, and the sadness returned. "If there's anything I can do to help the investigation, let me know." With that, he turned and walked out of the room. He didn't look at Kozlowski again.

"What an asshole," Kozlowski said when he was gone.

Flaherty nodded. "Yeah, you two make a great pair."

"What the hell did I do?" Kozlowski protested. "He was the one who was jerking us around from the start; pulling his hotshot lawyer bullshit. I'm telling you, I've got a nasty feeling about that guy. He's hiding something. Anyway, he needed to be knocked down a peg or two."

"Well, if anyone would be an expert on peg-knocking, it'd be you."

"You're not going soft on me, partner, are you? Did you see the look on his face before he left? Pure violence. Hell, if it wasn't for Little Jack, I'd be lookin' at this guy as our perp on the Caldwell murder."

Flaherty had seen the look; she couldn't deny it. But she'd also seen something else. Something more complicated, buried deep inside Scott Finn. She couldn't put her finger on it yet, but she knew it was going to gnaw at her until she did.

"Yeah, well let's focus on Little Jack for the moment," she said as she and Kozlowski walked out of the ME's office.

CHAPTER SEVEN

Finn got back to his office around six-thirty, although it felt much later. He was tired, and strung out, and confused. He'd been pushed too far by that asshole Kozlowski, and he'd reacted badly. It seemed that no matter how far he got from the streets, a piece of them remained. He couldn't change that—particularly when he was challenged.

Most of the firm's support staff cleared out at five o'clock, but the lawyers were still there. The days when big Boston firms were more "collegial" than their New York counterparts had passed. Law firms had all gone the way of big business, and the image of the Boston bar as a righteous and gentlemanly institution remained only as a facade. The focus was now on increasing revenue, and that put an inordinate amount of pressure on the young lawyers, who were counted on to accumulate ever higher billable hours.

Finn went to his office and closed the door. He sat at his desk for a moment with his head in his hands. *This isn't possible*, he thought. *It can't be happening*. But he knew it was. Any fantasy that the police had gotten it wrong and Nat was still alive had been shattered when the coroner pulled back the sheet to reveal her body. There was no doubt that it was Natalie on that cold, hard slab. *I'm not looking my best*, she probably would have joked if she'd been alive, but he knew her face too well for there to be any doubt. Every rise and fall to that beautiful face was etched permanently into his mind.

He shouldn't grapple with this here, he realized. If he let himself acknowledge how deeply he felt Natalie's death he'd lose control—a cardinal sin for a lawyer. Lawyers deal with other people's tragedies every day, and they're expected to remain unflappable. Finn was particularly good at it. Perhaps as a result of his brutal childhood, nothing ever got to him: not the tobacco plaintiff who had to answer questions at his deposition from his hospital bed through a computerized voice generator because he was missing most of his throat; not the widow of the steelworker who slipped from his sixth-story perch and fell halfway to the ground before he was impaled on a twenty-foot length of rebar—surviving for nearly thirty minutes as the fire department and the city works department debated the best way to cut him down; not the three-year-old who gamely crawled around on the two stumps that protruded from her hips, still unaware that her parents' insurance company's intractability had cheated her out of a normal life. None of it penetrated Finn's shell, and that's why he was so good at defending those accused of monstrosities. It was what made him stand out from the pack.

He had to get out of the office. If he was going to lose control, he wanted to do it in the privacy of his apartment, not in front of his colleagues. He began throwing some materials into a briefcase. Before he could finish, there was a knock on the door. He cleared his throat and steeled himself.

"Come on in," he shouted.

The door opened and Preston Holland's head peered around the corner. "How are you doing?" Holland asked. There was a look of deep concern on his usually stoic face. His thick white hair was combed neatly back from his forehead, and his trademark bow tie was neatly arranged over his pressed collar, but

Finn could feel his mentor's sympathy in the softened look around his eyes.

Finn took a deep breath and blew it out. If there was anyone at the firm he could be honest with, it was Preston. He'd been the one who pulled Finn out of the Public Defender's office and offered him a job at the firm—twisting the arms of many of his partners whose noses still turned up at anyone without at least one Ivy League diploma. Since then, he'd been openly proud of Finn's accomplishments, reveling in each new success the younger man tallied. Preston had become more than a mentor—he'd become a friend and a protector, giving Finn high-profile cases to work on, encouraging him in his practice, and steering him away from many of the obstacles that tripped up young associates in their climb up the firm's political ladder. It was the first time anyone important had believed in Finn, and he drew enormous strength from Preston's approval.

Finn was all the more appreciative of Holland's fatherly affection because of his stature in the Boston legal community. Preston Holland was a legend. He was shorter than Finn, and more refined, but still handsome and compelling, and his ability to sway a jury with the simple tempo of his voice and the strength of his oratory brought hundreds of clients to Howery, Black.

"I'm all right, I guess," Finn replied. "I've had better days, y'know? But I'll be fine in the end."

"Of course you will," Holland said. "We'll all be fine . . . in the end. But that doesn't make it any easier right now. I mean, my Lord, I met with Natalie just last Friday on a case. I can't believe this has happened. I keep thinking there's been some mistake."

"No mistake," Finn said. "I saw her down at the morgue."

Holland looked down at his feet. "I know, I just heard." He sounded guilty. "I'm sorry about that. I never would have given those police officers your name if I'd had any idea that they were going to ask you to do that. I can't even imagine how hard it must have been. I would have been willing to go down there myself if I'd known, but . . ."

"No, don't worry about it. I think it was probably a good thing. It brought home the reality of it all. I feel better knowing for sure there wasn't any mistake."

"Yes, I suppose I can see that. Still, it must have been awful."

"It was. That's why I'm thinking about calling it a day and heading home early." Finn looked at his watch. It was just after seven.

"I think that's an excellent idea. Go home and get a good night's sleep." Holland's expression was grim and his eyes seemed slightly damp as they peered out from his angular face. "Remember, we're all here for each other."

"Thanks."

Holland began to leave, then turned back. "By the way, stop by my office when you get in tomorrow. I have a favor to ask."

"Why not just ask now?"

Holland considered it for a moment, then shook his head. "I think it would be more appropriate to discuss it in the morning. You should go home and get some rest. This will keep, at least until tomorrow."

Something in Holland's tone piqued Finn's curiosity. "What's up?" he asked. "You might as well tell me now, or I'll spend the evening wondering about it instead of sleeping."

"Are you sure? It really can wait."

"Spit it out."

Holland paused, as though weighing his options. "It's about *Tannery v. Huron Security*."

Finn felt a jolt of adrenaline. The Tannery case was the highest-profile case in the office. Ed Tannery was one of the victims of the "Anniversary Bombing," as it had become known, and his widow was suing the company that had been in charge of security on the commuter rail line. As usual, Howery, Black represented the "black hat" in the case—Huron Security, Inc.

Finn had campaigned hard to be the senior associate assigned to the case when the firm had been hired six months before, but Holland decided to put Natalie on it instead. "She's a woman. You're not," he explained to Finn at the time. "Like it or not, the plaintiff is an attractive young woman—a widow. A jury will have an easier time hearing our side of the story if an attractive young woman helps present some of it. It will even our odds a little."

Finn had been disappointed. If the case could be won, it was a sure partner-maker, and he thought he had more experience than Natalie performing under pressure. At the same time, he trusted Holland's judgment, and even understood his point. Many lawyers viewed it as unethical to assign lawyers to particular cases based on their race, sex, or religion, but Holland viewed it as unethical not to exploit every possible advantage on behalf of his clients. Finn tended to agree.

"You're familiar with the case, obviously." Holland knew how disappointed Finn had been when it was assigned to Natalie. Finn nodded.

"As you know," Holland summarized needlessly, "Ed Tannery was one of the eight hundred victims of the terrorist attack last year. But Tannery isn't just any victim. He is the only victim whose family wouldn't accept the settlement offered to the victims' families by the Victims Compensation Act passed by Congress shortly after the attack. Instead, his widow's lawyers convinced her she could make more money by suing the state and Huron Security."

"How much did she pass up under the settlement?" Finn knew some of the Tannery case details but not all.

"Based on all the variables, she would have gotten more than two million if she'd settled."

Finn whistled. "That's a lot of cash. Why did she turn it down?"

"Who knows? She's still saying she wants an in-depth investigation into homeland security or some hogwash like that, but believe me, this is all about the money. Fred Barnolk represents her." Barnolk was a notorious plaintiffs' attorney whose courtroom skills weren't nearly as well developed as his media skills.

"Doesn't she know she has no case? Even if security was too light, she still has to prove an attack could have been prevented if other reasonable measures had been taken."

"I know, but Barnolk hopes to try this case in the press." Holland sighed heavily. "Every security expert in the world agrees it's virtually impossible to stop a well-trained terrorist who's willing to sacrifice himself in a massive attack. I know that. You know that. Her lawyers should know that. Legally speaking, she has no case. But she's not giving up, and it would take a judge with balls of steel to dismiss this thing before it goes to a jury. Can you imagine being the judge who denied a widow of the Anniversary Bombing her day in court?"

"Who's the judge?"

"The Honorable F. Clayton Taylor IV."

Finn shook his head in disgust. "Balls of clay, right?"

"Worse, he's a crusader. He was a high-profile plaintiffs' attorney in his former life before his political friends got him appointed to the bench. He thinks the first responsibility of a judge is to protect the little guy, regardless of what the law says."

"Great."

"Yeah, we've got a little bit of an uphill battle on this one, although we should prevail in the end. But that's why I have to ask a favor from you." Holland paused again. "I really wanted to talk about this in the morning. I feel pretty ghoulish bringing it up right after Natalie . . . well, you know."

"Hey, don't worry about it. I pressed."

"Yeah, I know, but still." He sighed again. "Anyway, we have depositions all next week, and I need someone who can get up to speed by then. I think that you're that someone."

Finn took a deep breath and considered his options. The Tannery case was a once-in-a-lifetime opportunity and couldn't be passed up easily. It felt strange, though, that he should benefit so directly from Natalie's death. Still, someone had to take over the case, and there was no reason it shouldn't be him. Natalie would have understood; she always believed everyone had to look after his or her own interests first and foremost.

"I'll take the case," he said finally.

Holland smiled. "Good." He lowered his voice. "In all honesty, I'm not sure I would have trusted this to anyone else here. If things go well . . ." He didn't finish his sentence. "I'll send the files down, and we can talk about the case in the morning. I'll also have Nick Williams stop by to fill you in on exactly where we stand. Nick's second-chairing this for me." He paused and looked Finn straight in the eyes. "It's good to have you on board. Now, you should clear out of here and get some rest."

Finn nodded. "I'll talk to you in the morning."

Once Holland was gone, Finn resumed throwing some papers into his briefcase. He knew he wouldn't look at them, but he would have felt naked walking out of the office without enough work to take up every moment between the time he left and the time he returned.

Before leaving, he turned toward the window again, looking out over the channel to the small area marked off by police tape on the other side. There were no police officers left. One corner of the yellow tape had come loose from the post around which it had been tied, and it flapped in the breeze. Soon, he knew, the tape would be gone—blown away by the wind or stolen by homeless scavengers who saw value in anything that could be gathered up and trucked away in their shopping carts. By the next day there'd be no way to tell that anything of consequence had happened there, and only the few who knew Natalie Caldwell would shiver when they passed. Life would go on, he knew, but it would be different for him. He'd lost one of the most important people in his life.

He took one last look from his perch high in the office tower above the water, still safe from the violent currents that had once directed his life. Then he turned off the light and headed for the elevator.

CHAPTER EIGHT

The Honorable William H. Clarke, governor of the Commonwealth of Massachusetts, sat at the kitchen table of his Beacon Hill mansion in his underwear and a rumpled T-shirt. A bathrobe was pulled around his shoulders, but he hadn't bothered to tie it at the waist. Clarke's hair stood on end, jutting out at impossible angles from his head, and the stubble of his beard was patched with gray. It was just after five o'clock in the morning, and it was hardly a photo-op moment for the middle-aged politician.

Wendyl Shore stood in front of the governor, nearly at attention. Even at this ungodly hour, Shore was dressed in pressed khaki slacks, a blue blazer, and a Brooks Brothers rep tie. He looked like a cross between an aging college a cappella singer and a marine sergeant. For all of Shore's idiosyncrasies, though, he was the best chief of staff Clarke could ever hope for. His loyalty, even when it was driven by self-interest, could not be questioned, and he was discreet in all respects. Certainly, Clarke knew, Wendyl had more than enough information to bring him down. For good or bad, the governor had entrusted him with all of his affairs.

"How bad is it?" Clarke asked.

"It could be better," Wendyl replied. "It would help if the police could find this 'Little Jack' killer. I think that would contain any fallout."

"We have people on that issue," Clarke assured him. "I expect it'll be taken care of very shortly. The commissioner has arranged for a female detective to run the task force, which will play nicely in the press. My understanding is that not only is this Lieutenant Flaherty poised, attractive, and presentable, but her investigative skills are top-rate. I doubt this 'Little Jack' will be at large for too much longer."

Wendyl shrugged. It was the closest to direct insubordination he'd ever come. "If you say so, sir. I think we might want to be more proactive, though."

Clarke sighed. "What do you suggest?"

Wendyl's eyes narrowed, and the governor could see schemes being laid behind his dark pupils. "Let me think about it," he said.

"Fine," said Clarke, nodding wearily. "You think about it. I have to get ready for work." He rose and crossed to the doorway that led into the hall. "You'll be in the office in a half hour when I need you?"

"As always," Wendyl replied.

"Yes," Clarke muttered to himself. "As always." He left his chief of staff to find his own way out and headed upstairs, passing the portraits of five generations of Clarkes that hung along the staircase wall.

CHAPTER NINE

Finn arrived at the office at eight-fifteen the next morning—late by his habits, which normally had him at his desk by seven. It took him nearly a half hour to listen to his voice mail. He couldn't remember the last time he'd gone to bed without checking his messages at work, and it made him feel like he was slipping.

He was listening to the last of the messages when Nick Williams appeared at his door. Finn waved him in and motioned for him to sit down. He jotted down a few notes in response to the rather long-winded message, then he hung up. "Sorry about that," he said to Williams.

"No problem," Nick said. He rubbed his neck as he looked at Finn. "How are you holding up?"

Finn gave a shrug. "I've got a lot on my plate right now, but you know how it goes, that's part of the job. It's nothing that should interfere with the Tannery case."

"I'm not talking about work, Finn, I'm talking about Natalie."

"I know you were," Finn admitted. He looked away.

"I mean, shit, I'm still shaken up by it, and I didn't know her half as well as you did." Williams leaned back in his chair and let a puff of breath escape his lips. "This job is bitch enough, Finn," he said. "Keeping your mind focused with all of this stuff going on in addition to the work seems like it'd be damned near impossible. Are you sure you don't want to take a little time before you jump right into a case like this?"

Finn looked at Williams. He was probably ten years older than Finn—mid-forties, Finn guessed—but still pretty well preserved. His brown hair was thinning, but it looked like he stayed in reasonably good shape, and his features were sharp enough to make his face attractive. All the same, he didn't have the drive Finn had. He'd made partner because he was an excellent tactician with a remarkable capacity to digest information, but he'd never be a first-rate trial counsel. He just didn't have the competitive fury. He was well liked, and Finn respected him, but he'd never understand that, whatever the circumstances, Finn couldn't possibly turn down an opportunity like this.

"I appreciate your concern," Finn said, and he meant it. "But concentrating on this case will help me deal with everything else. It's the only way I know to lose myself."

Williams shrugged. "If that's really the way you feel . . ."

"It is."

"All right, then let's talk about where we are in the case. You're familiar with the basics, right?"

"I think so," Finn said, nodding.

"Good." Williams leaned forward, fidgeting in his chair. "The two primary weaknesses of Ms. Tannery's case are the issues of negligence and causation. First, she has to show that our client, Huron Security, was negligent—that they did something wrong. Her lawyers will argue that Huron failed to adequately guard the railway yard."

"That's what I'd argue," Finn agreed.

"Of course," Nick said, nodding. "But Huron was following the guidelines laid out by the National Transportation Safety Board. And while those guidelines are very specific regarding how to deal with passengers and threats on the trains, they say nothing about how to guard the trains when they aren't running. If a mistake was made, therefore, it was made at the government oversight level."

"Seems logical."

Nick raised his eyebrows. "Let's just hope the jury agrees. To sell it to ordinary people, we have to make sure we have the right experts backing our position." He rocked back in his chair again. "The second issue we have to attack involves causation. Even if Ms. Tannery's lawyers are able to convince a jury that Huron was negligent in the way they guarded the trains, they still need to show that if it weren't for that screwup, the bombing never would have happened. To undermine that argument, we need to get into the mind of the terrorist, show that even tighter security wouldn't have prevented him from carrying out his attack."

"So we're arguing the terrorist couldn't have been stopped—stripping away any liability on Huron's part."

"Exactly. Our basic argument is going to be that nothing Huron could have done would have stopped this guy from killing. He could have strapped the bombs to himself, or he could have gotten shoulder-fired missiles, or he could have sabotaged the tracks—each of which would have had roughly the same result."

"Is it *too* simple an argument?"

"Not really," said Williams, shaking his head. "To make it sing to the jury, we have to show how dedicated these bastards are. We have to take the panel through hundreds of thousands of documents that demonstrate just how careful Huron was, and all of the measures they took." He paused, picking up a pen from Finn's desk and twirling it around in his fingers. "We also have to take them through hundreds of thousands of State and Defense Department documents that prove even the CIA and the FBI haven't been able to prevent attacks like this."

Finn stopped taking notes and put down his pen. "Looks like we've got our work cut out for us."

"More than you can comprehend." Nick scratched his chin as he looked across the desk. "This is a huge case for us. It's a real opportunity to show the partnership what you're made of. Are you ready for it?"

Finn took a deep breath. "I am."

Williams's eyes bored into him. "I hope you *are*," he said finally, then paused as if deciding whether to say something more. "I don't know if you know this, but you and I have something in common."

"What's that?" Finn asked.

"Well, like you, I wasn't born with a silver spoon in my mouth, and I never made it to an Ivy League school. I had to work my ass off in a state college, and then again in a city law school. I had to be better than everyone around me just to get a fair shake. Even though I never had Preston's courtroom presence, I made sure I was smarter and better prepared than the other associates, and that was enough to make partner."

He stopped fidgeting and leaned forward in his seat. "For guys like us, Finn, the big opportunities come around only once. I hope you take full advantage of it, because it would be nice to have another partner in the fold who came up the hard way."

Finn looked across the desk at his colleague. He knew exactly what the man was talking about. Finn had fought bitterly for every morsel of praise he'd ever received at Howery, Black, even when he was outperforming his peers. It made the ultimate prize of partnership all the more enticing. "I'll try not to let everyone down," he said after a long moment.

"Don't worry about everyone," Williams replied. "Just don't let *yourself* down."

CHAPTER TEN

The door to Captain Weidel's office was closed, and there was a group of officious-looking people Flaherty didn't recognize loitering outside. She was tempted to go to check her messages before she reported to the captain, but Weidel had been explicit on the phone earlier; he wanted to see her the second she got in. At least Kozlowski's desk was on the way to the captain's office, so she could drag him along for moral support. He looked up when she stooped over him.

"What's going on in Weidel's office?" she asked.

"Looks like some kind of weasel convention to me, but I wasn't on the invite list, so I'm not sure."

"Yeah, well, don't feel too left out, because I'm bringing you as my date."

"Shit. And me without my makeup."

"It's just as well. I wouldn't want you looking prettier than me, Kozlowski." She waved him over to the door. The sea of sycophants gathered there parted grudgingly. One young man in khakis and a blue blazer looked at the two detectives with particular disdain.

"Come in!" she heard Weidel bellow when she knocked. Flaherty opened the door and she and Kozlowski entered the room.

The first thing she noticed was that the office was crowded. She was used to dealing with Weidel one-on-one, as he chewed her out from behind his desk without the benefit of an audience. She wouldn't be so lucky this time. Weidel was at his desk, all right, but he wasn't alone. The room looked like a who's who of Boston politics and law enforcement. Bill Moyer, the Suffolk County district attorney, was leaning against a filing cabinet in the corner, next to the police commissioner, Randy Backton. Jimmy Tribinio, the recently elected mayor of Boston, was slouched on the low sofa facing the captain's desk. Also on the sofa was Rich Loring, the U.S. attorney for the District of Massachusetts, and sitting in the chair directly in front of Weidel was William Clarke, the governor of Massachusetts. It felt like an ambush.

"Lieutenant," Weidel began, "I think you know everyone here."

She stared at him, dumbstruck. "Not personally, no, but I believe I know everyone by reputation."

The men in the room looked at her from their perches with expressions that conveyed nothing but skepticism and superiority. Only Clarke rose to greet her.

"Lieutenant Flaherty, it's indeed a pleasure to finally meet you in person," he said, standing up and taking her by the hand. It wasn't as much a handshake as a hand press, the soft flesh of his right palm cradling her hand as he covered the grasp with his left hand, drawing her in toward his chest as he leaned in. It oozed of warmth, friendship, and trust, and it immediately put Flaherty on guard.

"You know, when this Little Jack unpleasantness started, I talked with Police Commissioner Backton, here, and I told him we needed the best investigator in the department leading the charge. He spoke to Captain Weidel, and they both agreed there was no one with more competence or a better record than you. I can't tell you how happy we all are that you're on the case." As he finished, the governor looked around the room, nodding, drawing reluctant agreement from everyone.

Flaherty had no idea what to say. She'd never been politically adept. Fortunately, Kozlowski made her look like a UN diplomat as he responded for her.

"Thank you, Governor, we've all been working hard to put an end to the 'unpleasantness.'" What the hell did he care, he already had his twenty years in, and he was never going to make lieutenant anyway.

Clarke looked at Weidel, who nodded venomously at Kozlowski. "Governor, this is Detective Tom Kozlowski. He's helping Lieutenant Flaherty with the investigation. For now." The last part was added with emphasis.

Clarke turned back to Kozlowski. "You, too, have all of our confidence, Detective."

Kozlowski shrugged.

The governor nodded as though a solemn pact had been reached between them, and sat back in his seat, spreading out like a king holding court. "Obviously, the last few days have brought a renewed urgency to this matter." He paused dramatically, like he was delivering a stump speech. "The loss of any life is a great tragedy, no matter how the first six of these women earned their living. But I think we're all even more greatly moved by the senseless killing of a young woman on the rise; a woman of promise who'd worked so closely with those of us in law enforcement. I never met Ms. Caldwell myself, but I'm told she was a top-notch lawyer and one hell of an investigator."

Flaherty was shocked. She spun on Weidel. "We haven't released the victim's identity yet," she said accusingly.

Weidel reddened just a little. "We haven't released it to the *press* yet, Lieutenant. Obviously, it's imperative the governor be kept in the loop with the most up-to-date information we have."

"That's pretty up-to-date. We only got a positive ID yesterday evening, and I don't think I've even had the chance to confirm that with you, Captain." A tone of accusation remained in Flaherty's voice. As the officer in charge of the investigation, she should have been notified of any information given out, even to the governor.

Loring, the U.S. attorney, got up out of his seat. "Look, Detective, I worked with Ms. Caldwell for two years when I was in the FBI and she was at the Justice Department. Are you suggesting the people in this room shouldn't be notified of events in the investigation as they develop? I thought we were all on the same team, but maybe I was misinformed."

"And I thought I was in charge of this investigation," Flaherty shot back. "But maybe I was misinformed."

"Just because you have jurisdiction here doesn't mean we shouldn't know what's going on. We have a right to be kept in the loop." Loring was raising his voice now, and clearly looking for a little turf in the investigation. Flaherty suspected he was more interested in furthering his own political fortunes than finding the killer of a junior colleague he probably didn't even know well. It pissed her off.

"Oh sure. The feds are always so forthcoming with the local cops, right? I remember all the times we were consulted on the Whitey Bulger case." Flaherty's barb found its mark, and Loring's ears went red with anger. Several years before, the FBI and the Justice Department had protected a number of informants high up in Boston's Irish mob who went on killing sprees with impunity. The most notorious was James "Whitey" Bulger, the head of the Winter Hill Gang. The local cops were left chasing their tails as they tried to clean up the mess.

Ultimately, Bulger was indicted on a slew of charges, including eighteen counts of murder, but escaped when his FBI handlers tipped him off before the state police and DEA could arrest him. Several FBI agents resigned. One was convicted of aiding Bulger and was sent to jail. The fallout was still radioactive, and even though Loring hadn't been directly implicated, he was the Special Agent in Charge of the FBI's Boston office at the time, and had signed off on the Bulger operation. The incident hadn't done permanent damage to his career, but he was still defensive about it. The mere mention of it was enough to make him seethe at Flaherty, but he kept his mouth shut.

"That's a pretty cheap shot at a guy who just lost a former colleague, don't you think, Lieutenant?" chided Commissioner Backton.

"I'm very sorry for your loss," Flaherty said to Loring, and the sincerity behind it took everyone in the room by surprise, defusing the tension that had been building. She took a deep breath. "Obviously I'm willing to keep people in the loop. But you've all run investigations, and you all know how important the control of information is to the success of the investigation. Everything must go through me." She looked Weidel straight in the eyes. "Otherwise, you can reassign the case."

"Now wait a minute. If you think you're in any position to dictate terms, Lieutenant, think again," Weidel began, but the governor cut him off.

"No, Captain, the lieutenant is right. It is *her* investigation." He looked at Flaherty with a calculating smile. The message was clear: the case was hers to live or die with—alone. "I think Lieutenant Flaherty is quite aware of how important this investigation is to the entire city, and I'm sure she'll use every means at her disposal to bring this sadistic butcher to justice. By the way, Lieutenant, where does the investigation actually stand at the moment?"

Flaherty was silent, caught off guard by the direction the conversation had taken. Suddenly she wished she hadn't been quite so territorial. It might be nice to have some political backing in this situation. After all, the investigation was stalled; they had no leads and no significant clues.

Everyone in the room was looking at her, waiting for an answer. She had no answers to give, and they all knew it.

"I have to wait for the coroner's official report before I can give you anything concrete," she said. It was weak, but it was the best she could do, and she hoped it would at least buy her a little time. Looking around the room, though, it was clear everyone there saw through her.

"Is there *anything* you can tell us?" Clarke asked.

Flaherty thought quickly. "Well, based on the wounds, we believe Little Jack may have had medical training. Because all of the victims have been white, he's probably white, too; most serial killers hunt within their own race." Great, she reflected. In Boston, with its dozens of leading hospitals, medical schools, and clinics, that narrowed the field of suspects to roughly fifty thousand individuals.

She took a deep breath and continued. "We also have reason to believe he may have met the latest victim, Ms. Caldwell, at a bar near Chinatown called the Kiss Club. Other than that, we're just going to have to wait for the ME's report."

"Anything else?" Clarke pressed.

Flaherty glared at him. "That's all we have right now."

Clarke looked at her for several seconds. The room was silent, and Flaherty could feel the walls closing in. Finally he spoke. "All right, gentlemen, let's clear out of here and let these people get on with their investigation. I trust you'll keep us informed, Lieutenant."

With that, the entire upper echelon of Boston's political and law enforcement communities got up and filed out of Weidel's office. None said good-bye, or even so much as looked at Flaherty on their way out. Then the door closed and she was alone with Kozlowski and Weidel. The captain was rubbing his hands over his face nervously.

"I sure as hell hope you get something from the coroner we can use. I'm not prepared to burn on this cross with you," he said.

"I think you're mixing your historical references, Captain," said Kozlowski.

"What?"

"A person either burns at the stake or hangs on a cross. You wouldn't burn on a cross." The detective kept a straight face as he said it.

"Kozlowski, I have no fucking idea how you ever made your twenty years without getting busted out of the department, but I'm not about to take your shit." The captain was letting his anger show now. "And you," he said, looking at Flaherty. "You're not going to have a chance in hell of making your twenty if you don't find this guy, and I mean fucking soon. I guarantee you that!" Weidel stormed out of his own office, slamming the door behind him.

"That went well," Kozlowski said.

"Yeah, I take you on the best dates, don't I? Sorry about putting us on the spot. You know you're now on the hook for this right along with me, don't you?"

"Wouldn't have it any other way."

CHAPTER ELEVEN

Hallelujah!
Salvation and glory and power belong to our God,
for true and just are His judgments.
He has condemned the great prostitute
who corrupted the earth by her adulteries.
He has avenged on her the blood of His servants . . .

He repeated the words over and over out loud. He no longer even realized he was doing it. It was one of his favorite passages, but there were so many others of equal power, and he could recall them all with such ease. They were the reason for his existence, and his existence would give rise to a new age of damnation for all but the chosen. That he was one of the chosen had been made clear to him years before, and now he'd been called to help clear the way for the plagues and the locusts and the great lake of fire. It made him important.

No one suspected. How could they? There was nothing to suggest the truth. And even if there were something, only the righteous would see it; and the truly righteous would understand, and would rejoice with him.

The house was unassuming; a small, freestanding wood-frame structure on the edge of the commercial district that spread between downtown and South Boston. His parents had left it to him. Their passing had been a painful blow, but in time it had given him clarity, and he knew they were watching him from their graves with pride, and waiting for judgment day to rise again.

The interior was sparse but clean, almost puritanical by bachelor standards. A few religious artifacts were spread around the rooms as the only decoration, but they weren't so prevalent as to draw attention—just enough to suggest a healthy respect for his religion and his God. He was deliberate about that, so that there would be nothing on the first two floors of the little house that would suggest the truth.

The basement was a different story. Concrete, white paint, and bright lights had transformed the space into an odd sort of medical bunker. Against one wall, stainless steel shelves held a wide assortment of medical tools, supplies, and bottles. In the center of the room, underneath a halogen light, a metal gurney was bolted to the floor, the mattress removed and replaced by a flat steel platform. It was less comfortable, but easier to clean, and he'd learned from experience that the latter was more important.

He was down there now, standing in front of the glass case at the far end of the room. It was his shrine. Six jars, lined up neatly, each filled with formaldehyde. This was his sanctuary, where he drew his strength and prepared to continue His work so that he'd be united with his parents again; so that they could all stand together among the trumpets in their white robes with the lamb of God as the others burned in an ocean of sulfur and acid.

Give her as much torture and grief
as the glory and luxury she gave herself.
In her heart she boasts,
"I sit as queen; I am not a widow,

and I will never mourn."
Therefore in one day her plagues will overtake her:
death, mourning, and famine.
She will be consumed by fire,
for mighty is the Lord God who judges her.

It was another favorite passage, and he repeated it for nearly thirty minutes before he pulled himself away from the glass case and locked the basement up tight.

CHAPTER TWELVE

"Roughly twelve hours," Farmalant said.

"Are you sure?" Flaherty asked.

"As sure as I can be. One thing is absolutely clear—the Caldwell woman was dead for a long time before her heart was removed. She was strangled to death, and then her heart was taken out later. I could be an hour off, give or take, but not more than that. You can be sure it wasn't near the time of her death."

"Shit," Flaherty muttered.

She was back in Farmalant's posh office. He'd called her earlier in the morning with the news that the autopsy was finally finished. "Why won't you just send the report over?" she'd asked. He'd been clear that she should come to his office.

"There are some things in here you're going to want to discuss," he'd said. At first she thought it was just a ploy to flirt with her again, but something in his voice told her there *were* things he really needed to explain in person. This was clearly one of them.

"You told me the other six had their hearts removed within a few minutes of their death, right?" she asked.

Farmalant nodded. "That's what I told you, but we've gone

back and run some more tests on the blood of the other victims, and I may have been wrong, *sort of*."

"What do you mean by 'sort of'? How long were they dead?"

"They weren't. At least not all of them. And the ones that were dead were only killed a moment or two before their hearts were removed."

"How can that be?"

"According to the results of the most recent tests, in each of the earlier victims, there was a mixture of muscle relaxants and local anesthetics. These were mixed pretty skillfully, so that Little Jack could actually operate on the victims while they were still alive. As a result, death didn't occur until the aorta was severed."

"Why would he do that?"

"You don't want to know," Farmalant said. When she scowled at him, he shrugged. "It looks like he was getting better and better at mixing the drugs. In the last three or four victims, prior to the Caldwell girl, the mixture was so professional that the victims could actually have been conscious while he was cutting them."

Flaherty felt sick. "You can't be serious. They were conscious?"

"Yeah, it's pretty twisted, isn't it? It looks like at least some of these women got to watch while this sicko reached into their chests and literally cut out their hearts."

Flaherty was glad Natalie Caldwell hadn't endured the horror of being sliced open while she was still conscious. At the same time, it was a significant departure from Little Jack's MO, and inconsistencies in method made the investigation harder. It also meant they had to consider again the possibility that this was a copycat killing.

"Anything else?" Flaherty asked.

Farmalant nodded. "I'm afraid so. We found semen inside the body."

"You mean she was raped?"

"Well, there's no way to be sure. She could have had consensual sex before she was killed—either with the killer or with someone else. We found some light bruising around her wrists that could be consistent with her having been bound, but the test wasn't conclusive. The circumstances of her death obviously suggest rape as a possibility, but there's no way to tell for sure."

"None of the others were sexually assaulted, were they?"

"Not a single one," Farmalant confirmed. "It's starting to look more and more like this is a different guy, isn't it?"

"Well, we still don't know. It may just be he was in a hurry, or something threw him off this time." Flaherty was rationalizing, and she knew it. The possibility that the killer had raped Natalie created particular problems. Murder motivated by or combined with a sexual impulse was a very different crime, psychologically speaking, from a ritualized serial killing. The absence of a sexual component in the first six killings, combined with the highly sophisticated manner in which the victims were dispatched, suggested a very distinct personality type: intellectual, patient, and controlled. The introduction of a sexual element was at odds with this particular profile. It suggested a lack of control and an absence of patience, and, like it or not, it seemed to support Farmalant's suspicion that they were dealing with a different killer.

On the other hand, Flaherty thought, there was no way to tell whether the penetration had occurred before Natalie Caldwell encountered her killer or after. If she had sex with some other person before Little Jack got to her, it would explain the state in which her body was found without being inconsistent with the method of Little Jack's prior murders. Still, Flaherty knew, it would only explain the crime's sexual element; it wouldn't explain the victim's being strangled to death before her heart was removed, or the difference in the skill with which the heart had been taken.

"Anything else?" Flaherty asked.

"That's not enough?"

"It's plenty, but I need to know if there's more."

"Nothing else startling. But these issues—" Farmalant cut himself short when he saw the look on Flaherty's face. "I just thought you should know."

"I appreciate it," she said, sighing. She got up from the plush leather chair and headed for the door. She paused when she got there, and turned around to face Farmalant. "What's your gut feeling?" she asked. "Is it him, or someone else?"

"You don't really want to hear my answer, do you?"

"Might as well. I don't have to agree with it."

"Fine." Farmalant took a deep breath. "In my opinion we're dealing with two different killers."

Flaherty nodded, and then turned and walked out the door.

CHAPTER THIRTEEN

Finn looked across the table at Antonio Patrick McGuire, the president of Huron Security. He looked slightly more like an Antonio than a McGuire, but having both Irish and Italian blood never hurt in Boston. Despite the facade of liberal politics that covered the city, its heart was still ruled by racial and ethnic divisions as old as the Freedom Trail. His dark hair was receding rapidly, revealing a flat, sloping forehead that ran down to a prominent brow above small, wide-set eyes. The eyes possessed intelligence; not the studied, cultivated intelligence Finn was used to seeing from in his lily-white, milk-fed clients, but something closer to cunning.

Finn was excited to be tasked with the responsibility of defending McGuire's deposition. It was a job that could easily have been taken by one of the partners on the case, but Preston was tied up in court, and Nick Williams was preoccupied with his analysis of the documents, so the responsibility fell to Finn.

"Have you ever been deposed before?" he asked McGuire.

There was a long pause before McGuire answered. "A couple of times. My divorce got messy when the shysters got involved, so I was deposed for that. Then I got sued by a tenant in a building I own and I was deposed again."

"What was the tenant lawsuit about?" Finn asked.

"Nothing worth talking about. I convinced the guy to drop it." McGuire said it with such finality that it foreclosed further probing. He was, after all, a client of the firm. As president of Huron Security, Inc., he ran one of the fastest-growing companies in Massachusetts. The growth was due largely to the contracts the company had secured from the state. Word had it that McGuire was a close friend of the governor's and that his inside track had won him the contract to staff the Transportation Safety Commission guards. It seemed odd to Finn. McGuire didn't look like someone who hobnobbed with the blue-blooded pillars of Massachusetts society. He looked like he'd be more comfortable in a pub in Charlestown or Southie.

"Well, at least you know the basic ground rules. We'll be in a conference room at the plaintiffs' attorney's office. There will be a court reporter and probably a few lawyers for the plaintiff who'll be asking you questions. You'll be under oath, so you have to answer truthfully. You should remember, though, that there's a big difference between answering questions truthfully and being useful. Your goal in this deposition is not to be helpful to the other side."

McGuire twirled a cigarette lighter around on the oak conference table. "I'm not sure I get what you're saying. Aren't you going to tell me exactly what to say? I mean, I don't want to screw this thing up. If you tell me what to say, I'll just say that and we can be done with it."

Finn sighed. He was dismayed at the regularity with which clients and witnesses expressed their willingness to be led to the "right truth." It wasn't that they were eager to lie, but they wanted to avoid saying anything wrong, and they were willing to bend the truth as much as necessary so as not to hurt the case. In the modern legal world, few people felt that being under oath really compelled them to tell the whole truth and nothing but the truth. Clients paying five or six hundred dollars an hour in legal fees expected to be told what to say so they'd win the case.

Finn had never crossed that line, and he didn't plan to. He'd walk the tightrope and play his games in the gray areas of the law, but feeding testimony to a witness was too much a betrayal of a system in which, despite his cynicism, he still believed.

"I can't tell you what to say, you have to tell the truth. I can simply tell you that there are ways you can tell the truth and still not be helpful."

"What do you mean?"

"Well, for example, listen carefully to the question, and don't answer anything that isn't asked. If they ask you, 'What do you do for a living?' you should give them the title of your position at Huron, not a full description of what it is that you actually do in that position. If they ask you, 'Do you have a direct superior?' you should simply answer yes and make them follow up with a question about what the name of your superior is. Remember, the less talking you do, the better off the company is."

McGuire smiled conspiratorially. "I can do that." Finn wasn't surprised. McGuire didn't look like someone who parted with information easily or made a habit of being helpful.

"Good. Also, don't guess. If they ask you a question and you're not absolutely sure what the answer is, tell them that you don't know. The worst thing you can do is start guessing. We can always supply them with the answers to the questions later, once the information has been vetted."

McGuire smiled again, more broadly this time. "There's a lot I'm not *absolutely* sure about."

"That's all the better. Hopefully it means you'll get out of this deposition quickly without giving them anything useful. Just keep reminding yourself that the less information, the better."

McGuire nodded. Then he leaned back in his chair and folded his hands together, putting them back over his head. He had huge knuckles, Finn noticed. The kind of knuckles that grow with continued use on docks, at warehouses, on construction jobs. Knuckles like that were only found around hard work requiring strength and indifference to pain and fatigue.

"Let me ask you something, Counselor." He drew the last word out into a slur, letting his contempt show. "What are these plaintiffs' lawyers looking for? The feds have already concluded no amount of security would have been able to stop this fuckin' towelhead. Even if we did screw something up in our procedures, the attack still would have taken place. Doesn't that mean these guys have no case?"

"It ought to, and it's likely we *will* ultimately win this thing for just that reason. But you've got to remember, this is a high-profile case, so the judge may want to let a jury decide it, and a jury has a lot of leeway in how it decides. Who do you think the jury is going to be more sympathetic to, the widow of one of the victims or the big security company hired by the state?"

"So we're screwed."

"If you weren't at least a little screwed, your company would never be paying the fees we charge."

CHAPTER FOURTEEN

Flaherty sat at her desk, staring at her computer screen, feeling defeated. She'd spent much of the morning in a meeting with the entire task force—more than twenty police officers in all—sharing information and analyzing what they'd come up with. Unfortunately, it wasn't much. They had no leads, nothing to guide the investigation. They continued to turn over rocks, only to find dirt underneath. Her eyes hurt. Her head hurt. Her muscles ached. But still, she needed to press on to find an answer. If only she could get a good night's sleep, maybe then she'd see whatever it was they were missing.

She suddenly looked up from her computer screen and noticed Kozlowski standing in front of her desk. He had this way of materializing without a sound that she sometimes found disconcerting. It was a useful skill as an investigator, though.

"What is it?" she asked.

"Nothing," he replied. He looked at her like he had something on his mind, though. "I ran the tox screens again—same result. I also had some uniforms do a house-to-house of all of the businesses and homes near where the Caldwell woman's body was dumped, just to see if anyone saw anything. Nothing. And I just spent the last two hours cross-checking our references, trying to find anything that ties these seven girls together—other than their being carved into pieces over the last four months. Zippo."

Kozlowski was thorough, but Flaherty already knew that. He wouldn't waste his breath on this kind of useless detail unless he had a point. He used conversation too sparingly for that. There was something else behind the visit.

"What's on your mind, Kozlowski?"

"You found anything in your magic computer there?" he asked. It sounded almost like an accusation, and Flaherty didn't like it.

"If I'd found anything useful I would have told you by now, Sergeant." She referred to him by rank on purpose. It was meant to remind him that, friends or not, she wasn't required to take his crap. "But then, you already knew that, didn't you? If you've got something to say, why not say it?"

She was letting her frustration show. It had been more than a week since she'd put both their heads on the chopping block in front of the leaders of every law enforcement agency in the state, and they were no closer to catching their killer. If anything, they had more questions now than they'd had before.

Kozlowski fidgeted a little, like he was trying to make up his mind about something. It was odd to see such a bull of a man fidget, Flaherty thought. Something about it seemed incongruous.

"What the fuck is wrong with you, Koz?" she asked, raising her voice, and several others in the squad room turned and looked in their direction. She didn't care; she was used to being scrutinized on this case.

Kozlowski hesitated just a minute longer. "I think we need to get a little more proactive, boss."

"How much more proactive can we get?" she asked incredulously. "I've got twenty-two cops running down leads, comparing data, looking for patterns. Everyone is busting his ass on this, including me. What is it exactly that you think we're not doing?"

Kozlowski looked at her, and it was clear that he was debating whether to take the conversation a step further. He had never doubted the team's commitment to the case, and Flaherty knew he certainly would never question her resolve and dedication, but she'd put his ass on the line right alongside hers.

"We should be out there," he said, nodding toward the window that looked out on Congress Street in downtown Boston.

"What do you mean?"

"I mean it's time to stop playing computer jock and get out on the streets." His voice was low and strong, and it somehow made Flaherty feel inadequate.

"What the hell are you talking about?" She meant to express indignation, but instead her voice seemed plaintive and small. "We've got cops in uniform knocking on doors all over downtown and Southie."

Kozlowski shrugged.

"If you've got any suggestions, I'd love to hear them." She was furious now, but she was also desperate. Kozlowski had no diplomatic skills, but his ability in the investigative realm was unparalleled.

"Let's start leaning on people," he said simply.

"Leaning on who?" she demanded.

"Local scumbags. Bartenders. Convenience store clerks. Anyone who may have seen something or might know something. It's time to get our hands dirty."

"'Local scumbags'? You don't really think there's a mob connection here, do you? There's nothing that even suggests—"

He cut her off. "It's not wiseguys doing the killing, but we need their eyes out there on the street. Somebody must have seen something. Or if nobody's seen anything yet, they will in the future, when this asshole kills again. We've got to make sure everyone who crawls in the gutter at night is taking this investigation seriously."

Flaherty thought about this for a moment. They hadn't been reaching out and putting the heat on their snitches because they weren't thinking of this as the type of crime where snitches could be helpful, but Kozlowski had a point. Boston still ran on its unseen connections, and Southie was the home of one of the oldest and best-organized crime networks in the country. It might be worth putting some pressure on the right sort of people.

"Fine," she conceded. "Set up a pressure cooker and see if anything pops. Anything else?"

"Yeah, let's get someone out at the Kiss Club in street clothes."

"What the hell for? You and I were both out there shoving Caldwell's picture under every nose we could find, and we got nothing. Even if that's where Little Jack found her—and we don't know that for sure—we've got no reason to think he'd go back there. How can we possibly justify an undercover operation?" He was really pushing it. They'd run that lead down as far as it would go, and they'd come up with nothing.

"You got any better ideas?"

They stared at each other for an eternity. She had no comeback, and he knew it. She could pull rank on him and simply say no without giving an explanation, but she knew neither of them would accept that. It would be like admitting defeat. She drew in a deep breath and pulled her brow down into an angry scowl, causing deep creases to appear on her broad, attractive forehead. Then she blew out a long exasperated sigh. In her position, she couldn't turn down any suggestions, and there was no question Kozlowski had the best instincts in the department.

She looked up at him and shook her head in frustration. "Just make sure it's someone who won't be recognized."

CHAPTER FIFTEEN

Finn sat in the conference room, listening intently as McGuire's deposition progressed at a snail's pace. It was all he could do to keep himself from wringing the necks of the plaintiffs' lawyers across the table from him, but at least the work kept him focused.

Work was the only thing keeping him sane in the wake of Natalie's murder. He found it to be more of a distraction than a passion now, but he welcomed the distraction with the desperation of a drowning man thrown a lifeline. He missed Natalie even more than he had anticipated. Even through their difficulties, she had provided an anchor in his life. A few times a day he still found himself picking up the phone to call her. And whenever something funny or odd or outrageous happened at work, he'd instinctively head out of his office toward hers, only to realize in an instant that she was no longer there. He'd walk by her office, which was now being used as a storage room until the fall, when a new crop of nameless, faceless law school graduates would start with the firm as first-year associates. Her nameplate still hung by her door like a tombstone or the plaque on a mausoleum entryway. It felt wrong that no one had bothered to take it down, as if the firm hadn't even noticed her death. But he couldn't bring himself to carry out the task.

The firm had, of course, noticed her death. In fact, it became a central topic of speculation and gossip in the weeks after she was found. The circumstances of her murder and the link to the murders of the six prostitutes tickled the other lawyers' hunger for sordid detail and appealed to their natural fascination with the dark side of human nature. Many of them showed up at her funeral, but Finn wondered how many had merely put in an appearance out of curiosity—like rubberneckers on the highway, eager for a glimpse of pain, and blood, and death. The interment had been delayed for a week, as a thorough autopsy pulled her body apart piece by piece, until there was barely enough left to sew back together. In the end, a closed casket had been required.

All of this was painful enough for Finn, who felt he was one of the few people who had been a true friend to Natalie, but what made it worse was that there was no one he could talk to about it. He was a natural loner, probably because of his past, and to the extent that he felt like he fit in at the firm, it was because of Natalie. He thought of talking to Preston about how he was feeling, but although they were exceptionally close, Finn was unsure how his mentor would react to such a show of weakness. He liked Nick Williams, but they certainly weren't confidants. As a result, he was left simply to churn through his daily routine.

There was a ton of work for him to churn through, though. That much, at least, was a blessing. The Tannery case was a monster to get his arms around. Between the state agency that oversaw the security program, and Huron Security, the lawyers at Howery, Black had overseen the disclosure of more than a million pages of documents, from simple purchase orders and requisition forms to complex reaction plans prepared in case of nuclear or biological attack. The case was a far cry from the relatively simple white-collar criminal and securities matters Finn was used to working on. Those cases usually involved fewer documents and fewer legal issues, and winning them depended on finding a simple hook that would resonate with the jury. By contrast, the Tannery case required exacting attention to detail. It became clear to him early on that, to win this case, he must acquire an encyclopedic knowledge of the facts.

He threw himself into the task with fervor, reading and analyzing every document, reviewing prior deposition testimony, and even visiting the security company's offices twice. He wasn't sure his efforts were paying off yet, though. His mind worked better with broad themes than with detail. That was another reason Preston had originally chosen to put Natalie on the case instead of him. Sure, it helped that she was a woman, but she was also better suited to the kind of work that was required here. Holland had pointed that out to him. "She's a great case manager," he had said. "You're a great trial lawyer, but your case management skills are not top-notch." It had hurt Finn to hear that, even more so because he knew it to be true. Now that he'd waded hip deep into the case, he felt renewed admiration for Nat and her skills.

His struggles in dealing with her loss made working on the Tannery case more difficult, too. Every day he came across memos or briefs bearing her name. Just when he'd lost himself in the case and had forgotten about her death, he'd notice her handwriting in the margins of a document, and the memories would come flooding back.

The clients didn't make things any easier. They were, without doubt, the most obstinate, obfuscatory group of people he'd ever dealt with. Finn supposed that that was normal in the security business, where secrecy and discretion were cornerstones, but it nonetheless presented significant difficulties.

He'd been working for two weeks straight, and still felt like he had no idea what the case was really about.

McGuire was particularly difficult to handle. He was a wily bastard—much more intelligent than Finn had initially given him credit for—and that made defending his deposition all the more difficult. As Finn sat in the conference room at the plaintiffs' lawyers' office, he knew he was about to have a battle on his hands.

"I can't recall," McGuire was saying again. Apparently he'd taken Finn's advice to heart; that was at least the twentieth time he'd professed his ignorance in the face of the most basic questions.

"What do you mean, you don't recall?" There was anger in Fred Barnolk's voice now. Fred was the lead attorney for the plaintiff, and a real character. He'd nearly flunked out of law school, and it had reportedly taken him three tries to pass the bar exam. Once he passed, though, a nose for big payoffs and a talent for righteous indignation had led him to represent high-profile plaintiffs against large corporations, and more than one jury had awarded his clients into the hundreds of millions of dollars. As their lawyer, Fred was entitled to one-third of that—an enormous amount of money by any standards—which he used to fund additional lawsuits. He had long, jet black hair that curled over the collar of his designer shirt.

"I mean I don't remember," McGuire said calmly.

"You're saying you don't remember how many people work under you?"

"That's what I am saying."

"Well, can you give me a rough estimate?"

Finn interrupted. "I'm going to object to that question, Mr. Barnolk. The witness is not here to speculate in his answers at this deposition, and he should only answer from his personal knowledge." He looked at McGuire. "You can respond to the question if you know the answer."

McGuire looked at Barnolk and smiled. "As I said, I'm really not sure of the exact number of workers we have, and I wouldn't want to guess."

Barnolk's face was now bright red, and contrasted nicely with the deep blue of his shirt. "Let me just say, Mr. Finn, that this is the most deplorable deposition behavior I've ever encountered in more than twenty years of practice. You may think that the best way to handle this case is to stonewall us, but you're dead wrong. My client and her family are victims of America's war on terror, and they're entitled to answers."

"Be careful, Mr. Barnolk," Finn interrupted. "It's starting to sound like you're blaming the terrorists who bombed the train instead of my clients whom you've sued."

"My client and her family are the victims of corporate greed in the manner in which the war on terror has been conducted," Barnolk corrected himself without missing a beat. "And they're heroes. They'll have their day in court, and they'll prevail regardless of whatever sleazy tactics you employ here."

"Mr. Barnolk, you may have noticed that there's no jury in the room. Nor are there any newspaper reporters present, so I'd suggest you save the speeches for your closing argument. As far as the witness's 'behavior' during this deposition goes, it's been exemplary. He's answered every single one of your questions honestly and without speculation. Furthermore, the specific information you are asking for is contained in the documents that we have turned over in response to your discovery requests."

"You turned over two rooms' worth of documents. We don't have the time or the resources to go through a production like that. We're not a big white-shoe firm like Howery, Black & Longbothum."

"Then you shouldn't have asked our client to turn over such a broad range of documents. Besides, I happen to know that with the tobacco settlement fees you received last year, partners in your firm made more money than the partners at Howery, so the David-versus-Goliath routine is a little disingenuous, don't you think?"

Barnolk turned back to McGuire. "Mr. McGuire, how many security guards were assigned to each train as of September 12, last year?"

McGuire leaned back in his chair and brought his giant hands together at the tips of his fingers, staring up at the ceiling as though lost in contemplation. "I'm not sure what the exact number was at that time, really. I'm sure I could look it up. It must be in one of the documents our lawyers gave to you guys."

Barnolk stared at McGuire with such malice it might have been disconcerting if he didn't cut such a comic figure in his tailored suit and oversized gold cuff links, his jowls hanging over his two-hundred-dollar Hermès tie.

"This deposition is over for today," he said finally. "But I want it on the record that Mr. Finn has, at best, failed properly to prepare the witness for this deposition, and has, at worst, prepared the witness specifically to frustrate the purposes of discovery and conceal relevant evidence. In either case, I believe that he has violated his ethical obligations to the judicial system, and we intend to bring this behavior to the attention of the court."

"Well, you can obviously bring whatever motions you want before the court, Mr. Barnolk," Finn retorted calmly. "But I have no doubt that the court will see clearly that the only reason you've become frustrated during this deposition is because you were woefully unprepared at the outset. That's obviously neither the witness's fault nor my fault, but it is something we can discuss with the judge. In any event, we won't make this witness available again unless the court orders it. You've had a full and fair opportunity to question him, and we will *not* allow the safety of other rail passengers to be jeopardized while you waste the time of those who are charged with the heavy responsibility of administering public safety."

Finn and McGuire were standing now, and they pushed their chairs out from the table and started walking toward the door. As McGuire passed Barnolk on the way out, he smiled at him again. He leaned over the prissy lawyer, and his huge right hand swung toward him. In a moment of horror, Finn thought McGuire was actually going to punch Barnolk. That would be difficult to explain to the judge under any circumstances. Barnolk clearly had the same thought, because he threw himself sideways in his chair, knocking his notes off the table, and almost falling out of the chair himself. It was only then that Finn saw that McGuire's hand was opened, and he was offering it in a handshake to Barnolk.

McGuire laughed heartily, and left his hand out. "It was a pleasure to meet you," he said through his own laughter.

Barnolk looked up, clearly still shaken. Tentatively, he held his hand out to shake, and McGuire's paw enveloped his.

As they shook hands, McGuire leaned in and whispered something into Barnolk's ear. When he turned back toward the door to head out, he was no longer laughing, but he was grinning from ear to ear. Over McGuire's shoulder, Finn could see that all the blood had drained from Barnolk's face.

Back in the street outside Barnolk's office, McGuire hailed a cab. He turned to Finn and held out his hand. "Thanks a lot, Counselor. I think it went pretty well in there. You were a pistol on those legal arguments."

Finn looked at the hand, caught in the memory of the bizarre exchange he'd witnessed up in the office between McGuire and Barnolk. He hesitated for just a second before he shook the hand. "Are you sure you don't want to go back to my office and do a little postgame analysis to figure out where we might have taken any hits?"

McGuire shook his head. "Nah, I gotta get back to my own office and see what's happening there. We did well today, though. I already know it." McGuire smiled again as he stepped into the cab.

Finn couldn't hold himself back from asking the question that was weighing heavily on his mind. "Hey, what was that between you and Barnolk up there?" he asked, trying to sound nonchalant.

"What was what?" McGuire asked.

"When you whispered to him, what did you say?"

"You don't need to worry about that, Counselor."

"I'm not worried, I'd just like to know," Finn protested.

McGuire laughed again. "I just told him you lawyers are the dumbest people I've ever had to hang around with," he said. Then he roared with laughter one more time. "Listen, Counselor, don't sweat it. You did great in there, and I'll make sure Holland knows it." With that, he nodded to the taxi driver to head out and closed the door.

As the taxi pulled away, Finn looked down at his hand, still lost in the feeling that he'd witnessed some moment of import in the office upstairs. Something about the exchange made him feel queasy, as if an event of significance had occurred right before his eyes and he'd missed it. He hated that feeling. It made him question whether he was really in control of the case. The uncertainty was all the more difficult to deal with because Natalie wasn't there to lend her support. She'd have been able to help him sort everything out. Of course, if she hadn't been killed, he never would have had this case to deal with in the first place.

Finn shook himself and started back to his office. The August heat was oppressive, and he loosened his collar and tie.

Everything had changed. The sky seemed a different color, and the buildings and people around him seemed less friendly. It had been more than a week since he'd had anything to drink, but he sure felt like he needed something now.

CHAPTER SIXTEEN

Tigh McCluen, a giant of a man with dark hair, sat on a stack of packing crates in a warehouse at the edge of Southie. The old man sitting in front of him was taking his time, as was his habit, reading every entry in Tigh's ledger with care, and adding the figures in his head with greater precision than any Harvard MBA.

"You got a few stiffs you're carrying here," the old man said at last.

"Long-standing customers," Tigh offered with a wink. Although he'd been in the United States for more than two decades, his accent still rang with the cadence of the shores of Donegal on the west coast of Ireland. "They'll pay, and in the meantime it gives me leverage to get whatever I want out of them."

"What could you possibly want from them?"

Tigh pointed at the ledger, halfway down. "That man there's a doctor at Mass General. Remember the tiff that Johnny and Viles got into last month?"

The old man nodded. "With Frankie's old crew, right?"

"Right." Tigh nodded. "Johnny took a slug in the leg. Nothing serious, it missed the artery, but it still needed tending. The good doctor was kind enough to pay a house call—off the record. At the hospital there would have been a police report, which would have presented a bit of an embarrassment."

He slid his fingers down to another red entry. "That man there is a waiter."

"What the fuck good is a waiter?"

"He's a waiter at Olives," Tigh explained. "It's the mayor's favorite restaurant. I told his Honor to ask for Sean whenever he goes to eat there. Sean cuts the check down to nearly nothing, and the mayor is very appreciative when we need him to be."

"How about this guy, here?" the old man asked, pointing to the bottom of the page. "Billy Zern?"

"That's a separate issue entirely," Tigh said, smiling. The old man looked at him expectantly. "I fancy his sister," Tigh explained with a wink.

The old man laughed. "I swear to fucking God, Tigh, if you didn't bring in as much money as you do, I'd have had you clipped years ago for that mouth on you." He shook his head. "You're just lucky you're good at what you do."

Tigh chuckled. "Funny, that's just what Billy Zern's sister said to me the other night. You two been sharing secrets, now?"

"You think that fuckin' charm can get you through anything, don't you?"

"It's worked so far," Tigh pointed out. "I stepped off the boat from the motherland when I was twelve with nothing in my pockets and no one in the world who cared about me. Now look at where I am." He waved his arms around the warehouse, which smelled of decay and had rats scurrying noisily in the corners. "Heaven!"

The old man shook his head again. "You do okay. Not as well as you would have in the old days, but you do fine." He rubbed his face in his hands. "When I was younger, all you needed were some balls and the muscle to back them up. Now the plays are bigger and you need more. You need brains. Guys like you and me are a dying breed."

Tigh scratched his head. "Like you said, I do fine." He nodded toward the ledger. "Everything all right in there?" he asked.

"Yeah, you're fine. Just don't give the stiffs too much rope, okay?"

"Understood."

"There's one other thing, Tigh. I got the word this morning that we need your help." The old man looked up from the flimsy card table that served as his desk.

"I'm listening," Tigh said after a moment of silence.

The old man blew out his breath heavily. "You know this Little Jack fuck that's been killing some of the local girls?" he asked.

Tigh nodded. "Only what I read in the papers."

"Yeah, well the organization wants him stopped. It's fuckin' up business and scaring the girls off the streets. Pussy ain't the meal ticket it once was, but it still provides a good, steady income stream. We'd like your help in putting an end to this fuck."

Tigh was silent for a moment, weighing his response. "What can I do?" he asked warily.

"You can do what you can do," the old man said. "You know the streets better than anyone. Hell, when you were younger you owned the streets. Get out there and find him. Talk to people . . . use those fuckin' connections you got."

Tigh shook his head. "I don't think my connections will be of much use," he said. "We're not dealing with a local hood, here, we're dealing with a psycho. I wouldn't even know where to begin."

"You can begin at the Kiss Club. Our friends in the department tell us that's probably where this guy bagged his last girl."

Tigh rubbed his neck. "This may slow down my collections," he offered.

The old man frowned. "Fuck that, Tigh. If you weren't carrying so many stiffs, that wouldn't be an issue. You figure out how to get both done."

Tigh got up and picked up his ledger. "Uncle Vinnie, it's been a real pleasure, as always."

The old man laughed again. "Boy, you got a fuckin' mouth on you." Tigh was nearly at the door when the old man called out to him. "Tigh!"

He turned around.

"When you find this little fuck, we don't want him talkin' to the cops—or to anyone else, for that matter. He can give his explanations to Saint Peter, you got it?"

"Sure, Vin. Any particular reason?"

The old man shook his head. "A psycho like this don't deserve a lawyer, or a fair trial."

Tigh studied the old man for a few seconds. "Is there anything else I should know about this, Vinnie?" he asked.

Vinnie shrugged. "I do what I'm told. Just like always, you know."

Tigh nodded. "Yeah, I know, Vinnie. Just like always."

CHAPTER SEVENTEEN

Officer Paul Stone sat at a corner table in the Kiss Club. He was dressed in his best bar-hopping clothes for the evening: black pleated slacks with a tight knit polo shirt, open at the neck. He stirred the soda water on the table in front of him and smiled to himself. This sure beat the hell out of walking a beat in Southie in his uniform. Finding that body was a stroke of luck, he thought. When the call went out for a young officer unknown to the usual players in Boston's nightlife to work undercover on the Little Jack case, Stone's prior connection to the case gave him an advantage and won him the assignment. It was also possible, he thought, that Lieutenant Flaherty might have felt badly about the way she'd treated him during their first meeting. Whatever the reason, Stone was just happy to be off the beat and doing real investigative work. It was an enormous opportunity for him, and he appreciated it.

Never mind, of course, that he had no idea what he was looking for. The Caldwell girl—Number Seven, as most people knew her—had been in this bar on the night of her death, that much had been confirmed by the bartender during the investigation. He hadn't been able to remember if she was with anyone, so it remained possible that Little Jack had met her here before he killed her. But so what? Even if Little Jack did meet her at this bar, Stone thought, what was the likelihood he'd return to find another victim? And even if he did, how was Stone supposed to differentiate between a serial killer leading a hooker to her death and a pervert leading a hooker to a hotel room?

That was what he'd been instructed to do, though: hang out at the Kiss Club every night to "see if anything turns up." Personally, he thought his presence at the club was an indication of how desperate the investigation had become, but he hadn't expressed that thought to the brass.

From his seat, Stone watched the patrons as closely as he could without attracting attention. The Kiss Club was a typically sleazy singles bar, with men and women sliding in and out of easy conversations in an endless game of musical chairs. Many of the men were still in suits or the contemporary equivalent "business casual" that dominated the modern workplace, clearly having come from work for a good time out. Judging from the amount of booze that was being tossed down, work might proceed at a slower pace the next morning, but that was to be expected. Other men fell into a different category—local wiseguys looking for a play, or conducting their own business.

The women were a similar mix. Some were regular young businesswomen out for a walk on the wild side, or looking for a story to share with their friends, or trying to prove to the men they worked with that they deserved membership in their boys' club. Others clearly earned their livings working in places like the Kiss Club—high-class prostitutes looking for clients. Most of the working girls sat at the bar, and although they were dressed a bit more provocatively, they were difficult to distinguish from their amateur counterparts. The line between sleazy and chic had been blurred by fashion trends, as satin chokers and shorter skirts became more popular. It was no longer the clothes that identified the professionals; it was the eyes. Stone could spot them a mile away. They scanned the crowd like those of sharks swimming in a school of fish; cold and dark and calculating.

"They're beautiful, aren't they?" The question came from Lou Salandro, seated at Stone's table. He'd noticed Stone looking across the bar at two of the better-looking barflies. One had shoulder-length brown hair braided down the back and was wearing stiletto heels that could pierce skin. The other was a redhead, her hair cropped close to her alabaster face in a retro-eighties style. They were both sitting at the far side of the bar with a good view of their prospects.

"You know, I could probably get you a freebie, if you're interested."

Stone turned his head to look at Salandro, evaluating him carefully. He was a small-time player in the Anguillo crew, which was an offshoot of New England's Patriarcha crime family and was fighting for greater control of the turf in downtown and Chinatown. It seemed like it couldn't even be called "organized" crime anymore, though. Too many factions had split apart and turned on one another, and the FBI's use of informants had succeeded in inflicting heavy damage on La Cosa Nostra. Salandro had been busted several years back by Kozlowski for selling heroin, and he'd become a fairly reliable informant for the Boston Police Department. He continued to work minor scams for the family, and was suspected of running girls and dealing marijuana, but he stayed away from anything the department considered "serious" crime. As a result, the police left him alone, and he provided Kozlowski with a stream of useful information. Kozlowski had set up a meeting between Stone and Salandro so that Stone wouldn't look out of place.

There was nothing about Salandro that Stone liked. He had big, thick lips that bubbled out in front of a round, red face and were kept moist by a thick tongue, which he slipped out of his mouth constantly. His chin seemed to recede in an unbroken slope from his lips to the bottom of his neck, and then from there into a concave chest. The inward slope was only arrested by the swell of Salandro's belly. Stone wondered how the Anguillo crew had survived this long with specimens like this running its errands.

He shook his head, indicating he would not need a "freebie" from the prostitutes at the bar.

"You sure?" Salandro kept up. "They do a tandem act you wouldn't fuckin' believe." He slipped his tongue back and forth between his fingers in an obscene gesture. Stone just looked at him, revolted. Salandro let rip a belly laugh that left him doubled up, coughing.

"Suit yourself," he said when he caught his breath. Then he whispered, "Just like Kozlowski—straight as an arrow, huh?"

"Yeah, I guess you could say that. But then, you could also shut the fuck up, if you knew what was good for you."

Salandro held up his hands in surrender. "No need to be uncivil. I was just trying to be cooperative."

Stone shook his head and returned his attention to the rest of the bar. Salandro was a worm. Stone had known people like him growing up in Southie, where walking a straight line was sometimes a challenge. But Stone's parents had drilled a sense of duty and morality into him, and he had managed to weather the temptations of his youth. He was willing to use Salandro if it could aid the investigation, but he'd never have anything but contempt for him. That he was giving information to the cops and betraying his friends in the process only made him more of a worm in Stone's eyes. In the end, with or without Salandro's help, Stone found it difficult to believe they'd accomplish anything sitting at this place.

He looked around the bar again and sighed. Maybe he was wrong. Maybe he was better off walking a beat.

Finn couldn't believe he'd found his way back to the Kiss Club. It had been at least two years, and he'd only been to the hole-in-the-wall once before—with Natalie. It was during that exciting time when he and Natalie were together. The intensity of their relationship had taken him by surprise, but so much of it seemed focused around their work lives. She was full of questions about the firm and its politics, and it took several weeks before she realized Finn would never be in a position to help her in the long run. She ended it soon after that, and he'd been wounded for a time. He'd spent his entire life on his own, though, and he knew he'd survive.

She'd surprised him back then by bringing him to the Kiss Club, but then, she'd surprised him in many ways. He remembered that she wore the tight leather skirt with the matching jacket and lingerie that night—the outfit she was found in. He realized at that moment that she indulged her passions more than he'd suspected.

The memories had brought him back here. He didn't know why. It felt like he was searching compulsively for something he couldn't put his finger on. He scanned the crowd for her face, recognizing the futility, but unable to stop himself. He was on his fourth gin and tonic, and the bar was becoming gauzy in his eyes. More than once he thought he saw her. Perhaps, he thought, he'd never been completely honest with himself regarding his feelings for Natalie. He was beginning to realize that he'd harbored the hope, unarticulated even to himself, that they'd be together in the end. It was absurd, he knew, given who she was. She was too tough to survive in any type of true, long-term romantic relationship—as he was, for that matter. But he felt her loss sorely nonetheless.

He was glad when the woman sauntered over and asked him for a light. It felt like she'd thrown a rope down into the hole he was digging for himself and dragged him back to reality. It took him a moment to respond, but the sound of his own voice reinforced the notion that he was still among the living.

He realized quickly that she was working him. She leaned in toward his shoulder, letting her breasts linger against his arm, laughing coquettishly when he looked down in surprise. She laughed at his lame attempts at humor, and hinted he should buy her a drink so that they could both be more comfortable. It was all too predictable.

At first he was hurt when he realized she was a professional. Like all men, he'd wanted to believe she was bowled over by his looks, or his humor, or his mere presence. It was the ego that the best prostitutes played to, not the libido. The temporal limitations of sexual gratification were more often than not overshadowed by the lingering pleasure of feeling strong, and confident, and irresistible. That illusion was shattered for him when she asked what he did for a living.

"I'm a lawyer," he replied.

"Ooh," she cooed. "I just love lawyers. They're so sexy."

At that moment he knew she was playing him. In his eight years of being a lawyer, not a single woman had ever found anything sexy about the law.

Nonetheless, Finn was grateful for the company. He needed human contact, even if she'd be angry when she realized he wasn't looking for sex. Besides that, he noticed she resembled Natalie. She had the same blonde hair, and there was something in her eyes that seemed familiar. In his inebriated state, it was enough. So, he bought her a drink, and then another and another, and let the drama between them play itself out.

It was one-thirty before anything happened. Stone hadn't moved from his table in more than three hours, and his patience with Salandro was wearing thin. While Stone continued to sip at his soda water, Salandro switched from gin to vodka to tequila. It was clear that the man had a remarkable tolerance, but as the evening wore on, he began slurring his words, and his comments became increasingly annoying. By one o'clock, he was sufficiently lubricated to share his opinions on law enforcement in general and the state of the Boston Police Department in particular. It was not a good idea.

"You see, the problem with the entire system is that the cops need the criminals to justify the money that's spent on law enforcement. The more crime you have in a city, the more the city will spend on cops. So, when you think about it, the cops have to make sure there's someone out there breakin' the law. It's just a fact."

Stone glared at him. Not only were his theories demeaning, but his tone and his diatribe risked blowing Stone's cover. The bar had cleared out to a degree, and there was no one sitting within earshot of their table, but that didn't excuse Salandro's behavior. If it wouldn't have caused a scene, Stone would have just beat the hell out of him right there. As it was, though, he had to sit there and take it.

"Just look at this 'investigation' you got here. One guy kills seven sluts and the city throws an endless stream of cash at the cops to catch him. Never mind that prostitution is illegal, so the guy is actually cutting down on the number of crimes that happen in Boston." He lowered his voice and leaned in to Stone. "Shit, the PD has already spent a couple hundred bucks on my drinks alone tonight." Salandro laughed at his own joke, slapping Stone on the shoulder. Stone shot daggers at him with his eyes.

"And in the end, it doesn't count for shit. The police department ain't gonna catch this guy; we're gonna catch this guy."

"What are you talking about, Salandro," Stone hissed. "There is no 'we.' You and I are not a 'we.'"

Salandro laughed again. "No, not you and me. I mean *we*. The organization."

Stone looked at him, not comprehending.

"The organization," Salandro said again. "You know, the family—or maybe those stupid Mick thugs in Southie. Those of us who actually live out here." He leaned in again. "Those of us who, whether you like to admit it or not, really control this town."

"Yeah?" Stone mocked. "And how is the family gonna catch this guy?"

"It's already happening, my friend. The word went out last week. Fifty thousand cash to anyone who nails this sonofabitch—an extra ten if he's brought in dead, so no fancy-ass lawyer can't get him a walk. I'm telling you, with that kind of incentive, someone is definitely gonna find this guy."

Stone looked skeptical. "Why would the mob want to get involved in police work?"

"I don't know, but that's the word. Hey man, look at it this way; who makes the money off the hookers? You start knocking them off, it's bad for business. Besides, the way the organization sees it, this pervert has no morals. When we kill, there's a reason that makes sense. It's over money or power or turf, and it's usually within the rules. This fucker just kills for the sake of killing; like it's fun or something. That's fucked up, and people around here don't like it. So they figure they've got to do something about it."

Stone couldn't believe he was actually listening to this lecture on "morality" from a scumbag like Salandro. It made him feel sick to his stomach. He was about to tell Salandro to get the hell out of his face when he noticed a commotion at the bar.

It started innocuously enough. A young man in his mid-thirties was sitting at the bar, talking to one of the working girls. The man didn't seem the type to rely on hookers to find companionship. He was good-looking and well dressed, with dark brown hair and a sharp, intelligent face. She was clearly working him hard, and had been for more than an hour. Stone had seen them earlier, but noticed nothing unusual, at least not for a couple in the Kiss Club. He certainly hadn't seen anything that would have suggested the volatile exchange at the bar.

Everything was fine for an hour or two. Finn continued to buy the young lady champagne cocktails as she leaned in toward him. The drinks were a small price to pay for the temporary illusion of companionship, and he found himself feeling a little better.

Then she put her hand on his thigh, and began rubbing higher and higher, dragging her fingernails across the fabric of his pants, grinding into him with her palm. Her face was just a few inches from his and her perfume was overpowering. It made him more light-headed than the alcohol. She whispered in his ear, "Let's get out of here and go to your place." As she whispered, her hand slipped fully up the inside of his thigh underneath the bar, and Finn felt himself tighten with desire.

For a moment he actually considered it. What would be the harm? He was a grown man, and the thought of human contact, even in its basest form, was undeniably appealing. No one could begrudge him the momentary escape.

He wouldn't do it, though. Even as he felt his desire swell, he knew with an unavoidable certainty that to accept her offer would demean his pain.

He smiled sadly as he gripped her hand under the bar and pulled it away.

"I'm sorry, I can't," he said.

"Why?" she asked. "Arc you married?"

He shook his head and almost laughed. "No," he began.

"Because I don't care," she interrupted. "I'm not going to tell anyone. It can just be our little secret."

Even in his drunkenness Finn realized that half of the

woman's appeal was her resemblance to Natalie. He was tempted again, but he bolstered his resolve and stood firm.

"No, I'm sorry, I just can't." He knew he'd never be able to explain it to her satisfaction, so he didn't even try.

"What the fuck do you mean, you can't?" She said it loudly, making Finn uncomfortable. He suspected that was her goal. "You've been sitting here for an hour and a half, buying me drinks and sending me signals, and now you decide you can't?" Her eyes scanned the bar, looking for another potential mark, but it was late, and the place had cleared out. She realized the evening was going to be a total loss and she was livid. She leaned in again and grabbed him between the legs.

"Do you know how much men pay me for an hour and a half of my time?" she said through clenched teeth.

"Sadly, probably less than they pay me," Finn joked. It was the wrong thing to say, but he was just trying to lighten the mood. Not amused, she gave a firm squeeze between his legs, pulling Finn's testicles away from his body, inflicting gut-wrenching pain in a quick, merciless strike.

He was taken entirely by surprise. He'd imagined she might be somewhat annoyed when he turned her down, but he never expected the violence of the retribution. He reacted instinctively, swinging his arm at her wildly and catching her in the side of the face with the back of his hand. The blow sent her sprawling off the bar stool and onto the floor. As she fell she released her grip, allowing him to breathe again.

His relief was short-lived, as a wave of nausea swept through his lower abdomen and he doubled over. At the same time, he could see two mean-looking bouncers moving in toward him fast, practically drooling at the prospect of pummeling him.

"You fuckin' faggot!" the girl was screaming. "I'll rip your goddamned balls off!" She was struggling to her feet, but it wasn't easy in the high-heeled shoes she was wearing. She looked like a mackerel flopping around on the barroom floor. At the same time, her hand was rubbing the growing welt under her eye.

"He fuckin' hit me!" she screamed at the bouncers. "That fuckin' faggot hit me because he couldn't get it up!"

Finn looked at the two giants headed his way. It was clear they had no interest in getting at the truth. They'd already chosen to side with the hooker, who probably spent four or five nights a week in the bar, and might even work for the same people they did. Finn couldn't blame them. If he'd seen a man strike a woman, he wouldn't be in the mood for excuses, either. He was about to take a beating.

He was still doubled over when the first bouncer reached him. The man grabbed Finn by the collar and pulled him into a standing position. Finn watched as the giant pulled his arm back, aiming his huge fist at Finn's chin in a controlled rage. Finn was powerless, and closed his eyes in anticipation of the blow.

"Hold up! Hold up!" Finn heard the yells and recognized the voice, though in the confusion of the moment he couldn't place it. It was a thick Irish brogue with a deep baritone pitch.

"Wait a minute! I know this man! He's all right!" the voice boomed. Finn could hear some additional yelling and a brief argument, but things were spinning out of control and he kept his eyes closed.

Then he felt himself being pulled by the collar. "I'll take care of this," the voice said, and Finn felt his shoulder being grabbed as he was steered out of the melee. His eyes were still closed and the nausea still permeated his abdomen as a giant hand shoved his head into the doorway and out into the street, where he crashed onto the sidewalk.

The entire altercation took less than two minutes, and then was seemingly forgotten in seconds. That was the way it worked in places like this, Stone knew. Although individual grudges could fester for decades, the collective memory was fleeting.

Only the girl was still at the bar, talking about the ruckus. The bartender had given her a bar rag filled with ice, and she was holding it against her cheek, cursing under her breath. One of the bouncers was looking at her with a critical eye, evaluating the damage.

"A little extra makeup and you should be able to work by Saturday night," he concluded.

"You think I'm coming back here with the kind of bastards you let in?"

The bouncer laughed. "Yeah, I do."

"Fuck you."

"How much?"

"More than you can afford, asshole."

She was tough, Stone had to give her that. She'd just gone a quick round with the guy at the bar and she was still shooting her mouth off to anyone who crossed her. But there was also something underneath the toughness. Something sad and desperate and familiar.

Familiar. That was most of it. There was something about the girl that stuck in his memory, like a phantom, just out of reach. Her shoulder-length blonde hair was tousled from the fight, and she radiated an energy, even in her acceptance of it all. He'd seen that energy before.

Suddenly she looked up and turned, staring straight at him. Her eyes were pale blue and full of intensity. Around her neck was a choker. Right then the memory fell into place.

Stone tossed some cash on the table and ran out the door, leaving Salandro behind. It was important he catch up to the man in the suit who'd attacked the girl. He'd gotten a good look at him, but he needed more: a name, an address, a license plate number— something that would allow him to check the guy out.

The street was empty. A light rain had come and gone, coating the neighborhood with a watery sparkle as the few lights in the adjacent buildings reflected off the bricks and the cars and the garbage piles. Stone looked up and down the block, half expecting some movement to give him a clue about which way the man in the suit had gone, but nothing happened. The rain hadn't broken the humidity, but instead had added to it. The air was thick, and he could almost taste the city in the damp atmosphere; dark and old and secret.

"Damn," he muttered to himself. The man was gone. Stone should have noticed him earlier—him and the girl. If he had, he would have paid closer attention to them at the bar. He would have anticipated something like this, and it might even have provided a break in the case. He should have noticed the resemblance earlier, but he hadn't seen the girl's eyes. The girl looked very much like Natalie Caldwell.

CHAPTER EIGHTEEN

"What the hell were you doing in there, Scotty?"

They were sitting at a small Formica table in Dynasty at the edge of Chinatown, waiting on a late-night dinner of fried rice and wontons. Finn was nursing his blossoming hangover as he looked across a sea of condiments at Tigh McCluen. He hadn't changed in eight years, Finn noticed. No, make that twenty years.

He was huge, as he'd been since the days of their youth. Six foot four, with broad, rolling shoulders and thick, immovable legs, he'd always been a great boulder of a man. Eyes that twinkled with mischief regarded Finn from the center of a large, round face, and beneath a dark goatee his mouth was torqued into a wry smile.

"Nobody calls me Scotty anymore," Finn corrected.

"Getting a little big for our britches, aren't we, lad?" McCluen snapped back. He'd never bought into any of Finn's "bullshite," as he referred to it; not when they first met on the streets of Charlestown as children—an orphan and an immigrant making their way on the meanest streets in New England; not even when Finn successfully defended him against a manslaughter rap resulting from a bar brawl several years earlier. "Don't you go forgetting where you came from, Scotty boy, or you'll lose your soul. It doesn't matter how nice your suits are."

"Sorry," Finn conceded. It was the least he could do after Tigh had saved him from the worst beating in years. "Thanks for pulling me out of there. I was in for a nasty time if you hadn't come along."

McCluen smiled. "Nothing compared to the old days, though, eh? And not that you wouldn't have deserved it—hitting a fine lady like that. I should take you across my knee myself. Not even your wife and you're raising your hand to her? Not exactly kosher, now, is it?"

Finn laughed. "What the hell would a Mick like you know from kosher?" Then he turned serious. "I told you, I didn't mean to hit her, but she grabbed my balls and was trying to crush them. I was just trying to get her off of me. I must've looked like a schmuck."

McCluen roared at that, his laughter drawing stares from several of the other late-night patrons at Dynasty. "Maybe you haven't changed as much as I thought, Scotty! Why the hell was she trying to make a gelding out of you, anyway?"

"She found out I wasn't a paying customer."

"You weren't looking for a free ride, I hope."

"No, nothing like that. I just needed someone to talk to, but I didn't want to pay for it."

"Ah, the worst of all economic crimes." McCluen was still chuckling as he regarded his old friend. He could see the bags under Finn's eyes, and the paleness in his cheeks. He'd lost weight, too. McCluen leaned in across the table. "Looks like something else's got you by the balls as well, hasn't it? You look like a hundred and eighty pounds of cow shit. What is it, Scotty?"

Finn shook his head. "It's nothing you can do anything about, Tigh. A good friend of mine was killed a couple of weeks ago. I'm having trouble picking myself up from it, that's all. That's why I was at the bar, I guess. She took me there once, and I thought that going back there might make me feel better somehow. I was wrong."

"A woman? And she took you to the Kiss Club?" McCluen looked sympathetic but skeptical. "It's not a place many respectable ladies frequent. She wasn't working you, was she?"

"No, nothing like that." Finn could still see the reservation in McCluen's eyes. "The world has changed, you backward Irish Catholic dinosaur. Women are allowed to go to more than church socials now."

"Well, I'll give you one thing: the world has changed, and not for the better. Even the priests have been feeling their liberty a little too well these days."

"I don't think it's their liberty they're feeling, that's the problem."

"True enough, the sick bastards." McCluen examined his friend again. The pain was obvious on his face, and there was a notion of defeat about him that concerned the big man. "If she was a friend of yours, Scotty, I'm sure she was every bit the lady. I'm sorry to hear of her passing, and for your sorrow. Is there anything I can do?"

"No, but thanks for the offer."

"Look, Scotty, I don't forget my friends, particularly my old friends. If it wasn't for you I'd be sitting on my arse in a tin can up at Walpole for that manslaughter rap they had me on. More than that, we go back to the first day I stepped off the boat. If there's anything I can do, I want you to be straight with me."

"No, really. If there was anything, I'd let you know."

McCluen continued to regard Finn for a moment or two, then shrugged. "All right, then," he said. He took out a piece of paper from his pocket and wrote on it, handing it to Finn. "That there is the number for my mobile. I don't give that out to many people, so keep it to yourself, but if you ever need anything the phone's always on."

Finn frowned. "What are you doing these days that you need a cell phone on around the clock?"

"Now why would a nice, respectable barrister like yourself want to know the answer to a question like that?" McCluen raised his eyebrows.

Finn nodded. "You're right, I don't want to know. Forget I asked."

"It's forgotten."

They sat in silence for a minute or two; just two old friends from a tough neighborhood who knew when nothing needed to be said. Then McCluen raised his half-empty glass of beer in a toast. *"Ná feic a bhfeicir; is ná clois a gcloisir. Is má fiafraítear díot, abair ná feadrais."*

"That's quite a mouthful. What is it?"

"An old Irish proverb."

"Sounds pretty. What does it mean?"

"Don't see what you see; don't hear what you hear. And if you're asked, say you don't know."

"Words to live by from the motherland?"

"As applicable in the new world as they were in the old, Scotty. Sometimes I think more so."

CHAPTER NINETEEN

Flaherty had never seen Captain Weidel so angry, and that was saying something. Weidel was not one to bottle up his emotions. She'd seen him explode with such force that it had driven dedicated officers to resign from the department. His acerbic tongue had reduced more than a dozen hulking rookies to tears. But this was something new, something Flaherty had never before witnessed. It was a simmering, contemplative sort of rage that bubbled under the surface of his skin, turning his forehead bright red as he worked a silent tongue back and forth in his mouth.

"Say that again," he said finally. It was more a dare than a request, as though if she didn't repeat it, it would be treated as if it had never been said. Flaherty considered letting it drop, but it was just not her style to back down from a fight.

"I said that the Caldwell murder might not be related to the others. It might not be Little Jack after all."

"You wanna tell me what the hell you're talking about, Lieutenant? And I use that rank for the moment only." Weidel's voice registered pure fury. "He took her heart, right? She had a gold crucifix around her neck, right? She was dressed like a hooker, right? So please explain to me why this murder is not related?"

"Well, it may be related in the sense that it could be a copycat killer."

"*May* be? *May*-goddamned-be? Let me tell you something, Lieutenant, if I hear you say anything like that outside this office, I'll have your fucking badge. We've got a city full of people locked in their apartments because of this guy, not coming out until we catch him, and you want to start telling them it's *two* guys they need to be worried about?"

"I'm just telling you that Farmalant thinks it's a different guy based on the autopsy results."

"Yeah, well you tell Farmalant that if I hear he's spreading that kind of rumor, I'll have him arrested for interfering with a police investigation, obstruction of justice, disturbing the peace, and any other charge I can come up with."

"Look, Captain, no one likes the idea that this may be a different guy, but the Caldwell girl was killed *before* her heart was taken out. It looks like she was strangled, then moved, and then cut up."

"So?"

"All the other girls were kept alive until their hearts were removed. They had a highly sophisticated blend of anesthetics in their blood. There was nothing like that in the Caldwell woman."

"Maybe he was in a hurry this time. Maybe she fought back and he had to beat the shit out of her before he was ready. Maybe she screamed and he had to shut her up. There are a thousand different *may*bes that would explain the difference. But no, you'd apparently rather scare the public with some new theory about multiple killers."

"Also, she was raped. The others weren't."

The anger bubbling under the captain's skin seemed ready for a major eruption. He said nothing, just glared.

"Trust me, Captain," she began again. "I'm not talking about making a public announcement. I just want to consider other possibilities while we continue our investigation. The Caldwell woman had a friend at her law firm who mentioned an older man she was dating. That opens up other possibilities that may be worth checking out."

"Let it drop, Lieutenant. You'll last longer in this job."

"I think we need to look into this."

Weidel threw his hands up in the air. "Fine, Lieutenant, have it your way. Look into this if you have to, but understand: I don't want to hear anything about it from anyone, got it? Just remember that shit rolls downhill, so if anyone starts dumping on me, you'll end up knee deep in it."

"I appreciate the support, sir. I'll keep that in mind." She put her hands on her hips in a defiant stance.

"Get the fuck out of my office," Weidel growled. Then he turned toward the window, giving Flaherty his back as she walked out.

She probably should have just let it drop, she knew. It was hard enough to chase down one serial killer without throwing additional variables into the equation. But something was eating at her about the Caldwell case. Nothing seemed to fit, and she didn't like it. She couldn't let it drop.

Kozlowski was sitting in the chair across the desk from her, leaning back in his patient, relaxed manner. Flaherty wished she could be that calm. She'd once asked him how he seemed not to let the ugly parts of police work get to him. "It comes with twenty-five years on the job and thirty years of Dewar's straight up," he'd explained. She wasn't sure if she'd make it that long.

"Any word on the street?" she asked.

"Nothing yet. We're still shaking the trees, though. And you'll be happy to know that we're getting a little help from our friends in the mob."

"What are you talking about?"

"The South Boston folks have put a bounty on this guy's head," Kozlowski said. Flaherty raised her eyebrows in disbelief. "Fifty thousand dollars is what we've heard. More if he's not alive to make it to trial."

"Great," Flaherty said. "Nothing like a little street justice. Do we get the reward if we catch him?"

"I don't think you meet the eligibility requirements. You've got to be a low-life scumbag."

"Well, you ought to qualify, anyway."

"Funny."

"Any word from Stone?"

"He's the one who found out about the bounty. Other than that, he hasn't come up with anything useful. There was a little dust-up at the Kiss Club the other night. Some john was smacking the heck out of one of the working girls—apparently a girl who looked a little like Natalie Caldwell—but it didn't amount to anything. Stone didn't get any kind of ID on the guy."

Flaherty looked at Kozlowski with a furrowed brow.

"What's up, L.T.?" he asked her. "You look concerned."

She sighed, almost afraid to raise the issue. "What do you really think about the Caldwell murder?" she asked finally.

"Personally, I'm opposed to murder."

"I'm serious. What do you think about how it fits in the investigation?"

"You mean, do I think Little Jack is responsible for offing everybody's favorite former federal prosecutor?"

"Yeah, that's exactly what I mean."

Kozlowski rolled his eyes. "You don't want to know what I think. Actually, that's not fair. I think you already know what I think, but you don't want to hear it."

"It doesn't fit, does it?"

Now it was Kozlowski's turn to sigh. "It's possible it's the same guy. There are a lot of ways to explain the discrepancies in the way she was killed. And there are still a lot of similarities between the Caldwell murder and the others that would be difficult to explain if it's not the same guy."

"But . . ."

"But my gut instinct is that we're looking for a different fish."

Flaherty nodded. "Mine too."

"So what do we do about it?" Kozlowski shrugged. "Splitting the investigation would cause confusion; not to mention a few heart attacks among the more political, upwardly mobile types who're just looking for a reason to squash us."

"I know. That's why *we* don't do anything about it. I was just thinking that *I* might take a closer look at the Caldwell murder myself."

"Off the record, of course."

"Of course."

Kozlowski chuckled. "Are you going to call up that good-looking young lawyer you were so smitten with a few weeks ago?"

"What the hell are you talking about? He's our best lead on the case." She felt herself turning red. "And I wasn't smitten. I felt bad for the guy."

Kozlowski couldn't wipe the smile off his face. "Smitten. That's what I call it, and I've known you long enough to tell the difference."

Flaherty shook her head in disgust. "That's fine, you can live with your twisted little delusions. Just don't tell anyone else what I'm doing. If the brass finds out about this, they'll have both our asses in a sling."

Kozlowski wagged his finger tauntingly at her. "I can't believe you're going against official departmental policy. You know, Lieutenant, if you keep hanging out with me, we may actually turn you into a rule-breaking malcontent with no hope for future advancement."

Flaherty picked up the phone on her desk. "I hope that doesn't mean I'll start wearing wrinkled, fifty-dollar suits from J.C. Penney like you, too."

"These are classics," Kozlowski said, pulling on his lapels as he got up and walked away from her desk. Once he was gone, Flaherty dialed the number from her case notes.

CHAPTER TWENTY

Finn sat in a conference room across from Preston Holland and next to Nick Williams. There were six junior associates and three paralegals crowded around the table as well—the trial team—ready to plan strategy in the Tannery case. Spread out in front of them on the mahogany conference table were the key documents and testimonial transcripts.

"This case, in the final analysis, is all about the experts," Holland was lecturing. "There's no debate about the facts. The Massachusetts Transportation Safety Commission hired Huron Security to provide security staff on commuter trains. Neither the commission nor Huron focused on the security at the railway yard—precisely because none of the federal security experts told them to. So the real questions to be dealt with at trial are: first, did the commission or Huron fail to take into account any information or advice they were given by the federal government on how to provide security? and, second, could either the commission or Huron have done anything to prevent suicide bombers from successfully carrying out an attack like this? The answer to both questions is no."

"Now we just have to convince a jury of that," Williams added. Finn had discovered that despite Williams's bookish nature, the man had a fondness for quips that might seem petulant coming from anyone else. Somehow, though, he carried it off.

"Right," Holland continued with a sideways glance at Nick. "And that's where our experts come in. They're willing to support every argument we make. We have the top people in the counterterrorism field ready to point out that it's virtually impossible for any agency to prevent a suicide bombing."

"Who are our experts?" one of the junior associates asked, obviously skeptical. Holland turned to look at his senior staffers, sending a clear message. Associates on the case were responsible for having complete knowledge of the facts. What might have seemed like an innocent question to most non-lawyers was, to the lawyers at Howery, Black, an admission that the associate wasn't doing his job. Preston's glare told both Williams and Finn he wanted an example made of the young man. Nick and Finn looked at each other briefly, silently deciding between themselves who'd step up to eviscerate the unwitting associate. When Williams raised his eyebrows in a challenge, Finn knew that he had to take the lead.

He glared at the junior associate with venom in his eyes, trying to remember his name. *That's right, Allen Spurler.* Spurler had graduated from Yale Law School two years earlier, but had spent time completing a couple of prestigious clerkships—including a one-year stint with the Supreme Court. He was very bright, but cocky. He'd be good to have on the team, but he needed to be knocked down a level or two.

"You haven't read the expert reports yet?" There was an accusation in Finn's voice that was evident to everyone in the room.

Spurler hesitated. "Uh, no, I've been busy analyzing the documents we turned over to the other side, trying to identify the ones that will cause us the most problems. Should I look at those reports now?"

Williams chortled, shaking his head at Spurler's misstep. "Wrong answer," he said under his breath.

Finn sat back in his chair. "Well, let me ask you this—if the key to our case is the experts, and you don't even know who our experts are, much less what they're going to say, how are you going to know which documents are the most important?" Out of the corner of his eye he could see that Holland was enjoying the show.

"I'm sorry," Spurler said, still trying to save himself. "No one told me I should be reading those reports."

Finn scoffed, going in for the kill. "This isn't law school, or some cushy clerkship anymore. No one's going to hold your hand every minute of the day, or lead you through what needs to be done. I would have expected that someone from Yale who clerked at the Supreme Court might have more initiative than that, but maybe we've all overestimated you."

Spurler nodded, accepting defeat at last. The room was quiet for a moment as Finn continued to stare at the chastised young lawyer. The other junior people were too scared to open their mouths. That was good, Finn thought. He'd made his point that no lapses would be tolerated.

After a moment, Holland resumed his speech. "In answer to Mr. Spurler's question, our primary expert is Leighland Slafsky, the former secretary of homeland security." Finn could hear the associates suck in their breath in awe. "Given his obvious qualifications and his outstanding record on domestic terrorism, we believe his testimony will be a bullet through the heart of the plaintiff's case. In addition, we have the CEOs of the two largest security companies in the country ready to testify. They have obvious concerns about any security company being held liable for the effects of a terrorist attack. At the same time, the jury will see the heads of Huron's biggest competitors on the stand testifying that Huron did nothing wrong. That should be fairly compelling."

"What about the fact witnesses?" one of the other junior associates asked. She was a third-year associate Finn had worked with before. Her name was Jane Mannerin—"Plain Jane," as she was known behind her back because of her severe looks and her simple, boxy suits. She was short and squat, and she wore large black-rimmed glasses with huge round lenses, giving her the appearance of a scholarly owl. What Plain Jane lacked in looks, she made up for in brains and stamina, though. She'd become a legend already by billing more hours than any other associate for three years in a row, proving her worth to Howery, Black's bottom line. Finn looked at Preston to see if he wanted another example made, but the older lawyer seemed satisfied with the earlier evisceration.

"Huron Security had more than one thousand security guards working on different commuter lines at the time of the terrorist attack," answered Holland. "The judge has ordered us to make ten of those security guards available for trial. We've already prepared a preliminary list—"

"I wanted to talk to you about that, Preston," Finn interrupted. "I found some notes in the personnel file with some additional names highlighted that I'd like to check on." He flipped through his notes. "Martinson, Phillipe, and Carter," he read off the names. "I've never heard of these guys before, but they may be worth checking out."

"We've already chosen our ten, Finn. I don't want to waste time plowing the same ground twice."

"I know, but these guys were singled out in Natalie's notes. She had pretty good instincts about which witnesses would present well to a jury." It still hurt him to say her name in public, but it was getting better.

Preston frowned. "All right, check them out briefly, but I don't want you to spend any real time on this."

"Will do."

"Okay," Holland said, turning to the larger group. "We've got two months until the trial starts, which is almost no time at all. I need everyone to dig in and dig in hard. This is one of the most important cases the firm has ever had, and the entire country is going to be watching us. We're all going to have to be ruthlessly efficient, always remembering that attention to detail is the key to any trial presentation. The show we put on for the jury has to be as seamless as a Broadway production: no surprises, no miscues." He paused dramatically.

"The Anniversary Bombing was one of the greatest tragedies in this country's history. Foreign nationals took advantage of America's generosity to inflict pain and suffering not only on those directly affected, but on the nation as a whole. Our hearts go out to the hundreds of people who lost loved ones—like Ms. Tannery—but we cannot allow the attack to divide the American people. The terrorists bear the responsibility for this great tragedy, not the good people who dedicated their lives to preventing terrorism. It's our job to make sure that allowing the blame to be shifted in the courts doesn't compound the injustice. Otherwise, the terrorists will have succeeded in making our judicial system another of their victims."

As he finished, all eyes were riveted on him. Finn marveled at the way Preston could control a room. He knew Holland was simply trying out various themes that he might eventually use at trial, but he didn't care. It was the power of the speech that Finn admired, not its sincerity. At that moment, he knew that Nick Williams had been right—the Tannery case was the biggest opportunity of his career, and he was determined to make the most of it.

Finn dialed the number for Daryl Carter first. He'd pulled Carter's personnel file from the stacks of Huron documents that were produced to the plaintiff in the lawsuit and had been piled neatly from floor to ceiling in the "war room," a large conference room dedicated to the Tannery trial. According to the file, Carter was thirty-one years old and had been with

Huron since the company first got the contract to provide security for the Massachusetts commuter rail system. The address listed was in South Boston.

As Finn waited for the call to go through, he flipped through the case notebook Natalie had kept before her death. He'd come across margin notations on the sheet that listed the witnesses identified by Huron. Normally he wouldn't have paid any attention to the scribblings, but they were hard to ignore. The names had been traced over repeatedly until they were marked in thick, dark lines. They'd then been underlined and highlighted, as if Natalie had kept coming back to them. It looked like she had had a good idea about some additional witnesses and couldn't let it go. She was tenacious, and always had been. Under any other circumstances he would have let the issue drop, but given the prominence of the marks in the notebook—

The phone ringing on the other end of the line interrupted his thoughts. Finn scanned Carter's personnel file again, looking for something to use so he could connect with him on a personal level. People were usually reluctant to talk to lawyers, and Finn found it helpful to establish a rapport before launching into more difficult questions. Before he could find anything, though, the line was picked up and he heard a familiar high-pitched tone whining in his ear. "We're sorry, the number you have dialed has been disconnected. We have no further information at this time," said the pleasant feminine voice recording.

Finn hung up. He checked the number in his notes and dialed it again. Once more, the recording told him the number had been disconnected. It was strange, he thought. Huron still had Carter listed at this number. Finn knew, though, that many security guards took the work temporarily, then moved on. It was very possible Carter had simply picked up stakes. Finn made a note to have one of his private investigators follow up.

Next, he picked up the file on Manuel Phillipe. The information from Huron listed him as forty-two years old, married with two children. He dialed the number. This time it was a male voice on the recording. "We're sorry, the call you have made cannot be completed as dialed. Please check the number and dial again."

Finn hung up and tried again but got the same result. He frowned. It seemed less likely that someone in his forties with a wife and two children would pick up and leave. Finn felt his puzzlement shifting to irritation as he moved on to the Martinson file. The man was listed as only twenty-two years old, and a recent graduate of a local junior college. Finn dialed the number listed, half expecting to get another phone company recording. He didn't, though. Instead, a woman answered.

"Hello?" she said. Her voice was low and gravelly.

"Hello, is John Martinson in?"

"Who?"

"John Martinson?"

"You got the wrong number, mister." And with that, the woman hung up.

Finn looked at the number on the Martinson file. *Maybe I misdialed.* He tried again.

"Hello?" It was the same woman.

"Hello, I'm trying to reach John Martinson."

"I told you, you got the wrong number." The woman sounded annoyed.

"I'm sorry, ma'am, but is this 555-1209?"

"Sure is, but there's no John Martinson here."

"I'm sorry again, ma'am, but can I ask you how long you've had this phone number? Did you get it recently?"

"Not unless you consider twenty years ago 'recently.'"

"And you've never heard of John Martinson?"

"Can't say I have."

Finn was deep in thought as he replaced the receiver. Why Natalie had focused on these three security guards was a mystery to him. He'd assumed she'd talked to them and decided they'd make excellent witnesses. That was, perhaps, still the case, but then why had they disappeared? Finn hated mysteries. He knew Preston was right when he said they couldn't afford to waste time chasing down rabbit holes, but he didn't think Holland would object if he sent one of the firm's investigators to do a quick check on the addresses of these three. He'd use Bostick, though. Finn and Bostick were close enough that he wouldn't even need to tell Preston about it unless they found something.

He was still lost in thought when the phone rang. He reached for the receiver and smiled when he heard the voice on the other end of the line. "Hello, Lieutenant Flaherty," he said. "It's nice to hear from you."

CHAPTER TWENTY-ONE

It wasn't a date, but it was the closest to one Finn had come in months. Flaherty had said that she had a few follow-up questions, and asked if they could meet. Finn was happy to do it, but explained that his day was too hectic to break away during work hours. "We could always talk over dinner," he suggested.

There was a pause on the other end of the line. "I'm not sure that would be appropriate," she said at last. Finn was disappointed at first, but something in Flaherty's voice told him that it wasn't her final decision.

"You have to eat, don't you?" he pressed.

"Yes."

"So how can it be inappropriate for you to have a working dinner? It's actually the most efficient use of your time. We can even go Dutch treat if it will make you feel better."

There was a long pause. Finally she sighed. "I'll meet you, but I'm not eating."

"Suit yourself," he replied. "Why don't we meet at Plaza Three Steakhouse in Faneuil Hall at seven-thirty. I *am* going to eat, and I'm in the mood for a good steak."

He was at the restaurant at seven-fifteen. It was unusual for him to be early for anything, but he was looking forward to seeing Flaherty again. He was sitting at the bar, sipping a Maker's Mark, watching the Red Sox fight out another close game, when he heard her voice behind him.

"Mr. Finn, I appreciate your meeting me." She was all business. Finn should have expected as much—after all, she was conducting a homicide investigation—but he felt disappointed.

"If you really appreciated my meeting you, you'd drop the 'Mister' and just call me Finn," he said.

She relented. "Finn," she said with a nod. "I just have a few questions about Ms. Caldwell. It shouldn't take much time."

"That's fine, but I'm starving so we'll have to do it while I eat." He nodded at the hostess, who waved to a waiter who led them to a table.

"I'm really not going to eat," Flaherty said as she sat down.

"So you've said," Finn replied. "Can I at least get you a drink?" He could see her wrestling with the offer.

"No thank you, I'm all right," she said.

Finn shrugged. "Okay, but I think this might be more productive if we dropped the formality. You must be off duty by now, at least technically." He smiled, trying to melt the icy front she was putting up.

"Fine," she said after some thought. "I'll have a chardonnay."

Finn chuckled. "I had you pegged as a scotch drinker, being a cop and all."

"That's what I drink when I'm out with other cops, but I thought we'd decided I was off duty. Besides, I'm counting on your discretion so that the people I work with don't find out I'm not really as butch as you apparently think I am."

"Touché," he said, chuckling again. "I'll try to keep my preconceptions on a leash for the rest of the evening."

"That would be nice, thank you."

Finn waved a waiter over to order her wine. "Now, Lieutenant, what did you want to ask me about?"

"The first time we talked, you mentioned that Ms. Caldwell was dating someone. An older man, you said. I wanted to see if you could give me any more information about him."

"I don't think there's anything I know that I haven't already told you. I only found out about it that Friday night, and our conversation didn't last very long."

"You don't remember *anything* else that she might have said?"

Finn closed his eyes for a moment and tried to visualize their last conversation. The few shards of memory that pierced his consciousness were blurry and ill-defined. He tried to focus on the sound of Natalie's voice during their last conversation, but it was no use; he'd felt so dizzy at the time that he'd effectively tuned her out while he tried to compose himself. He opened his eyes. "I'm sorry, I really can't remember anything more."

He *was* sorry, too. He wanted badly to help for Natalie's sake, but also for Flaherty's. He liked this woman.

She wasn't ready to let it drop, though. "Why did she bring the subject up that last night, do you think?" she asked.

Finn felt his face turn red as he remembered. The topic had come up when he'd made a pass at her and she was fending him off. It was humiliating, and he had no intention of reliving the moment in front of this beautiful police detective. "I'm not sure," he lied.

"Did it come up in conversation?" she asked.

"It must have." He shrugged evasively. "I just don't remember." He looked away, and she noticed how uncomfortable he was.

"There's something you're not telling me, isn't there, Finn?"

"I don't know what you're talking about," he replied, but he was unable to meet her eyes.

She looked at him as they sat in prolonged silence.

"You two were lovers," she said. It came quick and sharp, and it took Finn by surprise, slicing through his facade. It came from Flaherty as a statement, not a question, and he knew that denial was unrealistic.

He looked her straight in the eyes. "We were together for a short time," he said. He could sense her tension from across the table, and he took a deep breath. "It was a couple of years ago, and it never amounted to much."

"Just a quick roll in the hay between friends?" Flaherty tested.

"No," Finn said quietly. "No, it was much more than that. I cared about her, probably more than I've ever cared about any woman." He looked away again.

"How long did it last?" she asked.

Finn shrugged. "Not long. Natalie wasn't really the type to commit." He smiled ruefully. "She was great at some things, but intimacy wasn't one of them." Lowering his voice, he added, "I suppose, in some ways, we had that in common."

"What happened?"

"I thought there was something more. I mistook a friendship with fringe benefits for something more meaningful. She broke it off as soon as she saw it was something more than lust for me." He looked straight at Flaherty again and smiled. "She had bigger fish to fry."

"Did it hurt?" Flaherty pressed.

"Sure," Finn said. "I don't know how much of it was pride, and how much genuine feeling, but it did hurt at the time. If you really knew Natalie, though, you could hardly be surprised. She was remarkable in so many ways—a great friend, a great lawyer, a great wit—but she had her own agenda. I knew that, as much as I tried to ignore it, and deep down, I wasn't surprised. And because I wasn't surprised, we were able to stay friends."

Flaherty searched his eyes for some sign of deception, but

found only depth and confidence. Suddenly she realized she'd been staring into his eyes for an unusual amount of time, and she averted her gaze, feeling slightly self-conscious.

"Hey, listen," he said cheerily, trying to break the mood. "Can I call you something besides 'Detective'? It makes me feel like either a lawyer or an ex-con."

She hesitated. She knew she should avoid getting too close, but the honesty of his responses, and the depths of his feelings, made her feel like she'd already crossed that bridge. "Linda," she said finally.

"Linda." He tried it on for size and liked it. "Linda, why are you asking me all these questions? If Little Jack killed Natalie, then it was a random killing, right? What does it matter who she was dating or had dated in the past?"

"We don't know for sure that she *was* killed by Little Jack."

"Is there anything that makes you believe she wasn't?"

"No," she lied. "But we have to chase down every lead and angle."

He studied her face as she talked. She was pretty, and he liked her, but he wasn't convinced she was telling him everything. "Be honest. Something has happened, hasn't it?"

"I can't discuss the investigation. You were a defense lawyer once, you know that."

"Ah, so you've done a background check on me," he said, smiling. "C'mon, Linda. I was her friend, I deserve to know."

She looked long and hard at him. He was good-looking, she couldn't deny that, but then looks had never really attracted her before. Looks could never make her feel the way she was feeling. There was something more; something in the eyes. She decided to trust her instincts. "Look, Finn, you know I can't give you any specifics. All I'll say is that there are some differences about Natalie's killing that make it inconsistent with the others."

"What differences?"

"I've already said more than I should have, and you know it."

"All I know is that Natalie is dead, and you want my help in figuring out who killed her, but you aren't willing to share information with me."

"Nice try, but there's nothing I can do, so you might as well drop it."

Finn sighed. "Fine, I'll drop it." He looked at her again. "On one condition."

She folded her arms across her chest. "What?"

"Have dinner with me."

CHAPTER TWENTY-TWO

I should never have had wine, she thought as they walked along Devonshire Street up toward Chinatown. But then she'd done a lot of things that evening that weren't wise. Like ordering the twelve-ounce porterhouse.

"How can you possibly look this good when you eat like that?" he joked.

"I don't really look that good, you've just been drinking," she quipped. He had been drinking, but not to excess. No, it was more that he seemed enchanted. It had been a long time since she'd felt that from a man. "Besides," she added, "I don't normally get to eat like this on a lieutenant's salary."

"You mean I'm the only guy willing to take you out?"

"You didn't take me out," she corrected him. "I'm conducting an investigation."

"Good, then I still have our first date to look forward to." With that, he took her hand in his as they walked. It should have seemed such an odd gesture, clumsy and adolescent, but it didn't. It felt wonderful, and she hated how good it felt.

Damn you, Kozlowski, she thought as Finn's light conversation blurred into the rhythm of their footsteps. She might not have noticed her attraction to Finn if Kozlowski hadn't made a point of bringing it to her attention. Now it hung like a fog on her brain, mixing with the wine and making her extremities tingle.

"You're not listening to me, are you?" Finn's voice penetrated her thoughts.

"No, I am," she protested. "You were talking about growing up in Charlestown."

"I've been talking about myself all evening, haven't I?" There was disappointment in his voice. "I'm sorry, I hate it when people do that. I'm not normally so self-absorbed."

Flaherty hated when men did that, too; rambled on about themselves in an effort to impress her. This had been different, though. It didn't seem like Finn had tried to impress, but to connect. The rhythm of his voice had been easy, lacking the self-consciousness that so often accompanied other men's conversations. "You weren't that bad," she reassured. "Besides, you've led a more interesting life than most." He had, too. The stories of Finn's childhood sounded like something out of a Dickens novel, only without the charm. She couldn't imagine growing up without any family, without anyone to care for her, subject to the whims of the state and the cruelties of foster parents who all too often were more focused on the stipends provided by the government than on the well-being of their vulnerable charges. She was sure she would never have survived.

Finn had survived, though; more than that, he'd overcome, and kept his sense of humor to boot. So many men Flaherty knew defined themselves in shallow terms and were driven by cardboard notions of success—the perfect job, the perfect wife, the perfect car. She'd observed that firsthand long ago in her ex-husband, and the marriage had ended in less than six months. A fellow detective, he had been unable to see beyond her role as wife-as-possession, and his demands had strangled their relationship.

Flaherty saw none of that in Finn. He was driven to succeed, that much was clear, but there was also an even stronger need to *connect*—to someone or something—that was hiding under the surface.

"I want to learn more about you, though," he said, squeezing her hand.

She laughed. "I wouldn't have told you anything anyway." She pointed at a building up ahead. "Here we are," she said. They were walking toward an old converted warehouse in the leather district, just outside of Chinatown. "This is home."

Finn looked up at the dark brick building, with its hinged windows hanging high on the floors. "Nice place," he said.

"It's a loft," she explained. "I bought it before lofts were trendy, so it was affordable. And the neighborhood"—she looked around the narrow street, taking note of the trash piled on the curbsides awaiting the morning garbage trucks—"well, it's getting better, but let's just say I was an urban pioneer when I moved in."

"I like it," Finn said. He was looking at her when he said it, though, not at the building.

"Listen, thanks for dinner, and it was nice of you to walk me home, although it wasn't really necessary," she said quickly, patting her gun for emphasis. Her heart was racing, and she needed to get control of the situation fast.

"So that's it, huh?" Finn said, smiling. "You're just going to use me up for some dinner and information, then dump me on the sidewalk with the rest of the garbage?"

"Well, let's face it, you weren't able to give me any decent information," she pointed out. "Now, if you'd offered something really good—something I might be able to use—well, we'd probably already be upstairs between the sheets." She'd meant to keep it light, but the mention of the two of them in bed together, even in jest, made her blush. She was glad it was dark outside so he couldn't see her turning crimson.

He seemed taken with the idea as well. He cocked his head

to the side. "With an incentive like that, I'll try harder next time." He moved closer slowly, almost imperceptibly, and she felt her entire body tense. Then, as he was leaning in, he stopped. A thought seemed to crinkle his forehead. "There *was* something else, now that you mention it."

"Oh, *right,*" she mocked, but he'd pulled away from her and was concentrating hard, trying to kick something free in his brain.

"No, I'm serious. Natalie said at one point that she couldn't tell me who the older guy was, even if she wanted, but that she was learning a lot from him."

"What do you think she meant by that?"

"I don't know. God, this is frustrating. She said something else about him, but I wasn't paying attention. For some reason, though, I got the feeling he was a political mover and shaker—connected in some important way."

Flaherty frowned. "Who was it, do you think?"

Finn was staring off into space, trying to remember more, but there was nothing else. "I have no idea," he said at last. "Natalie certainly knew a lot of politically connected people from her days at the Justice Department, working on the Whitey Bulger case. She was also involved in last year's mayoral campaign, helping to get Tribinio elected, and she spent a bunch of time wining and dining with the party honchos." He searched his memory again. "I don't know who else. We traveled in different social circles, so it could be just about anyone."

Flaherty thought hard for a moment. "Can you come up with a list of some of the connected people you think she dealt with?"

"Sure, I can have that for you in a day or two."

"Great, that would really be helpful."

Finn smiled wickedly. "Really?" he said. "Didn't you say that if I gave you something useful we'd be upstairs between the sheets?" They were close to each other again now. It took Flaherty by surprise, and she could feel the electricity running through her. She wanted him, she realized. The closer together they came, the stronger the feeling was, until she was literally fighting to control the moment.

Their lips were only inches apart when she managed to speak. "You haven't given me the information yet," she protested, but her voice was breathy and desperate.

And then they were kissing. Finn leaned in and their lips brushed together; soft at first, his closed mouth moving over hers, tickling just the outer edge. Her lips parted on their own, without his prodding, and then they were locked in a passionate embrace; hands and tongues exploring desperately for a moment; then two; then three; until she could feel herself gasping for breath.

He pulled away from her finally, and they looked at each other, embarrassed, surprised, and excited. She didn't know what to say, which was unusual for her. Then he smiled and whispered into her ear, "I'll get you that list as soon as I can."

He kissed her cheek and backed away, still looking at her, and still smiling. *Say something*, she told herself. *Ask him to stay*, a part of her screamed. But she knew she wouldn't. She didn't know if it was the circumstances of how they met, or her Catholic upbringing, or some hidden cop's instinct, but she knew she wouldn't ask him to stay. Instead, she stood there in silence, watching him pull away, until he waved and turned around, heading up the street and around the corner.

CHAPTER TWENTY-THREE

The little house on Cypher Street was dark. Night had closed in around it softly, as if to avoid stirring the odd proclivities of its inhabitant. Cloistered in the windowless basement, he was oblivious to the dying of the light as he sat rocking on a small scrap of cloth in the far corner of the antiseptic room. In front of him, the makeshift shrine glowed with candles, seven in all. Six were placed in front of large jars, their contents deep red, surrounded by baubles and trinkets and locks of hair as talismans to guard against the souls of their former owners. The seventh candle sat apart, next to an open jar on a lonely corner of the shelf, its heat mixing with the formaldehyde fumes that wafted up from the jar, turning the air sickly sweet.

Rocking, always rocking, he repeated the verse like a mantra, blurring the words into one another until he was no longer speaking in a recognizable language, but in a gibberish; like an ancient tongue, secret and powerful.

> ***The waters you saw where the whore sits***
> ***are people, multitudes, nations, and languages.***
> ***The beast and ten horns you saw shall hate the whore.***
> ***They will bring her to ruin and leave her naked.***
> ***They will eat her flesh and burn her with fire . . .***

They will eat her flesh and burn her with fire . . .
Theywilleatherfleshandburnherwithfiretheywilleather fleshandburnherwithfiretheywilleatherfleshandburn herwithfiretheywilleatherfleshandburnherwithfire . . .

He'd settled his mind—or God had. That was what he liked to believe. It was time for another sacrifice. This was the time he most enjoyed, the anticipation of divine intervention—the feeling that he no longer controlled his actions, that they were guided by a force far greater than his own will. The abdication of control gave him a warm, protected feeling. It wasn't heaven, he knew, but that reward would come in time. And for now, this was the closest thing to heaven he could imagine. Sometimes, when he was in these trances, he could close his eyes and almost touch his parents. They were beaming at him with pride. Pride and acceptance; those two gifts he'd sought and been denied. They were his now.

When he was finished with his meditation, he left the candles burning and headed upstairs to get changed. The fear that gripped the city—the fear he'd created—made his task more difficult. The streetwalkers were wary. Many had taken to carrying weapons, or were staying off the streets entirely. He needed a new plan, and he'd spent days perfecting it.

There were places he'd researched on the Internet where prostitutes gathered in groups, looking to tempt men's weakness; bars that catered to ugly, discreet meetings and vile, no-strings-attached affairs. He'd use them as his hunting ground. It was thrilling to begin moving freely in public, fulfilling his duty in plain view of a city unaware of the approaching apocalypse.

Of course, hunting in bars meant he'd have to blend in. That had never been easy, and he'd spent a week working hard to look normal. The perversity of the need almost excited him. Almost.

They will bring her to ruin and leave her naked.
They will eat her flesh and burn her with fire . . .
They will bring her to ruin and leave her naked.
They will eat her flesh and burn her with fire . . .

As he walked upstairs, he was humming. As a child, he'd hummed when he was most happy.

CHAPTER TWENTY-FOUR

Stone noticed him almost immediately. He was in his thirties, short, with sandy brown hair that was thinning badly on top. In an attempt to make his hair look thicker, he'd grown it long in back and then brushed it forward over the bald spot on top. The effect was the opposite of his intent. He looked like the victim of some late-night infomercial.

Under normal circumstances, Stone wouldn't have given him a second look, but after losing the man who'd attacked the hooker a week before, he'd redoubled his efforts to scrutinize everyone at the Kiss Club. Mr. Infomercial caught his attention on the second pass.

The guy was sitting alone at a small table against the wall, his head turning on a swivel, taking everything in. He looked out of place with his forward-swept hair and his starched white shirt buttoned all the way to the collar, tight around his neck. But it was the look in his eyes that really startled Stone. The man watched each of the working girls strut by him with a cold, hard stare. Most of the men at the bar watched the women; there was nothing unusual about that. Men leered at their feminine parts with hunger. The stranger's glare was different, though. There was no heat to it, no yearning. It was judgmental and calculating, as though he were meting out silent justice.

Stone got up and moved to the other end of the bar so he could get a better look at this odd character. His new vantage did nothing to discourage his initial assessment, and he dedicated himself to watching the man closely for the rest of the evening.

The first thing he noticed was the smell. Lavender and musk and alcohol mixed with the more subtle odors of desire and sin to form a tapestry of desperation. The experience was so powerful it tickled something in his memory from before the death of his parents—before he'd changed. He couldn't quite put his finger on it, but it reminded him of the loss and pain he'd suffered, and it made him angry.

Put it out of your mind, he told himself. The time was coming, and he was the instrument of God's final will, but he needed to focus if he was going to be of any use. A young girl—no more than nineteen, if that, he guessed—walked by, looking down to smile at him as she passed. She was wearing a red silk dress, tight over her breasts to accentuate and reveal her lithe curves. From there it clung to her midriff and waist before letting go of her form to fall in a loose skirt to just above her knees. The skirt swished softly as she walked, and it brushed his hand as she passed close. He was surprised at the inner stirring it caused, and he struggled visibly to keep his composure.

He took a sip of his tonic water. She was too young anyway, he thought. She hadn't yet caused enough of God's children to stray. She would burn, no doubt, but not at his hand.

He picked up his head again and scanned the bar. There were so many to choose from, it was exhilarating. After several minutes of looking, he found the one he wanted—the one God wanted. She was sitting at the bar at the far end of the room, her legs crossed seductively, stirring a drink with the end of her finger. She did it sensually, running the pad of her finger around the edge of the glass, dipping it in occasionally to mix the drink, then lifting her hand to her mouth and dragging her finger over her lips, licking the moisture off with the tip of her tongue. It was a routine—a performance—that was clear, but it was also effective.

He stared at her for a few minutes, watching her practiced tease. She was older than most of the others—into her thirties, he guessed—but stunning in a sophisticated way. It looked as if she'd sat at that bar for an eternity, tempting the weak and destroying God's work. He hated her instantly.

After several minutes she noticed him staring at her. She looked surprised, embarrassed, and flattered all at the same time. She'd practiced that look in the mirror, too, he was sure. She smiled at him and then looked away for a moment, then returned her gaze and gave him a full smile that lacked any hint of inhibition or reservation. He couldn't bring himself to smile back at her, but simply nodded his head.

He stayed in his seat for a moment, wondering what the proper protocol was, whether he should cross the bar and approach her. She was the one God wanted, he knew that, but he had trouble bringing himself to initiate contact in public. He was still locked in indecision when she got up and started walking toward his table.

She swung her hips as she walked, and the dress showed off her legs and chest in a provocative way. Several men turned to watch her, but there was no doubt she was staring at him, and it was clear she was coming his way. A lesser man would be excited, he told himself, as he fought off the stirrings of lust, anger, and aggression.

When she reached his table, she sat down opposite him. She didn't wait for an invitation or an introduction, or even a smile or nod of encouragement. Just sat down as though it was her right to intrude on his evening. Her arrogance made him hate her all the more, and it made him happy for what God had in store for her.

Rejoice over her, O heaven!
Rejoice, saints and apostles and prophets!
God has judged her for the way she has treated you!

The words of the scripture screamed through his head, blazing a trail of white fury. They echoed in his ears and blocked out all sound, leaving him deep in isolation. She was smiling at him now, the whore, smiling as if she expected him to soil himself with her and debase his very essence—and pay willingly for the privilege. She was talking to him, talking as though she had a right to converse with the Lord's emissary on equal terms. She would pay for her arrogance in accordance with the prophecy.

He still couldn't hear her, since the screeching in his head was relentless, walling off the rest of the world, but he could understand her nonetheless. The words were simple enough to read on her thick, painted lips. "Hello," she said, still smiling. "My name's Eve, what's yours?"

Slowly, a smile came to his own lips, with the realization that God was with him, guiding his every move. He was tempted to respond with righteousness—*I am the Alpha and the Omega; the First and the Last; the Beginning and End*—but that would have been presumptuous, for he wasn't the Lord. He was merely a servant of the Lord, and a witness to the prophecy of the apocalypse fulfilled. Suddenly his smile broadened with a new revelation, and the screaming in his head subsided as he returned to his earthly task.

"My name is John," he replied.

CHAPTER TWENTY-FIVE

The odd-looking man was leaving with the hooker, and Stone had a decision to make. The man had done nothing overt to make himself a legitimate suspect, but Stone knew in his gut that something was off about him. He could sense it. The man seemed angry, bitter. There was a violence in the way he carried himself.

Of course, that would never stand up in court. So, for the moment, all Stone could do was allow events to unfold. This, he was beginning to realize, was the worst part of being a police officer. The restraints placed on him by the letter of the law often kept him from preventing a crime he knew was imminent. Every day on patrol, he'd seen the hoodlums standing on corners outside crack houses, their cell phones blaring. There was no doubt that they and their accomplices were loaded down with illegal drugs—drugs that were stealing youth and opportunity from an entire generation. He knew it. They knew it. And yet that knowledge wasn't enough to authorize action. Instead, the police were forced to wait and see if they could catch one of the dealers in a transaction. It was just as they whispered to you at the police academy: the law knows no common sense.

As the strange man left with his new companion, Stone

threw money on the table to cover the evening's soda waters and headed for the door. He needed to stay far enough behind to avoid detection, but close enough to keep the couple in sight. Maybe he was wasting his time. After all, anyone as awkward as this guy appeared would likely have to pay for sex. But Stone had decided to follow his instincts, and his instincts were telling him to follow them.

Outside he spotted the couple moving down the street and fell in step behind.

Eve. He smiled at the thought. Was it possible God had realized the depths of that first mistake, when he pulled the rib from Adam's chest and molded it into temptation? It was Eve who'd forced God to banish mankind from Eden. Perhaps it was Eve who held the key that would allow the righteous back in.

"So, what are you into, John?" She asked the question without shame or remorse, as though she were selling him an automobile rather than her most personal affections. It amazed and angered him and he had trouble hiding his disdain in the look that he gave her.

"Hey, not that it matters, as long as it's nothing too far out of bounds. I don't do anything involving animals or food, and I won't let myself be tied up. Safety issue, you know. After all, we just met." She smiled at him. "I'll tie *you* up if you like, though."

This time, he smiled back. They were getting close to his house, and his anticipation lightened his mood enough to feign kindness. He was growing excited about the things he'd do to her. Not the things she was anticipating, but things far more intimate.

> ***Give her as much torture and grief***
> ***as the glory and luxury she gave herself.***

"It's right up here, on the right," he said, pointing to his house, which was lost in the shadows between the streetlights.

"Nice. I like it out here. It's quiet," she said. They were standing on the stoop, and he slid the key into the lock, relishing the fit as the tumblers fell into place. Before he could turn the key and open the door, though, she put her hand on his as if to stop him. He was enraged at her audacity; laying her filthy hands on his sanctified flesh. "You know it's a hundred dollars, right?"

He actually laughed at that. "Don't worry. I have more money than you'll ever need," he said.

"Ooh, I like the sound of that!" she cooed. "Let's get started."

He pushed open the door and stepped back, allowing her to go in. She looked at him one more time, making her final decision. Then she stepped across the threshold.

CHAPTER TWENTY-SIX

Stone watched them go inside. He was standing on Cypher Street, a half block down from the little house at the end. He stood there for several minutes, debating what to do. The tension that had run through him when he first laid eyes on the strange man hadn't left yet. If anything, it had gotten stronger.

After a while, he wandered down the street, ambling as though he'd been drinking. When he arrived at the last little house on the right-hand side, he slowed his pace even more. The lights were still off inside, giving it a deserted look.

He looked over his shoulder to see if anyone was watching him. There wasn't a soul. The houses around him were shut tight against the darkness, drawn up from the dangers of the urban evening. Blue light from televisions flickered in many of the upstairs windows, and a few soft reading lamps cast a warmer glow, but these were the signs of lives turned inward, unconcerned with what might be happening beyond their doors.

He looked around one more time and, seeing no one, strode up the front steps of the house. Now the shadows of the small covered stoop gave him a feeling of protection against prying eyes, and he leaned up against the door, straining to hear any noises within. It was hopeless, he realized. The seal on the door was tight, and no sound escaped the dark little house.

He leaned over the railing and tried to look in one of the windows. Old lace curtains hung from the window tops, and cheap blinds were drawn all the way down, so he could only see a crack through the gauzy material. In the darkness, it was futile. He could make out almost nothing inside, just a lone chair next to a table with a plain white lamp on it. There was no detectable motion at all, and he found that odd. If the couple were having sex, he'd surely have seen some sign, a light going on upstairs, the rustle of a curtain. But there was nothing; just a dark, empty silence.

He looked at his watch. It had been nearly a half hour since he'd observed them going inside, and there'd been no sign of life since they stepped through the door. Something was wrong; he knew it. In the bottom of his heart, he had never been surer of anything. He looked around again at the quiet street. He'd have to make a decision soon. Otherwise the issue would become moot, and if another woman died without his doing something to stop it, he'd never be able to live with himself.

Stone sighed and shook his head. "To protect and to serve," he whispered as he pulled out a leather case the size of a cigarette pack. He unzipped a flap and pulled out a tool that looked like a tweezers and a long metal toothpick. When they taught the class at the academy on how to pick locks, it had seemed silly. Most of the boys he'd grown up with in Southie had mastered that art early. At the same time, it was good that the department encouraged him to stay in practice. He slid the tools into the lock, playing them back and forth as he pulled them out slowly. When he heard the tumblers click into place, he used the leverage between the two tools to turn the lock, sliding back the deadbolt. Then he repeated the same procedure with the lock on the door handle. The process took him less than twenty seconds.

He turned the handle, holding his breath as he listened for any disturbance inside. He heard nothing, so with great care he pushed open the door, wincing as the hinges let out a quiet squeak.

Still holding the door, he reached behind him and pulled his gun out of a holster hidden in the small of his back. Because he was working undercover, he had no flashlight, so he was going into the house virtually blind, but he was determined to go in nonetheless. It was too late now to retreat. He took a deep breath and stepped into the house like a swimmer slipping into water, letting the darkness swallow him entirely.

This was to be his masterpiece. He'd worked hard with each of the prior girls, searching for the type of pain that would best please the Lord and stop the screaming in his ears, but the relief had always been temporary and incomplete. Now he believed he'd found the key.

She was strapped down on the table, naked to the waist, as the chemicals in her blood pushed their way around her body, paralyzing her, carrying away the last of her ability to struggle. Only her eyes moved, wheeling around in terror. They spotted him at the counter, pouring sulfuric acid and other chemicals into a steel spray can, his own eyes full of excitement and satisfaction.

She will be consumed by fire,
for mighty is the Lord who judges her.
When the kings of the earth who committed adultery
with her
and shared her luxury see the smoke of her burning,
they will weep and mourn over her.

He looked at her again over his shoulder. Her eyes, now unblinking, strained to close. It was a last attempt at escape, but the potent cocktail of anesthetics had taken from her even that ability. So she stared unwilling at her tormentor, and from the corner of her left eye he saw a single tear trickle down the side of her cheek.

And then, almost as though to comfort her, he smiled and began reciting from the final prophecy:

> ***Blessed is the one who reads the words of this prophecy,***
> ***and blessed are those who hear it and take to heart what is within it,***
> ***for the time is near . . .***

Yes, he knew he would enjoy this.

CHAPTER TWENTY-SEVEN

Stone moved with deliberation, placing his rubber-soled shoes carefully to avoid any sound as he made his way around the first floor of the little house. It was dark inside. The shades were pulled on all of the windows, blocking even the pale filter of moonlight from the neat, uncluttered interior. The heat was unbearable as he moved from room to room, slipping silently along the walls with his gun drawn. All of the windows were closed, and he could feel the sweat pouring down his forehead, dripping off his nose.

When he came to the stairway leading to the second floor, he paused, listening for the characteristic muffled cries of sex coming from upstairs. There was no sound at all, though, and he began moving up the stairs. There were only three rooms on the second story—a bathroom and two small bedrooms. Stone stole into each of them, panning his gun around, edging it into the closets to make sure there was no one there. Once he'd satisfied himself that the upstairs was deserted, he crept back down to the ground floor.

He was at a loss. He knew that the strange man had brought the girl into the house, and he knew they hadn't come out. So where were they? He checked the back door. It was bolted from the inside and opened onto an enclosed patio with a couple of rusted chairs stacked against a high fence. It didn't look like anyone had been out there in years.

He walked back into the living room and stood still for a minute or two, his ears straining for any sign of activity.

That was when he heard it. It was a high-pitched whine, pulsing with a sick, familiar rhythm he couldn't place. He held his breath, trying to get a better fix on the sound. It was so thin it almost blended into the faint ringing in his own ears, but after a moment he guessed it might be emanating from back toward the kitchen. He moved there, stopped, and listened again. The noise sounded like it was coming from the far corner, behind a rack of coats. He tensed as he crossed the room, his palm opening and closing on the handle of his gun, which he now held tight to his side.

When he reached the coats, he brushed them aside and stared hard into the dark corner. At first it looked like nothing but a wall, covered in cheap faux-brick wallpaper, but as he peered closer, he could see the outline of a doorway. With his right hand, he leveled his gun, ready to open fire at anything that might come screaming out. With his left hand, he traced the sides of the door, looking for a handle or a doorknob. It took a minute or two, but he finally found a latch set flush to the door's surface. He dug his fingernails into the edge and worked it loose, hooking his finger into the small metal loop that protruded from the door.

He could hear his heart beating now, so loud that it drowned out the ringing in his ears and the high-pitched whine from behind the door. His breath came too quickly, and he steadied himself against the fear, forcing his chest to expand and take a full breath. Then, in one quick, silent motion, he swung open the door.

The tiny entryway flooded with bright light, and Stone had to shade his eyes for a moment as his pupils adjusted. Once they had, he could see a narrow stairway leading down to the basement. He was surprised at how bright and clean the stairway seemed, as though it was whitewashed on a regular basis. It almost reminded him of a hospital or a doctor's office, and for a brief moment he thought that perhaps he'd been wrong. Maybe there was nothing sinister about the strange man, or about the dark little house in which he lived.

Then he heard the high-pitched whine again.

It had stopped for a moment or two, he realized, but now it started up again. It pierced the air with its pulsating cry, mechanical and unrelenting. Something was definitely wrong here, he knew, and he stepped slowly down the stairs.

The first thing that hit him was the stench. It hovered in the air, and he passed into its grasp within a few steps from the top of the stairs. It was the foul odor of decaying flesh mixed with the sharp, acrid smell of chemicals. Stone was already feeling light-headed from the adrenaline coursing through his veins, and this new noxious smell was almost enough to keep him from moving on, but he steadied himself against the wall and pushed forward.

The second thing he noticed was the chanting. It was low and droning, overlaid by the endless whine. Stone couldn't make out the words, but it rambled on in singsong fashion, like the prattle of a small child fixated more on the sounds of phrases than their meaning or importance. It filled him with a new sense of dread.

But Stone didn't appreciate the full horror of what he'd stumbled on until he was nearly at the bottom of the narrow stairway, where he could see the entire room and take in the nightmare that was unfolding.

There was a steel medical-type table bolted to the center of the floor, and she was lying on top of it—at least what was left of her. She was entirely naked, and her arms and legs were strapped to the sides. A wispy mist of smoke drifted up off her extremities, which were stripped of their skin, as well as much of their muscle and soft tissue, as if they had been burned in a fire of such intensity that it had literally melted the flesh. The same was true of much of her torso and head, which no longer held any hair, and had lost most of its skin as well, so that the top of her skull reflected the white of the sterile room around her. Only the skin around her eyes seemed to have been left intact, and from beneath that small stretch of living tissue, the girl's eyes stared out in an agony too indescribable to comprehend.

Standing over those eyes was the man Stone had seen in the Kiss Club. A surgical saw was still whirring and whining and pulsating in his hand as it slipped through the girl's ribs, opening a chasm in her chest that oozed and coughed and bled.

It took a few seconds for Stone to recover his senses, so grotesque was the scene that played out in front of him. Then all at once he remembered who he was and why he was there. His gun flew up, pointing at the man's head.

"Freeze! Police!"

The man was startled. He'd been so involved in his work that he hadn't heard Stone as he came down the stairs. His shock quickly turned to anger when he realized he'd been interrupted.

"You can't be down here!" he yelled. "You shouldn't be here, you must leave at once!" His voice was indignant, as though Stone had committed some sacrilege, rather than the other way around.

"Shut up, you sick fuck! Put down the saw and move away from the girl, or I swear to God I'll blow your fucking head off!"

Now the man looked confused. "But I can't," he protested. "I haven't finished yet."

"I swear to God, I'll shoot you!" Stone looked at the girl again and saw that a new look had come into her eyes—a look of hope. It was so pathetic and useless he wanted to tear out his own eyes to purge the image. She couldn't survive this, could she?

"Oh, Jesus Christ! Oh, Jesus Christ! What did you do to her? You sick, sick fuck." Stone was beginning to lose it now. The horror of the scene was overwhelming whatever sense of reality he still clung to. He pulled out his cell phone and dialed 911, his gun still leveled at the man's head.

"Nine-one-one," came the operator's voice.

"Oh, Jesus Christ, I need some backup," Stone said. "I need an ambulance now! Oh, fuck! Please send someone now!"

"Calm down, sir. Where are you?"

"Cypher Street! I'm at 1027 Cypher Street in Southic. Freeze, motherfucker!" The man, saw still in hand, was bending down toward the girl again. Stone spoke back into the phone. "This is Police Officer Paul Stone, and I need backup and an ambulance, now!" He took in the scene in the basement again. "Oh my God, what have you done?"

"I did it for God!" the blood-covered man exclaimed. His voice was full of conviction. It was no longer angry or indignant, but calm and self-assured. "He is here with us now, and He wanted me to do this. He needed this to be done, and He needed you as His witness."

"Shut up, you sick fuck, or I swear I'll shoot you!" Stone wasn't sure how much longer he could last. "I need backup!" he yelled into the phone again. He didn't realize he'd already hung up.

"You know it's true, don't you? He told me to do this. He told all of us to do this. It's been written in the scripture, and so shall it be. The Revelation of Jesus Christ, which God gave to show His servants what must soon take place. He made it known by sending His angel to His servant, John, who has testified to what he has seen—that is the word of God, and the testimony of Jesus Christ."

"Shut up!" Stone's hand was shaking now, and he was having trouble keeping his aim at the man's head.

"Blessed is the one who reads the words of this prophecy, and blessed are those who hear it and take to heart what is written in it, because the time is near!" The man's voice was louder now, and clearer. It reverberated off the whitewashed walls of the sterile basement, booming out in a sermon of death and pain. *"Salvation and glory and power belong to our God, for true and just are His judgments!"*

"Shut up!"

"He has condemned the great prostitute who corrupted the earth by her adulteries!"

"Shut up!"

"He has avenged on her the blood of His servants! And again they shouted, Hallelujah!"

"I'll blow your head off!"

"The smoke from her goes up forever and ever!"

"You sick fuck!"

"He has sent His angel to me!"

"No!"

"The time is near!"

"Stop!"

"The time is near!"

"Stop!"

"The time is near!" With that, the man raised the surgical saw over his head, waving it with a flourish. His eyes were wide and staring, and he had a bright, toothy grin as he brought the saw down into the hole in the girl's chest. He was shouting as his arm came down. *"I am the Alpha and the Omega, who is and who was, and who is to come, the Almighty!"*

A fountain of blood erupted from the girl's chest, and Stone saw her eyes go wide and then fade. It was a mercy, he knew in his heart, for she could never have lived. She might have held on to life for moments, or hours, or even days, but it would have been a thin life filled with an agony no one should endure. There was a part of Stone that wanted her dead, because he wasn't strong enough to accept the possibility that her anguish would go on.

"No!" Stone screamed as the man raised his arm for a second time. He was still sermonizing, but the words no longer penetrated the howl that ripped through Stone's head. As the man's arm came down again in a broad, smooth arc, Stone pulled the trigger. He would never know how many times he fired his gun. It didn't matter. As the gun sounded, adding a mere fraction to the white noise that swirled in the basement, his vision faded and he lost consciousness.

CHAPTER TWENTY-EIGHT

Finn had trouble sleeping that night. The evening with Linda Flaherty had awakened feelings of need and dependence, emotions he usually kept at bay. He'd been a loner his entire life, and every experiment with an alternative way of living had ended in misery. Still, his mind played with the concept of love, like a child with a new toy, turning it over and over again to inspect it and see if it worked.

When he wasn't thinking about Linda, he was thinking about Natalie and the possibility that her death might not have been the result of a random attack by a serial killer, but a deliberate murder by someone she knew. Linda's questions had suggested it was a serious possibility, which stirred an anger in Finn that had been lurking just beneath the surface of his grief. As long as he believed that Natalie's murder was the random act of a deranged individual, the only place his anger could be directed was at God; and Finn had learned long ago that hating God was a waste of time and energy.

But now he could entertain the idea that Natalie's killing might not have been random. And if he could help find the killer, he could direct his anger and his energy toward that cause. After tossing and turning in his bed for more than two hours, he finally got up. Taking some action might make him feel better, he thought.

He walked through the living room of his Charlestown apartment and into the second bedroom, which he'd converted into an office. He sat at his desk and took out a pad and pen. He'd promised Linda a list of all of the "connected" people Natalie had worked with, and he thought he might as well get started on it.

He covered the easy ones first. There was Rich Loring, the U.S. attorney for the District of Massachusetts. Natalie had worked with him when he was the Special Agent in Charge of the Boston office of the FBI and she was an assistant U.S. attorney. She never talked about Loring much, but Finn knew they'd had contact on the Bulger case. He also knew that Loring was in his late forties, married, and very attractive. Persistent rumors in the tight-knit legal community had placed him in amorous relationships with several unnamed women in his office. Finn liked to think Natalie was too smart to consort with the likes of Loring, but there was no way to know.

Next, Finn wrote down Jimmy Tribinio's name. Tribinio was a local union politician who'd spent ten years carefully cultivating grassroots power and doling out support to other, better-known politicians until he had enough chits to run for mayor successfully. Because his power was based on his control over the local political machine, rather than on a defined public image, Finn knew relatively little about him, but Natalie had done some fund-raising for him as a favor to one of her friends.

Another possibility was Daniel Dolan. Dolan was a powerful political consultant who was based in Boston. He'd been credited with boosting the careers of several prominent politicians, and had connections at all levels of Massachusetts state politics. Natalie had represented him when he faced ethics charges under the Massachusetts lobbying statute.

Sheldon Seeley, the Middlesex County district attorney, also worked with Natalie for a few years at the U.S. Attorney's office in the criminal division before being elected DA. Natalie never talked about him very much, but Finn got the feeling they knew each other. Finn wasn't sure if Seeley was married or divorced, but he knew he had two children, because come campaign time they were paraded in front of the media.

Finally, there was Governor Clarke. Natalie had worked with him recently on one of his statewide Criminal Justice Enforcement initiatives. She had manned the phones and gathered necessary support from within the law enforcement community, helping to put the initiative over the top.

Finn sat back and looked at the list. Loring, Tribinio, Dolan, Seeley, and Clarke. It was quite a roster. They all fit the general profile of Natalie's boyfriend. All were older, and powerful enough to help Natalie in her career. All had political interests that could be damaged by news of an affair. Finn took another minute or two and jotted down the names of a few lower-level politicos who might possibly fit the profile, but he realized quickly that these first were the most likely candidates.

He tapped his forehead with his pen. Was he missing someone? It felt like there were others, but he couldn't think of anyone. Looking at the list, it seemed like there was a connection between them he should recognize, but he couldn't fathom what it was.

His head hurt, and his eyelids were getting heavy. He looked at the list one last time. He'd type it up and give it to Linda tomorrow. Maybe he'd even drop it off himself.

CHAPTER TWENTY-NINE

"I should have gone in sooner." It was a refrain Stone had repeated all night long. He couldn't let it go.

"You couldn't have gone in before you heard the screams. Don't beat yourself up," Kozlowski said. They were alone in one of the interrogation rooms at the station house. It had been a long night of gathering evidence at the little house on Cypher Street, and Stone had not yet had a chance to file his report.

"There were no screams, Detective. I just knew there was something wrong. I should have done something sooner." He was holding his head in his hands, rocking back and forth.

"Of course there were screams," Kozlowski insisted. "It must have been the screams that caused you to go into the house."

"No, Detective, you don't understand," Stone started to explain, but Kozlowski cut him off.

"No, Stone, you don't understand," he almost growled. "If there were no screams, then there was no probable cause for you to enter that house. If there was no probable cause, it was an illegal entry. If it was an illegal entry, then every piece of evidence that was collected tonight—including what was left of that girl that this sick bastard tortured to death—will be excluded from evidence. It would be like none of this ever happened, and he'll walk." Kozlowski grabbed Stone's shoulder and shook him. "Are you listening to me? This asshole will walk, and that means he'll most likely kill again, and we'll probably never find enough additional evidence to nail the son of a bitch. Can you live with that after what you saw in that house?"

Stone looked at Kozlowski, bleary-eyed. He was exhausted, and the shock of what he'd seen in the basement of that little, unassuming house still hadn't worn off. "No, I can't live with that," he said after a moment.

"Good. Then tell me about the screams."

"I heard screams. That's why I went into the house."

"Good. When did you hear the screams?"

"I don't know, right before I went in?" Stone asked.

"Think about this, Stone. Think long and hard about this. By the time you got down to the basement, the girl was in no condition to scream, so it must have been earlier than that, right?"

"Right, that's right."

"Did you walk around the house, maybe looking for a way in without picking the lock? That might explain the delay." Kozlowski was nodding at him as he said it, and Stone began nodding along.

"That's right. That's what happened," Stone said. "I was looking for an open door or a window so I wouldn't have to pick the lock."

"And it was only after you'd spent some time looking for another way in that you came back and picked the lock, right?"

"Uh-huh."

"And by then the screaming had stopped, right?"

"That's right, by then the screaming had stopped," Stone said, still nodding.

Kozlowski patted the younger officer on the shoulder. "Good. That makes sense, and it explains a lot. Just make sure you keep it straight in your report."

"I will," Stone was still nodding, but the thousand-yard stare hadn't left him. He looked lost as he rocked back and forth again, like he was in some sort of a trance. Kozlowski grabbed him and shook him once more.

"Hey, kid!" he said loudly. "Stay with me! You know that if you hadn't done what you did, we still wouldn't have caught this guy. We would have found that poor girl dumped somewhere in the harbor, and it would have been just a matter of time before we found another, and another, and another. You saved lives with what you did tonight. Be proud of that."

Stone looked up at him, and for the first time since Flaherty and Kozlowski found him unconscious at the scene, there was a spark of life in his eyes. It was like hope was returning, at least in some small part. "Yeah, that's right," Kozlowski said, feeding the spark. "You did good, kid. Real good. Don't screw it all up now by checking out on us."

Stone nodded again, but this time it looked as if he had a real understanding of what Kozlowski was saying.

"Okay, Stone, good to have you back."

Just then the door swung open and Flaherty walked in. "You guys ready for me?" she asked, looking at Kozlowski. He nodded.

"Yeah, Lieutenant, I think we're all set here."

"Good," she said. She sat down at the table across from Stone and took out a tape recorder, placing it on the table in front of him. "How are you doing, Paul, hanging in there?" she asked.

"I'm okay," Stone replied. His voice was a little shaky, but he seemed to be getting his legs back underneath himself.

"Good. Now, what I want you to do is just walk through what happened this evening so we have a record of it. You think you're up to that?"

"Sure," he said, although Flaherty noticed that the idea of reliving the evening's events didn't make the young officer happy. "Where do you want me to start?"

"Let's start from the time you first saw this guy."

"Okay." Stone nodded. He closed his eyes for a moment, steeling himself against the torrent of memories he now had to pick his way through, like the charred remains of a holocaust. Then he opened his eyes and began telling the story.

It took about forty-five minutes, and he spared no detail, walking through the entire evening's events, describing everything he could remember. The only lie he told was about the screams, and he touched only briefly on those, moving back to the truth as quickly as possible. Flaherty didn't press him on the issue, and at that point in the narrative Stone thought he saw her and Kozlowski share a knowing glance. He didn't care, though, and pressed on, eager to conclude his description so he could put the nightmare out of his head.

By the time he was done, he was exhausted. Flaherty seemed to understand, because she had few questions and soon dismissed him. "Go clean yourself up, Stone," she said. "We're probably going to have to go over some of this stuff a few times, but don't worry about that now. I'll have someone type this up so you can take a look at it later and see if you think you left anything out."

"Thanks," Stone said. He stood up and turned toward the door. "I need a shower more than I've ever needed one before," he said. "I feel so disgusting, I could scrub my skin off to get clean."

Flaherty nodded. "Stone," she said as he was headed out the door.

"Yeah?" He poked his head back into the room.

"Thank you. You did really good work out there. I know it wasn't easy."

"No, it wasn't. But it's part of the job, isn't it?" He shook his head. "I should have gone into real estate." He turned to head back out, then stopped and turned back to Flaherty. "I haven't even asked yet," he said. "Where is he?"

She hesitated. "He's at Mass General," she said after a pause. "They had to take two slugs out of his shoulder, and he lost a lot of blood, but they think he's going to make it. We'll get to interrogate him in the morning. It might be useful to have you there, so that you can hear what his story is."

Stone nodded, then headed down the hallway toward the men's locker room.

CHAPTER THIRTY

Man, this place is crazy, Finn thought as he walked into the station house for Area A-1. There were reporters everywhere, some setting up cameras and lights, others scribbling notes into floppy, well-worn notebooks, and still others scurrying to interview any cop at any level who was willing to talk.

"Excuse me," he said to the desk sergeant. The cop didn't hear Finn, or perhaps he'd heard him and was simply ignoring him. "Excuse me!" Finn said again, louder this time.

"Yeah, what the hell do you want, buddy?" the big, thick-jawed man responded.

"I need to speak to Lieutenant Flaherty," Finn said politely. He hoped that by using Flaherty's name he might get some deference. He was wrong. The desk sergeant just laughed.

"Yeah? You and everyone else in this place, I guess. Who are you with?" he asked.

"What?" Finn asked, not comprehending.

The desk sergeant looked impatient. He was a huge man in his late fifties, with a prodigious gut that folded over his thick police utility belt, making it difficult for him to get too close to the desk. "What outfit are you with?" he asked again. "The *Globe*? The *Herald*? ABC? NBC? Who?"

Finn shook his head. "I'm not a reporter, I'm a lawyer."

The desk sergeant's glare became hostile. "You're not representing this scumbag, are you?" he asked, pointing a thick finger at Finn's nose.

"What scumbag?" Finn asked. Then he thought better of engaging the sergeant; the man clearly had a bias against lawyers. He shook his head, waiving the question off. "I'm helping Lieutenant Flaherty on a case. She asked me to put together some information and drop it off."

The sergeant looked only slightly less suspicious. "What's your name?" he demanded, leaning over the counter and putting his jowly face too close to Finn's.

"Scott Finn," he replied.

The sergeant picked up the phone and pushed a button, then turned around as he spoke into the receiver so that Finn couldn't hear. After a moment, he turned back around and hung up. Without uttering a word to Finn, he went back to his paperwork.

"Excuse me?" Finn said politely again. The sergeant looked up, obviously perturbed. "Should I go in, or what?"

"I didn't tell you to go in, did I? You're supposed to wait out here and she'll be out in a little while."

"Did she say how long it would be?" Finn asked. He was pushing his luck, he knew, but he had to get to work.

The sergeant rolled his eyes. "No, buddy, she didn't say. Things are a little hectic around here today, so you'll forgive us if you're not exactly our first priority at the moment."

"I noticed. What's going on?"

The police officer frowned at Finn, as if in disbelief. "Didn't you listen to the news this morning? We caught the guy. We caught the Little Jack bastard who's been killing the whores."

Finn felt his heart skip a beat. "Caught him?" He couldn't believe it. He had no idea how to react. "When did you catch him?"

"Last night. He killed another girl, but we got him. Put a couple holes in him, too. Enough to put him on his ass at Mass General."

"How did you catch him? Is Lieutenant Flaherty all right?" A thousand questions streamed through Finn's head.

"What am I, your own personal news service? Why don't you pick up a paper and read about it? In the meantime, you can wait over there. I got a lot of work to do, and I don't have time to hold your hand."

Finn walked over to the corner and sat in an empty seat. All around him, the room buzzed with activity as reporters mined their sources for any nugget of information they could get their hands on. A television journalist began filing a report from inside the precinct house, only to be shut down and told to go outside by several large, surly officers. Finn noticed none of it, though. He sat dumbstruck, trying to work through the implications of the arrest. He'd lain awake nights over the past weeks, wondering what he'd do if they found Natalie's killer. He'd played out a thousand fantasy scenarios in which he found a way to get close to the man and kill him with his bare hands. He'd never do it, but that didn't make the fantasies any less satisfying.

He looked down at his hands in his lap. The list of Natalie's political contacts was typed neatly and folded into an envelope. *Linda probably won't need this anymore*, he thought. He was sorry he hadn't been more help in catching the bastard. Maybe he should just leave. He wasn't needed anymore, and Linda would contact him if there was anything more he could do. He *should* leave, he knew, but he couldn't seem to get his legs to work. In part, he wanted more information about the man they'd arrested. In part, he just wanted to see Linda again. They'd made a connection, and he wasn't willing to give that up, at least not yet.

He must have been sitting there for fifteen minutes before she came out. She was flanked by the Neanderthal—Kozlowski was his name, Finn remembered—and a younger officer Finn had never seen before. They were moving quickly as they came into the room, heading out the front door, but they were immediately swarmed by a mass of reporters shouting questions. The mob slowed them down, but Kozlowski and the other man locked arms in front of Linda, forming a wedge that drove through the wall of microphones and Dictaphones. Finn stood up, but hung back from the crowd, unsure what to do. He could see Linda over the bobbing heads of the reporters, and he waved to her, but her head was down as they pushed their way through. Halfway through the room the crowd of bodies became too thick, and even the wedge of muscle leading Linda was not enough to make significant headway. That was when Kozlowski pulled out his gun.

Finn was shocked when he saw it. Having met Kozlowski before, he feared the man wasn't pulling it out for show, but actually intended to shoot someone. The reporters must have had the same thought, because there was a collective gasp, and those closest to the officers immediately backpedaled. Instead, though, Kozlowski pointed the gun up in the air, as if he intended to fire a warning shot. The room got much quieter after the initial shouts of alarm from the press corps, and Kozlowski began giving orders.

"Ladies and gentlemen!" he shouted. "This is a police station, and we are charged with protecting the public safety! We will *not* have that role jeopardized by a press mob in the station house! We are *not* giving any statements at this time about any ongoing investigations, but there will be a press conference later this afternoon outside the station, at which time Lieutenant Flaherty will take a limited number of questions. Until then, please clear out of here and let us do our jobs!" He motioned to the desk sergeant, who gave a hand signal to those behind him. An instant later, several large uniformed officers materialized and began pushing the press corps back. There were initial protests, and Finn could hear the squeals of "First Amendment" from those being pushed, but they were to no avail, and within a minute or two the room was largely cleared out.

One of the uniformed officers moved over toward Finn with a menacing look. He had his nightstick out and was using it as a battering ram. "Clear out!" he shouted as he got close.

"Oh, no," Finn tried to explain, "I'm not a reporter."

The officer looked him up and down, still skeptical. "Who are you, then?" he asked.

"My name is Scott Finn. Lieutenant Flaherty asked me to stop by and drop off some information." He decided he was better off not identifying himself as an attorney.

The officer narrowed his eyes and held out his hand. "Give it to me, and I'll make sure she gets it," he said.

"I'm sorry, she asked me to give it to her personally," Finn explained. He was polite but firm, and the officer stared at him for a moment longer, debating whether a battle of wills was worth his time. In the end, he relented and turned toward the middle of the room.

"Lieutenant! There's a guy over here who says you wanted to talk to him!" he shouted.

Flaherty saw Finn and nodded. "It's okay, Jimmy!" she yelled back. She turned and said something to Kozlowski and the other man, and then walked over toward Finn. Finn could see the younger man talking to Kozlowski, gesturing toward Finn as Flaherty walked over. "What are you doing here?" she asked. He was thankful, at least, that she was smiling.

"You asked me to drop this off," he replied, showing her the envelope. "It's a list of all the politicos Natalie knew or worked with." Finn noticed she wasn't reaching for it. "It may be moot, now," he said, sounding disappointed.

"No," she said, taking the envelope. "We may as well have

all the information. But you're right, we think we've got our guy."

"Yeah, I just heard. That's terrific," he replied. "I guess you won't be needing my help anymore."

"Probably not, but I'll let you know what's going on as soon as we're sure ourselves. We're going to interview him right now."

"What do you know about him?"

Flaherty hesitated. "We're not releasing any information at this point," she said.

"I understand." Finn backed off.

"I'll let you know what we have as soon as I can, but I've got to go now."

"That's okay, we can talk later," he said. She nodded and started to walk away. Finn wanted to say more, so much more, but it didn't feel like the right time. He couldn't just let her walk away, though. "Linda!" he called out.

She turned around and looked at him, taking two steps back in his direction as he caught up with her. "What is it?" she asked.

"I know you're going to be swamped for the next week or two, and I'm not going to bother you, because you need to focus on what's going on here. But sometime after that, once you're starting to put this behind you, do you think we could have dinner again?"

She smiled. "I think I'd like that," she said. She looked over her shoulder and saw Kozlowski and Stone staring at them. "I'll call you," she said quickly.

He nodded, and she turned to go. This time he let her. He knew somehow he'd see her again.

Flaherty caught up to Kozlowski and Stone as they headed out the door. The two men exchanged a look. "What was he doing here?" Kozlowski asked.

"I asked him to put together a list of possible suspects for the Caldwell woman's older boyfriend. He was just dropping it off."

"You sure he wasn't just looking to get some information about the investigation?"

"He didn't even know we caught the guy until he got here."

"He doesn't read the paper?" Kozlowski scoffed. "He doesn't listen to the news?"

"I don't know. He was on his way to work. Maybe he doesn't read the paper until he gets in. Who knows? What difference does it make?" Kozlowski shook his head, which pissed her off even more. "What's up your ass about this guy, Kozlowski?"

Kozlowski nodded at Stone. "Tell her," he instructed.

Stone shrugged his shoulders and looked at Flaherty. "He was the guy from the bar," he said.

"What bar?" Flaherty asked.

"The Kiss Club. He's the guy from the Kiss Club. He knocked around a hooker who looked like the Caldwell woman a few nights ago. I reported it at the time, but I couldn't catch up with him to get any sort of ID. The man you were just talking to is the guy I saw that night, though."

Flaherty took a deep breath and tried not to show any emotion. "You're sure?" she asked.

Stone nodded. "I got a really good look at him."

The three of them walked in silence toward the parking garage. No one knew what to say.

"I thought you should know," Kozlowski said at last. "Sorry."

"Yeah," Flaherty responded. "Me too." *I knew it was too good to be true*, she thought.

CHAPTER THIRTY-ONE

Massachusetts General Hospital was only a few short blocks from the station house, but the ride seemed to last forever. Stone sat in the backseat, his hands gripping each other in his lap as the muscles tensed up and down his arms. He still hadn't come to grips with the evil he'd confronted only a few hours before.

In the front seat, Kozlowski sat behind the wheel, picking his way through traffic on the busy streets that ran along the back side of Beacon Hill. To him, the arrest of Little Jack was just another minor success in the ongoing struggle to hold back the tidal waters of depravity that were a constant force in life. He'd long ago given up any notion of "winning" the war against crime, opting instead to take solace in small victories.

Flaherty sat in the passenger seat, looking out the windows at nothing in particular. She was focused inward, watching a reel of regrets and calculations play out on the screen in her mind. This was a significant moment in her career, she knew. She'd been given the lead role in catching the most notorious murderer in Boston in the past thirty years, and she'd succeeded. Never mind that the success had precious little to do with her leadership, and was more the result of a wild rookie hunch combined with a search and seizure that was probably illegal. That wouldn't matter, she knew. She'd get the lion's share of the credit. Those ahead of her in the political pecking order—Weidel, the commissioner, the mayor, the governor—would each take their slice of recognition off the top, but her reputation was now guaranteed.

Why then did she feel empty—like an impostor living off lies and waiting to be unmasked? To her, the Caldwell case was still unsolved, and this latest revelation about Scott Finn had hit her like a baseball bat in the chest. She'd spent time with him and liked him. Hell, she'd kissed him. How could she have misjudged his character so badly?

For all her doubts about the Caldwell case, there was still a part of her that wanted to leave it all alone. Everyone in the city would be happy to lay the blame for the murders—including Caldwell's—at the foot of the monster who'd been caught in the act of torture; torture so unspeakable that rational explanation could be overlooked. No one needed any more mystery in this case, she knew. She could let the whole thing drop and simply walk away from Finn, and no one would ever know about their dinner together, or the kiss.

She couldn't do it, though. She had too many questions, and she was about to meet the one person who might be able to give her some of the answers.

They already had a working biography of Little Jack from the ten hours of investigation that had been conducted at his house. His name was John Townsend. The press would be thrilled that they could keep using "Jack" as the murderer's name, Flaherty thought. He was a thirty-three-year-old lab technician who worked at Beth Israel Hospital in Boston. He'd attended Tufts Medical School for two years in the late 1990s, but had dropped out after his parents died in a car crash that had left him with a broken arm. The house in which he lived—the house where he was caught—had been his parents', and he'd inherited it after the accident.

All of this information, Flaherty knew, only provided the most basic outline of who Jack Townsend really was. It might be that they'd never know more. He might clam up and refuse to talk, and watch as the police and the "experts" and the public searched for some explanation to hold on to—something they could all make sense of.

But then again, he might let them in. That was what Flaherty was hoping. She was praying he'd be the type of criminal who wanted people to understand him, or at least what he thought he was. That way, she might find out more about the other heinous things he had done. And she might get her answer about Natalie Caldwell.

These were her hopes as Flaherty stepped out of the car at Mass General and walked toward the entrance. Through the lobby and down a long corridor to the right was the Medical Detention Center, which treated patients who needed to be restrained for one reason or another. As she walked down the corridor toward John Townsend's room, she had the distinct premonition that the surreal journey she'd begun a few months before was nowhere close to ending.

CHAPTER THIRTY-TWO

He looked so frail. That was the overriding impression Flaherty had of Townsend. It almost made her laugh, but she reminded herself of what he'd done, and the humor faded. He was sitting upright quietly in his bed. His hospital gown was pulled off the shoulder where bandages covered the bullet wounds Stone had inflicted. His arms were at his sides, both attached by handcuffs at the wrists to the railings on the sides of the bed. The flop of sandy hair that he normally brushed forward was askew and stuck up from the top of his head like a rooster's comb, revealing a shiny bald pate. He looked so calm and harmless as they opened the door that they thought they might have the wrong room.

He turned as they walked in, looking at each of them for a long moment before moving on. His expression didn't change until he came to Stone. Then the slightest flicker of recognition flashed in his eyes, followed by a simple nod of his head, as though in respect.

"Mr. Townsend," Flaherty began.

"John," he said. "I prefer to be called John."

"My name is Lieutenant Flaherty, John. This is my partner, Detective Kozlowski, and this is Officer Stone."

"Yes, Officer Stone and I have met, haven't we?" He looked

at Stone with a placid smile. Stone shifted his feet uncomfortably and looked away. "We were never properly introduced, but it was Officer Stone who gave me this, I believe," he said, nodding downward toward his shoulder.

"Yes, it was," Flaherty said. Her voice was calm and reassuring. She'd instructed both Kozlowski and Stone not to speak unless she told them to. She'd undergone training in criminal psychology, and she knew that a confrontational tone was considered less effective than a sympathetic one in getting information out of a psychopath. That was what they were here for, she'd explained to Stone: information. The District Attorney's office would have to handle punishment.

"He didn't have many options at the time," she pointed out.

"Oh, I don't blame him," Townsend said. "He was only doing God's will. He could have done nothing else."

"Before we continue, John, I want to make sure you understand that you don't have to talk to us. Has someone read you your rights?"

"Yes, they have."

"So you understand that you don't have to say anything to us? And you're aware that, even if you want to talk to us, you have the right to have an attorney here with you? You understand these rights?"

"Rights are things that man invented so he could usurp God's role in the universe. I have no rights other than those given by God."

"But you understand that, legally speaking, you have these rights under the judicial system, right?"

"I don't mind talking to you, Lieutenant Flaherty."

It was the closest she was going to get to an explicit waiver of his constitutional protections, and Flaherty decided it was going to have to do. She wasn't going to keep pushing him until he got himself a lawyer. She was determined to press forward.

"John, we want to talk to you about the women you killed," she started.

"You mean the whores," he corrected.

"Is that why you killed them, John? Because they were whores?"

"That's why God killed them."

"But you were the one who actually killed them, John, not God."

"God was acting through me."

"Why would God want you to kill these women? Can you explain that to us so we can understand?"

"I can't explain it. But God can." Townsend closed his eyes and leaned back his head. He was the picture of contentment, Flaherty thought. And then he began to speak. His voice was slow and clear as he made his way through the recitation.

> *After this I heard what sounded like the roar of a great multitude in heaven, shouting:*
> *"Hallelujah! Salvation and glory and power belong to our God,*
> *for true and just are His judgments.*
> *He has condemned the great whore*
> *who corrupted the earth by her adulteries.*
> *He has avenged on her the blood of His servants."*
> *And again they shouted,*
> *"Hallelujah! The smoke goes up from her forever."*

He stopped speaking and looked at the three police officers as if he'd explained everything and no more needed to be said.

"What is that from?" Flaherty asked.

Townsend's eyes grew wide in horror at the question. "It's from the word of the Lord, the giver of life and death everlasting, from the book of Revelation, chapter nineteen. Don't you see, Lieutenant Flaherty? It's all made so clear for us, if we'd only listen."

The room was silent for a moment as Flaherty just stared back at Townsend, wondering what to say next. "So this was a religious act?" she asked at last.

"It was preordained by God. It was seen by me in prophecy."

Flaherty was struggling to remember her Bible scripture. It had been drilled into her as a schoolgirl by the nuns who were always eager to point out the sin they saw in young women. But it had been more than a decade since she'd been to church. It was coming back to her in dribs and drabs only.

"But didn't the words of the prophecy also tell us that God is the ultimate judge, and that it's not our place to take His justice into our hands?" she asked. It was one of the few things she remembered as making sense to her as a child, and she felt like it was the best ammunition she had to keep the conversation going.

Townsend nodded approvingly. "Yes, but we're also warned not to tolerate the whores of the world." He closed his eyes and began reading once again from the scripture in his head.

> *I have this against you:*
> *You tolerate the woman Jezebel, who calls herself a prophetess.*
> *By her teaching she misleads my servants into sexual immorality*
> *and the eating of foods sacrificed to idols.*
> *I have given her time to repent of her immorality, but she is unwilling.*
> *So I will cast her on a fire of suffering,*
> *and I will make those who commit adultery with her suffer intensely.*

They were dealing with a real psychopath, that much was obvious. Either that or he was a brilliant actor setting up an insanity defense, but Flaherty didn't think so. The words from the Bible rolled off his tongue freely; not like they'd been memorized as part of an act, but like they'd become part of him—as familiar to him as his own name. Flaherty noticed the look in Townsend's eyes and knew it would disturb her sleep for months. His eyes were narrow and intense and appeared ready to consume the world with their anger.

"But isn't it God's choice to take His revenge, not yours?" Flaherty asked, still fishing.

Townsend paused. He seemed unsettled by this suggestion, and his hands tugged involuntarily at the handcuffs, making them clink against the bed railings. His eyes went down for a moment, searching for an answer. Then the clinking stopped and he looked back at Flaherty. "God works through me," he said.

The answer seemed to calm him a little bit, but Flaherty could still feel the tension in him—an element of doubt that hadn't been there before. His posture had changed, and he now sat straight up in his bed, as if he were consciously keeping himself on guard.

"But if God works through you, why would He let us catch you?" she asked. "Why wouldn't you be permitted to go on killing?"

Townsend shook his head back and forth and smiled smugly, as if he'd been expecting that question and was ready with an answer. "That wasn't God's will! I've completed my task for God and cleared the way for the dawning of a new eternity. It was seven that He wanted, to make way for the seven angels of the apocalypse.

> ***The mystery of the seven stars that you saw in my right hand,***

and of the seven golden lampstands is this:
The seven stars are the angels of the seven churches,
and the seven lampstands are the seven churches!

"It's the seven angels and the seven plagues and the seven bowls of God's wrath that portend the coming of the riders of the apocalypse. For the seven angels to be reborn from the dead on earth, they must take the place of the living. That's what God needed of me. Even I didn't know the purpose of my actions, but it was God all along. He guided my hands. He brought Officer Stone to my house at the moment that the task was complete. We are all a part of the greatest moment in mankind's existence, and we should rejoice! The age of darkness is upon us, and the righteous shall emerge into the light! The seven bowls of the Lord's wrath are upon us, and the dead shall rise to be judged!"

Townsend's sermon was gathering speed as he reveled in epiphanies only he could see. Flaherty had to calm him down.

"But John, you didn't kill seven women, you killed eight," she said.

At this, Townsend began shaking his head violently, thrashing his body back and forth in denial. His wrists pulled at the handcuffs, and Flaherty could see the edges of the restraints cutting into his skin, but he didn't seem to notice. He was too busy throwing himself from side to side as his voice grew louder.

"The seventh angel poured out his bowl into the air, and out of the temple came a loud voice from the throne, saying, 'It is done!'"

Flaherty pulled out a picture of Natalie Caldwell. It was taken before the autopsy was conducted, and showed her head framed by the corners of the steel cutting table. The light from the surgical lamp gave her face an eerie glow, but the picture was clear and recognizable. Flaherty held it in front of

Townsend's face, moving it back and forth so he could see it as he thrashed around.

"Did you kill this woman?" she yelled, trying to break through the trance Townsend had worked himself into.

"The seventh angel poured out his bowl . . ." Townsend's wrists were bleeding now, as the handcuffs cut through his flesh. On his shoulder, the bandages that covered the gunshot wound had turned deep crimson as the stitches pulled away at the edges and the bleeding began in earnest.

"Did you kill this woman, John?" she yelled again, putting her face down close to his in an attempt to be heard through his rant.

". . . into the air, and out of the temple . . ."

"You killed her, didn't you, John?" she screamed.

". . . came a loud voice from the throne saying it was done . . ."

"Did you kill her?" Flaherty's fury was now approaching Townsend's, and Stone shot a look at Kozlowski. The older cop ignored him, focusing on the reaction Townsend was having.

Suddenly, Townsend seized. He started choking and throwing his head back against the bed. Blood was pouring from his shoulder, and the sheets near his wrists were stained red. Several buzzers attached to body monitors screamed, and his eyes rolled up into his head so that only the whites of his eyeballs were visible.

A nurse came rushing into the room. "What did you do to him?" she screamed as she hurried over to the bed and started checking various different readouts. "Code blue! Code blue!" she shouted into an intercom. Then she leaned over and pressed down on Townsend's chest, lodging her shoulder under his chin to keep him from biting off his tongue.

Kozlowski was tugging at Flaherty's elbow. "Come on, partner, let's get out of here. There's not much we're going to get out of him for the rest of today." He led her through the door as several doctors and nurses rushed in with a crash cart.

"Did you hear him?" Flaherty asked in a daze as they headed out.

"Yeah, I heard him," Kozlowski replied.

"Only seven. Not eight, only seven."

"Yeah," Kozlowski said, nodding.

"Are you thinking what I'm thinking?" she asked.

"Caldwell," he said simply.

She nodded. "Caldwell."

CHAPTER THIRTY-THREE

It had been nearly two weeks since Finn had last heard from Linda. That was all right, he told himself; she was swamped dealing with the Little Jack case. Besides, she was on television so often that it was like having her in the apartment with him. The gruesome details of Little Jack's capture had catapulted the saga from local preoccupation to genuine national phenomenon. Media outlets from around the country scrambled to get any piece of the story they could, from any source, credible or not. As the lead investigator, Flaherty was a national hero, interviewed repeatedly on all of the major networks. Finn felt sorry for her, though, noticing her obvious annoyance at being thrust into the media spotlight. Still, it wouldn't hurt her career.

The break allowed him the opportunity to concentrate on work again, which was good. The Tannery case was moving forward quickly, and it took all of his time just to keep up with the pace. As he sat in the office this afternoon, he was preparing an outline for the deposition of Amy Tannery, Edward Tannery's widow. Preston Holland would use the outline to conduct a deposition that would leave her no room to wiggle when she testified at trial. Finn had spent several days going through every piece of information their investigators had been able to find on both Tannerys, which now amounted to a file more than two feet thick.

If the American public knew how intensive this kind of litigation was, Finn thought, they'd probably vote to junk the entire judicial system and start from scratch. He now knew more about the Tannerys than they'd ever known about themselves. The firm's investigators had credit reports going back fifteen years. They'd subpoenaed Ed Tannery's entire work history, including every review he'd ever been given. They'd found all of the transcripts from both of their colleges and high schools, as well as the yearbooks from each school, and had interviewed many of both husband's and wife's former teachers. In all, Finn had notes from the interviews of more than one hundred Tannery friends, enemies, and acquaintances.

But the investigation hadn't stopped there. The firm's investigators had gotten hold of some of the Tannerys' garbage and had sifted through banana peels, cereal boxes, and diaper bags until they'd come across documents containing their social security numbers and credit card information. These provided the real window into the Tannerys' souls, since they allowed the firm's investigators to construct a nearly complete history of every purchase they'd made in a two-year period.

For the most part, there was nothing interesting in the information they'd gathered. The Tannerys were a fairly normal couple with the usual spending habits. Finn was able to learn, however, that they'd had difficulty conceiving their child, and had made several payments to fertility specialists during the two years prior to her birth. In addition, there was a two-month period when they were seeing a marriage counselor. Finn noticed that the payments to the marriage counselor were preceded by a three-month stretch when Ed Tannery's credit card had paid for several short stays in various local motels. It was possible he had been having an affair during that time, and that had led to difficulty in the couple's marriage. There was no way to tell for sure, but Finn made a note to ask Mrs. Tannery about it during the deposition. It might just make her reconsider settlement if she knew her husband's infidelity would be revealed during a trial.

Finn pushed the stack of reports away from him and leaned back in his chair, stretching his body against the effects of several hours hunched over his desk. This type of work made him feel unclean, a bit like a voyeur. Still, what he was doing was simply part of his job. Mrs. Tannery was the one who'd brought the lawsuit and opened up this particular Pandora's box. One of the goals was to make her understand that no one wins in a trial. If she insisted on pressing forward, she'd have her entire life laid out in front of the world. That was the price of justice, and she might as well know it now.

It was Finn's hope, however, that the case would settle before it came to that. He was beginning to find it hard to take any joy from the game. He wanted to feel clean again.

He looked at the phone. With two weeks having elapsed since that morning in the station house with Linda, why *shouldn't* he give her a call? He figured he wouldn't seem too desperate. Rather, he'd simply be confirming he was interested. That's what he wanted.

He picked up the phone and began dialing her number . . .

"Six hearts, all matching the first six victims. The hair clippings and skin samples found around the jars also matched the first six victims. The last jar was empty except for the formaldehyde. We assume he was going to use the jar to hold the last girl's heart."

Flaherty looked at the floor in despair as she received the report from Farmalant in the plush comfort of one of the leather chairs in his office. She'd known deep down that this was what he was going to tell her, but she still hoped there'd be something in the forensics that would link Townsend to Natalie Caldwell's murder.

"Was there anything in his house that matched the Caldwell woman?" she asked. "Any jewelry or clothing or anything?"

"Nothing," Farmalant replied.

"So, where does that leave us?"

Kozlowski was leaning against the filing cabinet near the door. "The captain wants this whole thing wrapped up in one neat package. So does the commissioner. So does the public. No one's going to be happy to hear we've only solved part of the case."

Farmalant looked incredulous. "I'm not really hearing what I think I'm hearing, am I? You'd really tank the Caldwell murder just because it's a PR problem? I thought you guys were better cops than that."

"I'm not saying we should tank anything," Kozlowski snapped. "I'm just pointing out that there are going to be plenty of pissed-off people when and if they find out we're continuing to investigate the Caldwell murder. That doesn't mean we shouldn't do it, it just means we should recognize what we're getting ourselves into."

"I get really nervous when you start to consider the political ramifications of something. That means we're in way over our heads," Flaherty said. She shrugged. "Maybe Townsend really did kill Natalie Caldwell, too, and he just didn't keep any mementos for some reason. We're dealing with a first-class psycho, after all."

"That's a bullshit rationalization, and you know it," Farmalant said. "There's another guy out there, whether you want to look for him or not."

Flaherty let her head fall into her hands. "Yeah, I know it. I just don't like it."

"Do you have any leads?" Farmalant asked.

Flaherty and Kozlowski looked at each other. "Yeah, a couple," Kozlowski said. "A friend from her law firm says she was sleeping with an older man—someone connected who might have had a great deal to lose if she ever went public about the relationship. That's one possibility. Either that or . . ." He paused and looked at Flaherty.

"Or her friend is lying and he killed her because he was in love with her," Flaherty finished.

Flaherty eyed with distrust the folded piece of paper containing Finn's list of Natalie Caldwell's political connections. It had been sitting on her desk since Finn gave it to her. She still hadn't looked at it. After hearing Stone's description of Finn slapping around a prostitute at the Kiss Club, she'd put this part of the investigation out of her head in the hope they'd find something linking Townsend to Caldwell. If they *had* found that linkage she would never have been forced to deal with her feelings for Scott Finn.

What feelings? she asked herself. *I had dinner with him once, that's all. I kissed him, so what?* That was hardly a sturdy foundation for a long-term relationship, or for real feelings. She could go back to treating him as she would any other suspect. She was sure of that.

Anyway, he was not the only viable suspect, she reminded herself. She had to keep an open mind until she knew more about Natalie Caldwell. There might be something to Finn's theory about Natalie's older boyfriend.

She picked up the sheet of paper and held it in front of her face without opening it. She could still turn back now and lay the Caldwell murder at Townsend's feet. That was what most people wanted—a clean, quiet end to it all. If she opened the piece of paper, any hope of that would be gone. She knew herself too well to believe she'd let the investigation drop once she'd seen the list of names.

She looked over her shoulder to see if anyone in the squad room was watching her. It was an odd thing to do, she knew, but she felt like she was somehow betraying the department by casting a shadow over the biggest public relations victory it had had in decades. Satisfied no one was spying on her, she slowly, deliberately opened the piece of paper and looked at the list of names.

She heard herself gasp as she read it. Every name felt like a punch in the stomach. One by one, she read the names and the brief descriptions of their connection to Natalie Caldwell. She was tied in, Flaherty realized, and tied in big-time. It looked like she knew or had worked with every person with any significant power in Boston. These weren't the kind of people who'd appreciate being investigated. *Jesus*, she thought, *even the governor is on the list.*

Wait, that's impossible, isn't it? Hadn't Clarke specifically said he'd never met Natalie Caldwell? She was sure he had. So it was possible Finn's list was wrong, wasn't it? Maybe she could ignore it. More than that, maybe it was possible that Finn was deliberately giving her false information—leading the police in the wrong direction to cover his own guilt.

There was only one way to find out, she knew, and it depressed her to think about it. She should have just thrown the list away. She hadn't, though, and it weighed heavily on her. Just then the phone rang.

"Lieutenant Flaherty," she said as she picked up the receiver.

"Is this the world-famous Detective Lieutenant Flaherty?" the voice asked. It was Finn. She felt her back stiffen, and it took a moment to compose herself. She was not sure what to say. "Linda?" he said after a moment.

"Yes, is this Mr. Finn?" she asked, trying to buy time.

"We're back to 'Mister'? How did that happen?"

"I'm sorry, I was just thinking about you."

"Well then, I guess great minds think alike, because I was

just thinking about me too. Specifically, I was thinking I'd like to see you."

"Yes, I think we need to talk." She was deliberately distant with him, and she knew he'd notice it. This wasn't going to be easy.

"Okay, do you want to do it over dinner at Il Panino?" he offered.

"I don't think that that will be possible."

"Well then, you pick a place," he pressed.

There was a long pause on the line. "I think I'd prefer it if you'd come down to the station house so we can talk here," she said finally. The silence on the other end of the line sent a cold shiver up her spine, and she had the feeling she had just destroyed any hope of their being anything other than enemies.

CHAPTER THIRTY-FOUR

"You're kidding, right?"

Kozlowski and Stone were in the interrogation room with Finn and Flaherty, but Finn directed the question to Flaherty alone.

"You were the last person we know of who talked to her," Kozlowski spoke up, somewhat defensively. "You were her former lover—a fact you neglected to tell us the first time we interviewed you—and you still haven't been able to give us a decent alibi. What do you expect us to think?"

Finn glared at him. "I don't expect you to be able to think at all, Detective. Just by looking at you, I understand that would be expecting far too much. But I do expect Lieutenant Flaherty to be able to think. And if she's thinking straight right now, she's remembering that the last time I saw Natalie was early on Friday evening, and I left the bar we were at without her. She's also probably realizing that the first time you interviewed me you never asked whether Natalie and I had had a physical relationship. You only asked what our relationship was at the time."

"So it all depends on what the definition of 'is' is? That excuse has been tried before," Kozlowski sneered.

Finn ignored him. "And she's probably also remembering

that I didn't hesitate to tell her about my past relationship with Natalie the second time we met, when she asked me about it. Finally, as far as an alibi goes, I dropped by several bars after leaving Natalie. I can name at least a few, and I'm sure I can find some people who saw me there alone—I haven't lined anyone up, because I wasn't aware I was a suspect until two minutes ago."

"Nobody said you were a suspect, exactly," Flaherty corrected. Her voice was flat, though.

"Then why, when you've got a guy in custody who was actually caught in the act of killing one of these girls, are you trying to jam me up for allegedly killing my friend?"

"We've told you, nobody's trying to jam you up. It's just that we haven't found anything that ties Townsend to Natalie, and he's claiming he didn't kill her. Normally, we wouldn't be too surprised or concerned that the main suspect denies being the murderer. But in this case, Townsend seems willing to admit to all of the other murders. So the question is, why does he deny killing Natalie Caldwell? That puts us in a position where we have to consider every possibility," Flaherty said. This time her voice was more reassuring.

"Fine, so look at every possibility. I gave you a two-page list of people Natalie worked with, and who fit the description of her boyfriend. Why not start by looking into that?"

"We do plan on looking into that, Mr. Finn," Kozlowski said. "But the only evidence we have that Ms. Caldwell was even having an affair comes from you. So before we go knocking on the doors of some of the most powerful people in Boston, accusing them of murder, we thought we'd get to know a little more about the guy who's pointing the finger at them."

"Besides," Flaherty continued, "we're pretty sure that at least some of the information on the list is false."

"What's false about it?"

"For example," Flaherty began, "we know Governor Clarke didn't know Ms. Caldwell personally, as your list suggests."

"How do you know that?" Finn asked.

"He told us so," she replied.

Finn looked at her, incredulous, waiting for more. "That's it?" he asked after a moment. "*He told you so?* He didn't even take a pinkie-oath on it or anything? Did he at least cross his heart and hope to die?"

Kozlowski scoffed. "He had no reason to lie to us when he said it. At the time, we weren't even considering that the killer might be someone other than Little Jack, so he wouldn't have had any reason to go out on a limb like that."

"Right," said Finn, rolling his eyes. "If he were the real killer, he'd certainly have no motive to foreclose any investigation into his relationship with her." The on-point sarcasm made Kozlowski feel a little foolish.

"We still have no reason to think he's lying, yet," Flaherty said. "We wouldn't have *any* reason to suspect him if it weren't for you."

Finn threw up his hands. "As I explained in the list I gave you, Natalie worked with the governor on one of his crime initiatives—I think it was the one aimed at domestic violence. Her name has to be on the legislation somewhere."

"We thought of that, but we haven't been able to find anything." Flaherty sounded almost sympathetic.

"Which means it's just back to your word." Kozlowski was back on the attack. "Besides, there are other issues we have to talk to you about."

"Like what?" Finn asked wearily.

"Like have you ever been to the Kiss Club?" Flaherty asked. The question was like a slap in Finn's face, and he physically rocked back in his chair. He looked back and forth between Flaherty and Kozlowski in a state of confusion.

"What does the Kiss Club have to do with anything?" he

asked. He had to take a deep breath to keep from becoming defensive. He didn't like the direction the interrogation was heading.

"The Kiss Club was the last place Natalie Caldwell was seen alive. Whoever killed her may have met up with her there." Kozlowski was in his element now, and he was enjoying turning the screws on Finn. "Have you ever been there?"

Finn thought for a moment. As a lawyer, he knew that the smart thing to do at this point would be to shut his mouth and answer no further questions. He'd always advised his clients to stop talking whenever it became clear they were a suspect in a crime, even if they were innocent. As a general rule, nothing good ever comes from talking to a police officer who believes you're guilty. But this was different, wasn't it? "I was there with Natalie once," he admitted.

"Ever been back there?" Kozlowski asked. From his tone, Finn had the feeling the detective already knew the answer.

"I was in there a week or so ago," he answered.

"You want to tell us about that?" Kozlowski asked.

"What's to tell?"

"Officer Stone saw you in there," Flaherty said, pointing to Stone in the corner of the room. "He witnessed you assaulting a working girl who apparently looked very much like Natalie Caldwell." She said it as fact, without any emotion, but Finn could still feel the anger and disappointment in her voice.

Finn turned bright red. "So that's what this is about?" he fumed. "Officer Stone saw something he took totally out of context, and now you all want to hang me for it?"

"Is there a context that would make this reasonable?" Flaherty asked, her tone exasperated.

Finn shook his head in disbelief. Then he turned to Stone. "Well, for starters, I'm guessing that Officer Stone didn't hear any of the conversation I had with the young woman, did he?"

Stone looked at Kozlowski, who held his palms up, indicating that he was free to answer the question.

"No, I didn't," Stone admitted. "But I don't see what—"

Finn interrupted him. "So you couldn't hear that the entire altercation started because she propositioned me and I turned her down, right?"

"Right," Stone said, "but—"

"And I'm also guessing that you were watching from an angle where you couldn't see what was happening underneath the bar, weren't you?"

"That's true."

"So you couldn't see that she reacted to my rejection by trying to crush my testicles, and that I was only acting in self-defense, could you?"

"Like I said, I couldn't see from where I was." Stone was backpedaling now.

"I see. So basically, you've all convinced yourselves that I murdered my best friend because I went to a bar that she took me to once and then rejected the advances of a prostitute who looked marginally like her. Do I have that about right?"

The three officers looked at one another silently. They seemed defeated, and each hoped that one of the others would find some leverage to go back on the attack. It was Kozlowski who finally spoke.

"That was a fine cross-examination, Mr. Finn. I can see why clients pay the fees that Howery, Black charges. But it doesn't mean shit in the real world. You're still the last person we know of who talked to Natalie Caldwell. You're still her former lover, and you still don't have an alibi. In my book, that means that we've got to take a long, hard look at you. If you have a problem with that, you'll just have to live with it. And until you can verify some of the information on this list you gave us, I'm going to take the governor's word over yours every day of the week."

Finn rolled his eyes and looked at Linda. "If I can prove to you that the governor really did know Natalie, will you stop leaning on me and take a harder look at the people on that list?"

Flaherty nodded. "If you can convince me the governor actually lied to us, then we might be persuaded to alter the current direction of the investigation slightly."

"Fine," Finn said, getting up out of his chair. "Come with me."

All three of the officers got up to follow, but he shook his head and pointed at Flaherty. "Just her," he said. "I'm not about to go traipsing around this city with the three of you in tow. She's less conspicuous, and you guys only need one person to verify my information."

Flaherty looked at Kozlowski and waved him off. "I'll be fine," she said. "You stay here and I'll let you know what I find."

CHAPTER THIRTY-FIVE

The station house was only a few blocks from Finn's office, so they walked. The silence between them was deadly, and neither could find a way to break it for a long while. It was Finn who finally spoke.

"You actually think of me as a suspect in this mess, don't you. After everything I told you that night, after everything that happened, you still think of me as a murderer."

"I don't think of you as anything, Finn. I hardly know you," Flaherty said. "We've got a murderer and a victim who don't seem to match up. I'd love to pin Natalie's death on Townsend, but we just don't have any evidence on him, so for the moment we have to keep an open mind about possible suspects. No one is saying they think you did it, it's just that you were the person closest to her. The first rule of a murder investigation is to take a good long look at the people who were closest to the victim. More than two-thirds of all victims are killed by their family or close friends, so we've got to investigate you."

"That's bullshit. You don't have to do anything you don't want to on this investigation. I find it bizarre that you think I might have done this." Finn shook his head.

"Yeah, and I find it bizarre that you were at the Kiss Club beating up hookers. I guess we're even," Flaherty said indignantly.

"I told you, that was self-defense. She attacked me first, and she attacked me precisely because I didn't want to be with her. I was depressed and lonely, and that bar was one of the places I'd gone to with Natalie when we were together, so I went back there. It was a mistake, but that doesn't make me a murderer." Finn felt like his head would explode soon.

"Yeah, it was a big mistake," Flaherty agreed. "And now we've just got to make sure you're not our guy. Once we're sure, we'll move on."

"Great, so you're expecting me to prove a negative?"

"That shouldn't be too hard. I'm sure you can find people who can vouch for your whereabouts at the time of Natalie's death."

Finn shrugged his shoulders. "Yeah, hopefully. But what if I can't?"

Flaherty thought for a moment, her brow furrowing. "It also wouldn't hurt if you provided us with a blood sample."

"What the hell for!" Finn almost shouted.

"We found semen inside of Natalie's body. We think she was raped before she was killed. If you give us a blood sample, we'll be able to tell if you were with her that night. It won't definitively rule you out as the killer, but it would take some of the pressure off you in the investigation."

Finn looked skeptical. The lawyer in him told him simply to clam up and provide the police with no information. That would be what he'd advise any client at this point. The more information you provide to the police, the more likely it is they'll have something to use against you. He could hear himself giving that same counsel time and again to clients when he was a public defender. He knew he should start listening to his own advice. At the same time, though, he wanted Linda to believe him. He needed her to believe him.

"I'll think about it," he said after a moment.

"Suit yourself," she said. "I'm just trying to help."

In spite of his innate skepticism, he believed her.

CHAPTER THIRTY-SIX

When they arrived at the office building that was home to Howery, Black, they stopped at the front desk to sign Flaherty in. The Anniversary Bombing had placed a renewed emphasis on security, and Finn now needed a separate building pass to get into the office. Bringing visitors involved filling out a pile of forms to verify identification, although Flaherty's badge helped bypass some of the hassle.

They rode the elevator in silence. Finn was glad there was no one else from the firm on it with them. Now that he was a suspect, he felt self-conscious about bringing the police into the office. He'd do it to clear his name, but he wasn't comfortable with it.

The door to Natalie's office was closed, and the room was stacked with boxes of documents from various cases. That it was still being used as a storage room Finn found repugnant. Of the original furniture, only the desk remained—the same basic L-shaped wooden one that all of the associates had. The room had been cleaned out by the police, who'd gone through all of Natalie's belongings looking for clues. They'd found nothing, and now all of Natalie's personal possessions were boxed up and stacked in a corner, waiting for someone to come get them, although she had no family members who might care enough to take her mementos home.

Finn picked his way through the clutter to Natalie's personal effects.

"What are you looking for?" Flaherty asked.

"Pictures," he said. He spoke over his shoulder as he dug through the boxes, pulling out little pieces of Natalie Caldwell's life as he went. There was a large framed seal from the Justice Department signed by all her coworkers—a traditional gift given to all departing federal prosecutors. There were diplomas from Harvard Law School and Yale University. There were letters, and workout clothes, and breath mints, and cold medicines—everything reminding Finn of the basic humanity of the woman with whom he'd once been infatuated.

"I'm not as evil as you may think," said Flaherty, interrupting his thoughts. "I do have a job to do, though."

Finn kept silent as he considered the feelings he sometimes had about his own profession. The irony was not lost on him.

"You brought this on yourself," Flaherty continued, faced with his silence. She was standing at the window looking out at the vast expanse of the southern Massachusetts shoreline that receded from Boston Harbor.

"That's bullshit," Finn shot back. "And what's worse is, you know it's bullshit. You want some sympathy? Fine. But you've looked into my eyes, and you should know in your heart that I didn't do this." He looked at Flaherty, and he could see she believed he was innocent. She knew he'd seen it, and she turned away. The only question was: did she believe it because it made sense, or did she believe it merely because she wanted to?

"So you can tell me you're just doing your job, and I'll accept that. But don't tell me I brought this on myself. A few weeks ago, I was just cranking through my life minding my own business. I might not be perfect, but I most certainly didn't bring this load of crap down on my own head."

Flaherty had no response. She wanted to say something, but the right words wouldn't come.

Finn pulled his hand out of one of the large cardboard boxes. "I found it," he said.

Flaherty looked down and saw that Finn was holding a picture frame. "She had a little wall of fame where she hung pictures of herself with all of the celebrities she knew," he explained.

He turned the frame around so Flaherty could see it. It startled her. She'd never seen a picture of Natalie Caldwell when she was alive, and while she knew Natalie had been a beautiful woman, she didn't realize how beautiful. She was standing there flashing a perfect ivory-white smile, her blonde hair falling to her shoulders, and those eyes—the eyes that Flaherty had first seen staring up at her from below the surface of Boston Harbor—leapt off the glossy picture and dragged Flaherty in.

She was so mesmerized by the image of the living Natalie Caldwell that it took a moment for her to notice the person standing next to her in the picture. There, with his arm around her shoulder, a wide, goofy grin on his face, and his chest puffed out like a robin in springtime, was William H. Clarke, governor of Massachusetts. There was also an inscription in black felt-tip pen across the picture's bottom. It read: *Natalie, Thanks for all of your help on the Committee. We couldn't have done it without you! Bill.*

"He lied," Flaherty said simply.

"I know," said Finn. "And I told the truth."

CHAPTER THIRTY-SEVEN

Tigh McCluen sat in his usual spot on the stack of crates in the warehouse in Southie. The graying wood creaked under the weight of his enormous frame, groaning with every slight shift in his posture. He was tempted to stand, but knew the movement would only draw the ire of the old man as he counted the cash in the envelopes. Tigh wasn't particularly worried about the old man's wrath; he'd been earning too well for too long on the organization's behalf to worry about the minor letdown with respect to Little Jack. Nonetheless, he had no interest in dealing with any more hassles than necessary.

"You're short," the old man said once he finished his counting. "Again."

Tigh nodded. "No more than to be expected with the volume I'm doing at the moment," he said matter-of-factly. He knew the money wasn't the cause of the old man's annoyance.

"I told you to cut the deadbeats loose."

Tigh's back stiffened. There was a delicate line between self-assertion and disrespect that he'd learned to walk a long time ago. "I run my end of the business properly," he said in measured tones.

"Not so well you can't fuck up," the old man replied sharply.

Here it comes, Tigh thought. "I also told you we needed to find Little Jack before the cops got to him."

"You did," Tigh said calmly.

"So what happened? You're always telling me nothing goes on out there on the street without your knowing about it."

Now Tigh rose, straightening his back to accent his full height, though careful to keep his arms loose, hanging from his shoulders in a nonthreatening manner. "From where I sit, there wasn't much chance to catch the man."

"The cops caught him," the old man pointed out. "You saying the cops are smarter than you are?"

Tigh shrugged. "Dumb luck," he said. "If you've got nothing but luck to rely on, you've got nothing but luck to blame."

"Another piece of wisdom from the fuckin' motherland, Tigh?" The old man was angry, but he barely raised his voice.

"What's this all about, Vin?" Tigh asked. "The sick bastard is off the street and the girls are safe again. What's it matter if the cops got the guy instead of us?"

The old man shrugged. "The bosses wanted him dead. Apparently he has some information that could hurt some of our people."

"What sort of information could a psycho like that have on any of our people?"

"How the fuck should I know? You think they tell me anything? All I know is that they were counting on you to take this guy out of the picture, and you fucked it up." Vinnie's face was red and his voice had grown louder.

Tigh looked serious as he crossed his arms. "If you've got a message to deliver, Vinnie, you'd better be out with it." He knew how the game was played, and he was ready to call anyone's bluff when it was necessary.

The old man held up his hands and shook his head. "Hey, no message here, Tigh. Our people may take a hit on this, but no one's blaming you. At least, not to worry about. I think the bosses are just a little disappointed, that's all."

"Oh, they're disappointed, are they?" Tigh's voice was more menacing, and there was no mistaking the message that he'd been pushed as far as he was willing to be pushed.

The old man leaned back in his chair. By all rights, he was Tigh's superior in the organization, but they both knew that meant precious little in the real world. In the real world, Tigh was young and strong and was worth far more to his bosses than the old man. "Don't worry about it, Tigh. It's not our problem anymore." He sighed. "I don't know what they expected in the first fuckin' place anyways."

Tigh was silent, but his glare was penetrating.

"Seriously, Tigh," Vinnie said. "Forget I mentioned it. You just go back to doing what you do so well, and you'll never hear another word about it."

Tigh relented at last, unfolding his arms and sitting back down on the crates. "All right, then."

The old man pulled on his earlobe and looked at him from across the room. "You may be able to help us on something else, though," he said.

"If I can, I will," Tigh said briskly.

"We need some information on a lawyer who lives in Charlestown, right on your turf."

Tigh's eyes narrowed. "What's his name?" he asked.

"Finn," Vinnie replied. "Scott Finn." He looked at Tigh closely. "You know him?"

Tigh was silent for a moment as he contemplated his answer carefully. Then he shook his head. "Never heard of him," he replied.

The old man stared at Tigh briefly, pulling on his earlobe again as he cocked his head to one side. Then he went back to stacking the bills on the card table. "It was worth a shot," he said.

"Why is the organization interested in this guy?" Tigh asked, sounding nonchalant.

Vinnie shrugged. "Like I said, you think they tell me anything anymore?"

Tigh regarded the old man sitting in the warehouse as he considered how far he could push the questions. Vinnie sat hunched over on a flimsy folding chair at the card table. It was such a pathetic existence to which he'd been relegated, sitting in a cold, stinking shell of a structure, counting out the cash in each greasy envelope that the local captains brought to him every week. Vinnie had once been one of the princes of Boston's underworld. He had everything then that "the life" was supposed to offer—power, money, women. But the modern world of Boston's organized crime had passed him by, and now he was stuck skimming what he could off the weekly take.

"Don't worry about it," Vinnie said, feeling Tigh's stare. For a moment, Tigh thought the old man had read his mind, until he realized Vinnie was still talking about Scott Finn.

"Are you sure?" Tigh asked. "I can always look him up."

"Nah," Vinnie said. "It's not your problem anymore. Leave it to the people who know what the score with this guy really is."

Tigh got up and walked to the door. He looked back at the old man sitting at the card table and saw a picture of his future. "You want anything, Vin?" he asked after a moment. "Lunch or a drink or anything?"

Vinnie looked up at him, pausing in his counting. "Yeah, some smokes and a six-pack'd be good," he said. Then he went back to his work.

Tigh opened the door. "Okay, Vinnie, I'll send someone over."

Vinnie grunted but didn't look up. Tigh looked at him for another minute—wondering what his own fate would be in another twenty years. Then he turned and walked through the door.

CHAPTER THIRTY-EIGHT

Finn was so relieved to have proved his point to Flaherty about the governor that he almost forgot where he was. The two of them walked out of Natalie's office and were almost run over by Preston Holland and Nick Williams, who were hurrying down the hallway in front of Natalie's door.

"Preston!" Finn exclaimed in surprise and embarrassment.

"Finn," Holland replied in kind. Then he turned and regarded Flaherty admiringly. Finn also noticed Nick looking Flaherty up and down with a remarkable lack of subtlety.

"Preston, I think you've met Lieutenant Flaherty, haven't you?" Finn asked, remembering it had been Holland who had directed Flaherty to him in the first place. "And this is Nick Williams," he said to Flaherty, "another one of the firm's partners."

Holland's approving assessment of Flaherty turned more respectful with the realization that she was the police officer he'd talked to before.

"Ah, yes, Ms. Flaherty, it's good to see you again," Holland said. "I believe congratulations are in order. I understand you caught Natalie's killer. I can't tell you how relieved we all are here. It will be a pleasure to see justice carried out in this case."

"Great detective work," Williams added ingratiatingly; he was still leering.

"Thank you," she replied to both men. "There are, obviously, a few loose ends we're trying to tie up, and Mr. Finn has been very helpful in that regard. We're appreciative."

"Yes, Mr. Finn is one of our best people," Holland said. "If he's helping you, I'm sure you'll be provided with whatever you need." The four of them stood in the narrow hallway looking at one another in awkward silence until it became unbearable. Then Holland said, "Well, we should let you get on your way, I know you've got a lot to do. It was a pleasure seeing you again, and good luck with whatever remains of your investigation."

"Thank you," Flaherty said. "Yes, I should be going."

"I'll walk you out," Finn said, nodding.

"When you're done with that, stop by my office, please," Holland ordered Finn. "I need to talk to you about the Tannery matter."

"No problem," Finn replied. Then he and Flaherty headed down the corridor toward the elevator banks as Holland and Williams continued in the other direction.

"I hope I didn't get you in trouble back there," Flaherty said as they waited for the elevator to arrive.

"Compared to being accused of murder, any work issues I have are beginning to seem minor."

"I never accused you of murder, Finn, but we do have to run down every lead on this case, and you're still the person who seems to have had the most direct contact with the victim."

"Fine, but you're going to check out Governor Clarke now, too, right?"

"We'll run down everyone on your list, but we have to do it carefully. These aren't the kind of men who'll allow themselves to be hauled down to the police station on minimal suspicion, you know?"

In contrast to me, he thought.

As the elevator doors closed on Linda, he stood quietly alone in the vestibule trying to understand his new situation. He remained a suspect. Flaherty didn't seem happy about it, but that didn't change the fact. More than that, if he couldn't find someone to provide him with an alibi, he would undoubtedly remain the primary suspect. Finding someone to corroborate his version of where he was when Natalie was killed was going to be difficult, since after several hours of bar-hopping that night he'd gone home and put the covers over his head until well into the next morning. Perhaps he should do a little investigating on his own. He wasn't sure he could trust the police to clear his name.

"What was that all about?" Preston Holland asked back in his office.

"She was just getting some background info on Natalie. No big deal."

"I wouldn't have thought there'd be much left to investigate. Didn't they catch the man as he was killing another girl?"

Finn acted nonchalant. "Yeah, well, there's still the sentencing. They're probably preparing a history on each victim." He was tempted to ask Holland for his advice, but he worried about preserving Preston's image of him. "What did you want to see me about?" he asked, changing the subject.

"We're deposing Amy Tannery in a few days," Preston replied.

"Yes, I know. I've been working up an outline for you to follow in the deposition."

"Good, but I won't have to follow it. I want *you* to take her deposition instead of me."

Finn was shocked. He'd taken hundreds of depositions before, but never one of the primary witnesses in a case this big. "Really?" he asked. "I'd love to do it," he added quickly, "but why?"

"I don't want her to be familiar with me or my style when I cross-examine her at trial. I'll sit in on the beginning of the deposition to get a feel for her, but this way she won't be comfortable when we square off."

"Why not have Nick Williams take it?"

"Nick is a remarkably intelligent analyst, and a fine lawyer," Preston explained. "But for this task we need someone with trial instincts, and I think yours may be better than his. Besides, he's working through the documents. His time is better spent there."

Finn was flattered, and nodded quickly. "Okay, I'll do it." For a moment, he forgot his troubles. This was the kind of opportunity he lived for, and he intended to make the most of it.

Holland must have noticed Finn's thoughts drifting because his voice suddenly took on a hint of paternal concern. "I know the last few weeks have been very hard on you, Finn. I know you and Natalie were close." He paused and held his subordinate's eyes. "If this case is too much for you to handle right now, just let me know. But if you're going to stay on it, I need your mind here, now. We're in the home stretch, and I can't do this alone. I need to know you're one hundred percent committed. Otherwise . . ."

"I'm committed, Preston," Finn said. "You've got me one hundred and *fifty* percent on this, and I won't let you down."

"Good." Preston seemed satisfied. "Now clear out of here and let me get back to work."

Finn closed Holland's door behind him as he walked out. He was glad to give the case all of his time and effort. This was the kind of legal defense that made legends, and if he handled it right, he'd be a partner by the time it was over.

Then he might be able to relax a little. He'd worked so hard for so long that he was determined not to screw this up. But to dive into the case fully, he needed to clear his mind of distractions. And to do that, he still needed to take care of some unfinished business.

CHAPTER THIRTY-NINE

Weidel's blood pressure was hitting a new high, Flaherty thought as she sat in his office. The captain had called in her and Kozlowski for an update on the Little Jack case assuming he'd be told that the police portion of the investigation was winding down and the District Attorney's office was taking over. For nearly two weeks, he'd been in what passed for a "good mood." From the look on his face, that mood had reached its end.

He sat at his desk with his fists pressed into his forehead, his elbows resting on a stack of overdue paperwork, looking at the two detectives. "I can't believe I'm hearing this. Tell me I'm not hearing this," he seethed.

"I know," Flaherty said. "We're disappointed, too." She hoped to make him an ally through commiseration, making it clear that much of the load was going to be borne by the two detectives.

"Don't you give me that shit, Lieutenant. You take the biggest arrest we've had in this department in two decades and throw it away, and then tell me you're 'disappointed'?"

"Now, Captain, we haven't thrown away the arrest. We've still got seven good murder charges on Townsend. He's not going to walk on those," Kozlowski pointed out. "It's just that it doesn't look like he's our guy in the Caldwell murder."

"Anything less than a conviction on every single one of these murders—all eight—is going to turn this thing into a public relations disaster," Weidel blustered. Flaherty could now see the prominent blue veins in his neck and on his forehead pulsing erratically. "I hope I don't have to remind you about the past perception problems this department has had with the public. This could have helped wipe some of that away."

"I know, Captain, but what are we supposed to do? We've got to follow the evidence, right?" Flaherty pointed out.

"I'll tell you what you're supposed to do about it, you're supposed to get out of here and do your jobs. Find something—anything—that will make the Caldwell murder stick to this Townsend asshole. It shouldn't take much, given the similarities in MO." Weidel looked straight at Kozlowski. "Search his house again. I'm sure you can find something—a shoe, a watch, some underwear—something that once belonged to Caldwell. You just have to look hard enough."

"You're not suggesting what I think you are, are you, Captain?" Kozlowski asked.

"I'm not suggesting anything. I'm merely pointing out that this Townsend guy is our killer. He's our only killer. As a result, there must be some evidence tying him to the Caldwell case. I want you to find it!" Weidel looked at Flaherty. "I'm also pointing out that some of the people on this investigation have had their faces plastered all over the television and newspapers bragging about what a bang-up job we did. Those people are going to have an awful lot of egg to wipe off if they go back on the air and have to explain that we got it wrong."

Flaherty and Kozlowski shared a look.

"This guy is our killer," Weidel repeated. "So let's make it happen." He was finished talking, and he looked at the two detectives, waiting for confirmation that they'd carry out his directions.

"What about that list?" Flaherty asked, pointing to a copy of the list Finn had given her, which was sitting on Weidel's desk.

"This list?" Weidel said, picking it up and waving it around his head. "This list is a fucking fantasy." He began tearing the paper into little pieces. "It's a joke, and I don't want to hear another word about it. Did you seriously think I was going to let you interrogate the most powerful law enforcement people in the state and start throwing around allegations? You've got to be insane, Lieutenant. I mean, Jesus H. Fucking Christ! Imagine if the press got ahold of that. What a nice headline that would make: 'Governor, U.S. Attorney Questioned in Little Jack Murders.' Trust me, that's not going to happen. Not while I'm in charge."

"So you want us to drop this?" Flaherty asked.

"Drop what? There's nothing to drop. And you better make damned sure this asshole Finn knows we're not buying into his bullshit. If I ever hear one word about this list from anyone, I'm going to assume he's been shooting his mouth off, and I'll nail his lawyer ass to the wall. If we were going after anyone in this case, it would be him. You better make sure he knows that."

"Okay, I'll make sure he knows. But just so we're clear, this is still my investigation, right?" Flaherty asked.

Weidel fumed. "You're pressing your luck, Flaherty. You know that, don't you? You've been hanging around this jackass for too long"—Weidel nodded at Kozlowski—"and he's been hanging around this department for too long. You're risking your career here."

"It's my investigation or it isn't, Captain," said Flaherty, holding her ground. "Which is it?"

Weidel threw up his hands. "It's yours. You do with it what you want." He shook his head. "But don't expect any cover if you start hurling accusations at our friends in law enforcement. The first time you get in a public official's face is the last time you'll have my support."

"Fair enough," Flaherty said, and walked out of the office.

Kozlowski lingered for a moment, taking a piece of Nicorette gum out of his pocket and popping it into his mouth, chewing slowly. "It's good to see we're all on the same team, Captain," he said.

"Kozlowski, you've never been on my team."

CHAPTER FORTY

Finn looked around his office, rubbing his temples as he felt a migraine spread. Documents from the Tannery case were stacked throughout the small space, some in folders, some in neat stacks, and some in splayed piles that had lost any pretense of organization—all awaiting his review and analysis. He wondered how he'd get through them all. Normally, the scale of the task before him would be of little concern. Through the years at Howery, Black, he'd acquired the stamina necessary to climb any documentary mountain, no matter how daunting. Today, however, he needed to be out of the office for a few hours, and for the first time in his career he worried whether the work would actually get done. He closed his eyes and rubbed his eyelids, desperate for relief.

When he opened them again, he saw Nick Williams over a stack of exhibits, standing in his doorway. Finn returned the smile and wagged his head back and forth as though shaking off a daze. This seemed to have become a routine of theirs. At least once a day, Williams stopped by to shoot the breeze while he took a break from his own tedium. Finn didn't mind. In fact, he usually welcomed the distraction, having discovered that Nick was far more engaging than he'd first thought. Nevertheless, at that moment he didn't have the time to spare.

"Sorry, Nick, I've got too much going on," he said, trying to wave him away.

"That bad?" Williams asked, moving a group of folders and collapsing into a chair.

"That bad," Finn said, nodding. He waited for Nick to get up, but his colleague leaned back his chair and propped his feet up on the desk. "Seriously, Nick, I'm swamped and I've got to get through this stuff."

"Hey, try not to bitch so much, huh?" Williams joked. "I got in at six this morning, and I've spent the last three hours staring at a pile of documents taller than most of the Celtics. It seems like the more I read, the bigger the pile becomes. It's as though I'm starring in someone's sadistic Greek myth."

"Sisyphus goes to law school?"

"Something like that. And if that weren't enough, I'm supposed to babysit you, make sure you're not fucking anything up."

That got Finn's attention. "Preston's nervous?"

"Well, the widow's deposition is a key piece of what we're doing. He just wants to make sure you're up to it." Williams paused and inclined his head toward Finn. "*Are* you up to it?"

"Of course I am. The deposition is the least of my worries. I still have to review all of the crap in these files for our witness outlines. That's what's got me concerned."

Williams shrugged. "Hey, these piles look pathetic compared to the document monsters that have taken over my office."

"What can I say?" Finn said. "You read faster than I do, and you're better at analyzing this stuff."

Williams feigned modesty. "Well, it *is* my specialty." He reached over and pulled three huge folders onto his lap. "What is this anyway?"

Finn looked at the files Williams was thumbing through. "Those are Natalie's old case files," he said. "Preston wanted someone to go through them to see if there's anything we can use." He rubbed his temples again. "I swear, I don't know how I'm going to get through all this." He didn't mention his appointment later in the day, of course, but it weighed heavily on him.

Williams seemed to be mulling something. "Fine," he said with mock exasperation. "I'll add these to my pile."

Finn looked at him incredulously. "But how can you—"

Williams shrugged. "Like I said, it's my specialty. And anyway, it's a drop in the bucket. This way, I can tell Preston that you're focusing on the deposition." He got up with the files under his arm.

"Oh man, I owe you big-time," said Finn. "If there's anything I can do . . ."

Williams turned around at the door. "Yeah, there is. Next time I stop by, try not to be such a whiny little prick." He gave a smile and headed down the corridor.

It was a twenty-mile drive up to the Massachusetts Correctional Institution in Concord, and the journey gave Finn some time to think. Living and working in the city, he often went weeks without driving, and it felt good to be behind the wheel. There was an instant feeling of control that he desperately needed at the moment.

He had the top down on his 1974 MG convertible, and the heavy summer air washed back over the windshield and through his thick dark hair, cooling him down. The car had been a gift to himself when he landed the job at Howery, Black. He'd received a modest bonus when he started—just enough to cover his credit card bills, not enough to pay off his student loans—but he'd decided to treat himself to a used car instead. Growing up on the streets of Charlestown, he'd developed an appraiser's eye for automobiles, the kind of instant evaluation skills that come from constantly weighing the chop-shop value of a potential boost against the likelihood of being caught. He'd always been partial to the foreign roadsters that were few and far between down in the area around the shipyards, and the feeling of owning one had been a thrill he still felt whenever he got behind the wheel.

He never really believed he'd be able to get into the prison to see Townsend. His years as a public defender had given him strong contacts within the prison system, but he never thought they'd be enough to get him in to see such a notorious prisoner. On a wing and a prayer he'd called Billy Parker, the judicial administrator in charge of case assignments at the Public Defender's office.

"Why the hell would you want to defend this guy, Finn?" Billy had asked. "Don't you have a professional reputation to protect now?"

"Yeah, but I never get into court anymore," Finn said, laughing. "I'm getting the itch. In all honesty, I'm not sure my firm will let me take this case, but I'd like to give it a try. I figured if I met the guy, I might have some ammunition to convince the partners to let me defend him."

"I'll see if I can get you in," Billy had promised. "It may be tough, but this guy is such a twisted nut I'd take any opportunity to get him off the PD's plate. No one here wants to deal with him at all."

Finn had no intention of representing John Townsend, and he knew damned well the firm would never let him take on a case as controversial as this—pro bono to boot. He felt guilty about lying to Billy, but he needed to meet with Townsend, just to see him face-to-face. Finn had spent enough of his life dealing with crooks and deviants and psychopaths, both as a lawyer and in his youth, that he had a pretty good sense of them. Twenty minutes with Townsend should be enough to make a judgment.

Of course, Finn was taking a serious risk with his career. If the partners at Howery, Black discovered what he was doing, there would be hell to pay. He'd survive the fallout, though, he knew. Preston would understand his need to see Townsend. Especially if he explained how much Natalie's murder was weighing on him and how he was driven to find answers.

Finn was passing through Cambridge now, with Harvard University's high brick academic buildings dominating the run up the Charles River. Long-haired students in tattered crimson wandered along the sidewalks carrying overstuffed backpacks. Along the river, joggers and Rollerbladers shared the wide path set aside especially for recreation, racing against the rowing shells that slid through the glassy waters, coxswains calling out a tempo to the hard-bodied rowers. This was a world that had always fascinated him, probably more so because it had been so out of his reach. He wondered what his life would have been like if he'd been offered the opportunities available to these fortunate few. He liked to think coming up the hard way had given him a drive other people lacked.

The bolt on the steel door sounded with a crash behind him, and the buzzer rang out twice before someone shouted, "All clear!" from down the cement corridor. Finn had heard these sounds from both sides of the impenetrable bars, and it still sent shivers up his spine when he returned to any prison setting.

He paced the room for five minutes before the buzzer sounded again and he heard the grating sound of metal on metal as the five-hundred-pound deadbolt was pulled back to allow entry.

Townsend entered from the other end of the room, bound in chains at the wrists and ankles. He looked tiny next to the two massive guards who held him by the elbows as he shuffle-stepped to the table in the center of the room. He'd just lowered himself into the wobbly plastic chair when one of the guards nodded at Finn. “You got fifteen minutes,” he said.

Fifteen minutes, Finn thought. *That should be enough*.

Once the guards were gone, he took a seat across from Townsend, who watched him with a calm, detached curiosity. Finn laid a pack of cigarettes on the table.

“Smoke?” he offered.

Townsend shook his head. “I went to medical school for a while,” he said. “Those things will kill you.” He smiled when he said it, clearly amused by the irony.

“Mind if I have one?” Finn asked.

“Suit yourself.”

Finn pulled a cigarette out of the pack and put it between his lips, taking a lighter out of his pocket and lighting the tip. Smoking was prohibited now throughout most of the building—a deprivation that seemed based more on morality than public health—but interview rooms were an exception.

“Do you know who I am?” Finn asked.

Townsend’s eyes narrowed. “I was told you’re a lawyer who may be representing me.”

“That’s right, my name is Scott Finn, and I’m a lawyer,” Finn said. “But I’m not just any lawyer, I’m your only chance at a fair trial. I work at one of the largest law firms in Boston, and if I take this case, you’ll have the best legal team in the business working for you. I’m here to figure out whether this case is worth our time.” Finn had rehearsed this speech in the car on the way up to the prison, but he still felt a rush of guilt as the lies poured forth. He silently prayed that his visit would never be reported back to the firm. “Because we’re considering representing you, everything you say here to me is privileged. Do you understand what that means?”

“Yes, I do,” said Townsend.

“So you understand that whatever you say to me, I can’t tell the police, and I can’t ever testify against you at trial?”

"I understand."

"Good." Finn examined the little man in front of him. His curious smile hadn't changed since he walked into the room. It gave him an incongruous air of confidence and untouchability. "Then I guess the only question I have for you is, why should I represent you?" Finn was trying to play hard-to-get, to draw Townsend into an attempt to defend his actions.

Townsend picked up the pack of cigarettes still lying on the table. He slid a cigarette out of the pack and began twirling it between his fingers. "Why do people smoke?" he asked, as if he hadn't heard a word Finn had said.

Finn sat back in his chair and shrugged. "I've been told it's because nicotine is addictive, but I think most people who smoke simply like to smoke. The addiction label just gives them an excuse."

Townsend looked up at Finn, still smiling his inscrutable smile. "I think people smoke because they are full of sin and self-hatred." The statement came out of his mouth with sympathy rather than self-righteousness.

The notion intrigued Finn. "Why do you say that?"

Townsend cocked his head. "This isn't the world God intended," he said. "The world God intended was pure, and bright, and wonderful. We ruined it. Mankind ruined it. God put sin and temptation into the mix, and we fell for it, and that sin and temptation has turned the world dark and *evil.* Mankind wasn't meant to be sinful, and that's why people feel guilt—when they do sin. The guilt makes them look for ways to punish themselves. Things like smoking and drinking and fornication, which they know is bad for them."

Finn took a long drag on his cigarette, drawing the smoke deep into his lungs and letting it linger there for a moment or two before opening his mouth and letting it drift out. "It's an interesting theory," he said. He took another drag and blew the smoke into Townsend's face. "Is that why you killed these women—to give them an escape from their sin?"

Townsend shook his head. "I didn't really know why I killed them at the time. I knew God wanted me to, and I assumed it was their sinfulness that offended him, but I was wrong. He needed me to kill them to make way for the seven angel-warriors of the apocalypse."

"So you think the apocalypse is going to start any minute now, is that it? It's a nice try at setting up an insanity defense, but do you really think anyone is going to buy that?"

Townsend smiled again. "That's okay, Mr. Finn, I'm not trying to sell it. Besides, the apocalypse has already begun."

"Really?" Finn asked. "Should I go to the window?"

Townsend laughed, and Finn was struck by the self-assurance the tiny man exhibited, as though he were laughing at a child who was still learning to perform the most basic tasks, like walking or talking. "Have you ever read the book of Revelation, Mr. Finn?"

Finn nodded. "Once, a long time ago. I had to read the Bible when . . ." He didn't finish the sentence. *I was at the orphanage*—that's what he was about to say, but he wouldn't give Townsend the satisfaction.

"It's the prophecy of the apocalypse," Townsend continued, "and it foretells the destruction of this flawed world. It describes a long and bloody war between the forces of good and evil, and nearly everyone is destroyed in the end—except the few truly pure."

"And you think this has already started?"

"Look around you, Mr. Finn. There's a holy war that has been gathering speed over the last decade. The Muslims are killing the Christians and the Jews, the Jews are killing the Muslims, the Hutus are killing the Tutsis, the Protestants are killing the Catholics, and it goes on *forever*. We're all drawn in. We're headed for the great cataclysm when the living and the dead alike will be judged, and most will be damned. Can you really look at the world around you and tell me it isn't already happening?"

Finn thought about it for a moment, but had no response.

"Why are you here, Mr. Finn?"

"I told you, I'm here to—"

"You're not here as a lawyer, Mr. Finn," Townsend interrupted. "And you're certainly never going to represent me, are you?"

Finn hesitated, reluctant to abandon his pretense so soon and risk losing a cover that might give Townsend a reason to divulge more information. But the man didn't want to talk about his case, that much was clear. He seemed to have no interest in his fate under the judicial system.

"No," Finn replied finally. "I'll never be your lawyer."

"Then why are you really here?"

Finn reached into his breast pocket and took out a picture. It had been taken a year before at a dinner party, and it showed Finn standing next to Natalie. Both were smiling and raising their glasses in a toast toward the camera. It was his favorite picture of her, and he had kept it with him since he'd learned of her murder. He held it up for Townsend to see.

"You knew her," Townsend said simply. "She's the one the police were asking me about."

"I need to know," Finn nodded.

"Were you married?" Townsend asked. From looking at Finn he knew the answer before it was given. "No, not married, but lovers. Sinners together." He raised his eyebrow. "The serpent of temptation claims another victim, right, Mr. Finn?"

Finn remained silent, and Townsend laughed. "You came here to escape, didn't you?"

"I need to know what happened," Finn pressed. "Did you kill her?"

Townsend shook his head. "That would be too easy for you,

wouldn't it? For some answers you need to look inside yourself." He picked up the picture and examined it closely. Then he looked at Finn, searching his eyes. The intensity of the look made Finn uncomfortable. "She was beautiful, and you loved her, but she wasn't yours," Townsend said at last.

"Bullshit!" Finn said, recoiling.

Townsend laughed again. "I'm sorry for you, Mr. Finn. Seven is the number God wanted, and seven is the number I gave him. Those seven did not include her. Search your own heart, and you'll find the answers if you want to." Townsend was smiling as he signaled the guard through the Plexiglas to open the door and let him out.

As he stood up from the table and began shuffling toward the door in his leg irons, he turned and looked at Finn. "As for this whore you mourn. I have no sympathy for her. God has shown us the way, if we would only choose to follow it. She was the filth that corrupted the beauty preordained by God. Her punishment in the corporeal world is but a fleeting taste of the torment she'll rightly suffer in the hereafter. *She will be consumed by fire, for mighty is the Lord who judges her!*"

Finn leapt out of his chair and grabbed him by the collar, throwing him against the wall. "You did it, didn't you! You bastard!" he screamed in his face.

Townsend shook his head. "I can't help you," he gasped.

"You're lying! Tell me what I need to know!" Finn lifted the little man off the floor and he could feel his fingers digging into Townsend's throat, but the only reaction he drew was a knowing, satisfied smile. It felt so good, like the days of his youth on the streets of Charlestown, letting loose his anger against a world that had cheated him so badly. The fact that Townsend didn't struggle made Finn even angrier, and he watched the smaller man's face turn bright red. The smug, superior grin hung on Townsend's lips as they began to turn blue, like a statement of secret victory as his life began to ebb away. *At least*, Finn thought, *I will be the one to wipe that smile off his face.*

"What the hell is going on here!" Finn heard someone shout from behind him. It was the guard. A few more seconds and it would be over. He could hold on that long, couldn't he?

But he knew he wouldn't. He wasn't a street thug anymore, and he couldn't go back to that. He pushed Townsend to the side as he released his throat, sending him sprawling into the corner, coughing and hacking and grasping his neck.

The guard watched the scene with malevolent amusement as Townsend fought to get air back into his lungs. Then he looked at Finn. "Are you all right? Do you want me to report any misbehavior?"

Finn shook his head.

The guard looked at Townsend. "What about you, scumbag? You wanna make any trouble for me?"

Townsend was hunched over on the floor in the corner of the room, still gasping for air. "No sir," he sputtered finally. "I was just considering Mr. Finn's kind offer to represent me as my attorney." The guard turned and looked at Finn quizzically, a new contempt for him evident on his face.

"Thank you, Mr. Finn," Townsend continued. "But I think I'm satisfied with my current representation." Then he started toward the door, dragging his chains behind him. When he got there, he turned around. "Thank you for coming," he said. "I hope you find what you're looking for, but I'm not in a position to help."

Finn watched him go, helpless. Wordlessly, he followed another guard out of the room, back down the corridor, and out of the prison, signing himself out along the way, and emerging into the cool night air in the parking lot. The breeze that cut across the open fields bordering the prison was the first break in the weather in weeks, and it chilled him in his sweat-soaked suit. He'd gotten his answer from Townsend, though it wasn't the one he was looking for. The bizarre little monster hadn't killed Natalie. Finn was sure now, and that knowledge was a dangerous thing, for it strengthened his resolve to find out who *had* killed her. As he climbed back into his car and pulled out onto Route 2, heading back to Boston, he worried about what he might uncover.

CHAPTER FORTY-ONE

"Objection!" Barnolk shouted. "Not even you can think this line of questioning has anything to do with this case!" The deposition had already taken over two hours, and everyone's nerves were beginning to fray.

Finn looked down at the copies of the credit card receipts that he'd just laid in front of Amy Tannery. Then he looked back up with a practiced expression of bewilderment. "What are you talking about?" he asked. "This line of questioning is highly relevant."

"What do some five-year-old hotel bills have to do with this case?" Barnolk was beside himself with rage.

"First of all, Mr. Barnolk, they're not *hotel* bills, they're *motel* bills. Second, you were the one who included a loss of consortium claim in Mrs. Tannery's complaint. As a result, you've asserted that Mrs. Tannery is entitled to cash damages based on her being deprived of her normal physical relationship with her husband. To define a measure of damages under that claim, we have to inquire as to the nature of that physical relationship." Finn's explanation offered a calm counterpoint to Barnolk's apoplexy.

"This is outrageous!" Barnolk exploded.

"No, that's fine, Fred," Mrs. Tannery interrupted. "He can ask his questions."

"But we haven't prepared for—"

"I hadn't prepared for *anything* that's happened in the last year. In comparison to what I've already been through, Mr. Finn's questions are a minor inconvenience." She looked directly at Finn. "Go ahead, lead us down whatever sleazy path you choose."

Finn was impressed with Amy Tannery. She played the role of victim with strength and dignity, but not so much so that it would obscure for the jury the depth of her pain and the genuineness of her grief. She was beautiful in an understated way—no makeup on her pale skin, and light brown hair that was neatly brushed, not styled. She wore no jewelry except a smallish engagement stone protected by a plain platinum wedding band. She'd make an excellent witness and would probably have a devastating impact on a jury if she ever took the stand. Finn felt even more pressure to convince her it would be better to settle her claims.

He fingered the motel receipts. "Have you ever seen these before, Mrs. Tannery?" he asked.

"No, I haven't."

"But you recognize the imprint from your husband's credit card?"

"Yes, I do."

"So it's fair to say that for a three-week period in 2001, your husband was renting a motel room at various times of the day on a fairly regular basis, isn't that right?" Finn asked. He was starting to feel dirty again, but he needed to know how far she could be pushed before she'd crack. She'd already kept her composure for longer than most.

"Assuming these receipts are accurate, then yes, that appears to be the case," she responded, her eyes never leaving Finn's.

"Do you know why?"

"No, I don't." Finn couldn't look away from her eyes. They were large, brown, and unflinching. They didn't even contain the hatred and anger Finn was so used to seeing in the eyes of the people he ripped apart during depositions. There was nothing there but simple dignity, a kind of regal acceptance.

"Did he meet *you* at this motel?" he asked.

"No, he didn't."

"Did he meet anyone else?"

"As I said, I don't know."

"So it's possible he was meeting someone else, isn't that right?" Finn was laying the groundwork, and it would be hard for her to fight the conclusion.

"Yes, it's possible."

"Is it also possible he was having an affair, Mrs. Tannery?"

The question made her flinch ever so slightly, but she didn't back away from it. "I suppose anything is possible, Mr. Finn. This entire year has been a lesson in the cruelties human beings are capable of."

It was a fine retort, and it made Finn blanch. "Do you know if he was having an affair?" he pushed. It was his job, he told himself.

"No, I don't. I only know that we were having problems at the time, the way all married couples have problems. We both worked very hard to get through those problems, and we succeeded. If there were any indiscretions on his part, I didn't know about them."

"I hope you'll pardon me for asking this, Mrs. Tannery, but you don't seem distressed at the prospect your husband may have been having an affair. Why is that?"

"I'll pardon you for nothing, Mr. Finn—that's not my job—but I'll answer your questions. You see, I came in here today fully expecting you to do everything you could to tear apart the memory of my husband. But I will not let that happen. I can't let that happen. I have a little girl who is only a year old, and all she has in this world is me, so I can't let this thing destroy me. All she'll ever have of her father are the memories I can share, so I can't let this destroy those, either. My husband wasn't a perfect man, but he was a good man—much better than you would have me believe. I suppose, if you dig deep enough, you'll find a hint of dirt on anyone. But no matter how much mud you throw at me and the memory of my husband, you'll never be able to take away my love for him. I won't let you." The last sentence came out with such quiet resolve that it moved even Finn. In all his years of wading through the cesspools of petty human emotion that so often collected during the course of civil litigation, he'd never come across someone with the strength of this widow sitting across the table. For the first time in his career, he felt a kind of self-loathing.

"Why didn't you accept the federal settlement in this case?" he asked impulsively.

"What do you mean?"

"Well, I mean that, according to our calculations, you would have received over two and a half million dollars under the federal settlement. All of that would have been tax-free. Now, with attorneys' fees and the cost of this litigation, not to mention the taxes on any noncompensatory portion of a possible monetary award, you need to have the jury award you more than five million dollars just to break even. It just seems like a huge risk. So I'm wondering why you didn't settle?"

Mrs. Tannery leaned back in her chair. "Do you know how long the federal investigation into what happened last year lasted, Mr. Finn?" Finn shook his head. "Seventeen days. Seventeen days was all the time that anyone felt was necessary. It's like people didn't even want to know what happened. Well, I want to know what happened."

"But even if you win this lawsuit, there's no reason to think that there'll be any further investigation," Finn pointed out.

Amy Tannery smiled sadly. "Have you ever truly loved

someone, Mr. Finn? Ever had a soul mate?" Finn said nothing. "I suppose it's an unfair question," she said, shrugging. "It assumes you have a soul in the first place." She paused to let her barb sink in. "If you'd ever had a soul mate, though, and that person were to be ripped away from you without any rational explanation, you'd understand why I'm doing this. I need to know the answers. And as long as the questions remain, I can't let it drop."

They stared at each other for a long moment, seeing in each other an understanding that went beyond the confines of their roles in the lawsuit. Finn knew why she was pursuing the case, and she could see in his face that he understood. He felt even more uncomfortable putting her through the hard questioning required by his job. He wondered if she comprehended that he had no choice, but then realized it didn't matter. What mattered was whether he understood.

"Are you done?" Barnolk asked, interrupting the silence between them.

Finn kept looking at Amy Tannery, the widow of a good man, making her way in a world that had broken its promises to her; a woman who was raising her infant daughter alone, without anyone to share the joys of her child's first step and each new word. He admired her. More than that, he realized, he cared for her in an odd way, which made what he was about to do even harder.

He turned and looked at Barnolk. "No, I have another hour or two of questions," he said.

CHAPTER FORTY-TWO

Rich Loring, the United States attorney for the Federal District of Massachusetts, was sitting at his desk when Flaherty walked into his office. It was a big mahogany piece with a leather top that oozed power and importance. The entire room did, paneled as it was in dark wood and papered in dark green. The thick, cream-colored carpet absorbed sound and gave the room a confidential feel. The windows looked out across the water from the new Federal Courthouse in Southie toward the taller buildings of downtown Boston. The courthouse had been completed in 1998, at the apex of an economy that seemed limitless, and the optimism of the time was reflected in the plush appointments afforded.

It was late afternoon on a Thursday, and it looked like Loring was getting ready to leave early for a long weekend—one of the perks of being the boss, Flaherty supposed. A small overnight bag rested by the side of his desk with a tennis racquet leaning up against it.

"A long weekend away with the family, I presume?" Flaherty asked, startling him. He looked up with the expression of a little boy caught in the act of some disobedience.

"How did you get in here?" he demanded.

"Sorry, there's no one out at your secretary's desk, and the door was open, so I thought I'd just poke my head in."

He was clearly annoyed. "Alice!" he called toward the open door, out to the empty vestibule where his secretary's desk was located. There was no answer. "Alice!" he called again, with similar results.

"She's not there, trust me," Flaherty assured.

Loring grumbled, "I'd fire her if they'd let me." Then he shrugged. "Try taking a job away from a civil servant with sixteen years seniority. It's easier to separate a pit bull from a big, meaty bone."

"Aw, the trials of being a political appointee in a bureaucratic world."

Loring actually smiled at that. "It's the truth." Then he turned serious. "Look, if Alice had been here, I would have had her tell you that I'm leaving soon and that you need to make an appointment for next week. I have to get out of here for a legal conference. Will you call her to set something up?"

"That's all right, I only need a minute or two. I can even walk you out while we talk."

Loring shook his head nervously. "That won't work, but I might be able to give you a quick minute—just a minute." He walked over and closed the door, glancing outside the office as he did, then returned to his desk.

"That's fine," said Flaherty. She sat in one of the upholstered chairs opposite him.

"I suppose congratulations are in order," Loring said grudgingly, leaning forward in his high-backed executive leather chair. "Catching Little Jack is a pretty big feather in your cap."

"We're happy we found him. Most of the credit goes to Kozlowski's and Officer Stone's intuition, but we're definitely pleased."

"That's odd. I haven't heard the media mention Kozlowski or

Stone when they interview you. It must be an oversight," he said with a wry smile.

"Actually, I've mentioned them in every interview I've given," Flaherty retorted testily. "Sometimes they edit it out, but I keep trying."

"They must think it makes a better story with a woman as the hero," Loring said, again letting his sarcasm show. He shrugged. "In any case, I'm happy you found him, particularly for Natalie Caldwell's sake. Hopefully, she'll rest easier now."

"That's why I'm here," Flaherty said. "How well did you know Natalie Caldwell?"

"We worked on several cases together in the two years she was at the Justice Department and I was at the FBI," Loring said. "We got along, but I wouldn't say we were particularly close."

"What cases did you work on together?"

"A couple of drug investigations," he offered. "Mainly ones involving the Asian gangs that run drugs up from Providence."

"Didn't she also work with you on the Bulger case?" Flaherty asked. She tried to make it sound offhanded, but it was too pointed a question to escape Loring's attention.

"Yes, now that you mention it, we did work on that case together, but I'm not sure how that's relevant to anything having to do with her death."

"Did you and Ms. Caldwell see each other socially?"

"What the hell does that mean?" Loring barked.

Flaherty refused to back down. "It means exactly what it says. Did you see her outside of work?"

"That's a highly unusual question, Lieutenant, and I'm trying to decide whether to take offense at it. I saw her when some of us went out for drinks after work, but nothing more than that. I'm married, you know."

"Yes, I know," Flaherty replied. "Other than that, you've never seen her socially? Not even since she left the Justice Department?"

"I don't think I like your tone, Detective," Loring said. "What's this about, anyway?"

"There are just a few discrepancies involving the Caldwell murder that we're trying to clear up."

Loring took a deep breath and brought his fingers together temple-style in front of his face, as if in deep contemplation. After a moment he said, "In that case, I think I *am* offended. I don't appreciate your coming in here with baseless inquiries about my relationship with a murdered woman, particularly since it appears you're simply looking for additional headlines in the media circus you've already created."

Flaherty shrugged. "I'm just following through with the investigation. I assure you, I don't pry into other people's personal affairs without reason. But we do need answers to these few questions."

"As I've said, there are no affairs for you to pry into here. And with respect to your questions, you have all the answers you'll get. You may leave now." Loring's tone was dismissive, setting Flaherty off.

"So you didn't see Natalie Caldwell socially, even after she left the Justice Department?" she repeated.

Loring looked angry now, but was too polished a lawyer and politician to lose his composure. "No, Lieutenant, I did not see Natalie Caldwell socially, even after she left the Justice Department. And, again, I'll remind you that I'm a married man, and I'd like to register my extreme displeasure with the manner in which you've approached me about this. I've worked very hard to get where I am, and I believe I'm entitled to a little more respect than you're currently showing me. I'll be talking to your superiors about this, is that understood?"

"Absolutely," Flaherty responded. "If you wish to make it public that your name has come up in the course of this investigation, you're more than welcome to. I'm simply following police procedure."

Just then the door swung open and an attractive young woman bustled into the office in midsentence. "What a fucking week!" she was saying. "I can't wait to get the hell away from here and relax in a—" She stopped short when she noticed Flaherty sitting in the chair in front of Loring's desk. Flaherty could see him turning bright red.

"I'm sorry, Rich," the woman stammered. "I didn't know you were in a meeting. I'll be back in a little while."

"No, it's okay," Flaherty said. "I was just leaving." She stood up and turned toward the woman in the doorway. She looked like she was in her late twenties, tall, with striking red hair and a pretty face. She had a large weekend bag slung over her shoulder and was gripping a tennis racquet.

Flaherty looked from the woman's bag to the duffel resting by the side of Loring's desk, then back to the woman herself. "I'm sorry," she said, "I don't think we've met." She extended her hand in a gesture that forced the woman to struggle with her racquet as she tried to free her own hand.

"I'm Janet Reed," she said, still shaken from the awkwardness of her entry.

"Ms. Reed is an attorney here in the Criminal Division," Loring offered weakly. "She and I are attending the same conference this weekend. It's a work function."

Flaherty looked again at the tennis racquet. "Well, it certainly looks like you two are in for a strenuous few days of professional activity," she said. Then she turned to Loring. "Thank you for your help, Mr. Loring. I apologize if my questions offended your sensibilities. I certainly wouldn't want to contribute to any unfounded rumors about your personal life." Loring fumed silently behind his desk, unable to defend himself.

Flaherty smiled. "I'll let you know if we need anything else," she said, squeezing past Janet Reed as she left the office.

CHAPTER FORTY-THREE

The view from the governor's office was spectacular. Located in the front of the State House, it perched on top of Beacon Hill in the heart of old Boston, looking down on the rest of the city as it ran from the hill toward the water on three sides. During the twentieth century, the skyscrapers had grown bit by bit from the lowlands in the financial district, eventually raising the altitude of the city's business institutions above the level of the seat of government. But even this metaphorical challenge to the State House's supremacy had done little to dampen the majesty of the view from the governor's office.

William Clarke stood facing the office's grand windows, looking out at the vast expanse of the Boston Common and the Public Garden that were a focal point of Boston's urban design. The phone was pressed hard to his ear and his grip on the receiver was too tight, as though he were trying to strangle the words coming out of the earpiece.

"I understand," he said. "Yes, that is disappointing," and then after another pause, "I'll let our friends know." He hung up the receiver by reaching absentmindedly behind him and placing it on one of the four phones that lined the side of his desktop, keeping his eyes focused on the city below him.

Wendyl Shore stood behind the governor. Even the creases

in his slacks and the shine on his loafers couldn't conceal the tension he was feeling. "Well?" he asked after several seconds.

"Apparently Flaherty isn't convinced about the Caldwell murder. She's not sure it was Townsend's doing, and she's still pursuing the investigation." Clarke's voice had a dreamy quality to it as he watched young lovers strolling through the Common, hand in hand past the Frog Pond.

"We have to stop her," Wendyl said flatly. He didn't want to think about what an investigation might uncover. He'd worked too hard to put the governor in a position where the political future was limitless. Some of the party elders were already whispering about the presidential nomination.

"How?" Clarke asked, more to himself than to his companion. "What possible precedent could there be for a governor to step in and stop a murder investigation? It would raise too many questions—questions I certainly couldn't answer." He paused, debating whether to share the other piece of news. "Besides," he said after a moment's deliberation, "we have another problem."

"What?"

"Scott Finn, the young man from the law firm, seems to be conducting his own investigation."

"What kind of an investigation?" Wendyl asked. This was clearly getting out of control.

Clarke shrugged. "Into the Caldwell murder. Apparently he's the one who fed Flaherty the information about Caldwell having a lover. And yesterday he visited Townsend in prison."

"What could he possibly want with Townsend?"

"Answers," Clarke said. "Mr. Finn didn't stay long, but our sources at the prison say it was an animated discussion."

There was a long silence between them. Outside, the sun had passed its apex and was beginning its slide to the west, tinting the sky a premature orange that would last for a few more hours. Autumn was coming, Clarke reflected. He couldn't wait. Autumn was a parodoxical time of rebirth in New England, where the residents identified themselves more with the dark winter months than with the heat of the summer. Every year after Labor Day a new cycle began, with children returning to school, businesses restarting their clocks on a new fiscal calendar, and the sins of summer disappearing under the brilliant autumn foliage.

"So, what should we do?" Wendyl asked, suddenly unsure of himself.

Clarke thought for a moment. "I think you and I can probably figure what to do about Flaherty." He turned and faced his chief of staff. "Mr. Finn is someone else's problem to deal with, however."

CHAPTER FORTY-FOUR

Peter Bostick stood on a deserted street in Southie, down near the water looking out at the harbor across to East Boston and Logan Airport. He hated this kind of work. After twenty years on the police force, being a private investigator for a big law firm was more boring than he could ever have imagined. However, Black's cases tended toward the respectable, and the work they needed him to do usually involved little more than errands. In this particular instance, Finn had asked him to track down some of the Huron security guards who'd worked on the commuter line before the terrorist attack. Tracking down witnesses was one of the dullest tasks he handled. Still, Finn was a decent sort—not like most of the snobs he dealt with. Bostick didn't mind doing the work for him, and the pay was always satisfactory.

He'd spent the morning running down the three addresses Finn had given him, with no success. He looked up at the battered old warehouse that was literally falling into the harbor, double-checking to make sure he had the address right.

It must be a mistake, he thought. Maybe the address had been entered into Huron's system incorrectly. That wouldn't be particularly unusual. A bad address was one of the most common reasons people hired him in the first place. He'd been told not to spend too much time on this particular errand, but he liked Finn. The young lawyer was one of the guys who referred good cases to him—ones that offered plenty of overtime and little effort. It wouldn't hurt to reach out to some of his contacts to find out where these people really lived—no extra charge.

Bostick got back into his car, pulled out his cell phone and address book, and started dialing.

CHAPTER FORTY-FIVE

Finn walked home that night, as he often did during the summer when the weather was nice. The walk took him three-quarters of an hour at a meandering pace, and brought him through several distinct and separate worlds. From his office downtown, near the harbor at the edge of Chinatown, he headed north through the business district, watching as the late-working, suited inhabitants scurried from their buildings like the last rats off sinking ships, bedraggled and serious. From there he passed through the Faneuil Hall area where the Thursday night crowd was already gathering steam at the open-fronted bars in Quincy Market, spilling out over the velvet ropes that loosely defined the establishments' borders; and then across the remains of the Big Dig, where the remnants of the raised expressway—a testament to the waste of modern government expenditures—separated downtown Boston from the Italian North End.

He walked with his head down, deep in thought; the footsteps on the bricks and cobblestones around him in the historic districts blended into his own, clapping in heavy time to a rhythm that had changed surprisingly little in the city's three and a half centuries. At the edge of the North End he turned onto Causeway Street, and from there onto the North Washington Street Bridge, which crosses the mouth of the Charles River into Charlestown. He walked in silent contemplation of his predicament. Many times in the past he'd stopped at the top of the bridge after postwork drinks and lit a cigarette, leaning against the railing as he looked out at the insular little neighborhood where he'd spent all of his years, marveling at the direction his life had taken. But not tonight. Tonight there was too much on his mind.

Townsend wasn't Natalie's killer. He knew that now with a certainty he couldn't deny. He'd tried to convince himself otherwise as he looked into the madman's eyes, but he'd been unsuccessful. Townsend would rot in hell, if he wasn't there already, but not for the murder of Natalie Caldwell; that's what Townsend's eyes had told him, and Finn was just beginning to grasp the implications. Natalie's killer was still out there, and Finn knew he couldn't rest until he found him.

It wasn't just that his own freedom was on the line—although he recognized that as a powerful motivator. The police, unable to pin Natalie's murder on Townsend, would keep looking for another suspect, and at the moment it appeared he was the likeliest target. But that practical concern was only a part of what was driving Finn. The other was a loyalty to Natalie he couldn't fully explain. For all her faults, she was still the person with whom he felt the closest connection. Even when their relationship was strained, she'd always been there for him, albeit not always in the way he wanted. There were so few people who'd ever stuck by him, and he was determined to stick by Natalie now.

Of course, his responsibilities on the Tannery case were becoming so overwhelming they allowed no time to follow through on these avowals. He simply couldn't take the time to investigate Natalie's murder without letting down Preston Holland and giving up everything he'd worked for at Howery, Black.

It was a quandary that resisted easy solution. All of these thoughts were swirling through his head as Finn walked through Charlestown on his way home. His apartment was in the fashionable Monument Square section. Only a few blocks from the housing projects off Bunker Hill Street where Finn had spent most of his youth, his two-bedroom duplex was nonetheless a world away from his roots. The line between the haves and the have-nots was clearly drawn in Charlestown, and he'd crossed over that line when he took the job at Howery, Black, leaving the desperation of the projects behind him. Tonight, as on many others, he took a long route home that led him up Bunker Hill Street, near the edge of his old neighborhood. The projects sat low and squat in rectangular huddles behind fences that seemed designed more to keep the inhabitants in than to keep others out. He walked past the walls, looking in on his past from the outside, like a voyeur, wondering about the other roads his life might have taken.

At Lexington Street he headed left, up Bunker Hill toward the monument. The change in atmosphere was instant, as the townhouses in brick and clapboard siding glowed with the warmth of comfort and security. His apartment was near the top of the hill, bordering on Monument Square Park, in what was known as one of the safest areas of Charlestown. He was almost to his door when he heard an unmistakable rustle coming up behind him.

It had been so long since he'd walked the streets in constant fear, always on guard, and his reflexes were slow, but he still managed to dodge the first blow. The rustle was the sound of two young men rushing toward him from behind—denim rubbing on denim, and black sneakers on pavement as they accelerated for the attack.

The first young man to reach him swung his arm just as Finn ducked, and Finn caught sight of a fist holding something dark and heavy. Instinctively, he shot his elbow out into his attacker's gut, catching the man in the solar plexus and doubling him over. As he turned to face the second man, though, he felt a sharp pain slice through his right shoulder as he was hit in the neck with a heavy club. He fell to his knees, his arm dangling free, numbed from the blow.

Finn could see the legs of the second attacker right in front of him, and he knew he had only a moment to act before another blow would land on his head or his back. He reached out with his one functioning arm and hooked the man around the knees, bending his legs backward and toppling him.

The man flailed about, trying to catch Finn with the club, swinging wildly. Finn continued to dodge the blows as he crawled up onto the man's chest. Feeling was returning to his right arm, and he managed to pin the young man to the ground. He raised his arm, making a fist and preparing to strike, but before he could bring down his arm, the first attacker, who'd recovered from the blow to his stomach, tackled him, wrestling him to the ground.

The fight was lost at that point, Finn knew. Both men fell on top of him, delivering repeated punches to the head and chest. Finn had been in enough street fights to realize that, without help, there was no way he could regain control of the situation. The only thing left to do was to protect himself as best he could. He curled himself into the fetal position, wrapping his arms around his head and pulling his knees up to his chest. This would help protect some of his vital areas, but it wouldn't stop the beating or prevent the pain. He'd have to live with that.

Through the fog of his agony, Finn could hear the two men hissing and wheezing as they wore themselves out delivering the pounding. One of them was standing now, kicking him in the ribs, having exhausted his arms. Finn wondered how long the beating would last.

Then, just as he began to worry they might actually beat him to death, the attack stopped. Finn could sense the men still there, though, leaning over him to determine if he was still alive. One crouched down low next to his head, but Finn kept his eyes closed. To his horror, he heard the sound of a switchblade opening, and a moment later he felt the knife on his throat.

"This was your warning," the man said. His voice was quiet and carried a strong Boston accent—the kind he knew so well from growing up. It was the rough, clipped accent of the streets, rather than the drawn-out Brahmin drawl of Beacon Hill. "Don't go sticking your neck out to protect that Little Jack scumbag. That shit's going to get what he deserves. Let the girl go—or we'll see to it that you die." With that, the knife flicked out along his throat, and Finn felt a sharp stinging sensation, followed by the warmth of a trickle of blood sliding down his neck.

Then, as quickly as they'd come, they were gone.

CHAPTER FORTY-SIX

Flaherty was at her desk going through two sets of files. The first was a background report on Scott Finn, Esquire. It depressed her. The most recent materials contained his bar admissions and some departmental reviews of his exemplary performance from his days at the Public Defender's office. But farther back in the files were numerous arrest reports and detention records. They were mainly for relatively minor offenses, but included two arrests for assault and battery. The files indicated that he'd cut deals in both cases, and spent several months in a high-security juvenile detention center for the second offense.

The second set of files was more interesting. They contained news reports of the Bulger case, and of the subsequent trials of FBI agents for their role in tipping off Whitey Bulger, an FBI informant, to state indictments. Flaherty had asked one of the assistants to pull together the materials so she could evaluate Loring's role in the mess.

The Bulger case was an indelible black mark on the Boston law enforcement community's record. Whitey Bulger had controlled much of the organized crime out of Southie in the 1970s, '80s, and early '90s. Although local law enforcement agencies committed significant time and manpower to building a case against him, he seemed to be clairvoyant, slipping out of any sting operation before the trap was sprung with a prescience that was confounding. It wasn't until the mid-1990s that the local police learned the truth: Bulger had been an FBI informant for more than twenty years, and his FBI handlers had tipped him off to investigations, allowing him to continue a crime spree that included murder, assault, and extortion. Even in the end, Bulger's FBI "angels" had been able to keep him safe from the law, warning him before the final warrant for his arrest was executed. Bulger escaped, went into hiding, and was later named one of the FBI's ten most wanted fugitives.

In 2002, one FBI agent, John Connolly, was convicted of aiding and abetting Whitey Bulger in his escape. A year later, one of the supervisors in the FBI's Boston office was indicted on charges of conspiracy to commit murder, although he died before he could be brought to trial. The entire Boston office of the Bureau had been given an enormous black eye, earning a reputation as the most corrupt federal office in the nation.

As Flaherty looked through the articles, she noted that Loring's name appeared in passing only, despite that, as the head of the FBI's office in Boston, he had oversight of the entire project. Whenever his name was mentioned, it was usually with the tagline, *The FBI's station chief in Boston has no comment on the matter at this time.* Somehow, however, Loring had escaped close scrutiny, and even came out of the ordeal with a reputation of a "reformer" by pledging to clean up the Boston office's practices. He'd weathered the storm admirably, and then, when the position of U.S. attorney for the District of Massachusetts became available, he'd convinced his political backers to get him appointed to the job.

Flaherty shook her head as she read the articles. Loring must have nine lives, she reflected. She wondered what a man like that would do to protect his reputation, and whether some illicit connection to Natalie Caldwell could have driven him to murder. The two had worked together at the Justice Department. It was possible she'd threatened to make public some of the details that were kept quiet during Connolly's trial. That kind of a threat might very well have been enough to push Loring to action, Flaherty speculated. At the same time, she knew, that's *all* it was—speculation. Without proof, it meant nothing.

She was reading some of the articles again, making sure that there wasn't something she was missing, when the phone rang. "Flaherty," she said into the receiver.

"Yes, Detective, this is Sergeant Gormand over in Charlestown."

"Yes, Sergeant?"

"We have a situation over here that might interest you." He was being obtuse, and Flaherty hated that. There were enough riddles involved in her work without beat cops playing guessing games with her.

"I don't know about that, Sergeant, I've got plenty keeping me busy right here in Boston."

There was a pause on the other end of the line. "Yeah, well this involves a lawyer named Scott Finn. He was attacked tonight, and he's asking for you."

"Tell me where you are, and I'll be there in ten minutes."

CHAPTER FORTY-SEVEN

Finn held an ice pack against the side of his face. It hurt to talk. It hurt to breathe. Nevertheless, he considered himself lucky. There'd been a few moments while he was being kicked when he thought he might not survive. He'd taken enough beatings over the years—and doled out his fair share as well—to recognize the thin line between being injured and being killed.

They hadn't intended to kill him; they made that clear. The wound on his throat was superficial, but skillfully placed. It was a warning, but a warning from whom?

Sergeant Gormand and one of the patrol officers were still in Finn's apartment, looking like angels of death, waiting dispassionately to see if he'd live. They'd offered to call an ambulance, but Finn was having none of it. A butterfly bandage held the edges of the cut on his throat together, and was covered with a gauze pad he found under his sink. His ribs were badly bruised, but not broken, so he wasn't about to spend the next twelve hours in an emergency room, waiting for some twenty-five-year-old intern to tell him what he already knew—he'd heal. With rest and time, he'd heal.

"You can't give us anything else on the description?" Gormand was asking without interest.

"No, Sergeant. Like I already said, they came up behind me.

After that, I was too busy trying to defend myself to jot down a sketch of their faces."

"And you don't know of anyone who has a grudge against you?"

Finn rubbed his forehead. "I spent two years as a public defender. Most of the thousand or so people I represented during that time spent some time in jail, so they might be a little grumpy." He looked up at the two cops. "I got some people off, too, and that usually doesn't sit well with your fellow officers. So, who knows?"

Gormand glared at him. "But you can't think of anyone in particular who might be angry enough to do this at the moment?"

"No one comes to mind." Finn hadn't told Gormand about the warning. He was saving that tidbit of information for Flaherty.

"Well then, I'm not sure there's much we can do here," Gormand said. "I called Lieutenant Flaherty like you asked, and she said she'd be here soon. Officer Harris is still outside looking for anything useful, but he's not likely to find anything. I'd ask you to come down to the station to look at some mug shots, but like you say, you were too busy to get a good look at these guys, so I'm not sure what purpose that would serve."

"Yeah, I'm pretty useless," Finn mumbled through the ice pack.

"I'm not saying that," said Gormand defensively. "I'm just pointing out that we don't have a lot to go on right now."

"I understand, Sergeant. If I think of anything else that might be helpful, I'll let you know."

Gormand nodded. "And we'll be in touch if anything develops in the investigation."

Yeah, right, Finn thought. He could tell from the look on Gormand's face that this case would be filed under "D.C."—for "don't care." The "investigation" would never get beyond

Finn's door, and would be over once Gormand passed through it on his way out.

Just then, Flaherty walked through the open door. "What the hell happened?" she demanded, glancing back and forth between Finn and Gormand.

Gormand held up his hands in surrender. "Talk to him," he said. "I gotta get back to the precinct and file one of the shortest reports in history." With that, the policeman was gone, and Finn and Flaherty were alone in the apartment.

"Well?" Flaherty asked again.

"It's nice to see you, too," Finn said, removing the ice pack from his swelling face.

"I'm sorry," she said. "Are you all right? Do you need an ambulance or anything?"

"No, thanks. The sergeant already offered. I'm fine. Just a little banged up, but I've been worse."

"Good," Flaherty said. "Then tell me what this is all about."

"I was jumped from behind by two men when I got home tonight." Finn shook his head in disgust. "I guess I'm not as agile as I used to be. In the old days I would have been able to take them."

"In the old days you would have been the one jumping someone from behind, isn't that more likely?" Flaherty corrected.

"What are you talking about?" Finn flared.

"C'mon, Finn, I can read a rap sheet, for Christ's sake."

"Still investigating me, huh, Lieutenant?" His voice was bitter as he looked away.

Flaherty crossed her arms. "I told you, until I know who killed Natalie Caldwell, everyone is a suspect. I didn't lie to you. Besides"—her voice softened a little—"you must have known we'd eventually run a basic background check on you."

Finn nodded. "Yeah." He looked up at her. "Some mistakes follow you your entire life."

"Two assault and batteries, three breaking and enterings, and a drunk and disorderly?" Flaherty raised her eyebrows. "Seems more like a lifestyle than a mistake."

Finn nodded. "Fair enough, but the assault and batteries were fair fights—not sucker-punch attacks. And the B&Es were to get back my own stuff after it had been stolen from me."

"Why not call the police to get your stuff back?"

Finn shook his head. "That's not how things work in the projects. You settle your own scores if you want to survive."

"What about the drunk and disorderly?" she asked sarcastically. "No excuses for that?"

Finn laughed. "Not a one. That was deserved." He shrugged. "Just boys being boys. You know how it is."

"I know I've seen boys get killed when they're 'just being boys.'"

"It was nothing like that," Finn tried to explain. "You wouldn't understand—you didn't grow up where I did."

Flaherty gave an exasperated sigh. "And tonight? Was this just two kids from your old neighborhood 'just being boys'?"

"No, this was something else," Finn said quietly. A moment of silence passed between them as he decided how much to share with her. She was still thinking he could be the killer.

"Well?" she said finally.

"I'll tell you," Finn began, "but first I need to know what you've turned up on that list I gave you."

Flaherty shook her head. "You know I can't give you that kind of information. How can I make it any clearer: you haven't been eliminated as a suspect."

"Fine, then there's no point in my telling you what happened here tonight."

"You're not helping yourself, Finn. Believe me, I want to clear you of this almost as much as you do, but I can't do that if you're keeping information from me. I'm going to follow this case wherever it leads, but I'm not going to give you a direct line into the investigation. It just can't happen that way." She looked at him with a somber expression. "And understand one thing," she said. "If you *are* guilty, I'm going to nail you to the wall. I won't protect you."

Finn thought for a moment. She was right, he knew. She couldn't possibly give him the information he wanted. At the same time, he needed to know what he was up against. "At least, tell me who on the list you've already talked to, okay?"

Flaherty glared back at him, considering whether to tell him. It wouldn't be like she was sharing any really confidential information, would it? "Fine," she said. "I've only talked to Loring. I don't know if he's told anyone else, though."

Finn rested his face in the ice pack again. "Loring," he repeated.

"Tell me what this is about, Finn. Right now, or that's the last piece of information you'll ever get from me."

He removed the ice pack and pointed to his eye. "This wasn't just boys being boys," he said. "It wasn't a mugging, or a gang initiation, either. This was a warning."

"A warning about what?"

"Natalie's murder," Finn replied. "One of the guys told me to stop asking questions or I'd wind up dead."

Flaherty was dumbstruck. She stared at Finn, not knowing whether to believe him. If it was true, it would go a long way toward clearing him, which was one reason to be skeptical. It would also have implications that she didn't even want to contemplate. She took a deep breath. "Start at the beginning, and tell me everything," she said.

CHAPTER FORTY-EIGHT

Flaherty was five minutes early for her meeting with Governor Clarke, and was asked to wait in a small room off to one side of the suite of offices that housed the governor and his staff. The room looked like it was decorated for high tea in the late 1800s. Two broad armchairs of ornate French design with yellow fleur-de-lis fabric flanked a high-backed loveseat in front of a large oval coffee table set low to the ground. The hardwood floors were covered with a thick oriental rug, and the heavy drapes let in only a hint of natural light from the tall windows along the wall. In a room like this, it was difficult to keep uncivil thoughts in your head, Flaherty thought. Perhaps that was the point.

It felt odd being there. She'd spent days trying to invent a pretext to meet with the governor, but nothing she could come up with seemed reasonable. Then, just when she was considering either giving up entirely or busting her way into the governor's schedule with all the finesse of an agitated moose, she'd received a call from Clarke's secretary, summoning her to the State House.

"Why does the governor want to see me?" she'd asked. It seemed a reasonable question.

"You'll have to take that up with the governor," was the curt reply from his personal secretary.

It seemed odd, but at least it would afford her the opportunity to ask Clarke some questions about Natalie Caldwell.

Flaherty languished in the waiting room for another fifteen minutes before a tall young man in a blue blazer came to fetch her. He greeted her in an overly friendly manner that failed to conceal his assumed superiority.

"Miss Flaherty," he said. "It's a pleasure to meet you. The governor couldn't be more pleased with the job you've done on the Little Jack investigation."

"Thank you," she replied.

He stood there, looking as if he expected her to say something more—as if a mere "thank you" was insufficient acknowledgment of the governor's compliment. But she stared back at him in silence.

"Please, come with me," he said after a painful pause. He led her through the catacomb of offices and anterooms in the governor's suite to the inner sanctum of Clarke's office. The young man, clearly displeased with her lack of solicitude, informed her that the governor would be with her shortly, and withdrew, leaving her alone in the huge office.

Flaherty was amazed. She'd never seen an office as large. In fact, she hadn't seen many apartments as large. It was long and wide, with several distinct areas. On the left side of the room, two deep leather couches faced each other across an antique oriental coffee table, like two aging bulls readying themselves for a confrontation. To the right, four large, comfortable wing-backed chairs bracketed two smaller tables, suggesting more amiable encounters. Toward the back of the room was a secretary's desk, complete with stenotype machine for transcribing conversations. And in the center of the room, against the far windows, was the governor's desk. It made Loring's power piece look like the desk of a schoolchild. It was huge, spreading out at least eight feet wide, with ornate etchings along the corners and elaborate inlays throughout the front panels.

She walked over for a better look, but forgot about the desk when she saw the view through the windows behind it. They looked out over Boston Common, toward the tall buildings downtown, and down in the direction of the harbor. Since Governor Samuel Adams and Paul Revere set the keystone to the building in 1795, the State House and its inhabitants had kept a watchful eye on the continuous growth of the city, checking its expansion through a patchwork of regulations and zoning ordinances, exacting a pound of flesh for each favor and privilege. Little had changed during that time, Flaherty knew. The skyline had risen, but so much of the city's foundation remained bogged down in the quagmire of local and state politics.

"It's a spectacular view, isn't it?" The voice came from behind Flaherty, startling her.

"It is," she agreed as she turned around to face Clarke. She hadn't heard him enter the room.

"Sometimes when I look out there, I'm overwhelmed by the responsibility of this great office. I never knew how humbling it could be, trying to guard the well-being of so many. In some ways, the governorship of Massachusetts is unique. The fortunes of the commonwealth are inseparable from the fortunes of Boston, and as I look out here at the city, I realize I have to balance both state and city politics to do my job properly." The governor was standing next to Flaherty now, gazing out the window in the same direction she had been.

"How does Mayor Tribinio feel about that?" Flaherty asked, which drew a laugh from Clarke.

"He's fine with it, of course," he said. "It's a delicate dance, to be sure, but one that governors and mayors have been doing with varying degrees of grace and success for three hundred years." He smiled. "No one has tripped over anyone else's toes—yet."

"That's some skillful dancing."

The governor laughed again. "It's all a matter of knowing where the spheres of influence lie. The mayor holds his power in the wards of Boston—in the day-to-day running of the city. He runs the machine, if you will. My mandate, on the other hand, is somewhat larger. I represent what the people want the city and state to be—the future they're searching for on a grander scale. I'm expected to be the visionary leader. As a result, the larger projects—the Big Dig, the airport and harbor reconstructions, major city infrastructure changes—those become my bailiwick even more than the mayor's."

"Sounds reasonable enough."

"It is. And it's why I asked you to meet with me today."

"Asked? That's funny. I thought I was ordered." The smirk on the governor's face told Flaherty he liked the perception and recognized the truth in it.

"I'm sorry you were given that impression. Sometimes my staff expresses my desires as edicts. I really just wanted to thank you for the job you've done on the Little Jack case. I challenged you—directly, intentionally—and you came through with flying colors. The city and the commonwealth owe you an enormous debt. As do I. You should feel proud of yourself."

"Thank you, sir. I appreciate that, but you should know that most of the credit belongs to the people who were working with me. They're the ones who broke the case open."

"It's the mark of a good leader that she shares credit with her subordinates. It engenders loyalty, and loyalty is the key to leadership," the governor commented. "But you shouldn't be too modest."

"It's not modesty, it's the truth."

"In any event, it was your operation, and you deserve most of the credit—as well as the lion's share of the spoils. Have you thought about what you'll do with your newfound celebrity?" Clarke raised his eyebrows in a provocative manner. Clearly, there was something on his mind.

"Well," Flaherty said, "first I have to finish the investigation."

"Finish?" Clarke frowned. "I would think that there'd be very little left to investigate."

"There are some open issues regarding the Caldwell woman that we still need to resolve." She watched him closely as she said the words, trying to register any reaction. As far as she could tell, there was none.

"I'm sure you could hand this small part of the investigation off to someone else if necessary, though, am I correct?" Again, Flaherty had the sense that Clarke was trying to entice her somehow, suggesting some as yet undisclosed agenda. She found it annoying, but it did pique her curiosity.

"Did you have something in particular in mind?" she asked, resisting the temptation to waggle her eyebrows back at him in mockery.

Governor Clarke smiled broadly. "Now that you mention it, there's a position opening up you might be interested in. You're familiar, of course, with the federal Department of Homeland Security." Flaherty nodded. "The president is about to announce the creation of parallel agencies at the state level to help in the fight against terrorism. The new Commonwealth Security Department in Massachusetts will begin with an annual budget of one hundred million dollars. The department will liaise with law enforcement personnel at all levels of both federal and state agencies to coordinate and direct investigations into terrorist activities, and will have its own five-hundred-officer police force."

"Sounds like a major initiative," said Flaherty, genuinely impressed.

"It is," Clarke agreed. "And whoever heads it up will have a very major, important job. As we in Massachusetts are particularly aware, terrorism is the greatest threat we all face. So the only question left to be answered is: are you a big enough person to take on the responsibility of heading up this new department?"

"Me?" Flaherty was shocked. She'd expected him to offer her a position as a deputy in the department. The thought of *heading* it . . . "I could never—"

"Lead this department?" Clarke interrupted. "Nonsense, of course you could. You have the required law enforcement background. You understand what needs to happen both on the prevention side of the equation and on the investigative side. Plus, I've been watching you on television throughout this entire Little Jack ordeal. You possess the poise and the political skills necessary to deal with other agencies, as well as the press. I've been very impressed. I know you can do the job. The only question is whether you're brave enough to take it."

Flaherty's head was swimming. It was the type of career opportunity that only came along once. More than that, it was the chance to do something really important—to take her training and her intuition and put them to work preventing crimes on a massive scale.

"I'd have to finish up the work I'm doing now, and that might take another month or so," she said hesitantly.

"I'm afraid that wouldn't be possible. The job requires you to start within two weeks," Clarke explained.

"That soon?" she said, showing her disappointment. "It's just that there are still some questions about whether Townsend actually killed Natalie Caldwell." Saying the words was enough to break the spell, and a sickeningly obvious thought crossed her mind. It made her angry. "That reminds me," she said, forcing herself to focus on the questions she'd come to ask in the first place, "I meant to ask you if you knew Ms. Caldwell."

Clarke shook his head. "No. I never had the pleasure."

"That's curious," Flaherty said in an offhand manner. "I was going through her personal effects the other day, and I came across a picture of the two of you standing together."

Clarke forced a smile and a quizzical look. "That's odd," he said. "Although, I appear so many places and at so many functions, and so many people ask to have their picture taken with me—particularly during campaign season—that it's quite possible she obtained that picture without our ever having been introduced."

"That's a possibility," Flaherty said, again filling her tone with indifference. She paused, and then crinkled her nose as though considering an inconsequential but nettlesome riddle. "Although, now that I think about it, I believe the picture was signed by you." Clarke's smile disappeared. "Yes, that's right, it said something about thanking her for her work on a committee, and it was signed 'Bill.' Does that make any sense to you?"

Clarke was doing an impressive job of keeping his composure, Flaherty noted, but his face had gone white, and his brow was slightly furrowed. "Really?" he said. "Well, there are literally hundreds of committees I have minimal involvement with, although I've probably met many of the committee members. I don't remember most of them, naturally. I'll have my assistant run through our records and see if Ms. Caldwell was on any of these committees. In any event, I have no recollection of ever having met the woman."

It was a weak story, and they both knew it as they stood there in the governor's office in front of the grand windows overlooking Boston Common. Neither of them, it seemed, had anything further to say.

"Well," Flaherty said finally, "it would be helpful if you could have your assistant check that out. We just want to be sure Townsend actually killed all of these women. We wouldn't want to find out later that we left a murderer walking around free."

"Of course," Clarke replied. "I'll have that information messengered over to your office by the end of the day." He swept his arm toward the door, inviting her to leave. "I'll walk you out," he offered. There was an uncomfortable silence as they made their way toward the door. As they neared the threshold, he turned to her. "Do you read much for pleasure, Detective?" he asked.

"Occasionally," she replied.

"You should read Machiavelli's *The Prince* if you ever get the chance. It's still considered one of the leading manuals for political survival, and it might help you if you take this new job."

"I'll be sure to pick up a copy."

He smiled again, but this time it contained no warmth. "You know, one piece of advice he gives is still as true today as it was five hundred years ago."

"Really?" Flaherty asked. "What's that?"

They were at the door now, and Clarke faced her fully, holding on to her arm at the elbow and looking straight into her face. "He advised that if you're going to plot to assassinate a prince, you'd better make damned sure you succeed."

This time it was Flaherty who smiled. "Good advice in any age, I suppose."

Clarke nodded. "I'll need an answer on the job offer within a week," he said. "You should seriously consider it."

CHAPTER FORTY-NINE

Finn took Friday off from work. He had to. The bruises on his face were too pronounced to hide, and he knew he'd never escape hard questions he couldn't answer. By Monday the swelling would be down, he reasoned, and he might be able to pass off his injuries as a basketball mishap.

Besides, the wonders of modern communication had made working from home realistic. Often he found he was able to get more accomplished when he stayed out of the office, away from the constantly ringing telephone and ever-pressing minor emergencies. At home, he could access his messages when he needed, and log on to the law firm's server directly. He called his assistant, Nancy, to let her know he wouldn't be in, and to contact him at home if anything really urgent came up.

"This isn't a Friday morning hangover, is it?" she asked playfully.

"No," he said. "I didn't have a single drink last night. I just can't make it in today. If Preston calls, or if there are any real emergencies, just call me here. If you can't reach me here, try my cell phone; I'll have that with me."

"Will do," Nancy said, "and I hope you feel better."

After he hung up he walked into the bathroom and looked in the mirror again. It wasn't pretty. His right eye was swollen and turning purple, the discoloration spreading like a tide from his cheekbone. His lip was split at the center, making it painful to smile, or frown, or eat, or speak. He touched his throat where the knife had slit the skin. The bandages were dark red from sopping up the blood, but there was no fresh bleeding, and the butterfly bandage was already pulling the corners of the gash together. He shivered as he thought about the knife edge slicing into his neck, close enough to the carotid artery to drive home the warning.

He sighed at his appearance, wincing as his rib cage contracted with the painful expulsion of breath, the bruises enough to make each movement an individual agony. It was better that he'd stayed home, he thought. The partners would have too many questions.

Looking into the mirror, for just a moment Finn saw a younger version of himself: a little thinner, and a little stronger, with the hunger of his childhood visible in his soul, and anger flowing through his veins. In many ways he'd left his stray-dog youth behind. Often he'd go days without thinking about his past. But it was always there, he knew; the skeleton of his prior life lurking beneath the well-fed layer that had covered it with the passage of time.

He opened the medicine cabinet and took out some ibuprofen, washing down three pills with tap water, then swallowing a fourth after a brief internal debate. He closed the cabinet, and as the mirror swung back into place, he was startled to see a reflection behind him, looming in silence.

"Tigh! For Christ's sake, what the hell are you doing, trying to kill me?"

Tigh McCluen smiled in the mirror. "It would take more than a start to kill you, I hope." He took a good long look at Finn's reflection, noting the cuts and bruises with some admiration. "Besides," he said, "it looks as if someone else has been giving it a bit more of an effort." He regarded Finn. "What the hell happened?"

"Disgruntled client," Finn quipped.

McCluen nodded. "I've always said you'd be better off in an honest profession."

"I'll give it some thought. How'd you get in here?" Finn asked.

"The door was open," Tigh replied with a familiar roguish look. "I let myself in."

"The door was locked," Finn corrected.

"Only once, Scotty boy. I consider a single lock practically an open invitation. So did you at one time." He winked at his friend.

"Why didn't you just knock? I'd have let you in, for Christ sakes."

"I thought you'd be at work. I was just planning on leaving you a note. I had no idea you'd be here—or that you'd be looking like haggis."

"That bad, huh?" Finn asked, feeling a rush of pride in his gruesome appearance. He often worried that his old friends thought he'd gone too soft, and he liked Tigh's seeing he could still take a beating and keep his sense of humor.

Tigh cocked his head to one side and held up his thumb, like an art critic appraising a new work, taking a closer look at the carnage. "Well, no matter," he said, laughing. "You were never much of a looker anyway."

Finn laughed. "What are you doing here?" he asked. "This is twice that I've seen you in as many weeks, and that after, what, three years? If I didn't know better, I'd say you were stalking me."

The smile disappeared from Tigh's face. "Not stalking you enough, as it turns out. I meant to stop by here yesterday, and the day before that, but I just couldn't seem to find the time. More's the point, I didn't know exactly what to tell you." He paused. "Lookin' at you now, it seems clear I should have come sooner."

Finn's hand went instinctively to his throat, probing the raw spot around the edges of the cut gently, then trailing up to evaluate the bruises on his jaw and cheeks. "You know who did this, don't you."

Tigh shook his head. "Not exactly. And certainly not to tell anyone."

Finn glared at his old friend. "What was that expression you told me the last time we spoke? *'Don't see what you see. Don't hear what you hear. And if you're asked, say you don't know'*?"

McCluen nodded. "That's it exactly, Scotty."

"It's a shitty motto to live by, Tigh."

"It's a shitty world to live in, Finn." He paused. "At least, it still is for me."

Finn sighed in understanding, if not agreement. He remembered the world Tigh lived in—the world from which Finn had escaped. There were rules that were inviolable, and chief among them was: *Silence is golden*. Tigh didn't make the rules, Finn knew, but he had to play by them.

"So why are you here if you have nothing to tell me?" Finn asked.

"To warn you," Tigh replied.

"My second warning in as many days."

Tigh nodded. "So it would seem. I can't tell you who did it, or who ordered it done, because I genuinely don't know. But I can tell you that I've heard your name bandied about in conversation in certain circles where it's never good to be known. I'm not sure what it is you've done, but it's pissed off the wrong people."

"I haven't done anything!" Finn yelled. "I'm just trying to figure out who killed my best friend!"

"Maybe that's a job for the authorities, Scotty. It certainly looks like it would be safer if you left it up to them."

Finn shook his head. "The authorities think maybe I did it, that's part of the problem. If I don't find out who killed her, I might end up in prison."

"There's worse things," said Tigh pointedly.

Finn glowered. "I'm *not* going back there, Tigh. Never."

Tigh held up his hands. "Just trying to look out for you, that's all." A sad smile slowly returned to his face. "You got any smokes, Scotty? I'm fresh out."

"Yeah, over there in my pocket," Finn said, pointing to the suit jacket thrown over one of the living room chairs. "I think there are matches in there, too."

"Don't need them." Tigh pulled a small silver object out of his pocket and held it up. "That's the other reason I came." He flipped the object quickly in his palm, producing a huge flame in what almost seemed like an act of magic. He lit the cigarette between his lips and flipped his wrist again, extinguishing the flame. "I found this in my drawer the other day, and I was going to leave it here for you." He tossed the warm Zippo lighter across the room.

Finn caught it with one hand and held it up. It was battered and dented, like some piece of well-used military equipment brought home and forgotten after years of active service. The inscription had faded as the years wore down the casing, but it was still legible. "*Chelsea Street Regulars*," Finn read out loud, and then looked up at McCluen.

"That there is a collector's item," Tigh said.

Finn nodded. "Only five ever made. I lost mine years ago."

"I know. And who knows where Jimmy and Joe left theirs. It's hard to get answers from corpses. As for Willie . . . well, once you've been in the joint for as long as he has, your brain turns to mush and you put away childhood dreams."

Finn laughed bitterly. "We were going to take over all of Charlestown."

"Indeed, we were going to wipe out the Winter Hill Gang

and make a name for ourselves," said Tigh. "Then we were going to take on those fuckin' wops in the North End. You know why?"

"Because, *Nobody fucks with the Chelsea Street Regulars*!" They both chanted their adolescent slogan in unison.

"I can't keep this," Finn said after he'd stopped laughing. "It's probably the last one."

"You keep it," Tigh said. "You and I are the only two left. I'm still here because I'm the biggest, meanest son of a bitch in this town. You're still here because you were the smart one and you got out. Now, I can't stop being mean. Can you stop being smart?"

"What does that mean?"

"Let this thing with the girl die like she did. Let the authorities take care of it. It's the smart thing to do."

"Who sent you, Tigh?"

"Nobody sent me, Scotty. I just came here to give an old friend some good advice. I'm hoping you're smart enough to take it."

"Fuck that, Tigh. And fuck you. You and I go too far back for this. Tell me who sent you."

"I'm being straight with you, Scotty. Nobody sent me, I'm here on my own."

"What have you become?"

"The same as you, Scotty—a survivor. That involves compromises no matter what your job title says, you know what I'm saying?" Finn didn't answer. "Now don't go getting all high and mighty on me. We've known each other too long to lie to each other like that."

"What if I can't let it drop?" Finn asked after a moment.

"Who knows for sure?" Tigh answered, shrugging. "But there's one thing I do know." He smiled. "You're not a Chelsea Street Regular anymore."

CHAPTER FIFTY

"What do you think?" Flaherty asked.

"I think this is getting messy," Kozlowski said. "Governor Clarke really threatened you?"

"Not directly, but the message was clear. There's no doubt he wants us to back off any investigation involving him. And if we continue, I'd say we'll be in an all-out war."

Kozlowski was sitting across from Flaherty in a booth at O'-Malley's across from the Fleet Center in the no-man's-land between downtown, Beacon Hill, and the North End. It was a cop bar, except on nights when the Bruins or the Celtics were playing at home. Then it turned into a smear of drunken jerseys singing the lament of the Boston faithful. Cops stayed away on those nights—too much hassle to deal with. But this was the end of August, when the Fleet Center was quiet except for the occasional rock concert.

As he sipped his scotch Kozlowski ran his fingers over the thick, ugly scar that ran down the side of his face. His medical insurance would have covered the simple plastic surgery that could correct his appearance, but he'd never bothered to have the operation.

"What are you thinking?" Flaherty asked.

"I'm just considering the possibility that the governor is not involved in this, and maybe we're making a mistake by pushing the issue."

"That doesn't sound like the Kozlowski I know," Flaherty said. She looked concerned. "What's this really about, partner?"

Kozlowski shook his head and took a long sip of his drink. He put his glass on the table and looked up at Flaherty. "I'm thinking about Tony Garibaldi," he said.

"Your first partner? 'The Legend'?"

"Yeah, my first partner. 'The Legend.'" Kozlowski played his half-empty glass back and forth between his fat, stubby fingers. "Have I ever told you how I got my scar?"

"No," Flaherty said quietly. She'd never asked, and he'd never offered. She was curious at one time, but then she began to see that to her partner it was more than just a physical scar, and she'd left it alone, respecting his privacy. She'd heard the rumors, and she knew it had something to do with the night that Garibaldi—a hero within the department—had been killed.

"It was the night Tony Garibaldi saved my life," Kozlowski began. "This was more than twenty years ago. Tony was about ten years older than me, and I was a rookie who worshipped him. He taught me most of what I know about being a cop." He took another sip of his drink, gathering himself as he launched into his pile of discarded memories.

"At one point, after we'd been riding together for about a year, we stumbled onto what we thought was a massive cocaine ring. It was going to be a huge bust for us—particularly for me, because I was the one who discovered it. The one hitch was, it looked like there were police officers involved. Tony suggested we take it slow and talk to some of the higher-ups in the department—cut a deal and take the drug dealers out quietly. But I was young, and full of piss, so I pushed him. I thought I could make a real reputation for myself.

"One night we finally moved in and busted four of the guys

during a score. One of the guys pulled out a shotgun and pointed it square into my chest. I knew right then I was a dead man. But as I saw the guy pull the trigger, Tony dove at me and pushed me out a window. That was how I sliced open my face."

"What happened to Tony?"

"He took the shotgun blast right in the head. He was dead before he hit the floor."

"They caught the guys, though, didn't they?"

"Yeah, they did. Three of them were cops. It hurt like hell losing Tony, but I felt like we'd done our job. You know, when you're young you can deal with the idea of death, as long as it seems to mean something—as long as there's a principle or a purpose involved."

Flaherty nodded. "There's something to that, though, isn't there? The sacrifices we make as cops have to be worth something, don't they?"

Kozlowski smiled, and the irony locked into his jaw gave Flaherty a pit in her stomach. "A year or so later I went to the jail to visit one of the cops we busted. He was a guy I knew—we were even friends. I wanted to know how it happened. You know what he told me?"

Flaherty shook her head.

"That Tony had been the ringleader of the group that was dealing drugs. He'd set up the whole operation. The night he was killed—he set that up, too. The plan was to murder me because I wouldn't let the investigation drop."

Flaherty frowned. "If he set you up to be killed, why save your life?"

Kozlowski shrugged, and his tired smile held more sadness than Flaherty could comprehend. "I've been wondering about that for the last two decades. I don't know. He must have changed his mind. Maybe, deep down, he knew he couldn't live with murder. Who knows? I'd like to think he redeemed himself in that last action. I'd like to think that when he's judged, that last impulse will be enough to get him off the hook for all the other shit he did. He meant so much to me."

Flaherty shook her head. "The guy in jail must have been lying to you," she insisted. "Just to get back at you for pushing the investigation and getting him busted."

Kozlowski smiled again. "I did my own investigation after that. Quietly, on my own. I found the money. I found the contact sheets. Tony was up to his eyeballs in the thing. I never told anyone, though. He was a hero in the department by then. The Legend. There just didn't seem to be any point in dragging his memory through the gutter and giving the whole department a black eye."

The two police detectives sat in silence for several minutes. Neither could think of anything to say. "So what do you want to do?" Flaherty asked at last.

"I want to take it slow," Kozlowski said. He pointed to the side of his face. "I kept this scar to remind myself that nothing is the way it looks at first. Not even me. It helps to reinforce that nothing is more dangerous to a cop than a partial picture. You need to have all of the pieces in front of you before you can solve any puzzle. So, we go on with our digging, but we dig carefully, and quietly." He looked at her and raised his glass in a pact. "And most important, we dig deep."

CHAPTER FIFTY-ONE

Finn lit his cigarette, wincing at the pain in his split lip as he inhaled. He held up the lighter in front of his face, reading the inscription over and over again. That part of his past was a blur to him now—the time when he and Tigh ran the show down on Chelsea Street. Screening his memories held no more reality to him now than watching a documentary. The images flashed briefly and then disappeared without letting him feel the grime under his fingernails, or smell the acid on the 3 a.m. streets.

Those streets had been filled with a lust and danger that no longer existed for him. His was a paper world now, he thought with a tinge of regret. He spent his days pushing mountains of paper back and forth, organizing the facts of others' experiences into neat written summaries for judges and juries. As a lawyer, he never really got his hands dirty. He never had to reach down and grab hold of the pain that the people he represented—or litigated against—felt. To him they were just numbers on a settlement analysis sheet.

He'd known the pain firsthand, once. He'd sat on an empty street, silent except for an excited dog braying in the distance following the fury, holding Joey's head as he bled out his young life into Charlestown's gutters, watching his best friend plead with him for one more day to make his life right. They'd been thrown together since before Finn could remember, and as little boys, defenseless in a world without compassion, they'd clung to each other in a pretense of safety. Taking their beatings together had somehow lessened the pain and the fear. Later, when they were in their teens, and they'd adopted the ways of their tormentors, terrorizing the residents of Chelsea Street, they'd relied on each other for the strength to be vicious. Without each other, they'd never have been able to fight their consciences to do the things that were necessary to survive.

On that night so many years ago, Finn had held Joey and listened to his best friend pour out a list of things he'd wanted to do with his life—a litany Finn had only suspected, within both Joey and himself. Then, after Joey's lips had stilled and his eyes had glazed over, Finn slipped away before the police arrived to ask questions.

He'd never forgotten the desperation in his friend's voice, though, and it had changed him. From that moment on, everything he did was directed toward getting out. Tigh had noticed the change, and at first tried to drag Finn back into the streets. But finally he accepted it, and gave Finn the distance he needed to succeed. It was, Finn knew, one of the greatest gifts he'd received.

Now that he was out of that life, he wondered what he'd really gained. Another friend had been taken from him, and he still felt the same helplessness and impotence he had nearly two decades before. His new life hadn't given him the power to protect Natalie, or even avenge her murder, and the pain that he felt now laid bare the dimensionless nature of the world he'd chosen.

Finn was so lost in his thoughts that he didn't hear the phone until the third ring. He reached over to the end table and picked it up. "Hello," he said dully.

"Finn, it's Nancy." Finn recognized his secretary's voice. He cleared his throat and tried to sound professional.

"Yes, Nancy, what's up?"

"Nick Williams stopped by, looking for you. He says it's urgent."

"Okay, can you give me his extension?" Finn asked. He wrote down the number. "Anything else?"

"The only other call was from Peter Bostick. No urgency, he said."

"You might as well give me his number." Finn jotted it down and hung up. He stared at the phone numbers in front of him. He had no interest in dealing with work at the moment. It all seemed so pointless. He thought back to the deposition of Amy Tannery. She'd been so strong, so determined. Finn wished he had a fraction of her strength. He knew though, that he had to push through the pain and do his job—if for no other reason than to not let down Preston. He looked at the numbers again, then he picked up the phone.

Finn waited patiently on the line until Williams's assistant picked up.

"Hi, Finn, yes, he's in his office. Let me just put you through."

"Finn, where have you been? I've been looking for you," Williams said when he came on the line.

"I'm just working from home," Finn said, somewhat embarrassed. In the macho world of big-firm litigation, lawyers took pride in not allowing minor inconveniences like illness, or childbirth, or holidays to affect their work schedule.

"Well, I've got some great news. Are you ready for this? They want to settle."

Finn hesitated. "Who wants to settle?"

"The widow Tannery. I got a call from Barnolk this morning. They're ready to cut a deal."

Finn was puzzled. "What are you talking about? They said they'd never be interested in any settlements." He remembered Amy Tannery at her deposition, the picture of determination. It seemed unlikely she'd settle the case for any amount of money.

"I know, I know, isn't it awesome? Man, talking to Barnolk he was practically begging me, he was so desperate to get out of the case."

"How much are they asking?" Finn queried. He remembered the calculation that, to break even as compared to the settlement Amy Tannery would have received under the Federal Victims Compensation Act, she needed to collect at least five million dollars.

"Barnolk opened at ten million, and I just laughed. He didn't even pause before he was down to seven and a half million. At that point, I thought he could be serious about settling. I let him sweat for a little before suggesting two point five might work. I swear to God, I hadn't finished my sentence when he dropped to five million. I still have to get sign-off from the client, but it looks like we're going to get out of this mess for three point seven five million!" Williams was clearly excited.

"Holy shit!" Finn exclaimed. "After taxes and Barnolk's cut, she'll end up with less than she would have gotten from the government!"

"More important," Williams pointed out, "it's well below Huron's insurance cap. They're going to get out of this thing without paying a dime."

"Other than our legal fees," Finn corrected.

"Well, of course. Justice must be served. But that's the best money they've ever spent. Not only is insurance going to cover this, but Huron will be done with the issue without any finding of negligence or wrongdoing."

"Does that really matter?" Finn asked.

"Are you kidding?" Williams blurted. "That's what matters most. Huron is competing for additional contracts—and not just in Massachusetts, but in other states as well. If there was ever a finding of negligence or wrongdoing, they'd have to close up shop. No one would ever hire them again."

"So the client's got to be pretty happy."

"You have a gift for understatement, Finn," Williams said. "The client is thrilled."

Finn was silent for a moment before saying hesitantly, "It's kind of weird, though, isn't it?"

"What do you mean?" Williams asked.

"It seems out of character for Barnolk, don't you think? I mean, the guy loves publicity, and this trial would have put his face on the nightly news for a month. And Mrs. Tannery seemed determined not to settle—acted as if the lawsuit had nothing to do with money."

There was silence on the other end of the line. "Yeah, I see what you mean," Williams said at last. "It does seem a little odd." He paused again. "Then again, I read the transcript of the deposition you took of Amy Tannery, and it was fantastic. You ripped into her pretty hard. It may just be that they realized that they had no case, and that taking this thing to trial was only going to drag her husband's reputation through the gutter."

Finn considered the possibility and rejected it. "I don't think that's it," he said. "She seemed pretty dedicated to the case. I think it's something else."

"Like what?"

Finn worked the possibilities in his mind. "How well do you know Tony McGuire?" he asked Nick.

"Huron's president?" Williams considered the question. "Not

well, really. I know he's one of Preston's biggest clients, and I know he pays the bills on time. Other than that, I've only met him a couple of times, and he seemed like a decent guy. He's a little demanding, but then, what client isn't?" There was silence on the line again. "What are you thinking, Finn?"

"I don't know, Nick. Something about Huron just doesn't feel right."

"Like what?"

There was no point in dragging Nick into his own paranoid delusions, Finn realized, and he really had nothing to back up his suspicions. "It's nothing," he said. "Don't worry about it."

"You gotta lighten up, Finn, you know?"

"Yeah, I know. Any way you look at this, it's a great victory for the client, and that's what really matters."

"It's not just a victory for the client, Finn, it's a huge victory for you. Don't think for a second this isn't going to give you a significant boost toward partnership. Preston already had a very high opinion of you, and your work on this case is only going to reaffirm that. I'd say your future here is pretty much guaranteed."

Less than a month before, that news would have thrilled Finn. It was what he'd been hoping to hear for more than six years. But now, somehow, it all seemed less important. It felt like he was being played by forces hiding in the shadows, and it set him off. He felt like he'd spent too much of his life running other people's errands, and doing other people's dirty work. He was tired and fed up. "Thanks," he said weakly.

If Williams noticed Finn's lack of enthusiasm, he didn't acknowledge it. "No problem, Finn, you deserve it. Just to warn you, though, you're probably going to be the one putting together the settlement papers, so don't get too comfortable hanging out at home on a weekday."

"I won't. Thanks again, Nick."

"I'll see you, Finn."

Finn hung up the phone, still stunned by the turn of events. He thought back to the deposition of Amy Tannery. Had he misread her? Was this lawsuit always really about money? No, he decided. There was something else going on. His mind kept drifting back to the exchange between McGuire and Barnolk after McGuire's deposition. He wondered what McGuire had said to Barnolk that shocked him so, and whether it had anything to do with Mrs. Tannery's willingness to settle.

He was still in shock when the phone rang.

"Finn here," he said into the receiver.

"Hey, Finn, it's Bostick."

"Hello, Bostick, I meant to call you to check in. How is everything?"

"Not too bad. As long as you keep feeding me work, I'll keep eating."

"Not that it matters particularly anymore, but did you ever get any word on the addresses I gave you the other day?" Finn asked. He'd been so busy with other issues, he hadn't thought to follow up on the issue.

"That's what I was calling you about."

"Well?"

"I'm not sure I want to talk about it over the phone. I found something a little screwy. Can you meet me?"

Finn looked at his watch and noted that it was already noon. He needed to go out to get some lunch anyway. "Where do you want to meet?"

"How about at the address you gave me for Carter in Southie. Do you have it?"

"Sure. Twelve forty-five okay?"

"Sounds good." Finn could detect some stress in Bostick's voice.

"Is everything okay?" Finn asked.

"Yeah," Bostick replied. "I just think we should talk about this in person."

"All right. I'll see you in a little while."

Finn hung up. He was puzzled. It wasn't like Bostick to get spooked—he'd spent too much time on the police force for that. And yet, that was how he sounded—spooked.

CHAPTER FIFTY-TWO

Finn drove to Southie. He wanted to get back that feeling of control that had deserted him again, and behind the wheel he felt, at least for the moment, powerful. Nothing made sense anymore. It seemed as if the world were closing in on him; like an ever-narrowing peephole crowding his vision. Maybe he shouldn't fight it. Perhaps he should loosen his grip and allow himself to be swept away in whatever currents were gathering against him. It would be easier, he knew, but it wasn't his way, and he knew that even better.

The drive into South Boston led through the heart of the city, and took him into the continuing construction of the Big Dig. The project had been approved by Congress in 1992 as a six-year, two-and-a-half-billion-dollar undertaking to sink under the streets the elevated interstate highway that snaked through Boston, opening up a thick ribbon of green space to encircle the city. Fourteen years and fifteen billion dollars later, the project was still not fully completed. Corruption and inefficiency had caused massive delays and cost overruns, and left an open scar on the city's cheek that seemed destined never to heal. To facilitate the construction effort, the streets that led across the gaping divide separating the two halves of the city were opened and closed without pattern or warning, and it took Finn two tries to make his way through the construction and around into Southie.

Once through, he headed toward the far end of the neighborhood, passing along the outcroppings of urban renewal that had sprouted up in this old, traditional, blue-collar section of the city. Housing prices in the heart of the city had driven many of the young, trendy, upwardly mobile residents to Boston's edges, and although the old-timers were putting up a fight, they were losing the battles for the streets that had been theirs for four generations. It was a silent campaign, fought with cold shoulders and angry stares, but without real violence, and the outcome was never really in doubt. The invading armies had better resources and more time with which to wage an agonizing war of attrition. Many of the older residents were already selling out and slipping away resentfully to points farther out on the urban sprawl.

Finn eased his car down Dorchester Street and took a left onto Preble Street, finally merging onto William J. Day Boulevard near the shoreline. He pulled up behind Bostick's battered blue Ford and got out. Bostick was leaning on the hood of his car waiting for him.

"What the hell happened to you?" the private investigator said, frowning when Finn came close enough for him to see the bruises on his face.

Finn rubbed his jaw nervously. It was time to test out his cover story. "I took a nasty fall playing hoops last night, caught the floor pretty hard," he said.

Bostick narrowed his eyes and took a closer look. The scrutiny made Finn even more self-conscious. Then Bostick whistled. "Looks more like the floor caught you, and more than once from the look of it—on both sides of your face, too." He looked again. "You didn't do anything to piss off this floor, did you? Hit on its girlfriend or something?"

"I don't want to talk about it."

Bostick shrugged. "Suits me, you're the one paying the bills. I'm just saying it might hurt less next time if the floor wasn't wearing rings on its fingers."

"So, what's so important you can't tell me over the phone?" Finn asked, trying to change the subject.

Bostick nodded at the derelict house in front of them. The shutters were kicked in, and the glass in the windows was broken. The falling-down structure sat at the edge of the road, close to the sidewalk, like something discarded on trash day. The only part that looked cared for was the mailbox, which gleamed in the afternoon sun.

Bostick handed Finn a piece of paper. "That's one of them," he said.

Finn looked at the paper. It was the list of three addresses he'd asked Bostick to check out. He looked over it, checking the street number. Sure enough, the crumbling structure was on the list.

"So which one of our boys lives here?" Finn asked.

"None of them," Bostick replied.

"What do you mean?"

"Just what I said. None of them lives here. In fact, I'm not even sure that anyone has been inside that building in years. This is supposed to be where Carter lives with his wife and two children. It's where they supposedly lived for the last two years while he was a guard for the Massachusetts Transportation Safety Commission Guard Unit, but I've looked in the windows and, trust me, no one has lived in there for a long, long time."

Finn thought for a moment. "Could it be just a bad address?"

"Yes and no," Bostick said.

"What does that mean?"

"It means that this is the correct address for this guy—this is where he's had his checks sent every week—it's just that the identification for the *guy himself* is all wrong."

Finn shook his head. "I'm not following you."

"What I'm telling you is that this is the correct information from Huron Security, but I've run this guy's name through every database known to man, and I've come up with nothing. I ran him through search engines, through credit files, through the IRS—I even had a friend at the FBI do a search, and every single search came up empty."

"Empty?"

"Empty. As in no information. As in, this guy doesn't exist, he's a phantom."

Finn looked down at the list in his hand and then back up at the deserted building, rechecking the addresses. They still matched, but he couldn't seem to grasp what it all meant. "What about the other names on the list?" he asked.

"Same deal. The social security numbers are all fakes, the addresses are dummies, and no government agency other than the Guard Unit has heard of these guys."

"So where do we go from here?"

Bostick rubbed his hands together as if they were cold, even though the temperature was still in the seventies. "I don't think you understand what I'm saying. I've already gone everywhere I know to go, and I'm not sure I want to go any further anyways. Do you know how hard it is to invent a whole person and get away with it?" He shook his head again. "I kept this all off the books—you're not gonna be billed a dime—but I'm bowing out of this investigation if it's all the same to you."

"Why?"

Bostick stared at Finn, conscious that the young lawyer still wasn't putting the pieces together. "Huron Security, which you represent, and which hired these guys for the Guard Unit, is one of the biggest companies in Massachusetts. It's also one of the most difficult to get information on. It's privately owned, and they don't disclose anything to anyone, other than what they put on their info sheets to the state. But I did some checking with folks I know in the security business. Huron is connected with some pretty shady people. I don't think I want this kind of company knowing I'm sniffing around. That's more than I'm willing to do at this point in my life."

"What is it you're worried about, exactly?"

Bostick started to get frustrated. "Hey, look, what do I know, huh? It's just that this company hires people using false identification, and then they disappear right after the Anniversary Bombing. These guys had access to the rail yard where the explosives were planted on the train that blew up. Who knows? Maybe these guys had a reason to disappear. I'm not sure I want to find out, y'know? What made you focus on these guys anyways?"

Finn hesitated. This was a complication he hadn't expected, and he wasn't sure how much information he wanted to divulge about the Tannery case. "Nothing in particular, they were just potential witnesses we couldn't put our hands on."

"Yeah, well, maybe there's a reason you can't put your hands on them. Maybe they had something to do with the bombing."

Finn shook his head. "That doesn't make any sense. What possible motive could Huron have for protecting these guys if they had something to do with the bombing?"

"Who knows? Maybe some wealthy Arabs paid Huron off. Or maybe they realized the security business would go through the ceiling if there was another attack. Or maybe they weren't aware of the deception until afterwards, and they got so angry they made these guys disappear permanently." Bostick drew his fingers across his neck in a gruesome gesture. "It doesn't matter what the reason is, Finn. All that matters is that this feels a little too hot for me to deal with. I'm out."

"I still don't buy it," Finn said. "There's got to be an angle we're missing." He frowned, thinking through the various scenarios. He'd found the guards' names in Natalie's notes, and sometime after she'd made those notes, she'd been killed. Finn wondered if there was a connection. "I need your help," he pleaded.

Bostick shook his head. "I told you, I'm out. It's not worth the paycheck."

"It's not worth the paycheck?" Finn echoed. "You said yourself you're keeping this off the books, so nobody's going to have any idea you're involved. Besides, you used to be a cop. I would think that if there really were some connection between Huron and the Anniversary Bombing, you'd want to find out about it."

"I was a lousy cop," Bostick said, shrugging.

"Oh, come on. If you really believe that these people had anything to do with the bombing, you can't be willing to let them get away with it, can you?"

Bostick rubbed his face in exasperation. It was clear he was less than enamored with the idea of becoming involved in this case, but Finn had stirred up something in his conscience. "Aw, fuck. All right, what do you want me to do?"

"All I want you to do is to run the names of more of Huron's security guards through the searches you did to see if there are more phantoms."

"Why?"

"I don't know, really, but something isn't right here. I need to know if these guards are anomalies, or if there's some sort of a pattern. It might also help us figure out if Huron had anything to do with the bombing. If not, it should let you sleep easier."

"Okay," Bostick said. "But how are we going to get the list of names?"

"We're going to my office right now to get it. We can use the computers there."

"You're going to go to your office looking like that?" Bostick asked, pointing to the bruises on Finn's face. "I've got to tell you, the basketball story doesn't hold water."

Finn thought for a moment. He really didn't want to be seen at the firm looking the way he did, but he needed answers fast, and the only way to get them was to go through the materials filed there. "It might not fool a former cop, but I think I can sell it to anyone we run into," Finn said of his cover story. "Besides, I'll try to keep a low profile."

Bostick nodded. "Okay, but after this I'm out, understood?"

CHAPTER FIFTY-THREE

"Is that the last name?"

"That's it."

"What's the total?" Finn was standing behind Bostick, who was seated at a computer terminal in the Howery, Black war room. They'd been there for five hours, and they were both bone-weary and red-eyed. They'd walked into the offices quickly and quietly, with Finn keeping his head down to avoid any scrutiny of his bruises, and they'd been lucky. They hadn't run into anyone who would have wanted to talk to Finn, and they'd managed to make it to the converted conference room without anyone noticing his appearance.

Now the nerves of both men were frayed from staring at the computer screen, but they'd completed their task, plugging all of the names of Huron's guards into various search tools and proprietary locator services. There were more than a thousand names in all, and it had been grueling work, but they'd done it—one by one—painstakingly investigating every individual. It was time to see how many of the names were fictitious.

"One hundred and seven," Bostick replied after a brief pause to tally the numbers.

Finn let out a low, astonished whistle. "One hundred and seven," he repeated. It was almost inconceivable.

"That's according to our searches," Bostick pointed out. "The search engines we used aren't perfect, although the social security database program that I accessed is pretty good. I would say that all these tools together have at least a ninety-nine percent success rate at locating people."

"So, any way you look at it, there are at least one hundred guards who don't exist, who have been getting paid salaries and benefits by Huron, according to our information."

Bostick nodded. "I'd say that's about right."

Finn whistled again. "Holy shit. We've stumbled onto some very dangerous information, haven't we?"

"I'd say so," Bostick agreed. "I don't get it, though. They wouldn't need this many false identities to facilitate a terrorist attack, would they?"

"No, but I don't think this has anything to do with terrorism. This has to do with money. I don't think these are false identities—I think these people never existed."

"But why?" Bostick asked.

"The starting salary for a guard in the Massachusetts Transportation Safety Commission is more than fifty thousand dollars. Multiply that times one hundred, and you have five million dollars. I think this was government fraud, pure and simple. Somebody was pocketing this money. You said before that Huron is connected to some pretty shady people, didn't you?"

Bostick nodded. "Mob," he said.

"That makes sense. This kind of government scam is right up the mob's alley."

"How could they possibly have thought they'd get away with it, though? Wouldn't they have known that someone would catch them?"

"Nobody did for more than two years," Finn pointed out. "If it wasn't for the Anniversary Bombing, I don't know that anyone would have ever noticed. The mob has enough control over the unions to keep them quiet, and as long as they've got someone involved on the government side, who's going to report them?"

"Do you really think they could get someone in the government to go along with all this?"

Finn thought for a moment about McGuire's friendship with Governor Clarke. It had always struck him as odd. Perhaps this explained it. He wasn't ready to tell Bostick, though. "I think it's possible," was all he said.

"I can't believe we're the first people to figure all this out."

We're not, Finn thought. Natalie must have discovered what was going on, too. She must have confronted McGuire or Clarke, and that was enough to get her killed. This had nothing to do with her older boyfriend, Finn realized; it was all about the litigation. And now that he knew about it, his life was in danger, too.

Bostick must have been thinking along the same lines, because he turned to Finn and said, "I'm definitely out of this now."

"I understand," Finn said. "You've already helped enough. Trust me, I'll keep your name out of all of this if anything comes up in the future. I really appreciate all you've done."

"It's no problem." Bostick tapped Finn in the chest with his finger. "You be careful if you're really going to pursue this. I spent a lot of time on the street when I was a cop, and I know what these people are all about. I'm not sure a high-priced lawyer like you can possibly know what you're dealing with, here. These people are vicious and brutal. They won't hesitate to take you out if you're threatening their money supply."

"You didn't know me when I was growing up. Trust me, I know exactly what sort of people I'm dealing with."

CHAPTER FIFTY-FOUR

Quietly and carefully. That was how Kozlowski wanted to proceed. It might be more easily said than done, though, given the public nature of the individuals they were investigating. He and Flaherty agreed that, other than Finn, Clarke and Loring seemed to be the most likely suspects. Kozlowski had some contacts in the Boston office of the FBI and the Justice Department, so he agreed to dig deeper into Loring's past. Flaherty agreed to put in the legwork on Clarke.

She started online, where most good investigators started in the modern world. There was no shortage of information on Massachusetts's ninety-fifth governor; the problem was distilling it into a useful quantity.

William Holloran Clarke was a descendant of Colonel Nathanial J. Clarke, who'd fought under General George Washington during the American Revolution. It was a storied lineage of privilege and sacrifice that included several early state senators, a leading abolitionist, and a Civil War general. The family had fallen on hard times in the second half of the nineteenth century, losing much of its wealth on speculative ventures out West, but the family's fortune had been revived by Clarke's father, who made millions liquidating the assets of bankrupt businessmen during the Great Depression. He had then parlayed that into an inestimable fortune by investing in real estate in and around Boston.

The restoration of the Clarke family to wealth and power had afforded young William Clarke every opportunity imaginable, and he took full advantage. He attended Phillips Andover Academy, where he was a star athlete and president of his class. From there, he took his degree at Harvard, across the river from his father's Beacon Hill mansion, where he graduated with highest honors. After that, he worked for two years before returning to Cambridge to get a joint degree in law and business. There'd been some controversy regarding his return to Harvard, coming as it did after his number had been selected in the military draft lottery, but strings were pulled, and his enlistment was deferred until after his graduation, and a sure tour in Vietnam ultimately morphed into a more mundane eighteen-month stint with the navy's Judge Advocate General's Corps. Few questions were asked.

Once released from the military, he took up a key role running the family's various businesses. His father passed away in the early 1980s, leaving an empire to his son, which William Clarke ran with efficiency and even, some would say, with compassion. While Clarke never failed to realize astonishing profits, he also became one of the city's leading philanthropists, establishing homeless shelters, schools, and youth programs. The family's extensive real estate holdings allowed him to couple commercial development with the dedication of public parks, works projects, and green space. The results were deemed not only good for Boston, but often resulted in enormous tax writeoffs for Clarke's businesses. He was a man who seemed to have the Midas touch.

It came as no surprise, then, when Clarke ran for the governorship and won handily. There were few knocks against him during the campaign, and all that his opponent had been able to come up with was some minor scandal involving an alleged payoff over the naming of a local park in Southie. It had never amounted to anything, and Clarke was elected in a landslide.

Since his election, Clarke had focused his energies on massive improvements in the commonwealth's infrastructure. The Big Dig was already under way when he took office, but he had broadened the project to include new secondary roadways and to increase the amount of green space planned. He'd implemented a plan to overhaul Logan Airport, and he'd created the Massachusetts Transportation Safety Commission, which had grown quickly into the largest bureaucracy in Massachusetts history.

The only real attacks on his administration seemed to concern its lack of fiscal restraint and oversight—a surprise to many who viewed Clarke as a brilliant businessman. The state budget had more than doubled in the short time he'd been in office, and several well-known economists were predicting dire economic consequences down the road.

Flaherty looked up from the news service printouts she'd been reviewing to see Kozlowski standing in front of her desk. She gave a start. "Damn it, Koz!" she yelled. "You've got to stop sneaking up on people like that."

He chuckled. "Sorry," he said, though it was clear he wasn't. "What have you got there?" he asked.

"Nothing yet. I was just doing a background check on our governor, trying to get a feel for what sort of skeletons he might have in his closets."

"And what are you finding?"

"So far, only the invisible kind."

"Nothing at all?"

"Not even an unpaid parking ticket. If this guy is doing something wrong, he's being very discreet about it." Flaherty noticed that her partner looked surprised. "I'm serious. Even when he was in the private sector he had the reputation of being a principled real estate developer."

"There's an oxymoron if I've ever heard one."

"No shit, but that's his reputation."

"How about his way with the ladies? Any possibility he and Natalie Caldwell were more than just committee members together?"

"It's always possible, but I can't find anything that would suggest it. He's been married to Emily Worthington Clarke for twenty-five years, and I can't find any hint of infidelity. Even if there were, I'm not sure it's the kind of thing he'd kill over. I mean, it's almost expected from a guy like him. I doubt a little extracurricular dabbling would hurt him politically." Flaherty shook her head in frustration. "I'm hitting nothing but dead ends. How about you?"

Kozlowski smiled. "I had better luck. It seems as though our friend Mr. Loring may have a few things to hide. For instance, it turns out he was more involved in the Bulger case than the media ever let on. He worked hand in hand with Connolly in developing relationships with mob snitches. He even met with Bulger a number of times over the years when he was still being protected by the feds."

"Wow," Flaherty exclaimed. "He certainly managed to keep that out of the news, didn't he?"

Kozlowski nodded. "That's not all. Apparently, Loring was developing other snitches on his own—high-level snitches in the various organized gangs in Boston. Some of those he kept secret from everyone else over at the Justice Department. As a result, no one over there seems to have a clear idea about how deep Loring was into these gangs. Apparently, the kinds of guys he'd lined up were into some really bad shit. Some people he used to work with in the government think he may still be in contact with these people—and that he might have turned dirty."

"If Natalie Caldwell had the evidence to prove those kinds

of allegations, it would certainly provide a good motive for murder, wouldn't it?"

Kozlowski agreed. "You should also know that he considers himself a bit of an office Casanova. He likes his women young, and apparently a couple have even liked him back."

Flaherty made a face. "I've seen him in action myself. It's not pretty."

"So, with Loring we've got a possible love-interest angle as well."

Flaherty shook her head in disgust. "Loring seems to be a better suspect than Clarke. Damn, maybe I should reconsider Clarke's job offer."

Kozlowski mused for a moment. "It's a great opportunity," he said. "And I can't think of anyone who'd be better for the job than you. How long did he give you to get back to him?"

"I can probably put him off for a couple of days, but no longer."

"All right, then. Let's get this case wrapped up before then so you can make up your mind without worrying you might be working for a murderer."

Flaherty smiled. "That would be nice, wouldn't it?"

Just then the phone rang. She picked it up. "Flaherty," she said.

"Linda, it's Finn," came the familiar voice on the other end of the line.

Flaherty looked up at Kozlowski and mouthed the word *Finn*. "Yes, Finn, what is it?" she said into the phone.

"I need to talk to you. I think I may have figured out who killed Natalie."

She paused, wondering if he was on the level. "Well, do you want to give me a clue?" she asked tentatively.

"Not over the phone," Finn replied. "Look, I'm at work now. Can you meet me at my apartment? I need to explain this to you in person."

"When?"

"As soon as possible. Now?"

Flaherty looked at her watch. It was six-thirty in the evening. "Okay, I'll be over as soon as I can," she said.

Finn was relieved. "Thank you. You won't be sorry. I'll get out of here as soon as possible."

Flaherty hesitated. "I'm not going to wait in front of your house, Finn," she said, somewhat annoyed.

"Please," Finn pleaded. "I need to talk to you. If I'm not there when you arrive, you can let yourself in and wait in the apartment. There's a key hidden in a slot underneath the mailbox."

Flaherty checked her watch again and sighed. "All right, I'll see you shortly." She hung up the phone and looked over at her partner with a raised eyebrow. "He says he's solved the murder."

"This should be interesting," Kozlowski said. "You want me to tag along?"

She shook her head. "I have a feeling he'll be more comfortable sharing whatever information he has if it's just me. You two have never seemed particularly close."

Kozlowski chuckled. "Still holding out hope for a romance, eh, Lieutenant?"

"He's not such a bad guy, Koz. If he's cleared in this case, I think you may actually grow to like him."

"Yeah, just remember that he hasn't been cleared yet. Be careful when you're dealing with this guy. You've seen his record."

"I love it when you worry about me, Dad."

"Hey, I'm not worried about you. Weidel is looking for an excuse to kick both of us off the force, and if you get yourself killed, I'm sure he'll blame it on me and try to have my pension taken away."

"Your concern is heartwarming."

"Just telling it like it is."

Finn hung up the phone and looked at Bostick. "She said she'd meet me," he said.

"Good," Bostick said. "But do you think she'll believe you? That's the real question, isn't it?"

"I don't know. I can only lay out what we've discovered. She'll have to make up her own mind."

Bostick nodded. "Well, this is where I bow out. Are you going to take these lists with you?" he asked, pointing to the notes they'd taken listing Huron's phantom employees.

Finn shook his head. "No, I'm locking those in the drawer of my desk so I can find them later. I'll make copies for Linda once I see what her reaction is to this information."

"*Linda?*" Bostick smiled. "Even when I was on the force, I never heard anyone call her anything other than 'Detective,' or maybe 'Detective Lieutenant.' How is it you get to call her 'Linda'?"

"Don't ask," Finn said. "Come on, I'll walk you to the door." They walked out of the conference room and headed toward the elevator bank. They were halfway there when Finn heard someone calling him.

"Finn! Finn!" came the voice from behind them. He turned and saw Preston Holland coming toward them. To his horror, he also saw that Tony McGuire was behind Holland. "Finn, glad we caught you," Preston said as he approached the two. He was brought up short when he noticed the bruises on Finn's face. "Good God, son, what happened to you?"

Finn had almost forgotten about his appearance. "I got elbowed in a basketball game and did a face-plant into the floor," he said lamely. Fortunately, Holland was preoccupied and just nodded sympathetically. By then, McGuire was standing next to them as well.

"Mr. McGuire, this is Peter Bostick, one of our private investigators. Pete, Mr. McGuire is the head of Huron Security."

Bostick's face was as white as a sheet as he held out a reluctant hand to McGuire. "Pleased to meet you," he croaked.

McGuire nodded as he regarded Bostick with suspicion.

"I didn't even know you were working on this case with us, Peter," Holland commented. Then he laughed as he looked over at McGuire. "I guess I've got to pay closer attention to the bills I send you, eh, Tony. Well, in any case, Mr. Bostick is one of our best, so you'd be getting a bargain."

"I was just doing a favor for Finn," Bostick said.

"It wasn't related to the Tannery case," Finn added quickly.

"Then I feel better," Preston said, winking at McGuire. "Finn, we had a couple of quick questions about this settlement Barnolk has proposed. Can we trouble you for a moment?"

"Sure," Finn said. "You can show yourself out, can't you, Peter?"

"Yeah, I'll be fine," Bostick replied, already moving toward the elevators.

"Why don't we go sit in my office," Holland said as he, Finn, and McGuire walked in the other direction down the hall.

McGuire was looking back over his shoulder at Bostick as he hurried into an elevator. "What sort of investigation was he doing for you?" he asked Finn, gesturing toward Bostick.

"Nothing that important," Finn replied. "He owed me a favor and I needed a little help with something."

McGuire's eyes narrowed as he looked at Finn. Then he smiled icily, sending shivers down Finn's spine. "It's always good to have some favors to call in."

CHAPTER FIFTY-FIVE

It took nearly an hour for Finn to meet with Preston and McGuire regarding the settlement, and he had trouble concentrating the entire time. Preston made clear that he expected Finn to take the lead in drafting the settlement agreement, and gave him detailed instructions on how it should be structured, but Finn's mind was elsewhere. He knew that he needed to get moving if he was going to meet Flaherty at his apartment.

Once he was released from the meeting, he hurried along the streets of Boston, back to his car parked near the office. He had to get to Flaherty to tell her what he'd discovered. How she reacted would determine his next move. He couldn't think that far ahead now, though.

It was nearing seven-thirty, and the sun had set to the west of the city, the glow on the horizon in that direction fading to light purple, then to blue, then to black in the east. It was the time of day and time of year Finn liked best. He could feel the wave of barometric pressure cresting and readying itself to crash upon the land, making way for the crisp, clean air of the fall. It felt like everything was coming to a head, and the world was preparing itself for a rebirth. *Who knows*, he thought, *maybe Townsend was right. Maybe the apocalypse is upon us and the crescendo of the summer will bring with it a new bibli-*

cal era. If that were to happen, Finn would need his answer to give to God. He was close, he knew, but he still needed closure. He owed it to Natalie.

Bostick lived in a small one-bedroom in the heart of Chinatown, only a couple of blocks from Linda Flaherty's loft, and a few more from the Kiss Club. He'd stopped into Coogan's Pub on his way home to grab a beer and calm down. The run-in with McGuire had shaken him, and he needed to be around other people for a while, even if it was in the anonymity of a crowded bar.

The first beer felt so good that he ordered two more in a half hour, letting the alcohol ease him into the evening. By the time the third beer had settled in his stomach, he was feeling better, and he decided to make his way home to grab some dinner. He slapped a ten-dollar bill on the bar, thanked Tommy, the bartender, and headed out.

Bostick could feel the pressure in the air, too. It was summer's last great gasp, as a wall of heavy, humid air pushed in from the northwest. This should be the last of the heat, he thought, looking forward to the crisper days of autumn.

The entrance to his apartment was in an alley off Atlantic Avenue, and he felt even better as soon as he made the turn into the narrow passageway. It was good to be home, he thought. He hadn't done anything he considered dangerous since the day he left the police force, and even while he was a cop, he'd never been in any really life-threatening position. As a result, the day's discoveries had been stressful, and he was looking forward to relaxing on his couch and watching a ball game.

He walked up the creaky wooden stairs that led to his apartment door—a remnant of the days when the building had been full of tenements, each housing several families of Asian immigrants. As he stood on the platform at the top of the stairs fumbling for his keys, he heard a creak behind him. It was an odd sound, as if the weight on the planks had somehow doubled. He might have turned around to look behind him, if only out of curiosity, but there was no time. He felt the steel of a silencer behind his ear, and before he realized what it was, he heard the muffled pop of the gun going off. Then everything was dark.

The killer stood over Bostick's slumped body in the alley in Chinatown. He looked down at the trickle of blood that ran from the back of the investigator's head, over his collar, and down onto the wooden stairs. There was less of it than he expected, probably because the wound was instantly fatal and Bostick's heart was no longer forcing blood through his veins.

Then the killer raised his arm and fired a second shot into Bostick's head, just to be sure.

CHAPTER FIFTY-SIX

Flaherty arrived at Finn's apartment before he returned. She knocked several times before taking the key from under the mailbox and letting herself in.

She felt guilty being in his apartment when he wasn't there, but he'd told her where the key was. She sat on the sofa in the living room for a few minutes, reasoning that as long as she was anchored in one spot, she'd be less tempted to snoop through the dwelling, as was her natural inclination. After a few moments, however, the stillness of the apartment and her own curiosity got the better of her, and she felt the need to stand up and move around.

She walked over to the living room windows to admire the view. Law firm life must be treating Finn all right, financially speaking, she surmised. The apartment had one of the best vantages she could remember seeing. It was a corner unit, and one side looked directly out at the Bunker Hill Monument, a granite spike identical in shape to the Washington Monument in D.C., only smaller. It rose from the top of the hill like some confirmation of conquest, overshadowing all of the other structures in Charlestown. The other side of the apartment looked down the hill toward the water. The tips of U.S.S. *Constitu-*

tion's masts were just visible from the window, down by the pier at the naval shipyard.

Flaherty took in the views then drifted around the living room, examining the various artifacts with an investigator's idle interest and analytical judgment. The room was sparsely decorated. The couch was a modern leather model with clean lines that cut in front of a glass coffee table. A low-backed armchair upholstered in an expensive designer fabric sat to one side of the sofa, with an end table in between. Facing the couch, two carved wooden chairs completed the set with a standing lamp in the middle.

The walls were largely bare. A few modern prints hung in those spaces that would otherwise have been too blank to suggest a life of any fullness, but they felt generic. Their colors were bold and matched the rugs and walls perfectly, as if a decorator had chosen them. Flaherty wondered if Finn had dated an interior designer at some point. It would certainly explain a lot, she thought. None of the furnishings seemed to reflect Finn, except insofar as they put her in mind of a man searching for an identity to be comfortable with. From what Flaherty knew of Finn's past, the image didn't really surprise her.

She moved from the living room to the kitchen, flipping on the lights as she went. The impact as she entered the room almost blinded her. Everything was bright white—the walls, the floors, the counters, the appliances—all of it so bright that it reflected the light painfully. It made her think briefly of the sterile atmosphere in John Townsend's basement, and she almost felt the need to leave. Instead, she made her way over to the refrigerator, opening the door with a notion of foreboding she couldn't explain.

It was almost empty. There were just a few condiments lingering on the door, lonely and forgotten. A few cans of diet

Coke and several bottles of beer were pushed to the back on one shelf, and there was a half-eaten pizza still in its box.

Not much of a chef, she thought.

She closed the refrigerator door and stood upright. She should go back into the living room and sit quietly until Finn got back, she knew. She should respect his privacy and end her snooping, but that just seemed too difficult. She needed to know more about him. As much as she fought to deny it, she had strong feelings for this man, and that didn't happen very often. She needed to know what it was she'd seen in him that captured her attention, and whether there was any chance to sustain those feelings. She wanted it to happen, but she needed more information about him. The rooms she'd seen so far were blank slates, yielding nothing.

She stood for a long moment, in an ethical quandary. And then, finally, she shook her head in disgust and walked out of the kitchen, through the living room, and down the hallway toward the bedroom.

When Flaherty got to the bedroom door, she paused. She flipped on the light and stood at the threshold, hesitant, looking around the room. As with the living room, the decor was sparse, but it felt less forced to her. A queen-size bed stood against the far wall, covered in sheets and a bedspread of simple country design. The bed had been made up haphazardly, simply by pulling the covers up to the top of the mattress. Beside it was a nightstand with a brass light and an old-fashioned alarm clock. A book was lying next to the light, and Flaherty walked over to take a look at it. *The Great Gatsby*. She opened it and flipped through the pages.

There was a dresser against the near wall at the foot of the bed, but the surface was clean and devoid of any objects of interest. In the corner there was a battered old six-string guitar leaning on a stand. The walls were bare except for a small mirror above the dresser, hardly large enough for Flaherty to see her entire face in.

Is this it? Was this all there was to the man who'd so affected her? It seemed like there should be so much more. Something was missing, like he was only part of a person. Something primal and necessary was conspicuously absent, but she couldn't put her finger on what it was, exactly. Then, all of a sudden, it hit her.

Pictures.

There were no pictures in the entire apartment—at least none she'd seen so far. Not a snapshot of friends at a party; not a memento from a trip hanging on the refrigerator; not a single image that would betray any sense of Finn's past or any connection to another human being.

In all fairness, she supposed it was normal, given his history. Growing up without parents, being shuttled from one foster family to another, with time in an orphanage in between, Finn must have learned that emotional investments in other people seldom yielded much return. It was sad, she realized. And still, he'd done a remarkable job of reclaiming his life. From just a glimpse at Finn's police record at age sixteen, Flaherty would have wagered that he'd either be long dead in the streets of Charlestown or spending time up Route 2 at the Concord correctional facility.

She moved over to the side of the room and opened the closet door. It was a small walk-in, and she flicked on the lights. There, lined up in perfect military order were Finn's suits. He liked his clothing; she could tell that about him from the few times they'd been together. He was always impeccably dressed in the latest business fashions. But she had had no idea just how much he liked his clothing. The suits looked like something out of a movie—there had to be twenty-five in all, arranged by weight and color. Pinstripes and glen plaids and worsted wool, from designers such as Hickey Freeman, Ralph Lauren, and Armani, were all waiting their turn patiently.

The shirts were almost as impressive. They hung on a different rack neatly, but with more vibrancy than the suits they faced. In addition to the traditional Brooks Brothers white and blue, there were shirts that beamed with colorful personality in lavender and orange and French blue.

She looked around again and something caught her eye. It was sitting on the shelf, up above the shirts. She could just make out the corner of a silver picture frame, turned to the side. She reached up on her toes to pull it down. The frame was antique, with ornate relief around the edges—vines of some kind winding their way around the image in the center. The face in the center was one with which Flaherty had become exceedingly familiar. Natalie Caldwell's eyes were hard to mistake, and they blazed out from within the matted frame. It was a beautiful picture. Even though she was looking at the camera, it seemed like a candid shot, her eyes showing surprise at having been caught unaware, and betraying an intimacy with the photographer not often found in pictures.

Flaherty wondered who the photographer was. Finn she presumed, and the thought made her shockingly jealous. Something about the way in which Natalie was looking at the camera made Flaherty long for an intimacy that was missing in her own life.

She could see what had attracted Finn to Natalie Caldwell. It wasn't just the obvious beauty; it was something more. There was something so open, and inviting, and sexual about her look that it made Flaherty blush. She suddenly felt guilty for her jealousy, and guilty for snooping in Finn's apartment. It would have been one thing if her motivation had pertained to the investigation, but it hadn't. This was personal.

The realization made her feel horrible, and she needed to get out of the closet—out of the apartment if she could. She realized she was too confused to view Finn objectively anymore. She reached up to put the picture back, and as she looked up at the shelf, her heart stopped.

She was frozen. She closed her eyes and tried to wish away what she'd seen, but it was still there when she looked up again. *It can't be*, she said over and over to herself, the fear and desperation growing. Even through her tears, though, she could see it dangling from the shelf, like a piece of thread that, once pulled, would unravel all her hopes about Finn. There, hanging from where it had become dislodged when she pulled the picture forward, was a piece of red ribbon—the kind that had been found around Natalie Caldwell's neck as she looked up from beneath the surface of Boston Harbor.

Flaherty reached up and pulled on the ribbon, and an entire roll tumbled over the edge. She held it up to look at it. *No, please, no*, she thought. Then she reached up again and ran her hand along the top of the shelf where she couldn't see. She was up on her toes, reaching as far back as she could when she felt it. It was hard and cold, and her fingers recoiled when they first ran across the flat surface. She looked around quickly for something to pick it up with, and grabbed a handkerchief off one of the racks in the closet. Then she reached up again carefully and brought it down. It was a knife; a professional-grade steel knife about ten inches long. The blade looked old and rusted, but when Flaherty looked more closely, it became clear that it was not old, it was just covered with a dark, flaky crust.

"God damn it," she said out loud. Just then, she heard the front door of the apartment open.

CHAPTER FIFTY-SEVEN

As Finn drove home, he tried to put the pieces of the puzzle together. The picture was becoming clearer, he thought. Huron Security was ripping off the state for millions of dollars a year. The company was charging Massachusetts for "guards" who didn't exist, and then pocketing the money. It was a minor amount in comparison to the billions that were being spent, but it still required inside help. Finn figured Natalie must have discovered the scam and confronted McGuire. As a result, McGuire had been forced to kill her, or have her killed, before she could report the fraud to anyone. The thought filled Finn with rage. He'd sat next to Natalie's killer, defended him at his deposition, discussed trial strategy and expert testimony, and he'd never known. McGuire acted as if nothing had happened—as if Natalie's murder was the same as any other business decision. It made Finn feel sick.

He needed to be careful in handling this, though. McGuire wouldn't have been able to pull off the scam without help from someone high up in the state government, and whoever that was would be working hard to cover his tracks. Without careful planning, Finn's knowledge could cause him more harm than good.

He guided his car through Boston and into Charlestown, up

Bunker Hill toward his apartment. As luck would have it, there was a parking spot open on his street near his building. He pulled in and put the top of the car up, all the while thinking through what he was going to tell Linda. She'd be skeptical at first, but he needed to find a way to convince her. Once she accepted the truth behind Natalie's murder she'd know the best way to handle the situation. Finn trusted her. He felt that once he had a chance to talk things through with her, they'd be able to come up with a plan.

He walked up the stairs and slid his key into the lock on his front door.

Flaherty heard the key in the front lock, then the sound of the door creaking open. She froze, her hand still holding the knife she suspected had been used to carve open Natalie Caldwell. She didn't want to believe it, but it was hard to avoid the conclusion that Finn had killed her. She shouldn't be surprised, she told herself. Murder victims were most often killed by those closest to them. It all made sense. So why did it feel so wrong?

"Linda?" Finn called out from the front hall. "Linda, are you here?"

Flaherty kept silent as her hand went to her gun and she rested the knife on the floor of the closet. Regardless of any doubts she might have, she couldn't take any chances. She peered around the corner of the closet door and listened as Finn moved from room to room, wandering around the apartment. She heard the refrigerator door open and close, and then purposeful footsteps headed toward the bedroom. She ducked fully back into the closet.

Finn walked into the bedroom and tossed his jacket on the bed, then started to pull off his shirt. He was holding a beer in his hand, raising it to drink, and as he turned toward the closet he saw Flaherty. He was so surprised he spit out a mouthful of beer.

"Holy shit! Linda!" he sputtered. "You scared the hell out of me!" Flaherty remained still and silent, partially shrouded in the shadows of the closet. "Didn't you hear me yelling for you? What's wrong?" Finn asked. Then he saw the gun clutched to her side. "What's going on?" he demanded.

"I found the knife," Flaherty said.

Finn looked confused. "What knife?" he asked, his consternation evident.

Flaherty was silent for a moment. "Don't make this any harder than it already is," she said finally.

"Don't make what any harder? Tell me what's going on." Finn moved toward Flaherty, as if to comfort a friend, and she raised her gun, pointing it straight at his chest. It hurt her to do it, but she had no choice under the circumstances.

"Don't come any closer, Finn."

Finn was clearly shocked. "I don't understand what's happening."

She raised the gun higher, her hand shaking ever so slightly. She wanted to talk to him, but she knew she couldn't. She was desperate to explain what she'd found, and to listen to him as he told her the knife was planted. She might even have believed him. In fact, a part of her knew that finding the knife in Finn's apartment was too easy, that it was quite possibly a setup. Nevertheless, she was painfully aware that, as a police officer, she had to treat him strictly as a suspect. She steeled her resolve and spoke in a clear, calm voice. "Take another step, and I promise I will shoot you."

"You can't be serious." Finn felt like his world was collapsing.

"I want you to move backward two steps and lie down on

the floor with your hands behind your head," Flaherty said, ignoring him. "Now!"

Finn hesitated, looking into her eyes, searching for the reason this was all happening. What he saw shocked him. All he could see were the eyes of a police officer, the eyes he'd seen so many times growing up. Those eyes assumed the worst, and were ready to strike without mercy, with an anger born from self-defense and too many disappointments in human nature.

"Now!" she yelled again. This time there was no hesitation in her voice, and she flipped the safety off her 9mm semiautomatic. He took two steps back and started to kneel down.

"Can I put the beer down?"

"On the floor. Keep your hands where I can see them!"

Finn put the beer down on the floor, and then lay facedown on the rug, placing his hands behind his head and locking his fingers together at the base of his skull. He did all of this in an eerily familiar sort of way, recalling the procedure from years before.

Flaherty emerged from the closet and stepped over Finn so she was straddling his torso, keeping the gun pointed at the back of his head. She reached behind her back with one hand and pulled handcuffs out of the case on her belt. Leaning forward, she clapped one of the cuffs onto Finn's right wrist.

"Put your hand behind your back," she ordered.

"Can I at least put my shirt back on?"

"I'll bring it with us, but right now I want you to put your hand behind your back."

Finn brought his right hand down and let it rest in the small of his back.

"Now the left one," Flaherty commanded. Finn obediently took his left hand and brought it down, resting his left wrist on top of his right. He winced as Flaherty snapped the second cuff onto his left wrist, leaving him facedown and helpless on the floor. Only then did she put her gun back in its shoulder holster.

She leaned down and hooked him under the shoulder, pulling him off the floor. "Get up," she said. Then they were both standing, and he was looking at her with pleading eyes, desperate for answers. There was nothing warm in her eyes anymore, though.

"I don't understand this," he said.

She looked away for a split second, and just for that moment he thought he'd reached her. Then she turned back to him, and he knew he was wrong. "Understand this," she said. "You have the right to remain silent. Anything you say can and will be used against you in a court of law."

"Why are you doing this?"

"You have the right to an attorney. If you cannot afford an attorney, one will be provided to you free of charge. Do you understand these rights as I have explained them to you?"

"You're making a mistake."

"Yeah? Well, that seems to be a pattern I've fallen into."

CHAPTER FIFTY-EIGHT

Finn paced back and forth in the holding cell. It was a single five-by-seven hole, and he was alone, surrounded by solid walls broken only by a steel door at one end. He'd been given his shirt back, which was a blessing in the damp, cool, concrete space, but he'd been stripped of his belt and shoelaces—a mandatory but humiliating precaution against suicide. He laughed bitterly. Suicide might be a viable option in the future, he thought. In the past he'd vowed to die before ever going back to jail. He wouldn't survive on the inside now. But suicide wasn't an option to consider yet. There was too much to do.

Without warning, the steel bar covering the peephole in the door slid back and an indifferent set of eyes appeared. "Finn? Scott T.?" the voice said.

Finn stopped pacing. "Yes."

"Somebody wants to talk to you." The eyes looked Finn up and down, evaluating the threat, and eventually concluding that the lawyer in the cell posed none. "Stand against the wall with your palms flat on the cement," the voice ordered. Finn did as he was told.

"Where are you taking me?" Finn asked as the door opened and a large skin-headed young cop appeared.

"Interview room," the man replied as he handcuffed Finn. For a split second, Finn thought about escaping. The young cop was big but careless, and he left himself exposed as Finn turned toward him. Finn was sure a well-placed elbow would drop the man instantly. *But then what?* He would never make it out of the station house, and even if he did, he'd be a hunted man with no way to prove his innocence. He decided to play along.

"Who wants to see me?" he asked.

The young cop was leading him by the arm out of the cell. He shrugged. "You'll find out soon enough."

Finn was deposited in the same room where Flaherty and Kozlowski had interviewed him a week or so before. He walked around, observing everything. Then he moved over to the one-way mirror and shaded his hand against the glass to see if he could look through to the other side. He was still in this awkward pose when the door opened and Kozlowski walked in.

"We've actually checked to make sure people can't see through that way," the detective said.

Finn turned to look at him, then stared back into the mirror. "It seems to have worked," he said. "But I figured it was worth a try."

"Sit down," Kozlowski ordered.

"Thanks, I'm fine," Finn said, his hands and face still pressed against the mirror.

"No, you're definitely not fine." Kozlowski shook his head. "Now, sit down."

Finn turned again to look at Kozlowski. He tried to fold his arms against his chest in defiance, but the handcuffs made the gesture impossible, rattling as he tried to bring up his hands.

Kozlowski looked like he felt some satisfaction at Finn's predicament. He leaned back and looked hard at him, as if he was deciding how to start the discussion. "We searched your apartment, and I think you can guess what we found," he led.

Finn tilted his head. Flaherty had said something about a knife before she shut off all information, but he thought it best to get Kozlowski to give him as much information as possible. "Let's assume I can't. Enlighten me."

"We found the ribbon."

Finn returned a blank stare and shrugged his shoulders. "What are you talking about?"

"The ribbon—the kind that was tied around Natalie Caldwell's neck when she was found. I'm no betting man, but if I was, I'd wager the lab boys are going to tell us it's an exact match."

Finn frowned. "I have no idea what you're talking about. I don't have any ribbon in my apartment. Even if I did, that hardly makes a case."

"You could be right," Kozlowski said, nodding. "But then, that's not all we found. We found the knife, too."

"You've lost me again. What knife? I have lots of knives in my kitchen. So does everyone."

"We didn't find this one in your kitchen, we found it in your closet. And wouldn't you know it, it looked like there was blood on it. Again, I don't gamble, but it would probably be a safe bet that the blood on the knife matches Caldwell's."

All of a sudden, Finn felt panic. It was a setup. It had to be. For a moment, he thought he was choking. His eyes bulged slightly, and he opened his mouth as if to speak. Kozlowski appeared gratified by his reaction.

"That's right, asshole. The case is made, with or without your help. The only question is, will we have to go through the formality of a trial?"

Finn regained his composure and sat quietly, considering his options as he worked to keep the muscles of his face from twitching. Kozlowski was right, he was in serious trouble, but he'd been around the criminal justice system long enough to know he was far from convicted. He also knew that the truth was on his side, which was a comfort. Not much, but some. One thing was clear—he needed help, and there was only one person to whom he could turn.

"I think I'll call my lawyer now, Detective," Finn said. It wasn't a request but a demand. Finn knew his rights, and he knew Kozlowski couldn't stop him from bringing in a lawyer at this point.

Kozlowski nodded grimly. "If that's the way you want to go," he said. "But wouldn't it be easier if you and I tried to talk this thing out and come to some understanding?"

"Please, Detective, spare me the carefully worded attempt to get me to waive my rights under the Fifth Amendment. I'm not some sixteen-year-old you grabbed off the street who can be bullied."

"Suit yourself," said Kozlowski, shrugging, though he was visibly disappointed. He stood up and walked out of the room, returning a moment later with an old beat-up rotary phone, which he put down on the table in front of Finn and plugged into a jack in the wall. "You've got five minutes," he said. Then he left the room again, and Finn heard the door lock behind him.

Finn thought carefully about what he was going to say. He knew he was risking everything he had left in the world—not just his career and a chance to make partner, but his relationship with Preston, who in the past had shown him genuine fatherly affection. Preston might very well hang up on him when he heard what was happening, and would have every right to. Finn silently prayed his mentor would believe in him enough to stick by him.

He reached the older lawyer at home. Even though it was

early Saturday morning, Finn knew that Holland would have risen hours before. "Finn, my boy," Preston boomed out cheerfully. "Getting an early start, I see. How's the Tannery settlement coming?"

Finn felt a rush of despair as he realized how difficult it was going to be to tell his mentor he'd been arrested. He almost hung up the phone, but he knew he had no choice. "I haven't actually gotten to that yet, Preston," he started weakly. "I'm calling about something else. It seems there's been a little confusion regarding Natalie's murder. I'm down at the police station."

"Confusion?" Preston sounded perplexed. "I thought they'd caught the killer? What more could they possibly want from you?"

"Well," said Finn, fumbling for a way to explain his predicament. "It seems like the investigation is continuing."

For the first time, Preston's voice registered concern. "Finn, what's happening?"

Finn paused for a long time before working up the courage to answer. "I've been arrested," he said finally.

"Arrested!" Preston shouted. "Good Lord, whatever for?"

"There's some confusion here, as I said, and it seems they think I had something to do with Natalie's death." He held his breath as he said the words.

"Nonsense!" Preston snapped back.

The surety of Preston's voice gave Finn hope. "I know, it doesn't make any sense, but they've actually got me locked up here." He leaned his head into his hand as he held the phone. "I'm sorry, Preston. I hate to drag you into this, but I had no one else to call."

Finn could hear the despair in his own voice, and he knew Preston would understand his concerns as he placed his entire professional future in the older man's hands. Preston's voice was unhesitating. "Finn, I don't want you to worry about that at all. You're the future of this firm, and if you're the subject of ridiculous accusations, we'll protect you." There was a pause, and then the older man added, with emphasis, "*I* will protect you. Anyone who knows you will see this for the absurdity it is."

Finn felt like a weight had been lifted off him—that for the first time since Flaherty had put the handcuffs on him, he felt like he could breathe.

"Finn," Preston said. "I'm going to get dressed and I'll be down there as soon as possible. You just sit tight and say nothing until I get there. We'll get this straightened out, I promise you."

Finn felt a lump form in his throat as he replied. "All right, Preston. Thank you—for everything."

Kozlowski returned a few moments later. "Did you get in touch with your lawyer?" he asked contemptuously.

Finn nodded. "I did. He should be here within the hour."

Kozlowski leaned up against the wall in a pose he clearly hoped conveyed his nonchalance. "You can still talk to us in the meantime if you want," he said.

Finn coughed out a laugh. "Why the hell would I want to do that?"

"Who knows?" The sergeant rolled his shoulders. "Maybe we could cut you a deal?"

Finn frowned. "What kind of a 'deal' did you have in mind?"

Kozlowski looked up, as if contemplating his options. "Maybe we could get your sentence reduced. Particularly if you killed the Caldwell girl in the heat of passion." He paused and gave Finn a sympathetic look. "But first you have to talk to us."

"I'll tell you what, Detective," Finn said, blowing out a sigh with his words. "I'd be willing to talk about this, but not with you."

"I'm hurt," Kozlowski grunted.

"Nothing personal," Finn said. "I'm just not convinced you have my best interests at heart."

"Okay, then who?"

"Lieutenant Flaherty."

Kozlowski wagged a finger at him. "She's not going to offer you a better deal than I will."

"I'll take my chances."

Kozlowski hesitated for a moment, debating whether to try again, but finally stood up. "I'll see if she's around."

"That would be nice of you," Finn said. "Oh, and by the way, Detective, if you plan to offer any deals in the future, you might want to have an assistant district attorney with you. Unless they've radically rewritten the rules since I was with the Public Defender's office, you don't have the authority to offer any deals. You might want to mention that to Lieutenant Flaherty as well."

Kozlowski paused at the door. "You know, you may be just a little too smart for your own good."

Finn nodded. "I may just be."

CHAPTER FIFTY-NINE

Flaherty walked into the room reluctantly. She closed the door behind her and stood silently for a moment as she and Finn looked at each other. Then she walked over to the table and sat down.

"Wouldn't this be easier for everyone if you just dealt with Detective Kozlowski?" she asked.

"Nothing's easy about this for me," Finn said. "And at the moment I really don't care about making this easier on anyone else. After all, it's my life on the line."

"You should've thought of that before you killed Natalie Caldwell."

"That's one of the reasons I wanted to talk to you," Finn said. He took a deep breath and looked at her hard. "I didn't do this."

"It's too late for that." She had to be firm. Any sign that she had lingering doubts would likely foreclose the possibility of a confession.

"I know how this looks, but I'm being framed."

"How could I possibly believe you?" She wanted to, but overnight the evidence had mounted, and she knew she had to put her personal feelings aside.

"Think, dammit! Why would I leave those things in my apartment if I really killed her? Am I really that stupid? Those things were put there by someone who's trying to frame me, and I know who it is."

"Nobody's trying to frame you, Finn. You're guilty. It's not just the evidence we found at your apartment. One of the bartenders at the Kiss Club has come forward and says he remembers you."

Finn looked confused. "I told you, I went there because I missed Natalie. I explained all that to you."

"No, not that night. The bartender remembers you from the night Natalie was killed."

Finn turned white. "No I wasn't! I wasn't there!" he shouted. "The bartender's lying," he pressed on. "Somebody got to him." Finn felt like he was falling into a deep, dark pit.

Flaherty shook her head. "Nobody got to him, Finn. It's over."

"It's not over," he objected. "This is all wrong, he's getting away with murder."

"Who is? Who is this person you think is setting you up? Tell me. Make me understand."

Finn was gripping the table now, and it was clear that he was trying to keep from losing his grip on reality; trying to keep himself oriented. "McGuire," he said after a moment. "McGuire is the one. He's pulling the strings."

"Who is McGuire?"

"He's the president of Huron Security. He's a friend of the governor's, and I think he's connected to the mob."

"What the hell are you talking about, Finn? You're delusional."

"No, I'm not. It's true. The company has been ripping off the state, and Natalie found out. That's why he had her killed."

"And I suppose you can prove this?"

"I can. I have documents that prove the company was stealing from the state, and I can prove Natalie found out about it just before she was killed."

Flaherty was shaking her head. "I can't simply take your word for it, Finn. I need some kind of confirmation."

Finn thought for a moment. "Bostick," he said.

"Bostick?"

"Yes, Peter Bostick. He lives in Chinatown. You've got to get to him. He can explain it all in a way that you might believe it."

"Peter Bostick? The former Boston police officer?"

"Yeah, that's why you'll believe him. All I'm asking is that you talk to him."

"That's going to be difficult."

"Why?"

"Because Peter Bostick was found murdered last night." She hesitated as she saw the shock and horror register on Finn's face. "It looks like a robbery. The whole precinct has been talking about it all day."

Suddenly it looked like the darkness had closed in around Finn. It was as if he could no longer see or hear anything, like he was lost in a whirlpool, spinning faster and faster.

"I have to get out of here," he said, more to himself than to Flaherty.

"You're not going anywhere. Tell me what Bostick has to do with this."

"I've got to leave," he said again. He got up and stumbled in the direction of the door. Flaherty stood up and grabbed him by the shoulders.

"Finn, talk to me! What's going on?"

He heard her this time, but he still wasn't able to focus on her words. "I've got to leave!" he shouted. "Don't you understand?"

"No, I don't understand." She pushed him back against the wall and he stumbled, hitting his head. "Tell me what this is all about! What does Peter Bostick have to do with this?" He struggled against her, but he was dizzy, and all of his strength had left him as the revelations piled up on one another.

"No, let me go!" he yelled.

"I'm not letting you go! Tell me what happened!" she yelled back.

Just then the door swung open. "That will be enough of that, Lieutenant!" a firm, strong voice boomed into the room, full of shock and indignation. Both Finn and Flaherty turned toward the voice, and there, standing next to Captain Weidel, both of them looking angry, was Preston Holland.

CHAPTER SIXTY

"Captain Weidel, I want to express my extreme displeasure at the treatment of my client. The days of rubber hoses have long since passed from our system of justice, or so I thought, and my client and I will be discussing very seriously the possibility of bringing charges against the department as a whole, and against Lieutenant Flaherty individually."

"What are *you* doing here?" Flaherty asked, still in shock from the sudden interruption.

"This man is my client, Lieutenant. Now, I would ask that you both leave us alone, please."

"I'll leave when I'm good and ready," she said defiantly.

"You'll leave now, or I'll have your badge by this afternoon!" Preston spouted back. "You're already in deep trouble for the illegal search you conducted of this man's apartment. If you want to salvage what's left of what was, until recently, a promising career, you'll be gone without another word, young lady!"

"Illegal search? What the hell are you talking about? He invited me in!"

"My understanding from your report is that he invited you in to wait for him. He did not give you consent to search his apartment—or his closet—and it's apparent you didn't get a warrant for that search. This is one of the clearest violations of the Fourth Amendment in the recent history of the Boston Police Department, and I guarantee that the case will be thrown out of court faster than you can say 'illegal search and seizure.'"

"But—" Flaherty began.

"Lieutenant!" Weidel interrupted. "Get out of this room immediately!"

Flaherty looked from Weidel to Holland to Finn incredulously. Then she closed her mouth and walked out.

Weidel nodded at Holland as he, too, withdrew. "Take all the time you need," he said, backing away and closing the door behind him.

Flaherty felt shaken as she sat at her desk. Finn was guilty. There was no other logical conclusion she could reach. He was the last person to see Natalie Caldwell alive; he was seen at the Kiss Club—where they had reason to believe Natalie Caldwell had been—on the night of her death; they'd found the ribbon and the knife at his apartment; and he had the perfect motive—jealousy. She couldn't imagine a simpler case.

So why didn't she believe he was guilty?

She sat at her desk for a long time, working through her feelings methodically. First, she had to recognize that she liked Finn. It had been a long time since she'd been drawn to anyone the way she was drawn to him. She forced herself to acknowledge that her hesitation might simply be a by-product of her *hope* that he was not guilty. She thought it was something more, though.

Part of it was that the case against Finn had become too simple. There was a certain compelling truth to what Finn had said. He struck her as too smart to keep the murder weapon barely hidden in the closet of his bedroom. The evidence just seemed too neat to be believed. That had been her first thought at his apartment, before the bartender at the Kiss Club came forward to claim Finn had been there the night Natalie was killed.

She was deep in thought when Kozlowski plopped down in the seat next to her desk holding two cups of coffee. He held one out to her. "So, how'd it go in there?"

"You weren't behind the mirror watching?"

He shrugged. "Someone has to fetch the coffee around here."

"It was interesting," she said after a brief pause. "He claims he didn't do it."

"Still?"

"Surprising, isn't it?"

"How did he explain the ribbon and the murder weapon we found?"

She raised her eyebrows. "He claims he's being set up by the real killer. He says that the evidence was planted, and that the bartender at the Kiss Club is lying."

"Did he have any suggestions for us about who the 'real killer' might be?"

"He did, actually. He has a very vivid imagination. He claims that some guy named McGuire, a bigwig at Huron Security, had her killed. You believe that? He's trying to shift the blame to one of his own clients."

Kozlowski frowned. "Tony McGuire?" he asked.

"I'm not sure, I don't think he gave me his first name. Why? Does it matter?"

"Probably not. It's just that when I was digging into Loring's past, Tony McGuire was a name that kept popping up. Loring apparently has an obsession with the guy, and he's been trying to bust him for years. It goes back to all of the trouble the Justice Department got in for using informants like Whitey Bulger."

Flaherty nodded. "Go on."

"Well, a lot of the recruiting was apparently done in an attempt to get this guy Tony McGuire, but it never worked and the guy slipped through the net every time."

Flaherty rubbed her forehead. "You think it's a coincidence?"

"I've been a cop for twenty-five years. I don't believe in coincidences anymore."

"What do you think, then?"

"We need to have a conversation with Loring and find out more about this Tony McGuire."

"I'm so sorry, Preston. I never meant to drag the firm into this."

Holland waved Finn off. "I think of this firm as a family, and when one of us is in trouble, we pull together behind him. You know how fond I am of you, both as a lawyer and as a person. You're one of the best associates we've ever had."

"I didn't do this, Preston. I swear to you, I didn't do any of the things they're saying. I could never have killed Natalie."

"I know it." Preston Holland patted Finn on the knee. "But the real question now is, how can we convince the police of that? Start by telling me exactly what you told them. I need to know everything."

"I told them what I just told you. That I didn't do this."

"And what about the evidence they found in your apartment? What did you say about that?"

Finn shrugged. "I told them it must have been planted there. That someone is trying to frame me."

"Good. Do you know who might be behind it? Anyone who has a grudge against you? Anything like that?"

Finn hesitated. Huron Security was Preston's client, and everything Finn had learned about the company and about McGuire was the result of Finn's participation in representing them. It suddenly occurred to him that, in telling Flaherty about his suspicions, he might have broken the law by divulging attorney-client privileged information. He hated to disappoint Preston any more than he already had. At the same time, though, he needed his boss's help too much to hold anything back.

"I think it's McGuire," he said, almost in a whisper.

"Tony McGuire?" Preston sounded shocked. "Nonsense," he snapped without a thought. Then he looked at Finn for a moment, as though he were considering the possibility, but he shook his head. "No. It just doesn't make sense. I understand Tony is not the most polished client the firm has ever had, but I can't believe he'd be involved in anything like this."

"I know how it sounds, Preston, but I can prove it. He's been stealing from the state, and I think he killed Natalie because she found out about it. Now he's trying to frame me for her murder."

Preston stood up and walked around the room, deep in thought. Then he spun on Finn. "You can prove this, you say?"

"I can prove that he's been stealing," Finn said. "I'm not sure I can prove yet that he murdered Natalie, but it makes sense."

Holland thought for a moment more. "What's your proof that he was stealing?"

Now Finn hesitated. "I don't want you to get too involved, Preston. You've already done so much for me, and I don't want to put you at risk. You just have to trust me; if I can get to the office, I can get the proof."

Holland nodded. "I do trust you, Finn. I do. It's just so incredible. Murder? Tony McGuire? It doesn't seem possible."

"If there's any way that you can get me out of here, I could prove it to you—and to the police, too."

Holland looked at his watch. "The problem is that it's ten o'clock on a Saturday morning. I could probably convince a judge that the search of your apartment was illegal, and based on that, you should be released. The only problem is that no courts are in session again until Monday."

"I can't wait that long," Finn said, groaning. "McGuire is trying to pin this on me, and at the moment he's doing a pretty good job. He's also clearly got a good deal of power. For all I know, they'll have someone in jail try to kill me before I can get in front of a judge."

Preston Holland rubbed his temples. "Maybe there's a way. I have several friends who are sitting Superior Court judges. I may be able to convince one to open a special session of court today just to hear this issue. If they did that, they could rule on our request for your release this afternoon."

"Do you think any judge would do that?"

"I think so," Holland said. "A couple owe me favors. I could call Harvey Whitehead. I was instrumental in getting him appointed to the bench in the first place." He leaned back in his chair and said in a confidential tone, "I also sponsored him for his membership in the Country Club in Brookline. He owes me big-time for that." He rubbed his chin. "It would involve calling in a huge favor, though."

Finn looked at his feet in shame. "I know it's a lot to ask."

Holland patted Finn on the knee again. "Don't worry about it. I have lots of chits out there on the table. I may as well have the fun of calling some of them in before I die."

CHAPTER SIXTY-ONE

Finn was on the street by four o'clock. Holland had made the call to the Honorable Harvey Whitehead, who'd grumbled, but ultimately called his bailiff and his clerk at their homes and agreed to hold a hearing at two-thirty that afternoon. Then Preston and Finn had sat together for an hour or so to prepare their argument.

"What exactly did you say when you told this detective she could enter your apartment?" Preston had asked Finn.

"I just said she could let herself in and wait for me there."

"So you didn't say anything like, 'Make yourself at home,' or 'Look around,' or anything like that?"

"Absolutely not."

"Okay, that's good. Now, I also need to know what you told the police when they arrested you and interrogated you. Did you make any kind of confession?"

"No. I told you, I'm innocent. I have nothing to confess to."

"Right, I know that," Preston said, though it seemed to Finn he'd forgotten. "Did you speculate at all about who really killed Natalie? Did you tell them anything about McGuire, or about your search for the real killer or anything along those lines?"

"No," Finn lied. He didn't want Preston to think that he'd

recklessly damaged his own defense by telling Flaherty about his theories.

"Good," Holland said. He stood up and adjusted his bow tie then smoothed his thick white hair into place. The hearing was in a half hour, but the police would bring Finn over to the courthouse. "All right," he said. "Let's get in there and kick some butt, shall we?" It was the line he always used before court appearances, and it made Finn feel normal for a brief moment. Preston smiled at Finn again. "I'll see you in court."

The hearing took less than thirty minutes, and Judge Whitehead ruled from the bench that Finn hadn't given the Boston Police Department permission to search his apartment by inviting Detective Flaherty to wait inside. The evidence found in the apartment was not in plain view and could only be found through an active search, the judge concluded. Furthermore, because Flaherty had failed to obtain a search warrant, the search was illegal, and all of the evidence found during the search would have to be excluded in any proceeding against Finn. Without the ribbon and the knife, the district attorney did not have enough evidence to hold Finn, and he was released.

The district attorney was livid. "Your Honor, I find it highly unusual that this hearing was called on a Saturday afternoon, and that this evidence is being excluded. It appears that the defendant is getting preferential treatment simply because he's an associate of Mr. Holland's law firm, and Mr. Holland is obviously an influential member of the bar."

Whitehead glowered from the bench. "And I find it highly unusual," he said, sneering, "that you would question the impartiality of this court—particularly in a matter where any first-year law student would recognize the weakness of the Commonwealth's position. Now, unless you'd like to be found in contempt and wish to take Mr. Finn's place in the holding cell for the remainder of the weekend, I suggest you figure out a legal way to collect evidence to build your case. Until then, however, this matter is dismissed."

The gavel came down, and Finn was free to go. Now all he had to do was figure out *where* to go.

First he had to say good-bye to Preston. Bostick's murder had demonstrated that Finn was in serious danger, and so were the people around him. He couldn't put Preston at risk, not after all he'd done for him.

Holland protested vehemently, offering to drive him to the office and help in any way he could, but Finn declined. He would take care of this on his own, he assured the older lawyer. He asked only one more favor of Preston. "I'm not sure I'll get around to the settlement agreement in the Tannery case this weekend," he said sheepishly.

Preston waved him off. "I'll have someone else at the office take care of that," he said. "You just focus on what you have to deal with here." Then they said their good-byes and Holland drove off.

Once Preston was gone, Finn needed to be sure he wasn't being followed. It would be a little tricky, he knew, but he remembered how to shake a tail from his youth in Charlestown.

He started out by walking a few blocks to a downtown bar he was familiar with. He walked in and sat at the bar, ordering a beer. As he sipped his drink, he watched the door, evaluating everyone who came in. Only two men entered within five minutes of his arrival. Finn looked them over carefully. One was a young man, in his mid-twenties, with an oversized Boston Red Sox jersey on over a T-shirt and loose jeans. The other was a slightly older man, in his forties, with a frumpy hat on his head and a gray windbreaker.

Either one could be a tail, Finn knew, but there was no way to be sure yet. He decided to play it safe.

After a few minutes of sipping his beer, he got up and walked back toward the men's room, out of sight from the main section of the bar. Once there, he passed the bathroom and walked out the back door. It led out to an alley around the corner from an upscale hotel. He walked quickly to the front of the hotel and hopped into one of the taxis lined up waiting for fares at the cabstand.

"I'm going to Central Square in Cambridge," he told the driver. As the cab pulled out into the street, Finn looked back down the side street that led to the bar. He could see the older man standing out front, looking up and down the street, scratching his head in frustration.

The taxi took Storrow Drive to Massachusetts Avenue, then cut across the river into Cambridge. Central Square was one of the busiest, most urban areas of Cambridge, right across the Charles River from Boston, which was why Finn had chosen it.

He paid the driver and got out in the heart of the square, then walked two blocks to another bar, checking over his shoulder the entire time for the man in the rumpled hat. Once in the bar, he repeated the procedure he'd used in Boston, sidling up to the bar to order a drink and watching to see if anyone followed him in. This time, no one did.

After ten minutes of waiting, he paid for his drink and left the bar through the back entrance, then walked five blocks to the nearest subway station to take the T back into Boston.

Finn knew where he was headed. He had to get the spreadsheets he'd stashed in his office. They'd prove to Linda that McGuire had been scamming the state for millions of dollars. With the actual evidence Linda would have to listen to him. The only question was whether he could survive long enough to show her the documents.

Governor Clarke stood at the giant window of his enormous office and watched the sun slide down on the horizon to the west of Boston. "He's on the street again?" he asked.

"Yes," Wendyl replied.

"I'm worried about what he may have told Flaherty."

"I doubt she'll credit his suspicions unless he has some hard evidence. Without something concrete to show her, he's just another murderer proclaiming his innocence."

Clarke looked at Wendyl Shore. He sighed, realizing he had to make sure the issue was taken care of. "What if he obtains hard evidence, and finds his way back to Flaherty?"

Wendyl shook his head. "That won't happen. As soon as he makes any kind of move, our friends will pick him up."

"I don't like this," the governor said. "I don't like this at all."

"Neither do I," Wendyl replied. "But we have to find out what he knows and who he's told. It's the only way."

The governor turned back toward the windows. The sun was gone, and the only evidence of its presence was a faint red glow that hung just beyond the Prudential Building. The lights in the buildings that ringed the Common twinkled on as Bostonians transitioned into night. He'd miss the view, if it ever came to that, Clarke knew. He suddenly wondered what it would be like to be a private citizen again. He couldn't let it come to that.

"Okay, make it happen," he said without turning around.

CHAPTER SIXTY-TWO

Flaherty called Rich Loring's home and discovered that the U.S. attorney was working that Saturday, so she and Kozlowski headed over to his office in the Federal Courthouse. He seemed less than thrilled to see them.

"Lieutenant," he said, greeting Flaherty with a cold glare. "I'm sorry you made the trip over here. I'm very busy today, and I don't have the time to be needlessly harassed on a weekend."

"I may have deserved that," Flaherty admitted.

"You did. Now, if you'll excuse me?" Loring gestured toward the door.

"Look, I'm sorry about the last meeting. I shouldn't have gotten personal, but we do have some questions we need to ask. This time I'll stay away from your personal life."

"Your apology is noted, but I still don't have time for this today. You'll have to come back some other time during business hours."

Flaherty shook her head. "This can't wait. There are people whose lives may be in danger."

"We all have our problems," Loring said, shrugging. "There are people whose lives are in danger every day. I wish I could help them all, but the reality is that there's only so much that one person can do." He swept his arm toward the door, more vehemently this time, indicating that the officers should leave. Flaherty looked at Kozlowski for help.

"Come on, Lieutenant," Kozlowski said, looking at Loring. "I told you he wouldn't be interested in our theories on McGuire. He's accepted that the man will never be caught. We'll just have to look for help with this someplace else."

"What did you say?" said Loring, taking the bait.

"McGuire. Antonio McGuire," Kozlowski said. "You know, that guy you've been trying to put away for years—unsuccessfully, of course. We have reason to believe he may be involved in Natalie Caldwell's murder, but it'll probably never pan out. I'll tell you what, we'll make an appointment for next week, and we can discuss how everything went." Kozlowski motioned Flaherty to the door and the two of them started to walk out of the office.

"Wait!" Loring yelled. He was out of his seat and around his desk quickly. "In what way do you think McGuire is involved?"

"At this point, it's just a theory," Flaherty said, "but Natalie Caldwell was working on a case for Huron Security at the time of her murder. There is a possibility she may have been killed because of something she learned about the company."

"What makes you say that?"

"We can't give that information out at this point," said Flaherty, shaking her head.

Loring considered Flaherty for a moment, weighing his options. "What a pity," he said. "For a moment I thought we were on the same side. I guess you'll just have to find someone else who's as familiar with McGuire as I am to help you out."

The two detectives looked at each other. They were at a stalemate with Loring and they knew it. Neither detective wanted to give up too much information about the investigation, but they needed Loring's help to figure out what role, if any, McGuire had played in Natalie Caldwell's murder. After a few seconds of reading each other's faces, they both nodded.

"Scott Finn made the claim."

"Finn." Loring considered this. "The lawyer who took over the Huron case after Natalie's murder?" It seemed he already knew more than the detectives might have thought.

Flaherty nodded. "At the moment, he's also our primary suspect in the case. How do you know so much about him?"

"We've been keeping an eye on him because of his connections to Huron and McGuire. We've been hearing his name mentioned by certain individuals with strong connections to organized crime." He thought for a moment. "If he's your main suspect, he may just be trying to deflect attention away from himself."

"That's our worry," Flaherty admitted. "What's Finn's connection to organized crime?"

Loring shook his head. "That's what we've been trying to figure out. We only know that certain dangerous people have been asking questions about him." Loring was pacing back and forth now. "Did Mr. Finn indicate what Natalie had discovered that led to her death?"

"He wasn't exactly clear," Flaherty admitted. "He simply said that Huron had been stealing from the state."

Loring raised his eyebrows. "Did he have any proof?"

She nodded. "He said he had documents. I asked him for confirmation and he told me to talk to his private investigator. Unfortunately, that PI was murdered last night. When I told Finn, he seemed shocked at the news. The PI's name was Bostick—a former Boston PD member."

Loring was becoming more agitated. "Do you know who killed Mr. Bostick?"

Flaherty shook her head. "I talked to the detective in charge of the investigation, and he said that they had no good leads. For the moment they're treating it as a random mugging."

"That would be a remarkable coincidence, wouldn't it?"

"Yeah, one among many. But I don't have enough information to move things in any other direction." Flaherty looked at Kozlowski, who had remained silent during the exchange. She wondered if she'd divulged too much information. The room was quiet for a moment as Loring paced back and forth behind his desk, doing mental gymnastics without taking any note of the two officers. Finally it was too much for Flaherty to take.

"Look, we've laid out our information, it's time you started giving something back. What do you know about McGuire? Who is he? And is it really possible he could be mixed up in all of this?"

Loring stopped his pacing and faced her. "Oh yes, it's very possible. I might even say it's probable."

"Why do you say that?"

"This is a very bad man we're talking about."

"We've dealt with bad men before," Kozlowski interjected, clearly annoyed at Loring's patronizing tone.

"With all due respect, Detective, you've never dealt with a man like McGuire before."

"What makes him so different?" Flaherty asked.

"Several things. First of all, he's brilliant. Most of the people in organized crime are nothing but street thugs with some violent supporters. Not McGuire. His schemes are often elaborate and well conceived. So well conceived we haven't been able to catch him at anything yet. He layers corruption on top of corruption in a pyramid that's almost impenetrable, so his finances are almost impossible to trace. He has a sophisticated mind that could have made him remarkably successful in almost any legitimate business. Unfortunately, he has some serious character flaws."

"Like what?"

"Like a love of violence and the absence of a conscience. He grew up in Somerville in the projects, and his father was fairly high up in the Winter Hill Gang. He was a sadistic son of a bitch and worked as an enforcer. Our reports indicate that he liked his work—and that he took it home with him."

"Child abuse?" Flaherty asked.

"That's a polite term for it. We have hospital records from back in the early sixties, when Antonio McGuire was a kid. He was in the emergency room almost every week. Broken bones, lacerations, burns that often resembled cigar tips, whip marks from leather belts, you name it."

"Lovely."

"Yeah. Apparently his father wanted to toughen him up. He did a good job. When McGuire was sixteen he moved out of his father's house. A week later the police found the senior McGuire hanging from a banister in the staircase."

"I take it from your tone it wasn't a suicide?"

"Not likely. More than twenty different bones had been broken in his body before he died. It looked like he was used as a piñata as he suffocated. The soles of his feet were burned off with a blowtorch, and his hands didn't resemble anything human."

"Did they ever find out for sure who did it?"

"There were rumors about it being a retaliation hit by La Cosa Nostra out of the North End, but it didn't fit. There was too much anger involved, and the wounds were too personal. Eventually, word began to trickle out that Antonio had taken his revenge on his old man. After that, Tony rose quickly through the ranks of the Winter Hill Gang, and later was a captain under Whitey Bulger. Eventually, though, he moved on to more sophisticated scams involving government and business fraud." Loring caught a look from both detectives. "That's right, just like the scam you're talking about. I've been trying to bust him for fifteen years, but he's a slippery bastard, and he keeps wriggling away."

"So it's possible Finn may be telling the truth?"

"As I said, it's definitely possible. If Mr. Finn actually has documents proving that McGuire has been embezzling from the state, it could provide the biggest break in a case we've been trying to make for more than six years. One thing's for sure, though." Loring looked at the two officers. "If McGuire even suspects Finn possesses incriminating evidence that he intends to share with us, the man won't last a day on the streets."

Flaherty looked at Kozlowski. "We need to bring him in. Now."

CHAPTER SIXTY-THREE

Finn closed the drawer of his desk and slipped the folded sheets of paper into his inside breast pocket. Getting into the office had been a breeze. No one at the firm other than Preston knew that he'd been arrested yet, and the office was quiet on that Saturday evening. He was also convinced that his circuitous route had thrown off anyone who was trying to follow him. He'd even told the cab driver to drop him off a few blocks from the office so he could see if anyone was still on his tail.

Boston was in its full glory that evening. Summer was yielding grudgingly to autumn as September matured, and the sun no longer baked the city's inhabitants mercilessly. Now it bit through the crisp, clean air at the tourists thronging Quincy Market and strolling past the ubiquitous statues evoking Boston's revolutionary past.

Finn walked over to the window of his office and looked out at the harbor. The last rays of the day twinkled off the casual ripples that graced the water's surface.

He loved this view. It made him feel as though he'd made it to the top of the highest mountain in the world and had staked a claim no one could nullify. Now he wondered if he'd ever enjoy the view again. The law firm of Howery, Black & Longbothum would suffer very seriously from the scandal if their client was involved in government corruption and murder—particularly if the evidence that sent the client away had been turned over to the police by one of Huron's lawyers. The partners would be looking for a sacrificial scalp, and Finn's would be the obvious choice.

He took another moment to memorize the picture from his window high above the streets of Boston. Several old wooden ships, with their sails playing in the breeze, shared the harbor with tankers and mammoth cargo barges, harkening back to a simpler time. Maybe it would all be for the best, Finn thought. Then he spun on his heels and headed out the door, turning off the light behind him.

Once out on the street he headed for the police station five blocks away. Even if Flaherty wasn't there, he'd wait for her. He couldn't go back to his apartment for fear he'd be followed, and for the same reason he didn't want to be on the street any longer than necessary.

As he walked, he rehearsed what he'd say to Flaherty. She'd be skeptical, clearly, and not without good reason, but he knew he could convince her. He had the evidence now, and she'd have to listen.

He thought carefully about every word he'd use to sway her—it was like constructing an opening argument, a trial, and a closing argument all at once. Tell the jury what they're going to see; then show it to them; then tell them what they just saw. It was one of the fundamentals of trial presentation. He just needed to make sure his presentation incorporated enough finesse to be convincing.

He heard the van door slide open as he walked by, but the meaning of the sound was lost on him until it was too late. Two men jumped out of the nondescript utility vehicle and were on him before he could react. One held out a black plastic baton with a wide opening and steel teeth at one end. Finn saw the electrical current buzzing between the metal teeth of the baton for only a split second before it was thrust into his side.

"No!" he tried to scream, but the current robbed his body of all control. As the electricity sped throughout his arms and legs, up his spine, and into the base of his skull, it felt like someone had screwed him into a light socket and thrown the switch. His eyes rolled up into his head, and the last thing his mind registered was the faint odor of burning flesh. Then his body went slack and he collapsed into the arms of his two attackers, who quickly slid him through the van's open side door and sped away from the curb.

The entire abduction had taken less than five seconds, and no one on the street noticed or cared. Across the street in Quincy Market, the tourists smiled in the early autumn evening, waiting for the leaves to change, reveling in the beautiful New England day.

CHAPTER SIXTY-FOUR

"There's no answer on his cell phone," Flaherty said.

"You've tried his office and his home as well?" Loring asked. They were still in his office, and the discussion had quickly turned to Finn's safety.

"I've tried all three places. I even had a patrol car go by his apartment in Charlestown to see if he might be there. Nothing."

"Does he have any family he might contact, maybe to go stay with during all of this?"

Flaherty shook her head. "He's an orphan, with no brothers or sisters."

"How about a girlfriend?"

"No," Flaherty responded a little too quickly.

"Okay, okay," Loring said, holding up his hands. "I'm just checking. I want to make sure we've considered every reasonable possibility before we start using my contacts."

"He's fallen off the face of the earth," Flaherty said, "and we need to use any means we have to find him. His life may be in danger."

"Finn's a big boy," Kozlowski interjected with a note of subtle reprimand. "He's been on the street before, and he can take care of himself."

"Not against these people," Loring said. "It's safe to say that if McGuire has gotten his hands on Mr. Finn, we don't have much time."

"What can you do?"

Loring hesitated. "As I told you, we've been keeping an eye on Mr. Finn because of his connection to Huron and the rumors we were hearing on the street. I may be able to locate him." Flaherty and Kozlowski looked at him expectantly. "There's a catch, though," he continued. "To find him, I'll have to risk compromising one of the best informants I've ever had—one of the best in the history of the FBI."

"Better than Whitey Bulger?" Kozlowski said wryly.

Loring scowled. "Bulger was a mistake," he said. "I knew he was shady, but I had no idea how far over the line he and Connolly were. I screwed up on that score because I wasn't paying close enough attention. People died because of those mistakes, and I have to live with that."

"But you're willing to make the same mistake again?" Flaherty demanded.

"No," Loring said. "This is different. This guy is on the level and only engages in some bookmaking to stay on the wrong side of the line with access to the bad guys. I have a personal relationship with him, and I've made sure he's never taken anything too far."

"How can you be so sure?" Flaherty asked.

"I had him tailed for more than a year in the beginning. Since then, I've put an agent on him periodically just to make sure there's been no backsliding. There hasn't been. This guy was looking for a way out on his own—it's not like he was busted and had no choice. He came to us and asked for a way out, and we gave it to him. Since then, he's been responsible for dozens of high-profile organized crime arrests in New England. That's a pretty good track record."

"It still seems a little dangerous in light of all of the past screwups the Bureau has had in Boston," Kozlowski noted.

"Oh, come off it, Detective. You know as well as I do that law enforcement depends on informants to get the job done. You can't tell me the police department would be effective without them."

Kozlowski thought for a moment. "No, I can't."

"There are always risks. The best we can do is to try to minimize those risks. The guy I'm dealing with here is clean. At least, he's as clean as any informant who can help accomplish anything is ever going to be. By the time he came inside with us, his reputation on the street was so nasty he didn't have to mess with people anymore—because no one messes with him." Loring could see the detectives were still skeptical. "Believe me, I hate to expose this guy. He's the best pipeline of information we've ever had. More than that, he's put his life on the line by working with us, and now we're going to have to ask him to expose himself and make himself a target. I hate to do it, but if Mr. Finn has evidence that can make a case against McGuire, it would be worth it."

"Why would this guy agree to put himself in that kind of danger?" Kozlowski asked.

"Trust me, he has reason enough."

"Make the call," Flaherty said.

Tigh McCluen sat behind the counter at the Downtown Liquor Outlet in Charlestown, leaning into the *Boston Herald* sports pages that were laid out in front of him.

"Sox lost again, huh, Mr. McCluen?" Billy Shea said as he stocked liquor bottles on the racks nearby.

Tigh smiled through his goatee. "That they did, son."

"So you must be having a pretty good day then, right?"

"Ah, Billy, you've got to learn never to take joy in someone else's misery. In this business, you can't be making moral judgments about who should win and who should lose. It's a business plain and simple. All you can do as the house is balance the odds and take your cut."

Billy nodded. It was a slow day at the Outlet, but that wasn't that unusual. While the liquor business generally turned a tidy profit, the store's real value was as a cash funnel for more lucrative, illicit enterprises. The store generally cleared more money in a day in the rackets than it did in a month on sales of booze. Billy, a skinny street teen with the look of a beaten pound dog, worked the register and kept the store running. Tigh, who was nominally the store manager, used the place as his office for running a gambling operation. Day after day he sat behind the counter, getting up occasionally to use the stockroom for any transaction that was better suited for privacy.

"Still," Billy pushed, "you must've done all right, right?"

Tigh smiled again. "The fans in this city are very loyal," he said. "They bet with their hearts, and that gives anyone who plays the odds well an advantage."

Tigh stopped talking as a customer walked in and began to browse through the discount booze that was displayed prominently at the front of the store: Mad Dog, Thunderbird, Old Crow. These were the brands that moved the fastest off the shelves in the small shop that stood across Water Street from the projects. He kept a couple of cases of chardonnay in the back to provide some cover for the wealthier heavy betters from up on Monument Square, but it was the cheap stuff that made the store itself profitable.

It wasn't a bad life on the whole, Tigh reflected. He didn't miss the danger of the old days, when he was out on the street as one of the most feared enforcers for the Winter Hill Gang. His size and his tolerance for pain—both the pain he inflicted on others and the pain others inflicted on him—made him a legend on the street. He reputation was so well established that no one had challenged him in years. He preferred being off the streets; preferred even the cracked linoleum and yellow lights of the Liquor Outlet to the endless battles and posturing and bullying that were such a central part of his past.

The buzzing of Tigh's cell phone interrupted his thoughts. He flipped open the cover and held the phone up to his ear. "Hello?" he said in his typically gruff voice.

"We need to talk."

"Now?"

"Right now."

Tigh took the phone away from his ear and looked around him. Billy was leaning against the counter behind the register idly flipping through the pages of one of the particularly graphic pornographic magazines the store sold from behind the register, along with cigarettes and lottery tickets. It was a one-stop vice shop, Tigh had commented once. You could get your booze, your bets, your smokes, your lotto, and your porn. He got up from his stool and walked to the back of the store.

"Billy, if anyone's looking for me, tell them I'm in back, and I'll be out in a minute, all right?" he yelled as he walked.

"Okay, Mr. McCluen."

Once in the back storeroom, Tigh spoke into the phone again. "We're on a cell phone, remember," were his first words. They were unnecessary, but Tigh said them in every conversation nonetheless. It made him feel safer.

"We've got a problem with your friend."

"Shit. How serious?"

"As serious as it gets. We're going to need your help with him." There was a pause on the line. "And Tigh?"

"Yeah?"

"This could be the ball game, you know what I mean?"

Tigh shook his head. Sometimes, no matter how hard you tried, you could never escape your past. "Pick me up at the usual spot in thirty minutes," he said. Then he flipped the phone closed before the caller could respond.

He had dreaded this possibility from the outset, but he knew he had obligations from which he couldn't run. Slowly, without enthusiasm, he stood and walked back out into the main part of the Outlet and looked around, taking in every detail. He'd probably never be back, he knew.

CHAPTER SIXTY-FIVE

Finn heard the ringing. He was eight years old and all he wanted was sleep, but the noise wouldn't stop. He flailed out from his bed, trying to locate the snooze button on the clock to stop the alarm, but he'd only been with this foster family for a few days, and he still didn't know where things were in the dark. His arm swung out and caught the lamp by the side of the table, sending it crashing to the floor. Suddenly there were voices everywhere.

"I'm sorry!" he screamed, but to no avail. They were coming for him, and he could already feel the heavy sting of the leather belt on his back.

"I'm sorry! It was an accident!" he yelled again, knowing it would do no good, and might even prolong the beating.

"Please! I'm sorry!" he cried again in the darkness, frightened for his life. His eyes were shut to try to keep out the pain, shut so tight he could see shapes forming on the insides of his eyelids: flashes of light in red and yellow and white mixing to form an image that was becoming clearer and clearer until Natalie Caldwell's face hovered before him, the eyes sad and desperate, and so full of life.

"I'm sorry!" he yelled again.

Finn opened his eyes. It was dark and cold, and it took a

moment for him to get his bearings as he tried to remember where he was. Every muscle in his body ached as if he'd run a marathon. Then he remembered the two men who'd attacked him in the street, and the electricity they'd sent through his body to incapacitate him. He rolled his neck in memory of the pain, and tried to rub the back of his head, but something was preventing him from raising his arm. He felt down and realized, even in the darkness, that he was tied to a chair with plastic wire restraints.

He wiggled himself back and forth in the chair to test the strength of the plastic, and determined that his legs were similarly bound. The plastic was strong, and cut into his flesh when he pulled against it, so he rested for a moment and concentrated on acclimating his eyes to the darkness.

There wasn't much he could tell about where he was. The room he was in seemed huge—so huge he couldn't tell where it ended in the darkness. He could also hear the echo of dripping water off the cold stone floor, and he could smell the mildew on the damp walls.

Suddenly, just as he felt his eyes were adjusting, someone flashed a bright light directly into them, blinding him. He screamed out in shock and pain as his eyes snapped shut reflexively. It was at that moment that he heard the laughing. It was low and deep and sinister, coming from some point just beyond the light source.

"Who is that?" Finn demanded impotently. The only response was an increase in the laughter, turning it from a chuckle to a cackle that died down again to silence.

"Who is that?" Finn yelled again as panic began to set in. He tried to calm himself, but it was no use. This was bad, he knew. He was in more trouble than he'd ever been in before, and there was nothing he could do. He started to struggle against the restraints again. He knew it was pointless, but he couldn't stop himself. He pulled so hard that he felt himself bleeding from his wrists and ankles, but he didn't care. It gave him an added sense of control, and if he caught an artery and bled to death, at least it would be by his own hand, not by the hand of his captor beyond the light. He continued to struggle until he heard the voice, clear and strong.

"Relax, Counselor, we just want to talk to you."

Finn stopped struggling and he could feel his body go cold. He recognized the voice—and the sarcasm. "Oh shit," he whispered.

"Good to see you, too," the voice replied.

CHAPTER SIXTY-SIX

Tigh McCluen walked slowly along the road, lugging a thick duffel bag over his shoulder. It was well into the evening, and his giant frame, caught in the lights from the cars, cast long shadows that grew and sharpened, then disappeared as the cars passed. He made his way along the O'Brien Highway, which headed into Cambridge from Charlestown, keeping an eye out for his ride. At the same time he took in every visual detail of the neighborhood, memorizing the town that had been his home for more than two decades, ever since the first day he stepped off the boat. This might be the last time he ever saw this place, he knew.

On his way out of Charlestown, he passed Sullivan's Tavern, a pub established in 1756, whose wide pine flooring and heavy oak bar still held the aura of revolution. That was where they often used to celebrate, in a private room in the back. They'd gather together, a dozen or so of them, and toast their violence and thievery.

The first time Tigh had been included was when he was eighteen, having only recently been recruited as an enforcer. It was right after the Chelsea Street Regulars broke up—right after Joey's death. Finn was still on the streets, but he'd already begun to drift away, and Tigh felt truly lonely for the first time in his life.

As a newcomer to the elite world of organized crime, he sat quietly at the edge of the crowd, drinking it all in, wondering if this would be his new family. Bravado poured forth from the older crowd as they swapped stories from the days of the long-running gang wars.

After a few hours, Whitey Bulger made his way over to Tigh and sat next to him, introducing himself as though anyone didn't know who he was.

"You don't say much, do you, kid?" he said after a moment or two of trying to draw Tigh out.

Tigh shrugged. "I guess not." He was still a little self-conscious about his accent.

"That's good." Bulger nodded. "The less you say, the better. If you want to survive in this game, you're always better off keeping your mouth shut."

Tigh nodded back at him, but said nothing.

"Good," Bulger said. Then he stuck out his hand. "Glad to have you on board. If you ever have any problems, come see me, okay?"

Tigh shook his hand. "Okay, Mr. Bulger," he said. Then Bulger got up and walked away, heading back to the other end of the table. Tigh wouldn't find out for another fifteen years that, in exchange for protection, Bulger was already supplying information to the FBI about his enemies.

Tigh didn't turn for another decade, and when he finally did, it wasn't for personal gain or to secure immunity down the road. It was out of anger.

He'd spent much of the 1990s running an extortion racket with Freddy Miller, one of the favored sons of the Winter Hill Gang. Freddy was the heir apparent to the Charlestown crew, and he was ruthless. There were few people in the world who'd ever made Tigh nervous, but Miller was one of them.

He enjoyed the act of inflicting pain, and was crazy enough to lose his composure over the slightest provocation.

Miller had one redeeming quality, though: his girlfriend, Nikki Raymond. Tigh could never understand what she was doing with him. She was smart and tough and good-looking. She and Tigh became friends, and Tigh often wondered if they might have been more than that if it weren't for Freddy. Both were well aware, though, that Freddy would have killed anyone who went near her. At least Tigh got to spend time with her, and sometimes it even seemed like that was enough.

Then one day, suddenly, Nikki stopped coming around. When Tigh asked Miller about it, he was nonspecific. "We broke up," was all he'd say, and Tigh knew not to ask any more questions.

Later that day, Tigh snuck away and went to Nikki's mother's house. The mother opened the door in tears. "Get out of here, you bastard!" she shouted. "Haven't you done enough already?"

Against her protests Tigh pushed his way into the house and made his way to the back bedrooms. He found Nikki curled up on her bed in a room that obviously hadn't changed much since she'd been in high school a few years before. Pennants and out-of-date rock star posters hung on the walls.

He barely recognized her. Her nose was broken and her jaw was wired shut. Her eyes were frightened little dots surrounded by raw tissue turned bright purple, still oozing from the edges of her wounds. Above her eyes, stretching from her forehead into a shaved patch of skin in her hairline, was a gash that had been stitched together with thick surgical sutures.

When she saw Tigh, she pulled away in fear, crying.

"I'm sorry," was all Tigh could say before he left the room quickly. Two days later he turned over a cache of incriminating information on Freddy Miller to a cop he'd known growing up. With that, his career as a police informant had begun.

Now it was ending, he suspected. After tonight, he'd probably be exposed, and returning to the streets would no longer be an option. His old life was over.

"So who's this guy we're going to pick up?" Flaherty asked as they drove through Charlestown.

"He was once an enforcer for the Winter Hill Gang," Loring replied. "Now he runs a bookie operation out of the Liquor Outlet in Charlestown, and he has big-time contacts. He's been feeding us reliable information for almost ten years. I trust him." Loring was driving the car with Flaherty riding shotgun. Kozlowski was bundled into the backseat.

"And you think he knows where Finn is?"

"He should. I asked him to keep an eye on Finn. They were friends growing up, and I thought we might be able to get some leverage if we used him."

"You're a manipulative son of a bitch, aren't you, Loring?" Kozlowski interjected from the backseat.

"Yes, thank you," Loring spat back.

"What's he like?" Flaherty asked.

"You can judge for yourself," Loring said. "That's him up on the next corner."

The dark blue boxy Ford four-door sedan slowed and pulled to the curb in front of him. *Why not just wear a fucking sign that says "Cops Inside"?* Tigh thought. Not that it really mattered. After tonight, his cover would likely be blown anyway. He opened the door and got in the backseat.

"Loring," he said, nodding at the U.S. attorney. "You didn't mention we'd have company."

"Tigh McCluen, this is Detective Lieutenant Flaherty. Lieutenant Flaherty, this is Tigh McCluen."

Tigh nodded at Flaherty. "I've seen you on the news, haven't I? You're the one who caught Little Jack, right?"

Flaherty heard Loring chuckle as she shook her head. "My partner and another officer had more to do with that than me."

"She just took the credit," Loring jabbed.

"What have you got to do with this, then?" Tigh asked.

"It may just be that this mess is connected to one of the murders we've been assuming Little Jack committed," Flaherty responded.

Tigh nodded. "I still don't like strangers," he said pointedly, looking at Loring.

"And we don't like snitches," Kozlowski interjected.

"You haven't been properly introduced," Flaherty said, looking over her shoulder from the front seat. "This is my partner, Tom Kozlowski. We bring him along to handle public relations. You'll have to excuse his manners."

"Don't apologize for him, lass. None of us like snitches."

"Then why do you do it?" Kozlowski asked.

"We all have our role to play, now, don't we? Sometimes the role chooses the player, not the other way around."

"Did you get a location on Finn?" Loring butted in, eager to prevent the conversation from straying too far in the wrong direction.

Tigh shook his head. "I haven't had time yet, but I brought the tracker with me. It's here in the bag," McCluen said, opening the duffel on his lap. He pulled out what looked like a laptop computer and booted it up.

"What's that?" Flaherty asked.

"It's a portable GPS tracker," Tigh said. Then he looked at Kozlowski. "That's a Global Positioning System tracker for those who're less educated."

"That's funny," Kozlowski said, sneering. "You planning on doing stand-up in the joint?"

"Where did you get it?" Flaherty asked, trying to push the discussion over the potholes.

"I gave it to him," Loring said. "Makes it easier for Mr. McCluen to track certain people we're interested in."

"One of my many talents," said Tigh, winking at Flaherty.

"Where's the transmitter?"

"I put it in a lighter I gave Finn a few days ago."

"How do you know he still has the lighter with him?" Kozlowski challenged.

Tigh looked at Kozlowski the way you might look at a dog who's just passed gas. "You didn't grow up on the street, did you?" He didn't wait for an answer. "Trust me, if Finn's still alive, he's got that lighter with him."

The computer screen flickered on, and after a moment a map appeared. Tigh worked the keyboard in the backseat, pressing buttons to reposition the map and cross-reference the coordinates that appeared on the screen. Finally a bright red signal showed clearly in the center. "Jesus, Mary, and Joseph," he said under his breath.

"What is it?" Loring asked as he drove the car. "Did you find him?"

"I found him," Tigh replied.

"Where is he?" Flaherty demanded.

"He's at the Castle," Tigh said. He looked up and caught Loring's eyes in the reflection of the rearview mirror.

"That's bad, isn't it?" Flaherty asked, witnessing the visual exchange between Loring and McCluen.

Tigh nodded. "It doesn't get much worse, lass."

CHAPTER SIXTY-SEVEN

The voice came out of the darkness beyond Finn's sight, which was severely limited by the light that was being directed into his eyes. He now understood why some cops still liked to use bare lightbulbs in their interrogations. It was effectively disorienting. He felt helpless as he strained to make out the shadows that kept shifting just beyond the corners of the fireball that burned his irises. He could tell there were two, maybe three other people in the room, but they looked like faceless phantoms. Still, he recognized the voice.

"McGuire," he said simply.

Finn saw the shadows behind the light shift, and McGuire moved forward so that his silhouette was more clearly visible. He pulled up a folding chair and sat within a few feet of Finn. "How's it going, Finn?" he asked evenly.

Finn looked down at the plastic restraints binding his arms and legs. Then he looked back at McGuire. "I'm not sure," he replied, feeling his way into the conversation. "What do you think?"

McGuire arched his eyebrows and tilted his head noncommittally. "I guess that's what we're here to find out, isn't it." He leaned forward and put the tips of his fingers together contemplatively. "You should have listened to the warnings, you know? You're a decent guy for a lawyer. It's a shame things had to come to this."

The fear sent a shot of adrenaline through Finn's body. "In Charlestown?" he asked. "Your guys?"

McGuire nodded. "It would have been better if you'd paid attention."

Finn looked down at his hands and legs again, twisting them slightly to test the bindings for weakness, but they held tight. He sat there for several seconds as McGuire regarded him in an oddly detached way. Finn wondered what would happen next, but the silence stretched out endlessly, until he could stand it no longer.

"What do you want?" he asked, thinking that the best defense in the situation might very well be a strong offense.

"What do I want?" McGuire considered the question. "I want world peace. I want an end to starvation in Africa. I want the Red Sox to win the World Series again." He leaned forward again. "But most of all, what I really fucking want is to know what the fuck you were doing with this." He reached into his jacket and pulled out a sheaf of paper. It took a moment for Finn to realize he was holding the list of names Finn had retrieved from his office.

Finn looked at the papers nervously, but could think of nothing to say. "How did you know?" he asked at last.

McGuire laughed. "Oh, Finn," he mocked, "you're not nearly as smart as I thought you were. It's my business to know things, and I've got the right people on my payroll."

Finn stared at McGuire without comprehension. "Who?" he asked feebly. But even as the question escaped his lips the answer became plain to him. He felt dizzy as his mind spun through the events of the past days, and the realization of his betrayal came into focus. *It can't be*, he thought, but he knew it was true, and the force of the truth was almost too much to bear.

He looked up at McGuire, who was watching him closely. The man laughed again, shaking his head. "You really are a fucking patsy, Finn. You know that?"

At that moment, that's exactly how Finn felt.

CHAPTER SIXTY-EIGHT

Fort Independence sat low and heavy at the edge of the water, a stone pentagon on a peninsula jutting out from the edge of South Boston, guarding the entryway to Boston's Inner Harbor. The first fortress built on the strategic spot stood from 1634 until the British burned it during their retreat from Boston during the Revolutionary War. It had been rebuilt several times, and the current incarnation was commissioned during the presidency of Andrew Jackson in 1834. The five-turreted stone and earthwork structure covering the nine acres of Castle Island had long ago been given the nickname "the Castle," and its lore had been secured when a young Edgar Allan Poe was stationed there, and later based his descriptions of the catacombs in his short story "The Cask of Amontillado" on the fort's layout. No longer a military installation, it was run by the Massachusetts District Commission as a tourist attraction.

Flaherty, Kozlowski, Loring, and McCluen parked on Day Boulevard at around 11:45 that Saturday night, about a half mile down the access road from the giant structure.

"It's a perfect spot for this sort of thing," Tigh pointed out. "Because it's out there on the peninsula, there's really only one approach, and that's down this long bottleneck, so they can see anyone coming. There's a boat tied to a jetty at the waterside, so they can always get away quickly if there's a need. And it's remote enough that there's little chance anyone will overhear them as they work people over."

"How the hell do they get in?" Loring asked.

"The city posts a civilian guard at night, but it's a patronage job, and the Southie representatives in the State House are always told who to give that job to. Right now, it's Lefty Sullivan."

"Howie Sullivan's son?"

"The very same. So you can see how he might not object to some of his father's associates using the place when needed. He gets paid on the side, too, to act as a lookout, although they usually leave a little muscle by the entrance with him, just in case."

"So how do *we* get in?" Flaherty demanded, impatient with all the talk.

"I'll be walking in," Tigh replied, rubbing his fingers across his chin. "They know me, and Lefty's afraid of me. It shouldn't be a problem."

"That'll be enough for you to get in?" Kozlowski sounded skeptical.

Tigh shrugged. "We'll see. I'll tell them I have some important information about the man they've got in there."

"Okay, that takes care of you, but there's got to be several of them in there, so how do the rest of us get in?" Flaherty demanded.

"I've been thinking about that," Tigh said. "On the other side of the fort, down near the water—just to the left of the jetty—there's a door that leads to a tunnel. The tunnel comes up through a trapdoor into an old storage room in the heart of the Castle. It was designed as a way to sneak supplies into the fort if needed during a siege. Other than the front door, that's the only way in."

"Won't they see us as we walk down the road toward the fort?" Loring asked.

McCluen pointed to the high wooden fence that bordered the access road. "That fence was put there to block the view," he said. "On the other side is a commercial shipping yard's holding area. The fence runs all the way to the water down by the Castle. I'll give you a ten-minute head start, then I'll go in the front door. You need to get yourselves down to the water, around through the tunnel, and into the storeroom. That room is about twenty yards away from the place where they take people for questioning. When you go out of the storeroom, go to the right, and then stay out of sight and wait for my signal."

"What's the signal?" Flaherty asked.

"I'm not sure yet," Tigh admitted, "but I'll make it obvious enough that you'll have no doubt."

The epiphany left Finn devastated, and he had to struggle to keep his composure.

Preston.

He searched his mind, fumbling with the pieces of the puzzle. How could he ever have missed it? How could he have been so stupid? Natalie told him she was sleeping with someone older—someone who could help her with her career.

Preston.

Besides Linda, only one person knew that Finn suspected McGuire and Huron of scamming the state.

Preston.

Only one person knew that Finn was going to the office to collect the evidence he needed to prove his suspicions to the police.

Preston.

The puzzle was coming together in his mind now. Finn had never even considered that Preston might be involved in any of this mess, because he viewed him as untouchable. He was the paragon of everything to which Finn aspired. More than that, he was one of the few people who'd ever given Finn a chance. Preston was his mentor, and his friend, and the thought that he'd betrayed him felt like a knife carving out his heart.

But it all made sense. Preston was in charge of all of Huron's legal work, and the security company was one of Howery, Black's largest and most profitable clients. In addition, Preston had the political connections necessary to protect Huron.

All of a sudden, Finn felt more lost than he ever had before. When Preston had showed up at the police station to help him, Finn had drawn such strength from his unwavering belief in him. Now he understood that Preston was only interested in having him released so he could lead McGuire to the evidence. He'd believed Preston when he said that Finn was the future of the firm. Now he knew that his boss had merely been playing him, much the same way others had played him throughout his life. Until that moment, Preston had been the only figure in his life worth looking up to. Now that image was gone, and there was nothing to take its place. There seemed to be no hope left, and so little to live for. With Preston helping McGuire, Finn would simply disappear, and Natalie's murder would be pinned on him. No one would care.

"Let's talk about this list," said McGuire, interrupting Finn's thoughts.

Finn looked at the papers again. He sighed heavily. "What do you want to know?"

CHAPTER SIXTY-NINE

"Do you know how to handle a gun?" Kozlowski asked Loring.

He nodded. "I was certified when I was with the FBI."

Kozlowski reached down to his ankle holster and pried loose a snub-nosed .38.

"I'm sorry to take your spare piece," Loring said.

"No problem, that's why they call it a spare," Kozlowski replied.

They were standing with Flaherty at the foot of the wooden fence separating the access road to Fort Independence from the shipyard. The fence was tall—clearly meant to discourage unwanted visitors—but hardly insurmountable. There was no barbed wire at the top, and it was only eight feet high. It seemed that aesthetics were the primary purpose behind its construction, rather than security.

"All right, let's do this," Kozlowski said, dropping to one knee and locking his giant knuckles together to give Loring a place to put his foot. "I'll boost you up to the top, and you help pull the lieutenant up. Then, if you both reach down, you'll be able to pull me over."

Loring nodded and put his foot into the cradle created by Loring's hands. He gave a hop, and Kozlowski straightened his knees, giving him a boost like an Olympic weight lifter performing a clean and jerk. Loring was amazed at the man's strength, as he almost catapulted fully over the fence to the other side. He managed to hold on to the top, though, and he straddled it to give himself some leverage. Then he reached down to grab Flaherty's hand and lifted her up.

Now came the hard part, they all knew. Balanced at the top of the fence, Loring and Flaherty reached down and each took hold of one of Kozlowski's hands. He was much heavier than either of them, and Loring thought for a moment that they weren't going to be able to pull him over. It took some time, but they managed to get him to the top. Then they all dropped to the ground on the other side.

Once on the ground, the three looked around to get their bearings. The shipyard was quiet. Giant cargo containers twelve feet high and fifty feet long were lined up as far as the eye could see, stacked like some gargantuan child's Legos.

Flaherty nodded toward the containers and whispered, "Do you believe they only check one in every twenty of those for weapons?"

Kozlowski looked back at the fence. "Yeah, but at least the security is airtight," he mocked. "It's a wonder we haven't had more terrorist attacks."

"Are we going to debate national security policy, or are we going to get inside that fort?" Loring snapped. As part of the federal government's law enforcement structure, he felt a certain embarrassment at the lack of a coherent security plan. Flaherty and Kozlowski both nodded and kept silent as they set out.

The fence ran the entire length of the shared border between the shipyard and Castle Island, and the three of them hurried along it down toward the water. It ended on a pier that extended ten feet into the harbor. Kozlowski crawled out onto the pier to take a look around the fence.

"I can see the door to the tunnel," he said when he got back.

"Unfortunately, I can also see a boat tied to the jetty right near it, and it doesn't look like the guy standing watch is a fisherman."

"A guard?" Flaherty asked.

"More like a wiseguy, it looks to me."

"What do we do?" Loring asked.

"We take him out," Kozlowski replied without hesitation.

Tigh waited for several minutes before he started walking down the access road out toward Castle Island. He couldn't take Loring's car, he knew; it practically advertised his association with law enforcement. It might seem odd to Lefty that he was showing up on foot, but that was a risk he had to take.

As he neared the fort, he thought about how he should approach the situation. The first priority was simply to get inside and make sure Finn was still alive. Once he accomplished that, he figured he'd improvise the rest.

The road leading down to Castle Island was narrow, bordered on the left side by the fence that protected the shipyard, and on the right by a seawall that ran along Pleasure Bay. Toward the end of the peninsula, it opened up slightly to form a narrow parking lot for the tourists who frequented Fort Independence, particularly during the summer. The lot was empty at night, though. As he walked through the parking lot, Tigh looked up at the huge stone edifice that sat on top of the hill at the end of the road, thinking of the history of violence and horror associated with the Castle.

At the far end of the lot, where the blacktop gave way to a curb and then to a grassy hill that led up to the fort's gates, there was a building that housed a concession stand, designed to serve the visitors. As Tigh passed the stand, a flashlight clicked on to his left, and the beam was directed into his face.

"Turn it off," Tigh growled.

"Park's closed, sir," came Lefty Sullivan's voice.

"I'm not sightseeing, Lefty. Now turn that damned thing off before I shove it up your arse."

"Holy shit. Tigh," Lefty said, recognizing him. He didn't turn off the light, but he lowered it so it brightened Tigh's chest rather than his face. He stepped out from the shadows of the concession stand.

Even in the dim light, his appearance was almost comical. As a child, Lefty had contracted a rare form of palsy that had stripped the right side of his body of its strength and retarded his growth. The paralysis eventually passed, and he'd regained the full use of his arms, but the impairment to his stature was permanent, as was his nickname. He stood no more than five foot three, and most of that was his upper body. As a young man, he'd become a compulsive weight lifter—to overcome the inferiority felt from childhood—and as a result, his chest, arms, and shoulders were oddly large for someone his size.

He wore an MDC guard shirt and khaki pants, cinched tight at his waist and covered with a huge utility belt that held a .45 automatic, nightstick, handcuffs, and Mace, all bulging from their various holsters. MDC guards were generally not permitted to carry firearms, but Lefty's powerful father, Howie, had impressed on certain of his friends in the legislature the importance of his son's ability to defend himself, so a special exemption had been passed as an addendum to a local highway bill.

"What are you doing here, Tigh?" Lefty asked, letting his hand rest on the butt of the huge gun hanging from his waist.

"I need to speak to McGuire," Tigh said.

"What makes you think he's here?"

"We both know he's here, Lefty, so why don't we skip the malarkey. I need to speak with him." With that, Tigh started heading up the path toward the giant door to the Castle. Lefty stepped in front of him, raising the light up into his eyes again.

"I'm sorry, I can't let you go up there, Tigh," he said. He was directly in front of Tigh, only a foot or so away. Tigh reached out his giant paw of a hand and slapped at the light, knocking it out of Lefty's grasp and sending it skittering out toward the parking lot.

"Now you see here, you little shite of a man, I don't care who your father is. I need to talk to McGuire, and I'm going to talk to McGuire. I've been in this organization since you were only this high"—Tigh set his hand an inch or so below Lefty's current height as an insult—"and if I say I need to do something, you'd better damned well listen and stay the hell out of my way. Got it?"

Lefty's hand tightened around the butt of his gun. "I said you can't go up there," he said, but Tigh could hear his voice wavering.

"You're wrong. I can, and I will," Tigh said. He could tell he'd won the stalemate. Lefty would do nothing, and his hand relaxed around his pistol. Tigh began walking past him, when he heard another voice coming from the shadows under the concession stand.

"No, Tigh, you're wrong."

Tigh looked to his left and saw Johnny Mullins emerge from under the awning where the public restrooms were. Tigh realized instantly that Lefty was merely the first line of defense, and that McGuire had left Mullins to handle any problems too big for Lefty to deal with.

Johnny Mullins was twenty-five years old, and was making a reputation for himself in South Boston as a brutally efficient enforcer. At six foot six, he was taller than Tigh, but leaner—still with that young, hungry look that Tigh had lost some time ago. Much of his reputation stemmed from the rumor that he was responsible for the particularly gruesome killing of Manito Sanchez, the point man for a South American syndicate that was beginning to make inroads in the drug trade in Somerville and Revere. Mullins had been tasked with sending a message and resolving the conflict. To make sure there'd be no further misunderstanding, it was rumored Johnny had castrated Sanchez before killing him, and sent his trophy to one of Sanchez's associates as a warning he'd be better off returning to South America. There'd been no further problem with that particular syndicate, and the story had made an instant legend of Johnny Mullins, who'd supposedly enjoyed every aspect of the task.

Tigh regarded Mullins, who was coming toward him and Lefty, lighting a cigarette as he walked. "Johnny," he said, smiling. "It's a little past your bedtime, isn't it?"

Mullins laughed. He stuck out his hand. "It's good to see you again, Tigh McCluen. It's been a long time." Tigh took the hand and the two locked each other in a mutual stare.

"It has been," Tigh said, still smiling. "The last time I saw you, you were still roughing up the other kids for quarters at the arcades down at Revere Beach." He raised his eyebrows. "I guess things change, don't they?"

Mullins nodded. "And the last time I saw you, you were the most feared man in the entire city of Boston." He shrugged. "Yeah, I guess things do change."

"Maybe not so much as you think," Tigh said, and he started walking toward the doors of Fort Independence again.

Mullins stepped in front of him. "I can't let you go up there, Tigh. Tony was clear about my orders."

Tigh looked at him. "Look here, you pea-brained fool, I have important information for McGuire—information that may prevent us all from getting busted. That means my neck is out there on the line right along with his. I'm going up there to talk to him, and I won't be stopped by some upstart with a testosterone problem." With that, he stepped around Mullins and continued up toward the fort.

Mullins thought about it for a moment and then put out his

arm to stop Tigh. It was a mistake. If he'd pulled out a gun, Tigh might have reconsidered his options, but by extending his arm, he merely made himself vulnerable.

Tigh grabbed Mullins's wrist and, in one clean, quick, brutal motion, he swung his other fist up from his waist, connecting perfectly with Mullins's elbow. The force of the blow combined with the leverage of Tigh's other hand gripping Mullins's wrist, bending his elbow back, snapping the bones at the joint, and leaving the arm flapping helplessly. Then, just as quickly, Tigh grabbed the shocked man by the collar, holding his head steady, and drove his own forehead hard into Mullins's face. Blood erupted from the man's nose, and it looked as though the right side of his face had caved in. Tigh let go of his collar, and the younger man fell to the ground, unconscious.

He looked at Lefty, who'd gone pale and was backing away. "You got a car, Lefty?" he asked.

"Yeah, Tigh, I do," he stammered.

"Then go get it and bring it here. Pile this piece of crap in and take him to the hospital."

"But I've got to stand guard out here."

"There's no one going to storm the place tonight, and the only alternative is to call an ambulance. Do you think McGuire would appreciate having to explain what we're all doing here to an EMT?"

"Okay, I'll take care of it," Lefty said after thinking for a moment.

"Now, I'm going up to the Castle to talk to McGuire," Tigh said. Then he paused, and added, "That is, if it's all right with you?"

"Sure, Tigh, that's fine with me. Whatever you say." Lefty nodded enthusiastically as he scurried off to get his car.

Tigh watched him go. Then he looked down at the crumpled wreckage of Johnny Mullins. He knelt for a moment and whispered into the ear of the unconscious man, "A word of advice, my boy: you should never take as much pleasure in this line of work as you appear to. It's unseemly."

Then he stood up, turned, and headed up the path to the huge iron doors that led into the Castle.

CHAPTER SEVENTY

Kozlowski crept along the rocks down near the shoreline, inching closer to the jetty, always careful to stay low and out of sight. When he reached the wood planking suspended from the pilings, he caught his breath and looked back toward the shipyard to see if he could make out Loring and Flaherty, but the night was dark and every feature of the shoreline seemed obscured. That gave him some comfort.

It hadn't been easy to convince Loring and Flaherty to stay behind, but logic ultimately prevailed. "The more people we have out there on those rocks, the more likely it is we'll be seen," Kozlowski reasoned. "Once I'm there, taking the guy out will be easy. Any way you look at it, it's a one-man job." In the end, his reasoning had been persuasive, and the other two agreed to hang back. Kozlowski knew, though, that somewhere behind him in the darkness, Flaherty had her gun trained on the cigarette burning at the end of the pier, hovering near the boat tied to the jetty.

Kozlowski poked his head up above the pier to evaluate the situation. The jetty was fifty feet long, but the darkness made it seem endless. He could see the silhouette of what appeared to be a heavyset man reclining in the captain's chair of the thirty-foot Sea Ray, his feet up on the console as he leaned back and looked out at the planes taking off and landing at Logan Airport across the harbor.

It was clear Kozlowski wasn't going to be able to take him by surprise. The pier was too long, and Kozlowski knew he'd be spotted long before he got to the boat at the end of it. He decided that a strong bluff was the only chance he had.

He looked up and waited until an inbound plane was directly overhead on its approach to the airport, and hauled himself onto the pier as it passed so that the roar of its engines would cover any sound he made. Then he positioned himself on the pier so that it would look like he was coming from the Castle.

He was halfway out on the pier when the man on the boat saw him. "Who's that?" he demanded.

Kozlowski kept strolling nonchalantly toward the boat, his hand clutching his revolver down next to his leg, out of sight. He knew in the darkness, from a distance, it would be difficult for the man to tell who he was. "McGuire told me he needs you inside," he said. It was a risk, but a calculated one. It was always possible McGuire wasn't actually in Fort Independence himself, in which case the shooting would likely start soon. He was hoping he'd guessed right, though.

"What for?" the man asked, drawing a sigh of relief from Kozlowski.

"How should I know?" he responded, drawing ever closer to the man at the end of the pier. "He told me to watch the boat."

The man grunted as he lifted his gut up and climbed out of the captain's chair. "Okay. You know what to do if the cops show up?"

"Yeah, I know," Kozlowski said. He was at the boat now, and he reached his left hand out to help the man off.

"I don't know you, do I?" the man said as he stepped onto

the jetty and accepted Kozlowski's hand. "Are you with Johnny's crew out of Somerville?"

As Kozlowski helped the man up with his left hand, he brought his gun up under his chin with his right, pinning him back against a piling. "No, I'm with the police commissioner's crew out of Area A-1," he said. "And you're under arrest. I'd read you your rights, but we're a little pressed for time, so I'm just going to assume that you are familiar enough with our criminal justice system to know your rights already."

"Fuck you!" the man said, swinging his arm across his face, knocking Kozlowski's hand and causing the gun to discharge as his arm jerked away. At the same time Kozlowski heard the gun go off, he felt a warm, wet blast on his face, which he quickly recognized as blood.

He was stunned. Had the man really killed himself with such a stupid move? The huge body in front of him lurched back against the piling, and Kozlowski let go to wipe the blood off his face. As he opened his eyes, he caught a brief glimpse of the huge man's arm swinging toward Kozlowski's head in a rage, and he ducked to avoid the brunt of the blow.

Looking up again, Kozlowski realized that the man wasn't dead, but he was very angry. The force of his arm had been sufficient to knock Kozlowski's gun out from under the center of his chin before it fired. As a result, rather than blowing a hole through the roof of his mouth and out the top of his skull, the bullet had merely destroyed the side of his face, ripping his cheek and ear away from the bone, leaving them flapping in the night breeze, secured to the bone only by a thin sliver of sinew.

The man was swinging his fist blindly again, and Kozlowski ducked once more. As the fist passed over his bent head, the detective reached out and thrust his head forward, driving it into the man's solar plexus. As the wounded man doubled up from the blow, Kozlowski snapped his head back up quickly, and the back of his head slammed into the man's chin, knocking him unconscious.

Kozlowski felt the man's weight topple forward, and he managed to redirect the mass with his arms over the side of the pier and back down onto the floor of the Sea Ray, where it landed with a crack that seemed louder than the gunshot.

The detective rubbed his sore head as he stepped down into the boat to see if the man was still breathing. He was. *Thank goodness for small miracles*. The paperwork required to clear an officer-involved homicide was endless. He took out his handcuffs and was busy cuffing the man's hands to the boat's railing when Flaherty and Loring finally arrived.

"What the hell happened?" Flaherty demanded. "I thought you said taking this guy out was going to be a piece of cake."

"Thanks, Lieutenant. I'm fine," Kozlowski said, looking up at Flaherty with a grin.

"Oh my God!" she exclaimed as she looked down at her partner and noticed his face was covered in blood. "Koz, are you sure you're okay?"

He nodded. "It's his blood."

"So what happened?" she pressed.

"What happened was that this asshole is a giant moron with a death wish—one which I was unfortunately not able to grant." He looked down at the still-breathing carcass. "Better luck next time," he said.

"Both of us should have taken him out," Flaherty said.

"Oh please," Kozlowski said, sneering. "It would have made no difference."

"You don't know that," she retorted.

"Detectives!" Loring interrupted. "I'd suggest you finish this later. Right now we need to get inside."

"He's right," Kozlowski said. "For all we know, they may have heard the gunshot from inside."

"I doubt they could hear it through those walls; that's over ten feet of stone. But we should still get moving," Loring said.

All three hurried back up the pier and scrambled onto the rocks toward the thin beach at the edge of Fort Independence. After following the seawall that ringed the shore for twenty yards or so, they came to a rusted iron door.

"This must be it," Flaherty said doubtfully. The door looked impenetrable.

Kozlowski ran his fingers around the edges. "I don't think it's locked," he said, wiggling his thick fingers under the steel catch. He pulled, and the door budged an inch or two out, and then slammed back shut, nearly taking his fingers off. "Damn, it's heavy," he said. "I think we're all going to have to do this." He looked at Loring. "You go high, the lieutenant can take the bottom, and I'll pull on the side."

They nodded, and all three attacked the door, working their fingers under the sides. "Ready?" Flaherty asked once she had a strong hold on the bottom edge.

"Ready," Loring confirmed.

"Okay, on the count of three," Kozlowski said. "One, two, three."

They pulled for all they were worth, throwing their backs into the task and straining the delicate muscles in their fingers, which screamed out in pain. Finally the opening was wide enough for Kozlowski to slide his whole hand into it, and he repositioned himself to get better leverage, pulling on the door with both arms.

The massive iron gate swung wide open and crashed against the seawall, revealing a tunnel much narrower than the size of the door suggested.

Flaherty peered into the blackness.

"McCluen said the tunnel is fifty yards long, and there is a trapdoor at the end of it," Loring said.

“I hope his information is good,” said Flaherty. She looked apprehensive.

“It always has been before,” Loring assured.

“Well then, I suppose there’s no reason to stand around here,” Kozlowski said. And with that, he stepped onto the threshold, crouched down to fit his bulk into the opening, and disappeared into the black tunnel.

CHAPTER SEVENTY-ONE

"We need to know, Finn," McGuire said.

"What?" Finn asked. He felt disconnected from the world. So much so that he couldn't tell how much of the disorientation was from the electric shock he'd sustained when he was abducted, the surreal nature of his circumstances, or the realization of Preston's betrayal. In any case, he wasn't sure he had the strength left to fight.

"How you found these names, Finn. We need to know." He was still leaning forward, within the circle of light cast on Finn by the powerful beam shining in his eyes. Finn could see other shadows moving behind McGuire, and wondered if Preston was in the room. He supposed it didn't matter.

Finn thought for a moment, focusing on McGuire's question. It seemed like years ago that he and Bostick had made the list. In his foggy state he was having trouble remembering how the whole exercise started in the first place. "They were in the case notes," he finally mumbled. "Three of them were, at least. I thought they might make good witnesses."

"Make good witnesses?" It was clear McGuire wasn't following Finn's point. "What the fuck are you talking about?" He leaned in farther. "Whose notes were the names in?"

Finn's head lolled slightly to the side, as if he were drunk.

That's how he felt. "Natalie's," he said. The mere act of mentioning her name brought him back to the reality of his situation. He looked at McGuire, his apathy hardening into anger. "Why?" he asked with discernible hostility.

McGuire seemed startled by the shift in Finn's demeanor, and he leaned back in his chair, allowing some space between them. "Why what?"

"Why did you have to kill Natalie?" Finn's question was asked with a hatred so fierce it caught McGuire by surprise.

He glared at Finn as he considered his answer. "I didn't," he said at last.

Finn's eyes never left McGuire's. "Who did, then? Preston?" He spat out the question, watching carefully to see McGuire's reaction. McGuire didn't flinch, but Finn thought he saw a shift in the shadows behind the mob boss. After a moment, McGuire smiled—a thin, toothy, evil grin that successfully conveyed a sense of superiority Finn hadn't guessed at. Finn was starting to realize how badly he'd underestimated McGuire.

"I don't know what you're talking about, Finn," he said. "And I think we are getting a little off track here. I need *my* questions answered, and I need them answered quickly. If I have to, I'll start presenting you with some motivation, but, trust me, you don't want it to get to that point." He paused and looked at the list. "I gather you found some of these names in Natalie Caldwell's case notes, but how did you find the others? Was that Bostick's role in this?"

"Bostick." Finn nodded as he felt the guilt of having dragged Bostick into the mess that led to his death. He should have listened more carefully to the ex-cop's concerns. "Another person you killed for no reason," Finn commented. "What's this whole thing worth to you? A few hundred thousand? A million? You're so fucking pathetic!"

Finn was so preoccupied with his own anger, and McGuire moved so quickly, that Finn didn't even see the punch coming.

McGuire's massive fist smashed into his nose, and Finn could hear the cartilage pop. Seconds later he felt the rush of blood down his face.

McGuire was already leaning back in his chair by the time Finn realized what had happened. McGuire looked down at his hand, examining his knuckles for a moment. Then he sighed heavily. "I don't have any interest in hurting you, Finn. You seem like an okay guy, so don't make me do that again. You can't be so stupid that you'd think this was simply over a million dollars, or even several million. And you should keep in mind that I wasn't the one who got Bostick involved in this situation; you did that all on your own. As for Natalie, all I'll say is that I didn't have anything to do with her death."

"I don't believe you."

"Yeah, well, fortunately for me, I don't give a fuck what you believe. What I do care about is what you can tell me. Let's get back to this list." He tapped the papers in his lap. "Who else knows about this?"

"Fuck you," Finn hissed defiantly.

"Wrong answer," McGuire said. He reached over and grabbed the pinkie finger on Finn's left hand, bending it backward with a brutal twist. Finn heard the bone break before the pain shot up his arm, spreading through his body like a wave.

Finn screamed in pain. "No one!" he yelled in agony. "No one else knows!"

"No one?" McGuire seemed ready to pounce, and, when he leaned forward, Finn could see the gun holstered underneath his jacket. He suddenly realized he might have signed his own death warrant.

He shook his head. "No one yet," he said.

"Now, that's very interesting," McGuire said. "What should I assume from that?"

Finn was having trouble concentrating because of the pain coming from his finger. He gulped for air as his mind worked quickly. "I made copies," he lied. "I made copies and I put them in a safe-deposit box. If I die, they'll be found eventually."

McGuire frowned. "Where?" he growled.

"I can get them for you."

McGuire grunted in disgust. "What do you think? I'm going to let you go so that you can gather them up and bring them back to me?"

"I was hoping," Finn conceded.

"I don't think so, Finn," McGuire said after a moment. "Instead, why don't you tell me where you hid these supposed copies, and I'll send someone to check out your story."

"You can't," Finn protested. "The bank requires a photo ID, and they have my picture on their computer system to verify who I am. Even if I gave you the key, you couldn't get in, and they'd call the cops to investigate."

"Well then, Finn, it looks like we've got ourselves a problem, doesn't it?" McGuire thought for a moment more. "I'll tell you what, why don't you give me the name of the bank, and I'll have someone check it out."

The pain emanating from Finn's broken finger was exquisite, and yet his brain no longer fully acknowledged it. He'd reached the point of fear beyond pain, where his only focus was on survival. As he regarded McGuire, he knew for certain that he was dealing with a man unencumbered by a conscience. He couldn't be manipulated, Finn was sure. He had to find someone else to bargain with—someone who might think twice before putting a bullet in his brain. Suddenly, he focused on the shadows hovering behind McGuire.

"I'll tell you the name of the bank," Finn said. "But only if I can talk to Preston first." He looked at McGuire again. "Where is he? Is he here?"

McGuire's eyes narrowed. "What makes you think Holland is involved in any of this?" he asked.

The pain in Finn's finger was overwhelming. "Oh come on," he said. "Just cut the bullshit. Preston's your lawyer. He was having an affair with Natalie. He's the one who knew I was going to the office to get the list. Is he behind you?" Finn spoke in the direction of the shadows. "I see him face-to-face or you get nothing out of me."

McGuire scratched his head for a moment, as if considering his options. Then he shook his head and leaned forward again. "Sorry, that's strike two, Finn." He grabbed the next finger up from Finn's pinkie and snapped it like a twig.

Finn screamed in agony. It was a loud, piercing scream that filled the entire room and echoed off the walls. McGuire screamed right back into his face—a horrible, bloodthirsty scream that shocked Finn almost as much as the pain. "See, no one's going to hear us out here." McGuire leaned forward again and punched him hard in the mouth, almost knocking him off the chair. "Wise up, Finn. It's only going to get worse from here on out."

Finn could feel the blood running down his chin from the corner of his mouth. The metallic taste sent a new wave of terror running through him. It took all his concentration not to break, but he knew he had to hold on if he had any chance of surviving. He had to get Preston involved. His eyes watered as he fought back the fear. "Is he here?" Finn croaked. "Can't he even face me?"

"Tell me what I want to know, Finn, and we can end this little morality play," McGuire said, although Finn could read in his eyes that he hoped the game would continue.

"Fuck you, McGuire!" Finn spat.

"Fuck me? No, I don't think so. I think fuck you. I think you don't want to be pissing me off any more. I think you want to be making friends. I want to know where this bank is. Now."

"Not until I talk to Preston." Finn held out in spite of his agony. "I want to see his goddamned eyes when he tells me how he killed Natalie!"

"It's not going to happen, Finn. What's going to happen is, we're going to keep going round and round, and I'm going to keep hurting you until you tell me what I want to know."

"Then I guess you've got to do what you've got to do," Finn said with all the bravado he had left. "I'm not talking until Preston comes out of the shadows." He kept telling himself that if he could just get Preston involved in the interrogation, he might be able to talk his way out of his predicament.

McGuire shrugged. "Have it your way." He reached forward again and pulled back Finn's middle finger, pausing just as he reached the point at which the bone was ready to break. He smiled at Finn. "Last chance," he said.

"Fuck you." Finn almost choked on the words as he tried to brace himself. McGuire pushed the finger back and it snapped instantly, drawing a fresh round of screams from Finn. He was beginning to wonder how much longer he could hold out. His will had just about ebbed and he was on the edge of blind panic.

"Preston!" he screamed. "You bastard! Let me see your face!"

"Let it go, Finn," McGuire said.

"Fuck you! Preston is the one who started this! He's the one who killed Natalie! He's the one I want to see!" Finn was beginning to lose it.

McGuire shook his head.

"Preston!" Finn screamed out again.

"You really want to go for a fourth finger?"

"Preston!" Finn's screams were starting to dissolve into agonized sobs as the pain and exhaustion began to overtake him. For a brief moment the only sound in the room was that of Finn gasping for breath.

Then, just as Finn was considering giving up, one of the dark figures behind McGuire spoke. "Preston didn't kill Natalie, Finn. I did."

Finn recognized the voice, and wondered if he was hallucinating.

CHAPTER SEVENTY-TWO

The tunnel was cold and damp and cramped. Kozlowski led the way, hunched over, slogging his heavy legs forward as his flashlight crept over the dark walls of the crypt, illuminating the nitre that hung glittering on the damp stone. Flaherty could almost hear Fortunato's cough echoing from within the imagination of a young private stationed at Fort Independence more than a century before.

The passageway was much longer than they'd anticipated, and the going was slow in the darkness. More than once their progress was interrupted by the squealing of rats as Kozlowski accidentally upset a nest.

Flaherty was behind him, and could see almost nothing. Occasionally she let her hand brush against her partner's suit jacket to make sure of where she was. She noticed that Loring, who was following her, was in a similar predicament, although she was not wearing a jacket. As a result, Loring's hand periodically brushed against her hips, or the area just below the small of her back. She had a brief thought of Janet Reed, the young woman she'd seen in Loring's office, tennis racquet at the ready, and wondered whether Loring was being more aggressive than necessary in keeping his bearings. She let the thought pass, though, so that she could concentrate on more immediate concerns.

She couldn't keep her mind off Finn, and the thought of what might be happening to him turned her stomach. She wished she'd listened to him. She'd been so careful not to let her personal feelings bias her in Finn's direction that she may have let herself become biased against him. *Please let him be alive,* she prayed silently.

She no longer even considered the possibility that he was guilty, that he'd actually killed Natalie Caldwell. She couldn't. She'd been back and forth too many times on the issue, and had consciously decided to land on a position once and for all, if only to save her sanity. Finn was innocent, and that's all there was to it.

Suddenly, Kozlowski stopped short. "I think I've got it," he whispered.

Flaherty looked up. Just in front of Kozlowski on the ceiling was a break in the stone. A steel and wood square was cut into the granite, like a hatch cover on an old ship.

The sergeant moved the flashlight from the trapdoor to the faces of Flaherty and Loring. "Are we ready?" he asked.

"Ready as I'll ever be," Loring said. He looked a little green to Kozlowski, but at least he had his gun drawn.

"All right," Flaherty said. "You handle the door, Koz, and I'm coming right up underneath your arms with my gun, just in case there's someone waiting for us."

"Be ready to shoot," Kozlowski said. "If McCluen got this wrong, there's a possibility that we're coming up right into the room where McGuire's holding Finn. If that happens, the only advantage we'll have is the element of surprise—and that will only give us a few seconds."

"I know," Flaherty said. "I'll get through the opening quickly, you guys just make sure you're right behind me." Loring nodded and flipped the safety on his gun.

Kozlowski handed the flashlight to Flaherty, who took it and held it parallel to the barrel of her gun in a two-handed grip, and then pointed both at the trapdoor. "Ready when you are," she whispered.

Kozlowski squatted under the hatch cover. The tunnel was only around four feet high, so all he needed to do was to straighten his legs and push the door over his head and there would be plenty of room in which Flaherty would be able to maneuver. He put his hands on the rusted steel ties that held the trapdoor together, took a deep breath, and fired his weight upward.

As soon as the door was raised, Flaherty popped her head into the opening, following the beam of light that guided her gun in a sweep around the room.

"All clear," she said quietly after a moment. Then she pulled back into the tunnel, and she and Loring helped Kozlowski push the hatch cover out of the way, sliding it on the stone floor above.

One by one they pulled themselves through the opening into a small, dark room. Gray steel government-issue filing cabinets and desks were stacked along the walls. Apparently the room was a storage area for files and other junk that would likely never again see the light of day.

"Tigh said that the room where they conduct their interrogations is only fifty feet away to the right," Loring reminded.

Flaherty nodded. "Let's go."

"Tigh said to wait for his signal," Loring warned.

"Are you kidding?" Flaherty hissed. "For all we know, they could be killing Finn right now. We're not even sure if McCluen ever made it into the fort. We can't wait."

"Look, if we go busting in there without knowing what we're up against, we're just as likely to get everyone killed—including Mr. Finn," Loring argued back. "Believe me, Tigh McCluen is very resourceful. We'll be better off if we wait for his signal."

"Are you crazy! We're right here, and we're not going to do anything? That's insane. Koz, tell this asshole we're going in now."

"No, I think he's right, Lieutenant. We're better off waiting to see if McCluen pulls off his end of this."

"What are you saying? We should just sit here?"

"I'm saying we should wait." Kozlowski looked at his watch. Then he looked up pointedly at Loring. "For five minutes."

Fort Independence's heavy metal door was open just a crack. Tigh looked up at the giant edifice—twenty feet of stone hanging over him, foreboding in the darkness. Even from that steep angle, he could see the long grass growing from the earthen ramparts on the top of the fort. He breathed heavily twice, taking in the heavy sea air and enjoying it as if it were his last. *It's been a damned good run, Tigh*, he said to himself. Then he pushed the door open a little wider so he could slide his huge frame in.

It was pitch-black inside, or so it seemed at first. The only windows in the Castle were the raised wedge-shaped openings on the water side, designed to allow the soldiers to fire on any enemy vessels that might approach Boston from the sea. There were no openings near the giant door, and it took a long moment for Tigh's eyes to adjust. Even after they had, it was so dark he could barely make out the outline of the wide corridor running off the entryway, down the interior side of the fort. Still, Tigh knew where he was headed. He was ashamed at the number of times he'd been to the Castle before, and he felt a sharp stab of guilt at the pain he'd inflicted within the stone labyrinth. It helped somewhat to remind himself that he'd had few choices in his life, and that most, if not all, of the men he'd tortured were people who'd joined the game freely. Since civilians caught in the web of organized crime almost always caved in to the threat of violence long before a trip to the Castle was necessary, this particular spot was generally reserved for rival gang members or those of their own crew who were suspected of treachery.

These were rationalizations, Tigh knew, though, and they ultimately provided only shallow relief from the sins of his past.

He worked his way along the dark corridor, walking softly and following the stone walls around the first two corners. When he came to the third corner, he could see a faint light filtering down the stone hallway, and he heard low voices coming from an anteroom off to the left.

He crept close, hugging the wall as he stole to within feet of the doorway, listening until he was sure he heard Finn's voice mixing in with others coming from the room. He breathed a sigh of relief. At least Finn was alive. Now Tigh just needed to figure out how to get him out of there.

CHAPTER SEVENTY-THREE

Finn's voice was hoarse from the screaming, and the pain had sapped him of almost all of his strength. "Nick," was all he was able to say.

Nick Williams took a few steps forward so Finn could see him. "Yes, Finn. It's me."

"I don't understand," Finn stammered. "What about Preston?"

"Preston has nothing to do with this," Williams said, smiling. "He's actually the sanctimonious prick he pretends to be. He'd never let his precious reputation be sullied by becoming involved with anything that shades over even the technical limits of the law."

"But how did you know how to—"

"Find you? It wasn't that difficult, really. You told Preston you couldn't work on the settlement, so Preston called me to ask me to pick up the slack. When I asked him what happened to you, he said you had some personal business to attend to, and if I ran into you at the office, I wasn't to bother you."

Finn breathed deeply. Preston hadn't betrayed him. At least, not on purpose.

"You believe that?" Williams said. "He was worried I might bother you." He laughed. "A little ironic given the circumstances, don't you think?"

Finn looked at McGuire, who was intently watching the interplay between the two lawyers. Then he turned back to Williams. "So what now?" he asked.

"That all depends on you, Finn," Williams replied. "You have some choices here."

"Really?" Finn was doubtful. "You want to tell me what they are?"

Williams tapped McGuire on the shoulder and beckoned him away. The two pulled back beyond the point where Finn could see, and while he couldn't make out their words, he could hear them whispering angrily to each other. When they returned, Nick pulled up a chair and sat down next to Finn. "Okay, Finn," he said, "let's lay out the possibilities. Your first option is to continue with your obstinacy, in which case I'm sure Tony will continue to ruin any chance you have of ever playing the piano." He nodded toward the twisted wreckage of Finn's left hand.

Finn forced himself to look down at his fingers, taking in the damage that had already been done. The pain was so excruciating that it no longer seemed limited to his fingers. The entire side of his body was racked with an agony he'd never known before. "What's my second option?" he asked after a moment.

Williams hesitated, looking back at McGuire before he answered. "You could join us," he said at last.

Had he not been in such intense pain, Finn would have had to stifle a laugh of his own. "Join you?" he asked incredulously.

Williams nodded.

"Why should I believe you'd make it that easy?"

Williams's expression became earnest. "I know much more about you than you might think, Finn. I've done my homework. You and I have more in common than you'd ever believe."

Finn's breathing labored against the pain. "I'm listening."

"I grew up in Somerville—in the rough part of Somerville.

My father was a drunk who used to drive a delivery truck in between beating the hell out of my mother and me. At nine years old I thought it was a blessing when he ran over a kid and got sent upstate to Walpole. Mom and I went onto welfare, and it didn't take long before I was hanging out in the local gangs, running drugs and numbers for the Winter Hill crew." He paused for effect. "Sound familiar?"

"It's making me homesick," Finn replied, gritting his teeth against the pain. "What's your point?"

"My point is that by the time I was fifteen, it was pretty clear I was eventually headed to jail or to the morgue, just like you. But then a funny, fortuitous thing happened. I met Tony McGuire." He gave a nod back to McGuire.

"He told me I was wasting my time. He told me I was smarter than everyone I was running with, and that if I ever really wanted to make anything of myself in the organization, I had to use my head. As it turns out, he was right. Then he made me a deal. He told me that if I was willing to work hard, he'd front me the money to go to city college."

Finn looked back at the shadowy figure of McGuire. "I never would have pegged you as Santa Claus," he said.

McGuire glared back at him. "You better learn to keep your fuckin' mouth shut," he said.

Williams shook his head. "You've got it all wrong. He wasn't trying to do me a favor; he was doing himself a favor. He's a goddamned genius, whether you believe it or not. You see, he was thinking big—and thinking ahead. He recognized that the various gangs in Boston had plenty of muscle, which was fine for running drugs, and extorting money from liquor stores. But he also knew that the real money was in big business—and that was a cash cow the gangs hadn't even thought of milking. The only problem was access. He had no access. To find a way in, he didn't need more brainless soldiers, he needed MBAs and CPAs . . . and lawyers.

"When I got out of college, he paid my way through law school, then used his connections to get me a job at Howery, Black. Since then, I've used the information at my disposal to get him on the inside of some of the biggest businesses and deals in Boston. And there are a dozen others just like me across different industries doing the same thing. We're not talking about millions of dollars, Finn, we're talking about *billions* of dollars. Tony has a hand in every major construction project from the Big Dig to the rebuilding at Ground Zero. He controls trucking and shipping and security up and down the East Coast, and we get a cut of all of it. I'm telling you, he's the smartest man you'll ever meet."

Finn looked down at his hand. "You'll forgive me if I'm not rushing to join his fan club."

Williams smiled, almost apologetically. "Admittedly, many of the old methods are in his heart and soul, but his head is focused on business. Trust me, we're going to be bigger than all but the biggest companies in the Fortune 500."

"So if things are going so well, why do you need me?"

"We don't need you," Williams said. "We *want* you. I had one of Tony's acquaintances get me access to your police file—very impressive. And talking to some of our friends in Charlestown, it seems you made quite a reputation for yourself."

"That was a long time ago," Finn pointed out.

"Come on, Finn. Guys like us never really change our spots. I've seen that same viciousness at the law firm—in the way you rip witnesses to shreds, or handle cases for the partners. You're a take-no-prisoners kind of guy. It's a more genteel world, but your instincts are still there. Plus, you're smart, and you've got some of the best trial skills I've ever seen. A guy like you could be a huge asset to the organization."

Finn glared at him. "Do you really think I could join you, knowing you killed Natalie?"

Williams threw his hands in the air. "Oh please, Finn. Let's not go there, okay? Natalie wasn't exactly a saint—you know it as well as I do. Do you know what her first thought was when she found out about the Huron payroll scam? Do you?" He looked at Finn, who was afraid to hear the answer. "She was trying to figure out how she could use the information to make partner early!"

Finn looked confused until Williams continued: "Like you, she assumed Preston was involved, and she was trying to figure out how to blackmail him. She would have blown everything for us, so I had to stop her." He laughed. "She actually asked if I'd help her with the blackmail because she had no idea I was involved with Huron."

"Why would she go to you?" Finn asked, still trying to avoid the truth.

"Because she and I had been sleeping together for months. It was lucky for me too, otherwise she might have gone straight to Preston, and it would have caused serious problems." He actually looked proud of himself.

"Once she was dead, I called Tony to help me take care of the body. I was just planning on dumping her, but Tony came up with the plan to make it look like she was another of Little Jack's victims. He has a guy on the payroll who's very good with a knife."

"The knife you planted at my apartment," Finn surmised.

"Yeah, that's right," Williams admitted. "You just wouldn't give up, so we needed to take care of you. The cops were already looking at you as a suspect, so we figured this would kill two birds with one stone. I was going to put in an anonymous call to the police, but then that Flaherty woman actually found the knife on her own, so I didn't need to bother. But, you see, if you start working with us, we can make those allegations go away."

"Like you made the Tannery lawsuit go away?"

Nick nodded. "In the end, Mrs. Tannery decided that protecting her daughter's life was a higher priority than investigating her husband's death. We were pretty sure that would be an easy decision for any parent." He shook his head in disgust. "I spent weeks combing through Natalie's files, trying to figure out how she discovered what was going on."

"The names were in the files I had," Finn pointed out.

"I was guessing. That's why I offered to take them off your hands, but I still couldn't find anything."

"You only took the ones I hadn't looked at yet. The notes were in a different set of folders that I'd already gone through."

Nick Williams nodded in understanding. "I guess that was bad luck for both of us . . . unless you're willing to be smart." He looked at Finn hopefully. "What do you say? Partner?"

"You're scum, Nick. You know that, don't you?"

"Good God, Finn, don't throw away your one chance to walk away from all this. Not for the memory of someone like Natalie Caldwell, and not out of some misplaced pity for a widow who's going to be a millionaire anyway! Don't you realize how big this thing is? It goes higher than you could even imagine, and you can be a part of that, don't you see?"

"All I have to do is play ball?"

Finn caught Williams looking back at McGuire. "That's right," Williams said after a moment.

Finn looked at his coworker. "You've got it all figured out, haven't you, Nick? You killed Natalie. You had Bostick killed. You scared Amy Tannery into settling her case against Huron. And now you're offering me the world on a silver platter."

Williams was silent.

"There's only one problem. You're right, I *was* very much like you once. But that also means I know how your mind works. It all sounds so good, but I know *I'd* never have let someone with all the information I have simply walk free, no matter what. The only way you can be sure that your plans are safe is to make sure I never leave here alive." He looked straight at Williams, searching his eyes for the truth.

"Is that a chance you really want to take, Finn?"

"Let me put it to you this way, Nick. Fuck you, and fuck your offer. Just make sure you keep looking over your shoulder."

"You can't mean that, Finn," Williams insisted.

Suddenly McGuire walked out of the shadows. "Fuck this," he said.

"No, Tony," Williams protested. "We still need to know if there are copies of the list."

"Bullshit." McGuire pulled a 9mm pistol out from under his jacket. "There are no copies of the list. I can read it in his eyes." He looked at Williams. "You gave it a try your way. Now we're going to finish this."

Williams considered McGuire with a look of resignation. "Fine," he said at last. "He didn't fall for it." Then he turned to Finn. "Looks like Tony has made up his mind, Finn, so I guess I'll just say my good-byes. But before you go, there's something you should know about Natalie." He smiled.

"What?" Finn spat.

"She was a cheap piece of ass. I know you already knew that, but I wanted to remind you. I let her believe I could help her make partner, and the little whore was all over me. That's what she was about. I didn't care what she thought, as long as she kept wriggling up and down on me the way she used to." He looked at Finn. "I know you know what I'm talking about."

Finn could feel his face burning as his rage grew.

"That's right," Williams said, "you remember." He leaned in close to Finn and whispered to him. "Even after I realized I was going to have to kill her, I couldn't resist fucking her one last time. I swear to God, the look in her face when she was tied up and she realized what I was going to do was the biggest turn-on I've ever known." Williams was enjoying the memory of murdering Natalie, and it made Finn sick. Then he pulled away.

"Okay, Tony. I'm through with this piece of shit."

McGuire pulled back on the barrel plate to cycle a round into the chamber, making an unmistakably sharp, definitive sound that Finn knew signaled the end of his life. Then he pointed the gun at Finn's head. Finn closed his eyes and took one last breath.

That's when he heard Tigh's voice.

CHAPTER SEVENTY-FOUR

"McGuire!"

Tigh's voice boomed through the cold stone room, reverberating off the walls and making everyone there jump. McGuire's hand recoiled, and it appeared for a moment that the startled muscles in his hand might inadvertently squeeze the trigger.

"McGuire!" Tigh shouted again. He could see from the arched doorway that he'd arrived just in time. Finn was tied to a chair in the middle of the room, brightly lit by a portable high-beam spotlight, like some grotesque work at a deranged performance artist's opening. He looked bad. His white oxford shirt was stained a rusty magenta in the front, and his chin and neck were covered with drying blood. His left hand hung lifeless from the chair, and Tigh recognized instantly the distinctive quality of McGuire's handiwork.

Standing around Finn, like voyeurs at an accident scene, were Tony McGuire, his bodyguard Henry Schmitt, and a respectable-looking man in an expensive, neatly pressed suit whom Tigh didn't recognize. They were all looking at Tigh with a mixture of shock and anger.

"Tigh?" McGuire finally managed to spit out, sloughing off the moment's paralysis. "What the hell are you doing here?"

"I have to talk to you, Tony." Tigh squared up his shoulders to send a subtle message that he wouldn't budge until he'd been heard. He was by far the largest man in the room, and his presence made the space seem smaller. He'd long ago learned to use his size to his advantage.

McGuire waved his gun around the room, as if to say, *Can't you see what we're in the middle of here?* "It'll have to wait, Tigh. Johnny should've never let you in to begin with."

"Don't blame Johnny, he did his best," Tigh said with an edge in his voice that made his point clear. McGuire frowned and his eyes darkened. Tigh shrugged. "I had no choice, Tony. This is important—and it concerns him," he said, nodding at Finn.

McGuire looked back and forth between Finn and Tigh as if making up his mind about something.

"Excuse me," Nick Williams interrupted, his concern growing, "but who is this?" The question drew Tigh's eyes away from McGuire and they came to rest on the lawyer. The power of Tigh's glare was impossible to ignore, and Williams seemed to shrink from it involuntarily.

"He's Tigh McCluen," McGuire responded. "He runs some of our operations in Charlestown." Williams grunted. "Tigh," McGuire continued, "this is Nick Williams. He's one of our lawyers."

Williams scowled, and addressed Tigh in a lawyerly tone. "What is your business here, Mr. McCluen?"

Tigh continued to stare through Williams. "My business here is with Tony," he said flatly. "As I said, I'll talk to him alone."

"We don't have time for this kind of shit right now, Tigh," McGuire said, exasperated.

"It's important, Tony. Otherwise I wouldn't be here. And Johnny wouldn't be in the hospital."

McGuire looked from Williams to Tigh, and then glanced at Finn, still awaiting death under the spotlight in the middle of the room. Finally he lowered his gun and walked over to Tigh. "Fine," he said. "But it had better be quick, and it had better be good."

The light still shone in Finn's eyes, preventing him from seeing beyond a short radius, so he couldn't see Tigh, who was standing near the door. Tigh hoped that his friend would have enough sense to keep his mouth shut and let him handle the situation. He had tried to warn Finn before, and he had refused to listen. Now they had one chance for survival, and Tigh silently willed Finn to keep quiet.

McGuire reached Tigh at the far end of the room. "Well?" he asked.

Tigh leaned in to talk softly into McGuire's ear, keeping a close watch on Schmitt, the bodyguard, who was shifting nervously on his feet. "I knew this man, growing up in Charlestown," he whispered, "and there's something you need to know about him."

McGuire looked concerned for a moment, like he thought he might have missed some important piece of information about Finn—some intelligence that might come back to haunt him. "So?" he asked. "What is it?"

Tigh paused, letting the moment draw itself out as he watched the reactions of those around the room, gauging the level of danger each posed. Then he leaned in again to McGuire and whispered, "He's a friend of mine."

McGuire looked confused as he waited for Tigh to say more. "And?" he said after a moment.

"And he's a very good friend of mine," Tigh said, this time with emphasis.

Tigh's explanation failed to wipe the look of bewilderment off McGuire's face. "What are you trying to tell me?" he asked, adopting a more aggressive posture as his annoyance grew.

"I'm trying to tell you that you can't kill this man. I protect him."

McGuire took a step back from Tigh and looked at him closely, trying to evaluate what the huge man had said. Then he gave a quiet laugh. "You're full of shit, you know that?" He laughed again, harder this time, and shook his head, looking at the ground in disgust. "You really had me going for a minute there."

Tigh moved in with lightning speed as McGuire's head was down. He pulled out his gun and brought it up to McGuire's temple, grabbing him around the neck as he did.

"What the fuck!" McGuire shouted. "Tigh, have you lost your goddamned mind?"

Tigh didn't answer. He was busy swinging McGuire around so he provided a shield against Henry Schmitt, who'd pulled out his own gun and was taking aim. "Put it down!" Tigh yelled. Schmitt seemed confused and looked at McGuire for guidance. "Put it down!" Tigh yelled again. Then he spoke directly to McGuire. "Tell him to put it down, or I swear to Jesus I'll blow a hole straight through your head, Tony."

McGuire knew Tigh well enough to know he didn't make idle threats. He made a hand motion to Schmitt to lower his gun. Schmitt put his arm down, but held on to the pistol.

"You too, Tony. Toss your gun toward the wall." McGuire did as he was told.

Then McGuire spoke. "Now, everybody's going to calm down here, and Tigh is going to stop this crazy shit, and we can all go back to being friends, right?" He looked at Tigh over his shoulder, but Tigh pressed the barrel of the gun harder to his head, turning it back around.

"Any minute now," Tigh said, smiling. He looked at Schmitt. "Untie him," he said, nodding at Finn. Once again, Schmitt looked uncertain, so Tigh pressed the gun even harder into McGuire's temple. "Now!" he yelled.

Schmitt pulled out a switchblade, and in four quick movements he'd cut Finn's plastic restraints, freeing him. Finn moved with evident difficulty, trying twice to stand without success.

"You just signed your own death warrant, Tigh!" McGuire yelled, ignoring the gun to his head. "You know you're never getting out of here, don't you?"

"Perhaps not," Tigh said, "but there's always the hope, isn't there?" He was careful to keep McGuire between himself and Schmitt, who still hadn't dropped his gun.

Suddenly Tigh heard another voice. "Hope sometimes fades quickly, Mr. McCluen. Let Tony go immediately."

It was Nick Williams speaking, and Tigh turned into the barrel of a .357 Magnum revolver being pointed at his head from less than four feet away. He'd made a terrible miscalculation, Tigh realized instantly, by focusing only on McGuire and Schmitt. It never occurred to him that the lawyer would be armed. Because of his oversight, Williams had been able to maneuver into a position where he had a clear shot. Tigh knew he only had one chance.

"Have it your way," he said, letting go of McGuire and diving to his left as he began firing his gun. He didn't even bother to aim at anything in particular. He knew he couldn't hit both Williams and Schmitt, so instead he just tried to get off as many shots as he could, filling the room, and the entire Castle, with explosion after explosion as the gun fired and the shots ricocheted off the stone walls, multiplying the cacophony.

He was sure he'd gotten off at least four shots before he felt the first bullet enter his chest.

CHAPTER SEVENTY-FIVE

When the shooting started, Flaherty was the first to move. The five minutes had already expired, and she, Kozlowski, and Loring were in the corridor approaching the cold stone room where Finn was being held. They could see the light filtering out from the doorway, and hear the sound of voices trickling out from the room. It had been difficult to persuade Loring to take action, but Flaherty was beginning to think he wasn't going to be much help in this situation if things got ugly anyway. When she heard gunfire, she was running before she knew it, her heart pumping wildly as she realized something had gone terribly wrong.

"Lieutenant! Wait!" Kozlowski yelled after her, breaking into a run himself. Loring was behind the two, but moving with less enthusiasm.

Flaherty charged toward the bright light that was casting confused shadows on the stone floor outside the room. She knew it would be more prudent to assess the situation before running in, but there was no time; if she hesitated, the fight would be over before she got there, and Finn would no doubt be gone. She couldn't let that happen. If he really was innocent, then she'd put him in danger, and she'd never forgive herself if anything happened to him.

She passed through the door and into the room at full speed with her gun drawn, yelling, "Police! Everybody down!"

Kozlowski saw Flaherty sprint into the room. She was probably only fifteen or twenty feet ahead of him—a few seconds at most—but he knew that a few seconds could mean the difference between life and death. He increased his own speed and flew into the room after her. He didn't even bother identifying himself as a police officer. Flaherty had given fair warning and an order to get down on the ground. To Kozlowski's way of thinking, that should be enough; anyone still standing could be presumed to be on the wrong side of the law. There'd be no time in a situation like this for deliberation.

As he came around the corner, the room was in chaos. The first thing he noticed was Flaherty on the ground to the left of the doorway. *Oh my God, she's been hit!* he thought initially, but then he quickly realized she'd thrown herself down to avoid a hail of bullets. Just then he felt the wall next to his head explode in two small pops, kicking out stone and mortar as shots just missed him. He dove to the right, so that he and Flaherty were flanking the doorway.

As he lifted his head, the room came into better focus. A spotlight in the middle of the room had been knocked to the floor, and its reflection off the stone walls cast an eerie glow. He could see a giant figure topped with dark hair lying near Flaherty to the left—Tigh McCluen, he assumed—and he could see Scott Finn lying in the center of the room. Other than that, there were three people, and at least two were armed. *This is going to be unpleasant.*

Across the room, he could see a large, balding man in his forties. He was standing calmly, squeezing off round after round. *A professional*, Kozlowski could tell instantly. His demeanor was far too controlled to be anything but, and as a professional killer, he was likely to pose the greatest threat. Kozlowski rolled onto his knees, his body reacting to the moment without thought or awareness. He brought the gun up, leveling it with his eye in a steady, two-handed grip. He sucked in a breath and held it as the muscles in his forearm tensed, pulling the trigger and firing twice, his shoulders and elbows reacting subtly to compensate in his aim for the gun's recoil. The man went down on the second shot, as Kozlowski took him square in the chest, knocking him off his feet.

Kozlowski swung his body around to find another target. He saw McGuire drop to the ground across the room, grasping for the gun at his feet. Kozlowski brought his gun up again, aiming for the center of McGuire's body. He had McGuire in his sights, and once again he felt the muscles in his arm and hand contract to pull the trigger, but before the gun went off, he heard a loud explosion to his right, and he saw his right elbow shatter, splattering blood over his shirt and sending his gun to the ground.

It took a moment for him to realize what had happened, and as he turned to the right, he saw a man in a suit taking aim at his head. Kozlowski threw himself to the floor and rolled to his left to avoid the shot. He winced and groaned as his broken arm connected with the stone floor, but pushed himself through the pain. Having lost his gun, he knew it was only a matter of seconds before the next bullet found him.

Flaherty was on the ground as well. She'd burst into the room only to find herself dodging a series of shots from the heavyset man at the far end. She could see Finn in the center of the room. He was moving, but there was no way to tell exactly how badly he was injured. In any case, as long as she was pinned down, there seemed little she could do. It was only after Kozlowski had taken out the professional killer that she was able to stand up and join the fight.

As she lifted her head, she saw Williams shoot Kozlowski, and a rage grew in her like nothing she'd ever known before. The lawyer was setting himself again, and taking aim at her partner, who was moving as quickly as he could to make a more difficult target. She spun around on Williams and fired without hesitation. The bullet hit him in the shoulder and knocked him back. He screamed out in pain, but stayed on his feet, clutching his gun to his side.

"Drop the gun!" Flaherty yelled. Williams looked at her with an odd expression of amusement and anger. He was barely keeping his feet as his knees buckled, causing him to stagger. Flaherty's mind raced through her options. "Drop it now!" she yelled again. Williams refused to comply, standing in front of her with a strange smile, his gun hanging down from his arm loosely. Then Flaherty thought she saw him flinch, and she fired twice without thinking. The first shot hit him just below the sternum, and he staggered back two steps more. The second shot hit him in the center of his forehead and ended his life instantly.

She hadn't even realized what she was doing, and the shock at her actions froze her as she looked at Nick Williams lying in a bloody heap. It was the first time she'd taken a life, and she stood there, momentarily stunned.

"Lieutenant! Look out!"

The warning came from Kozlowski, and caused Flaherty to turn to her left. McGuire had picked his gun up off the ground, and the barrel was now pointed directly into her eyes from six feet away.

What the hell am I doing here? Loring was asking himself.

He was standing in the damp corridor outside of the room,

listening to the gunshots ring out as the sweat poured down his face. *I'm a lawyer, not a cop!* It was true, and he knew it for certain now. For years he'd gone to the FBI firing range and practiced his marksmanship, bragging to agents and other lawyers alike that he was prepared for anything—the complete law enforcement officer.

But his bravado was a sham. His mastery of the mechanics of firing a gun aside, he'd never trained for an actual confrontation, and he knew now he was unprepared for one. Other than in his childish daydreams, he'd never even contemplated the notion of risking his life in a gunfight. He wasn't sure which he was more petrified of—being killed or having to kill another person—but he knew that if he didn't act, he'd never be able to live with himself. He could hear Kozlowski's voice calling out between the gunshots, and he knew he couldn't let the others down.

He came around the corner of the door with his gun drawn, and he was amazed by the scene. Tigh and Kozlowski were on the ground, as were three men he didn't recognize. Only Flaherty and McGuire were still standing, and McGuire was pointing a gun straight into Flaherty's face. Loring knew he was too late, that he'd never be able to aim and fire his gun at McGuire in time to prevent Flaherty's death. He felt a rush of guilt as he realized his hesitation had probably cost Flaherty her life.

He was bringing his gun up and trying to lock McGuire into his sights when he saw one of the men lying on the ground lunge toward McGuire. The man moved quickly, kicking out with his legs and catching McGuire in the knees, throwing him off balance. A shot rang out, reverberating off the stone walls, but the bullet missed Flaherty and ricocheted off the wall behind her.

Now Loring had his chance, and he fired his gun without thought or warning. McGuire seemed surprised, and Loring couldn't tell at first whether he'd hit him or just startled him.

The U.S. attorney was about to shoot again when he saw a trickle of blood start from the corner of McGuire's mouth. Then McGuire's arm dropped, and the gun slid out of his hand. He stood there, hovering for a moment, as if caught in indecision, then he fell forward hard onto the ground.

All of a sudden, the room was deathly quiet.

CHAPTER SEVENTY-SIX

Finn rolled onto his side and struggled to sit up. Every part of his body ached so badly that the pain seemed to reach into his soul and overwhelm him with an old, familiar feeling of despair. McGuire's body lay at his feet, at the spot where Finn had thrown himself into the mob boss's legs, saving Flaherty's life.

He looked around the room. It seemed as if an invading army had laid siege to the place, with the dead and wounded piled around the room. A man whom Finn recognized from bar association functions as Rich Loring, the U.S. attorney for Massachusetts, was still standing with a gun in his hand, frozen for a moment, until he moved over to Kozlowski, who was just starting to sit up, his arm covered in blood. "Are you okay?" Loring asked the police detective.

Kozlowski gave a pained smile. "I will be." He tore through the sleeve of his shirt, revealing the wound. It looked as if at least one of the bones had been badly broken, and blood was dripping down onto the floor. Kozlowski winced as he tore a long piece of cloth off his shirt and wrapped it around his bicep, tightening the tourniquet by pulling with his left hand and his clenched teeth, and tying it off. "See? Good as new."

Flaherty was standing over the lifeless body of Nick Williams, looking down at it with an odd mixture of satisfaction and horror.

After a moment, she pulled her radio off her belt and double-clicked the handset, speaking into the unit. "This is Lieutenant Flaherty. We have an officer down and multiple casualties at Fort Independence off Day Boulevard. Request backup and emergency units immediately. Over." Then she spoke to Kozlowski. "Don't be a macho asshole, Koz, how are you really doing?"

Kozlowski looked at his arm. "I don't think it hit any arteries," he said. "It hurts like a bitch, but I'll be all right." He took a deep breath and blew it out through clenched teeth. "Don't get me wrong, I have no problem with your asking the EMTs to hurry just a little bit."

Flaherty nodded, then she hurried over to Finn and knelt down next to him. "How about you, Finn? Are you all right?"

Finn opened his mouth to speak, but nothing came out. His mind wasn't yet able to process all that he'd been through, and he recognized that he was in shock. Time seemed to slow to a crawl as dark images floated through his brain.

"It was Williams," he said finally, in a hushed tone, nodding over to the body of the dead lawyer.

"Who?"

"Nick Williams," Finn repeated. "He was a partner at my firm. He killed Natalie."

Flaherty looked confused. "I thought McGuire killed Natalie."

"So did I," Finn said. "But I was wrong, it was Williams. He and Natalie were . . ." He couldn't bring himself to finish the sentence. The lightbulb went on in Flaherty's head and she nodded in understanding. "He was working for McGuire, and he killed her because she found out they were defrauding the state. McGuire was . . ." but Finn's voice trailed off as he struggled to deal with the enormity of what he'd learned.

Flaherty nodded again. "Finn, I don't know what to say," she began. "I'm—" But she never got to finish the sentence. From across the room, Kozlowski was shouting into his own radio.

"We need that ambulance, now!" he was yelling. Both Flaherty and Finn looked across the room and saw Loring bent over Tigh McCluen. Loring had his hand on the huge man's chest, and he was trying to stem the bleeding.

"Oh my God! Tigh!" Finn struggled to his knees, and then to his feet, and hobbled over to his friend, kneeling down next to his head. He looked down at him, and could see the dark blood pooling underneath his enormous body.

"Hang in there, Tigh, we're going to get you out of here," Finn said.

Tigh gave a weak smile. "No you're not."

Finn held his own hand to the hole blown in Tigh's chest, which was still oozing freely. "Are you kidding?" he said. "I've seen you do worse than this while shaving."

Tigh coughed out a laugh and a river of blood ran down his cheek from the corner of his mouth. "That's why I grew the goatee," he said.

"I always thought it was just to cover up your ugly mug."

Tigh patted Finn's hand. Then he closed his eyes and opened them quickly, swallowing hard. "It's not that bad," he said to Finn. "I'm lucky. I made it long enough to try to set some things straight. Not everyone we grew up with got that chance."

"You did more than that," Finn said. "You saved my life."

"I wonder if Saint Peter will count that against me?" Tigh winked as he said it. Finn could hear a pronounced gurgle in Tigh's chest as he fought to breathe. "Given my past, it's likely to be a lengthy debate in any case."

"You could always talk your way out of anything, you big, dumb Mick. But shut the hell up and focus on staying here. Saint Peter can wait."

Tigh shrugged. He closed his eyes again and his breathing

became shallower. "Do you remember the time we all went to that beach in Newport?"

Finn laughed softly. "Before Joey was killed?"

"Yeah, that's right." Finn had to lean in to hear Tigh now. "We went out there in our ragged old shorts and dirty T-shirts . . ."

"And that guy tried to chase us away," Finn continued.

Tigh smiled. "So we threatened to drown him and bury his body in the sand if he didn't get out of our sight."

Finn laughed. "I've never seen anyone run so fast in my life."

"It was a grand day. Sitting on that perfect beach, looking out at the water, dreaming about all the things we were going to do with our lives . . . Now, when I dream, I dream about the past, not the future. I think that's when you know you've run your course, Finn—when your happiest thoughts are of the past."

Finn could hear the sirens getting closer outside. "Hang in there, Tigh, the ambulance is almost here."

Finn could barely hear Tigh breathing anymore, and his voice was nothing but a whisper. "You got out, Finn. Let all the crap from your past go, and live your life." Tigh's chest hitched twice, and Finn could hear that his lungs were taking in more fluid than air. He thought he was gone for a moment, but then Tigh opened his eyes and looked at Finn with a smile that was filled with all of the life left in him. For a moment, Finn saw the Tigh he knew in his youth. His face was thinner, and there was a twinkle in his eye that was unmistakable. Finn remembered how much they'd shared, just to survive in the streets, and he knew that, as much as he'd hurt Tigh when he found his way out, the friend within him had always cheered for him.

"Where the hell are the paramedics!" Finn yelled to no one in particular.

"They're here, Finn," Flaherty said quietly. "They're just trying to get to us." Finn could hear the resignation in her voice and it angered him, mainly because he knew she was right, and there was nothing that could be done.

"Hang on, Tigh, they'll be here any second," he said.

Tigh waved two fingers toward his face, drawing Finn in closer so that he could hear him. "Promise me you'll never forget one thing, no matter what happens, Finn?"

Finn nodded. "Anything, Tigh. What is it?"

Tigh smiled a mischievous smile, one last time. "Nobody fucks with the Chelsea Street Regulars."

Tigh was gone before the paramedics made it to the dark stone room in Fort Independence. Finn watched as they pulled and prodded, trying to coax some sign of life from the huge body, but to no avail. One paramedic was taping Finn's broken fingers together on splints as the young lawyer watched them pull the sheet over Tigh's head. With that final statement of mortality, Finn got up to leave the room.

"I still need to examine your other wounds, sir," the paramedic said in a slightly tired and petulant voice. "And then you have to go to the hospital."

Finn turned around and glared at the man, who got the message quick enough. He shook his head in resignation, as if to say, *I'm not wasting my precious time on you, asshole.* Finn didn't care. He just needed to get out of there, to be alone.

He walked out of the room and into the corridor, which was filled with police and EMTs and park rangers. Flaherty was there, too, waiting for him. She walked up to him and put her hand gently on the area between his chest and his shoulder. It struck him as an oddly intimate gesture. She looked at him sadly.

"Finn, I'm—"

But he interrupted her by taking hold of her wrist and moving it off his body, pushing it back toward her as he shook his head.

"But Finn—"

"No," he said, and it was definitive. He walked through the sea of law enforcement personnel, which parted before him as people looked on in silence.

"We need to talk, Finn!" Flaherty called after him. "If not now, then later!" she yelled, her voice sounding desperate.

Finn kept walking. He had too much to deal with himself before he could answer anyone else's questions. *Besides*, he thought, *nobody fucks with the Chelsea Street Regulars.*

EPILOGUE

Finn sat outside at a small harborside restaurant on the shore of Boston's North End. A light breeze brushed back his hair as he sipped a Budweiser on the back deck of the bistro, looking out at the Boston skyline. He loved this time of year. Always had. It was only four-thirty, but already the October sun was low on the horizon and cast a watery orange glow on the city. He breathed in deeply and could taste the crisp leaves, ripened to the point of decay, as they mixed with the salt air. To Finn, the renewal had begun.

He didn't hear her when she joined him. She slipped into the chair next to his without a word, and waited for him to speak first. The waitress arrived before either of them had worked up a notion of what to say.

"What would you like?" the waitress asked Flaherty.

"I'll have a glass of chardonnay."

The waitress headed back into the bar, leaving them alone again in silence. It was Flaherty who finally broke the stalemate.

"It's been more than a month, and you never returned my phone calls," she said.

Finn bristled. "I gave my statement at the police station the day after everything went down. You weren't there. I figured that if you needed to talk to me for the investigation, you'd have sent someone to pick me up."

"I wasn't calling about the investigation," Flaherty said, sighing.

Finn took a sip of his beer. "I know."

Another extended silence set in. Out on the water, a racing sloop drifted by, tacking gracefully upriver as if nothing had changed in the city for three hundred years.

"I'm sorry," Finn said at last. "I had a lot of things to work through on my own before I could really deal with anyone else's questions."

Flaherty looked at him. "Were you successful?"

Finn shrugged. "Tough to say. I still have a bunch of things to think about." He paused and thought about what to say next. "I fought my way out of the projects, and I thought once I made it into the real world, I wouldn't have to deal with all the shit that goes on there—the cruelty, and the anger, and the viciousness. It turns out I was wrong. I didn't escape anything. Even some of the people I cared most about were screwed up."

"Like Natalie?" Flaherty asked.

"For starters," Finn admitted.

Flaherty let him catch his breath while she considered her next question. "You really loved her, didn't you?"

He blew out his breath contemplatively. "Yes," he said after a moment. "And no." Flaherty looked inquisitively at him, and he continued. "It's hard to explain, even to myself. She was a fantasy to me—an ideal. She was everything I always wanted but could never have. She was smart, and beautiful, and successful, and funny. I think I believed she'd somehow make me better—happy, even."

Flaherty thought about that. "I'm not sure anyone can fill in a part of us that's missing. They can only help us live with the things that are hardest."

"I guess I found that out the hard way," Finn said. He looked off into the distance, toward the south where Fort Independence jutted out from the shoreline like a sentry. Flaherty followed his gaze, and seemed to know what he was thinking.

"I'm sorry about Tigh," she said.

"Yeah," Finn responded. "Me too." He looked down at the table, lost in thought. "When we were running together in Charlestown, he was the most feared guy in the neighborhood. I saw him do awful things to people—really brutal things. But even then, there was a part of him that was fighting against it. I think that's why he understood why I had to get out. In the end, he saved us all."

Flaherty nodded. "Nothing is ever exactly what it seems to be," she said, echoing Kozlowski's warning. She gave Finn an embarrassed smile. "I learned that about you the hard way." She hung her head. "I'm sorry I didn't believe you. You have every right to hate me."

Finn took another sip of his beer. "How could you have known? McGuire was pulling all the strings with such skill that he had everyone fooled."

"It's nice of you to say, but it doesn't stop the guilt."

"Don't bother with guilt," Finn said. "It's a waste of energy."

Flaherty smiled. "You sound like my old partner."

"How is the Polish prodigy doing?" Finn asked.

"Ornery as ever." Flaherty laughed. "He's being forced to retire because of his arm—it'll never fully heal—and he keeps threatening a lawsuit. I think the brass would be willing to go to court just to keep him off the force and out of their hair."

"What will he do?"

"What do all old cops like Kozlowski do? He'll get a private investigator's license and start causing real problems."

Finn laughed. "That will be frightening, won't it? I can't imagine how dangerous he'll be once he can start doing things his own way."

"I know," Flaherty said. "He could put the rest of us out of business."

"I'm guessing he's awfully proud of you, though," Finn said, nudging Flaherty across the table. "Director of the Commonwealth Security Department, huh? Pretty impressive."

Flaherty shrugged. "I think the new governor wanted to put some distance between himself and the old administration."

"Can you blame him? I read the newspaper reports on what your investigation uncovered about Clarke. Turns out he was up to his armpits in McGuire's shit, huh?"

"Maybe not his armpits, but his shoes were certainly covered with it. All he really did at first was take mob money for his campaign. That's the thing about politicians, though, they can't just get a 'little' dirty."

"It's like getting a little pregnant," Finn agreed.

Flaherty nodded. "Once McGuire had his hooks into him, Clarke was helpless. He even supplied the information McGuire's people needed to make Natalie look like one of Townsend's victims."

Finn thought about that for a moment. "Can you imagine how much more power McGuire would have had if Clarke had ever been elected president? I heard a rumor he was on his party's short list before all of this."

"I know. It's more than a little scary to think about. That's why the new governor thought it was so important to put as much distance between himself and Clarke. One way to do that was to hire the person credited with bringing Clarke down. For good or bad, I was the one the press focused on."

"That's being a little modest, isn't it?" Finn pointed out. "You deserved most of the focus. Without you, the investigation would have ended the minute John Townsend was under arrest. And Clarke and McGuire would still be in business."

"Maybe, but there were other people involved who didn't get the recognition they deserved. Including you." She looked out at the water. They were across the harbor from the spot where Stone had found Natalie floating by the embankment, her eyes still somehow vibrant and penetrating, hovering under a thin veil of water. It was such a waste. "So what are your plans now?" she asked Finn after a moment.

"I was offered a partnership at Howery, Black," he said.

"That's great. I'm very happy for you." Flaherty sounded disappointed.

"I turned it down," Finn said.

She looked at him. "Why?"

"I don't know, really," he replied honestly. "Preston has been great throughout all of this. His friendship is probably the only positive thing that I've held on to as a result of this mess. But I'm not sure I can go back there. It feels like I've spent the last eight years doing other people's work—handling cases for other lawyers' clients. It's a little like when I was young and working the streets in Charlestown; I was always doing someone else's bidding. I'm tired of being a pawn."

"What now, then?" Flaherty pushed.

Finn took a deep breath. "I think I'm going to start my own firm—hang out a shingle back in Charlestown and see what happens."

"That's a little risky, don't you think?"

Finn nodded. "Yeah, it is," he admitted. Then he looked back at her. "But I'm through playing it safe. Preston got the firm to agree to a generous severance package that will help get me started, and he'll refer some clients to me as I get on my feet. If I'm ever going to be a really good lawyer, I've got to get out there on my own and get my hands dirty."

Flaherty looked at Finn and decided she liked what she saw. She'd always been attracted to his humor, and his strength, and his intelligence, but now there was something more. There was a fire in Finn she'd only seen hints of before—a passion that had seemed muted and dampened. Now he seemed complete.

"I guess that just leaves us," she commented after a minute.

He sipped his beer as he looked out at the water again. "I guess so," he said noncommittally.

She was still looking at him. "Do you think there's a chance for us?" she asked. As soon as the words left her mouth she held her breath.

He turned to look at her. Her dark hair shimmered in the waning light, and she looked beautiful. He raised an eyebrow and smiled. "Given our history, don't you think that would be more than a little risky?"

She held his gaze for a moment or two. Then she reached out and put her hand over his. She could feel the strength of his fingers, and it felt comfortable to her—sturdy and reassuring. She looked out toward the water, but left her hand on his as she closed her eyes and smiled into the last rays of autumn. "I'm through playing it safe, too."

ACKNOWLEDGMENTS

The following people have provided invaluable advice, support, and substantive comments without which this novel would never have been possible: Joanie Hosp, Richard Hosp, Martha Hosp, Joan McCormick, Gary Mitchell, Ted Hosp, Betsy Hosp, Jeff Atwood, Jen Atwood, Breck Masterson, Elizabeth Masterson, Gus Coldebella, Tony Feeherry, John Englander, and Lynne Sollis.

I would also like to thank:

My partners and colleagues at Goodwin Procter, LLP, who, over the past nine years, have made me a better writer, a better lawyer, and a better person;

Frances Jalet-Miller, whose insight and editorial skill was invaluable in preparing the initial draft of this novel;

Larry, Jamie, Jimmy, Michele, and the entire Warner Books family, whose support I will always appreciate;

Rick Horgan, who did such an exceptional job of editing the near-final draft of the manuscript; much of any success I have with this book can be credited to him;

Lisa Vance, my agent (and the rest of the outstanding crew at the Aaron Priest Literary Agency), whose patience, perseverance, good humor, and hard work have already brought more success than I ever could have hoped for;

Maureen Egen, who took a chance on an unknown lawyer-turned-first-time-novelist and has been a great supporter, friend, and final editor; I am honored to have the opportunity to work with her; and finally,

Aaron Priest, who was the first person "in the business" to read the initial manuscript and agreed to represent me; without his belief and encouragement, none of this would have been possible.

Also by David Hosp

INNOCENCE

Attorney Scott Finn has returned to the tough Charlestown streets of his youth, where he ekes out a living from any legal work he can get. But nothing has prepared him for a case as twisted as the one he now faces.

Fifteen years ago doctor and illegal immigrant Vincente Salazar was convicted of a brutal attack on a female undercover cop. Now he wants a new trial, and Finn is the only man willing to fight to find the truth.

Allying himself with maverick detective Tom Kozlowski and delving into the past, Finn peels back layers of corruption and secrets that stretch from Central America to Boston's suburbs. Before Finn and Kozlowski know it, it will be *their* lives that hang in the balance as they search desperately for the thin line between guilt and innocence.

'Red-hot fiction rooted in stone-cold fact – a legal thriller to rival the best from Grisham or Turow' Lee Child

AMONG THIEVES

On the night of the St Patrick celebrations in 1990, some of the world's most famous and valuable paintings were stolen from Boston's Isabella Stewart Gardner Museum. They were never recovered, and there were no clues as to their whereabouts – that is until now.

When Boston attorney Scott Finn takes on well-known thief Devon Malley as a client, he gets much more than he bargained for. Not only is he asked to care for Devon's teenage daughter, Sally, while Devon awaits bail, but his investigations into what he believed was a case of petty theft lead him to the underworld of Boston's organized crime gangs, links with the IRA and the realization that he may be close to solving the mystery of the stolen paintings all those years ago.

But an Irishman who, at nine years old, saw his entire family murdered before his eyes is determined to avenge their deaths. His commitment to the cause is frightening and unrelenting, and he will never give up until the job is finished . . .

'Hosp is a born storyteller, a master of quirky character and detail who enthrals through the simple, but elusive, expedient of never seeming to write a dull sentence'

Daily Telegraph [Review]